INTO HELL'S FIRE

Douglas Cavanaugh

www.into-hells-fire.com

ISBN: 97-8-0-9854684-1-5 (paperback: Kirostar Publishing)
ISBN: 978-0-9854684-0-8 (ebook: Kindle)
ISBN: 978-0-9854684-2-2 (ebook: epub)

Into Hell's Fire
Kirostar Publishing
2637 Kelling St.
Davenport, IA 52804
USA
kirostar@mail.com

Printed in the United States of America

First printing, 2012

This book is a work of fiction. Names, characters, places, and incidents
either are products of the author's imagination or are used factiously. Any
resemblance to actual persons, living or dead, events, or locales is entirely
coincidental.

Author's Note

This novel describes the dreadful collapse of the former Republic of Yugoslavia in the early 1990s. The intent of this story is neither to incite nor inflame the emotions of those who personally experienced this tragedy firsthand, but rather to entertain readers who enjoy tales of espionage and adventure.

I would like to emphasize that this is a work of fiction. Similarities to real people or events are purely coincidental. All names and locations were selected at random; the entire plot is a creation of the author's imagination.

PART I

The old Bosnian lay dazed by the side of the road. He was still damp with the sweat he had worked up while tending to his sheep earlier that day. He was also wet from splattered blood and from a clear fluid that was seeping from his ears. His right leg was useless; its lower portion was bent unnaturally just below the knee. Beside his mangled limb rested a banged-up German Mauser Karabiner rifle, a relic he had kept hidden in his barn since seizing it from a dead German soldier during World War II.

The wounded man was conscious, but largely unaware of his surroundings as a result of the grenade that had detonated just a meter or so away from him. The ringing in his ears was so loud he could not hear anything else. His nervous system had shut down, and he was now incapable of defending himself. Yet as they closed in around him, the enemy advanced with extra care, fully aware of the fight he had put up without showing the slightest hint of fear.

By the time the Serbian soldiers finally surrounded him, he was stretched out on his back; his torso was propped up off the ground by his flexed elbows. He was mumbling incoherently and obviously in shock. They knew immediately that he no longer posed a threat to anyone.

Seconds later, the group's new commander appeared, and even though he was not dressed in regular military attire, he approached the nearest soldier and began barking orders at him. When the soldier did not respond to his furious tirade, he turned quickly toward another and repeated his performance. Again, he was ignored. Horribly frustrated, it wasn't long before he broke into a violent rage and dropped one of the soldiers to the ground with the butt of his gun. The air was thick with tension.

Little time had passed when a Mercedes-Benz appeared on the scene and suddenly screeched to a stop less than ten meters away. All at once, the soldiers' attention became focused on the passenger inside the car and their postures changed accordingly. Without hesitation, the troop's troubled leader hurried over to talk with the Serbian officer in the back. As he approached the car, the electric window in the rear slowly went down.

"What the fuck is taking so long, Mr. Obrenović? I want this mission completed before it attracts any attention. It must be done professionally. Do you understand me?" said the officer inside.

"I fully understand, General. And that's exactly what I'm trying to do. But these new recruits don't appear to understand the program. They haven't quite figured out why they should carry out such drastic measures under the guidance of a civilian," answered the general's henchman.

"Let's see if I can help. Call that big one over here," said the general.

A moment later, a heavy-set private in a wrinkled uniform came near and stood at attention. He had only been in the army for a few months, but he knew very well when to be alert and pay attention.

"Now listen up, you insubordinate prick. Your new commander gave you orders to clear the village. He wants these people disposed of at once. He just informed me that your outfit is refusing to carry out his orders. What is the meaning of this?" the general asked.

The youth replied, "Sir, our orders are to search out and destroy any resistance in the area. He wants us to kill that old man, but he isn't resisting. He couldn't hurt a fly anymore. He needs medical attention."

"Listen closely, you fat son-of-a-bitch," interrupted the general. "I don't want to hear another word. Your orders are to do exactly as you are told. He takes his orders from me and you take your orders from him. I want this village cleared...as in *cleared*! Understood?"

"Yes, sir," the young soldier answered. He knew that he was now in the worst possible position; a wretched position from which there was no escape.

"Now I want you to act like the soldier that you are. Put a bullet through that bastard's head and bury him in the forest. That's an order!" snapped the general through clenched teeth.

Against his will, tears began to fill the young soldier's eyes. "But sir, the old man is harmless now. He was just protecting his...."

"Enough!" shouted the general. "I don't have time for a debate. What is it with you - all gut, but no guts? I have a war to win, you big pussy. That man is your enemy. He would kill you right now if he could. You will carry out the orders I just gave at once, or you and your group of malcontents will be next in the firing line."

The soldier was trembling as he began to retreat in the vain hope that his squad would support him. But before he got very far, the general's civilian enforcer cocked his pistol and pointed it at the private's head, stopping him in his tracks. Together, they marched over to the old man while the rest of the unit looked on.

General Parenta sat back in the car. His hands were wringing in restless anticipation. The tactics he had imposed over the past few weeks were winning accolades from his superiors in Belgrade. He estimated that with a little more time, he would be promoted to the top of the chain of command. Unlimited money, benefits, and recognition would follow. It all seemed so easy.

Before the young soldier could carry out the order, the general tapped his driver on the shoulder and instructed him to drive away. He did not want to be in the vicinity of the act when it was committed. Any suspected involvement by him in the offense would be likely to impede his campaign and possibly jeopardize his future. It was better to have his trusted subordinate, Dragoslav Obrenović, ensure the job was finished in his absence. As the Mercedes sped away, a single gunshot was heard in the distance and a broad smile spread across the general's face. The war was going in his favor, and this was just the beginning.

As the car wound around the twisted roads leading out of the burning village, the general's heart rate returned to its normal level, and the atrocity that had occured only minutes ago quickly vanished from his mind. Analytics and logistics now consumed his thoughts. In the coming days, a whole new devastating campaign would begin and he needed to be certain it would start without a hitch.

●●●●●

Winter was unpredictable in Bosnia, and the young general knew it. Not enough time had been allowed to properly prepare for the most recent orders issued by his Belgrade superiors, and it troubled him deeply. Or at least it did for a little while. To the politicians, it didn't matter. They didn't care about schedules, punctuality, or attention to detail – and many in the Balkans shared their indifference. Fortunately for the general, he was aware of this and had learned to deal with it accordingly.

The most important obstacle for his army to avoid was the kind of snowstorm that could bog down his assignment for days or weeks, as even the slightest delay might tip off the enemy to his strategy. The general had earned his reputation as a reliable commander who could be counted on no matter how difficult the orders were that he received. He could not, however, control the weather.

From its origin in eastern Croatia, the Yugoslav National Army (JNA) convoy had moved southward during the late winter months, stopping along the way only to assist and supply other JNA units and civilian paramilitary outfits in northeast Bosnia. By early March 1992, his units had progressed to where the thirty-nine-year-old commander felt comfortable that the mission could be completed.

●●●●●

Stevan Parenta was proud to be the youngest general in the Serbian army. He viewed his recent promotion as a great honor and considered it the opportunity of a lifetime. He never referred to himself as an officer of the Serbian military, but rather, as General Stevan Parenta of the Federal Republic of Yugoslavia's National Army. Just two years ago, he was an assistant to the director of the Bank of Belgrade. It was a respected position he obtained through a contact of an army buddy he had known since fulfilling his required military service many years ago, long before Yugoslavia had fragmented into warring nations. Prior to satisfying this obligation, he had earned a degree in economics at the university in Belgrade. A bank position seemed to be his calling in life. He enjoyed working with money and all the pleasures that wealth created. He earned enough income to support his family and to provide his wife and two children with a comfortable lifestyle. Yet the job offered no prospect of advancement. His status was not uncommon. Before the country's breakup, the Republic of Yugoslavia prospered and its citizens enjoyed satisfying lives, but opportunities for social advancement rarely surfaced. Stevan Parenta wanted more. When war in the republic became inevitable, he saw unlimited possibilities in his future.

After fighting broke out in Croatia in 1991, Parenta used his college education and military background to attain the rank of major upon re-enlistment. It seemed like a logical move to make. His nationalistic tendencies, combined with a distinguished military record, would provide for favorable advancement opportunities when the fighting stopped and a 'Greater Serbia' was established.

Major Stevan Parenta moved quickly up the chain of command. Ruthlessness and aggression agreed with his personality. The visual stimulation that results from the brutality of war, such as dead and decomposing bodies, parentless children, and innocent civilians whose lives had been torn apart, bothered him less with each passing day. At first, he justified the atrocities he ordered his men to commit simply as obeying orders given to him by his superiors. Carrying out the acts was necessary to achieve the recognition he needed to obtain a better life for himself and his family. Later, he would explain it to his peers as something he was naturally good at, something he enjoyed.

The young officer was a skillful planner and quickly earned the respect of the army's older, obsolete officers. He was imaginative and decisive, often drawing quick praise from the politicians about how critical situations were handled with minimal moral consequences. In effect, he performed the dirty work that more seasoned officers were reluctant to carry out, and he executed these orders promptly and unquestioningly. These traits of ferocity and loyalty did not go unnoticed by Belgrade's controlling powers. The civilian leadership soon decided that many of the conventionally trained generals needed to be replaced by a newer, more ambitious prototype that could complete the difficult assignments deemed necessary for victory.

By mid-1991, when the campaign to seize Croatia's Slavonian province had stalled, two-thirds of the ineffective generals had been relieved. They were replaced by less experienced, more aggressive commanders, of whom Stevan Parenta was the most celebrated.

Stevan Parenta had been awarded the rank of general after only a year of active duty and granted the highest honors issued to any current JNA officer in that same time span. At his promotion ceremony, he received his most cherished possession: a hand-engraved, .357 magnum, Crvena Zastava revolver that never left his side. From Napoleon's gold-trimmed flintlock pistol to Patton's ivory-handled Colt 45 peacemakers, it was his belief that all great military leaders were remembered by the weapons they carried while in uniform. Now he would also be admired for the Serbian-made firearm that he flaunted on his hip.

Within days of taking control, General Parenta implemented cold-blooded tactics that suited his superiors' strategy. He armed Serbian civilians, encouraged vigilantism, and promoted disregard for established law and authority in Serbian-dominated regions. General Parenta was determined to break the Croatian resistance in Vukovar, and it was under his direct orders to eliminate any future opposition after its collapse. When the city finally fell in November 1991, he ordered the soldiers under his command to clear the hospitals of potential combatants. All patients, military and civilian, were slaughtered and their remains buried in mass graves outside the devastated city. General Parenta proclaimed himself to be the Serb who had regained Vukovar as Serbian property and his superiors looked on with delight. The Belgrade politicians were satisfied. They had found the man who could accomplish the most difficult of tasks. Now the next phase of Serbian expansion could be initiated, and General Parenta would be called on for its implementation.

By the time Vukovar had been captured, the Belgrade regime had already determined the next course of action to enlarge their territorial ambitions. When heavy fighting broke out in the rest of Croatia, Belgrade opted to seize the whole of Bosnia in order to clear a path to the Adriatic Sea. After this region was under control, they calculated, Croatia's highly coveted Dalmatian coastline and tourism industry could be acquired. Accordingly, the Serbian leadership shifted their military support to the Serbian populations concentrated in Croatia's Lika region, and they planned to annex the majority of Bosnia and Herzegovina soon after.

To achieve this last objective, a majority population of ethnic Muslims in Bosnia would need to be displaced or destroyed. The smaller cities and villages, they plotted, could be quickly demolished and ethnically cleansed. The larger cities would be taken over time. The military moved methodically, refusing to take on projects considered too large until the timing was ideal. The Serbian politicians presumed that Western intervention would be slow to come.

●●●●●

Early in 1992, as heavy fighting spread across the Bosnian countryside, the capital city of Sarajevo remained spared from war. In Sarajevo, the population was almost fifty percent Muslim, and the Serbian leaders knew they had to be cautious about how to deal with the metropolis. As spring of 1992 approached, the West's diplomatic efforts to stop the hostilities within Bosnia stalled. The ensuing "wait and see" political approach allowed the Serbian leadership the opportunity to strike. It was quickly decided by the Serbian leaders inside Bosnia that when the snow stopped falling, General Parenta would be ordered to pound the capital city into submission. Before long, the ambitious general reconfigured the entire strategy. He decided to bring Sarajevo down first, predicting the rest of Bosnia and Herzegovina would then crumble with ease.

The time it took for the JNA units to move from northeastern Bosnia to Sarajevo's central location was not wasted in transit. Along the way, the general consulted with other JNA officers and added heavy artillery, tank, and field units to his command. He ordered the construction of detention centers for prisoners of war and devised plans for concentration camps to hold civilian populations during a relocation process. These camps would eventually dot the landscape. His units also assisted other units in securing areas from the Croatian army and Muslim militia. Several times his detachment was ambushed and lost numerous confrontations to smaller groups of Muslim rebels in the remote hills. Usually, revenge was taken at the nearest village. This revenge always followed the same pattern. First, the mosques and minarets were destroyed. Then, the government buildings, schools, and houses were demolished. Afterwards, the villagers would be separated. Men of fighting age were often taken away, executed, and then buried in mass graves. Other times, they were marched to concentration camps that were secluded in remote areas. The women were usually held against their will. Some were beaten and raped, others killed on the spot. As time passed, the urge to control the lives of others grew in the newly promoted general and narcissistic feelings overtook him. In the uncontrolled atmosphere of war, he was free to do as he pleased, and the soldiers under his command responded to his leadership.

●●●●●

As winter ceded to spring in 1992, a legitimate feeling that Sarajevo could be spared from the fighting remained intact. The European Community was slated to vote soon on whether Bosnia and Herzegovina would be recognized as an independent state. Of course, the Bosnian-Serb government was adamantly opposed to this. Mounting tensions and hidden anxieties spread throughout the city as the voting deadline neared. Weeks prior to the EC vote, General Parenta had been ordered to have his forces in place. The Serbian leaders were convinced that any necessary military action would need to be swift and overwhelming. By April 1, the final phase of the general's military maneuvering was taking shape.

In the end, the city's location sealed its fate. Spread along the banks of the shallow, winding Miljacka River, it is surrounded by the Olympic Mountains, from which it was all too easy for JNA artillery units to surround it and look down on it from above. Hundreds of tanks, mortars, and heavy artillery took aim on the Bosnian capital from their elevated positions.

As the EC voting deadline neared, several JNA convoys of military equipment and personnel were still in transit from other areas of engagement. The lack of troops forced the general to recruit Bosnian Serb civilians to man the weaponry. These paramilitary units were unofficial combatants composed of nationalists, warmongers, and criminals, all eager to rid the region of Muslim dominance and seize the territory so the Serbian population could emerge as the controlling power.

Besides pounding the city's civilian population into submission, General Parenta's plan included securing the city limits to curb any resistance. All roads leading into and out of the city would be blockaded within days. In addition, several units of Serbian militia, armed with Yugoslav-made M-76 sniper rifles, would infiltrate various neighborhoods and create chaos. These unofficial soldiers would be delegated to isolate the resistance so that the tanks and artillery could dismantle it from above. The strategy was so simple that it was foolproof, the general mused. The city's food and water supply couldn't hold out for long; a resulting surrender was inevitable.

•••••

On April 5, 1992, the day of the European Community's vote for independent statehood of Bosnia and Herzegovina arrived. Late that morning, General Parenta and his second-in-command, Colonel Vladimir Nikolić, were standing together and talking while Dragoslav Obrenović, the leader of the paramilitary fighters, paced nearby. All three had been watching the demonstration below unfold through binoculars. Civilian protestors, who had gathered in the city center, were pleading for a peaceful independent statehood. The citizens chanted and marched for a nonviolent response to the EC's coming decision. When the activists reached the Sarajevo's governmental headquarters, Obrenović, on the orders of General Parenta, gave a signal to a hidden assassin that shook the world. High above the marching civilians, the sniper opened fire on the crowd from a nearby building. It was an obvious act of intimidation directed toward the population and the EC officials who were preparing to cast their votes a short time later. Not long after, the dazed and confused inhabitants waited anxiously for news of the voting results. They would find out only too soon what lay ahead.

During the demonstration's frantic disbandment, fear and panic overwhelmed the crowd's leadership. Before the protestors' frazzled nerves could be calmed, mass hysteria broke out. In haste, the population armed themselves to take revenge against their aggressors. Minor skirmishes and larger firefights erupted in various parts of the city. That same day, irreversible damage occurred after the final ballots were tallied. The EC minister's count did indeed recognize the Republic of Bosnia and Herzegovina as an independent entity, much to the chagrin of the Serbian nationalists watching the events from afar.

•••••

It was later that afternoon when General Parenta received the call on his cellular telephone. The units under his command had been in place for most of the day, awaiting orders to begin the operation's next phase.

Colonel Nikolić and Dragoslav Obrenović stood together in silence, nervously chain-smoking to help pass the time. Their superior, sitting in the back seat of his Mercedes-Benz several meters away, was speaking at length with an unknown voice on the telephone's other end. After a short time, Colonel Nikolić inched toward the vehicle in a covert attempt to eavesdrop on the conversation. Reluctant to make a spectacle of himself, he drifted as close to the car as possible, desperately wanting to know the details of the conversation. He leaned his shaved head as far forward as his thick neck would stretch, and avoided eye contact until he was convinced the general was not annoyed by his presence. Colonel Nikolić looked through the windshield as his agitated leader ran his fingers through his salt-and-pepper hair. Inside the vehicle, the telephone conversation became heated, and at times, General Parenta gestured wildly with his free hand while shouting into the mouthpiece. Colonel Nikolić deduced that his superior was desperately trying to explain the military position to a Belgrade politician. Whenever the JNA general stopped to listen to the party-leader's directives, he took long drags from his cigarette. As the conversation's pace slowed, the stocky colonel was certain that final orders were being issued, and that his commander was calculating how best to act them out. The tension and suspense mounted as the dialogue wound down. In time, a look of cold determination showed on the general's face. When the call ended, he dropped the cumbersome cellular phone on the car's front seat. He then finished his cigarette and relaxed a moment before returning to the company of his officers. Once again, the three stood and stared through their binoculars. A foggy haze now limited visibility. In time, Colonel Nikolić collected the courage to question the general openly. Finally, the silence was broken.

"And so, General…what are our orders?" he asked.

"Are the units properly positioned? Is the artillery loaded?" the general asked, answering the colonel's question with two of his own. He continued surveying the Bosnian capital through his binoculars.

"Since seven o'clock this morning. What will you have me tell the men, sir?"

"Tell them to open fire on all predetermined targets. Bring the city to its knees."

"Immediately, sir!" Colonel Nikolić responded. He flicked his cigarette onto the rocks below and scurried off.

II

It wasn't that the news arriving that evening was a complete surprise, but there was an element of shock in its coming.

There was only an hour and a half left before sunset, yet the humidity remained intense, so Lucas Martin decided to leave the beach for the more agreeable atmosphere of his air-conditioned apartment overlooking Patong Bay. Compared to the haggard mess he had been when he arrived in Thailand from the Balkans just a few months ago, Lucas felt like a new man. That harrowing assignment hadn't been his first in Eastern Europe. It was, however, intended to be his last.

Lucas had set aside enough money for early retirement. He had dreamed for years about losing himself in the sights and sounds of Southeast Asia, with its exotic sights and agreeable climate. The first country on his list was Thailand. Malaysia was next, and then Indonesia and the Philippines. Since he was now independent, both financially and professionally, and because expenses in that part of the world were ridiculously low, Lucas planned to spend his retirement years in a state of perpetual travel. In the mornings, he would drink coffee, read newspapers, and relax on pristine beaches. At lunchtime, he would feast on foreign cuisines and drink iced tea by the sides of pools. In the afternoons, he would travel, sightsee, or rest, depending on the weather. This he would follow with refreshing swims after the day's hottest sun had disappeared. After the exercise, he would enjoy fine meals of fresh seafood and other local delicacies. Here in Thailand there was the additional attraction of unlimited nightlife: Muay Thai kickboxing, cold beer, a constant stream of tourists and expats to mingle with, and friendly local girls to flirt with late into the night. This was how he had imagined living life after turning fifty-five. This is what he had saved for; what he had planned and prepared for. Now it had become reality. He considered it his reward for the sacrifices he had endured serving his government, serving his country. This life of leisure, he had decided, was owed to him.

●●●●○

It was early evening when Lucas stopped at the edge of the beach to beat the sand from his feet. After slipping on his sandals, he started through the village and headed for home. Along the way, he kept his eyes averted from the persistent shopkeepers hawking their wares, and lowered his head to drown out the incessant honking of the tuk-tuk drivers trying to drum up business. He went into a 7-11 to buy drinking water and an international newspaper, and a bit later, stopped to chat with an old woman cooking vegetables and rice at the side of the road. This had become his routine since his arrival several weeks ago. The two had become friends. Lucas was her best customer. They exchanged small talk in Thai, and then switched to English when he began to struggle. When the conversation stalled, Lucas said goodbye and continued on his way. As the pair parted company, the woman turned abruptly, with a stick in hand, to chase off a stray dog that had nosed its way to her outdoor kitchen. Lucas watched the spectacle play out, smiled, and then kept walking.

Soon he came to his building and climbed the steps to his third-floor rental. As he walked down the open-sided hallway, he stopped to admire the view and smell the sea breeze. He studied a tourist parasailing above the nearby bay, only to lose sight of him a moment later when the parachute vanished behind a row of palm trees flush with young, green coconuts. When he reached his apartment, he removed his sandals at the doorway, a custom he had retained since completing an assignment in South Korea several years before. He entered the flat, flipped on the air conditioner, and then picked up the TV remote control. As he grabbed a cold bottle of Singha from the refrigerator, he pointed the infrared beam and pressed the power button on the remote. As the screen flashed to life, CNN International, received via satellite, was interrupting its scheduled programming to update a breaking news story. At first, Lucas watched with indifference. Yet as the story unfolded, he straightened up, squared himself, and froze in his tracks. Soon his eyes opened wider and he looked on with astonishment.

The screen was filled with images of horror. The live feed showed multiple explosions ripping through cinder-block buildings and fragments of glass, metal, and concrete being hurled several stories below. Fires burned out of control, their flames jutting from broken windows of large apartment buildings. The windows' white frames had already been scorched an evil charcoal-black by the blaze. On the streets below, old men in plaid shirts and woolen pants hustled urgently past the camera's lens while younger men in faded denim helped pull the wounded from the carnage. Crowds of people pushed and shoved as they ran for their lives. Multicolored skirts and silk headscarves littered the streets, the result of Muslim women shedding their restrictive traditional clothing to escape the terror. The CNN correspondent, clearly out of breath, sounded as if he had been running to gain a better position, or sprinting to escape the attack. He desperately tried to describe the mayhem, reporting in flurries between gasps of air. The network's picture shook repeatedly, a result of the camera being jarred by the repercussions of incoming artillery rounds.

Lucas remained upright, his eyes transfixed.

"Oh, you fucking idiots," he muttered in disbelief. The city where he had spent most of the last seven years was under attack. The siege of Sarajevo had begun.

III

When the telephone rang at nine-thirty that evening, the surprise in Lucas's voice wasn't the result of who was calling or when, but rather that the telephone had rung at all. No telephone connection was part of his lease, and he wanted it that way. He had insisted on it to the landlord—almost demanded it.

"Hello?" he asked suspiciously, his voice just above a whisper. Lucas had just stepped out of the shower; he was barefoot and wrapped in a freshly ironed towel.

"Oh, Lucas, my old friend, how are you this evening?" replied a voice—a voice that was familiar, although muffled just enough to leave Lucas with a trace of uncertainty.

"Morton, is that you?"

"Yes, it is, Lucas. It's good to know you're still in top form...as sharp as ever. Well done. Tell me...what have you been keeping busy with these days, my good friend?" Morton asked. His East Coast accent had an artificially sweetened tone.

The last time Morton Riggs had spoken to Lucas in this manner, it was because he wanted something, something big. Lucas foresaw trouble ahead and proceeded cautiously.

"How did you get through on this line, Morty? It hasn't been connected."

"Well, obviously it has, Lucas. It has also been scanned, rerouted, and secured. It's amazing what Bell Labs can do for you if you know who to ask."

"So this conversation is of the 'official business' variety?" Lucas asked, though he was already convinced it was. When Morton offered no denial, Lucas's suspicion was confirmed. He regrouped, and then continued bitingly, "You know I'm on permanent vacation. I can't imagine why you took all the trouble of bothering Ma Bell when you know I have no interest in hearing from you. All the details of my retirement were made explicit and left in no uncertain terms. This was agreed upon by everyone, including all the department heads."

"Lucas, don't be so defensive. Take it easy; we're all on the same team here!"

Lucas grimaced and bit his tongue. *Not this again*, he thought to himself. Then he answered, "Listen, Morty, let's skip the pleasantries and get down to business. Just tell me why you are interrupting my life of leisure."

From halfway across the world, Morton Riggs played along coyly, knowing that proper presentation was vital in order to get what he wanted.

"Lucas, did you see the developments on television earlier today?" Morton stopped a moment to recalculate the number of time zones between them; if it was mid-morning in Washington, it would be late evening of the same day in Thailand. "It seems as though all hell has broken loose in Bosnia and Herzegovina, and the administration is more than a little perplexed about how best to proceed. Public outcry is mounting and the U.N. Security Council is breathing down our necks. The Croatian and Slovenian-American populations are pushing hard for U.S. intervention. Those populations represent millions of voters and the president wants this bag of shit to appear as being under control before the election gets any closer. Christ, every day this thing escalates gives the opposition that much more ammunition with which to attack us. Those bastards are quietly standing off on the sidelines with this one grinning from ear to ear. All contact with the delegates from the involved countries seems to complicate the matter. And worse yet, the team of diplomats we have in place are so far out of their league they couldn't negotiate a settlement between a group of fucking first graders fighting over who goes to recess first. Lucas, I'm calling because we need some guidance. We need your expertise, advice, and direction."

Morton waited patiently for a response. None came.

"Lucas, please. You are our resident authority on the Balkans, and we need to hear what you can tell us. Everything we've tried has failed. There seems to be no logic at work here, not even common sense, *especially* not common sense. The only success has come with the use of bribes and payoffs, but that's only been a temporary fix. We've approached this thing from every angle. The single definite conclusion that we've drawn is that these people look like us, but they don't act like us, think like us, or resemble us in any other way."

Lucas grinned knowingly, and then followed through firmly. "It's all in the report I filed before submitting my resignation, Morton."

"Yes, my friend, we covered the highlights and applied your conclusions to the areas of concern, but, frankly, we found that report to be long-winded and not entirely relevant," Morton confessed unappreciatively.

Lucas retorted instantly, "I spent six hours a day for three weeks in a two-star hotel room in Belgrade, pecking at a broken-down Yugoslavian typewriter that was a piece of shit when it was new, and you mean to tell me that you didn't bother to analyze every word of that report before deciding to disturb me?" Lucas's voice began to rise in concert with his temper, a quality Morton Riggs picked up on instantly. He silently shifted gears, plotting to use Lucas's emotional ties to his favor. Meanwhile, Lucas continued: "It was all there, Morton, all of it. Today's events, tomorrow's events, next month's events, and next year's events; all of what has happened, and all that is going to happen in ex-Yugoslavia is in that report. The State Department blew it, Morty. You and the self-serving idiots at the Pentagon and CIA, all spending your billions to help the Afghanis dig tunnels and fight the Russians. And the NSA, swapping arms and building armies in the Middle East to control the price of oil, but in the meantime creating dictators who turn the tables and attack whomever they please. So now, Morty, a situation has developed in a country where the United States has few 'special interests,' a situation that has been allowed to escalate to a level beyond control, all on your watch. And the best you can do is to call me and ask me what to do? Are you mentally disturbed? A little bit senile, old man?" Lucas paused to gather steam, and then followed through in a built-up rage, "At this point, I doubt there is anything I could recommend that would make a difference. If you had studied the report for more than a few minutes four months ago, you could have foreseen this coming and done something meaningful to prevent it. A lot of innocent people are going to die now, Morty. Lives are being ruined every second, and it's on your head!"

As the two men sparred, the television coverage continued, now showing live footage of a makeshift hospital inside a school. Pandemonium owned the moment. Small children sobbed loudly as mothers held their bandaged heads and cried out for help. All faces in the camera's range appeared to be in shock. Some were darkened, stained red with blood; others were hauntingly white from lack of it.

"Still the dramatic type, I see, Lucas," Morton rebuffed calmly, dodging the accusations with the skill and experience of a seasoned veteran. "Can we stop the finger-pointing long enough to develop a consensus as how to rectify this situation, or does your permanent vacation qualify as too important to help save these poor Slavic souls? You do still have some family and a few friends living in those parts, don't you? I imagine that to help their plight would be reason enough to persuade you to make your services available. Is that a fair presumption? If not, you could always do it to spite me for my alleged inactions."

Lucas did not respond.

Morton pressed on, taking care to push his case, but not too strongly. "My friend, as far as the White House is concerned, this is the European Community's problem and always will be their problem.

The irony with this is that it seems no European country wants to get off its ass and take charge of the situation, no matter how hard we push. It is unbelievable how they turn to us and piss and moan about how something should be done about a tragedy occurring in their own backyard. It sounds to me like the inconvenience of the war is interrupting their fucking vacation time." Morton stopped for a moment, leaned back in his leather chair in his State Department office, and drew a puff from a Dominican cigar. Lucas, still enraged but now a bit calmer, seized the moment to resume a lecture.

"Listen, Morton, I realize being a U.S. undersecretary of state doesn't require a doctorate in world history. Nevertheless, a little background knowledge of this region is of paramount importance in managing this crisis. It would be helpful if you had some. Of course the Europeans aren't eager to get involved in this quagmire. They've been dealing with these people and these problems for centuries. This is nothing new for them, and they had a very good idea how the situation would play out from the beginning. If you would have taken a full day or so to review more than the summary of my report, you would already know this."

The sixty-nine-year-old State Department official took the lecture with an air of dignity, then attempted to steer the conversation in a more favorable direction.

"Look, Lucas, for now things really may not be as bad as they appear. If we can get some cooperation from the goddamn Serbs, then maybe we can lean a bit harder on the goddamn Croats, and give the goddamn Muslims a chance to work out some sort of settlement," Morton paused briefly to gather his thoughts. "What we can't seem to do is to get the Serbs to stand by an initial agreement for more than two days before we hear about another fucking uprising. Either they are all jerking us around, or the individuals who claim to be in charge are really in control of nothing. The only success our team has achieved was avoiding the destruction of a village in northeast Bosnia that was rumored to be the next JNA target. And that was by a stroke of good luck. The Serbian general in the area actually broke rank and promised not to attack if the United Nations agreed to let him fly to Cyprus for a weekend of R&R. In return, U.N. troops were allowed to move in and relocate the refugees to a more secure zone."

Lucas wondered silently a few seconds, then followed the undersecretary's admission with a question. "Morton, aren't there sanctions in place barring all warring parties from leaving the area of conflict?"

"Officially there are. But in this situation, we decided it prudent to overlook certain commitments that may cause more problems than they solve," responded the diplomat.

"Did you at least have him kept under surveillance?" queried Lucas with dismay.

"Of course we did. You know the routine as well as anyone."

"And so?" Lucas pressed further.

"And so what?"

"Did he meet with anyone? Make any phone calls, or establish any personal contact in Cyprus?"

"No, my friend, as far as we could tell, the young general spent the entire weekend living it up with a gorgeous creature from Novi Sad. And a fine taste in women he has, too. We all agreed."

"And did *she* talk with anyone?" Lucas continued, still unsatisfied.

"The only anomaly we detected was a lengthy discussion she had with the manager of the resort where they were staying. The general didn't participate in the conversation, and our sources couldn't follow the dialogue. They were speaking in either some strange dialect or another language altogether. Could have been Greek, Bulgarian, maybe Macedonian," said Morton. Then he waited nervously. "Why? Is there something I should know?"

"Morty, you did exactly what you were not supposed to do. Those restrictions are in place to prevent the trafficking of arms into the region or the smuggling of large sums of cash out of it. Either one would be next to impossible to achieve from inside ex-Yugoslavia. The JNA probably had no intention of destroying the village, and the general likely moved hordes of German marks to secret foreign bank accounts via Cyprus," Lucas said bluntly. "I can almost guarantee you the general did just that. He threw out the bait and your team bit. He controlled the circumstances and got something for nothing," Lucas added. "You still don't get it. You're not just dealing with two demented politicians who are trying to enlarge their national boundaries. It's more than that, Morty. That story is for the newspapers. These are the Balkans we're talking about. Things work differently there than in the other parts of the world. They have a different way of doing business, and the sooner you understand this, the sooner you can gain some ground."

When Morton didn't interrupt, Lucas's sermon continued. "The people in power are pathological liars, Morton. In the Balkans, it permeates all the way down to the bottom. People there lie for sport. They lie when the truth sounds more unbelievable. They are constantly sizing up your strengths and testing your weaknesses. Don't try to outmaneuver them with logic or reason. The only thing they respect is superior power. If you don't scream, you won't be heard. You've got to play hardball with them. That's how the communists did it, with good, old-fashioned spankings. People there understand that. They respect and need that. They *like* that!" Again, Lucas stopped, caught his breath, and prepared for the next segment of his rant. His blood pressure shot up as his patience dropped off. A rejuvenated passion was bubbling within him. Morton Riggs cued in on it immediately. It was the signal he had been waiting for.

"If you try to negotiate with them with Western-style tactics, you'll get nowhere. They'll look you in the eye, agree to your terms, and sign your pacts. They'll shake your hand. Then, the second your back is turned, they'll smile, tear up the agreement, and raise a glass of the finest local brandy to toast you. Afterwards, they'll do as they please. And believe me, when you hear them say 'no problem,'- problems are guaranteed to follow. This is the mentality you are dealing with, Morton. It is the level you must place yourself on so you can oppose each other on an even playing field. Only then can real progress be made. Is your team prepared to do this?"

Morton edged forward in his chair, thoughtfully searching for an angle to present his proposition.

"Lucas, we have reached a critical juncture in the crisis. Our objectives are in place, and we have the full cooperation of the United Nations, NATO, and our allies in the region. What we now need most of all is concrete information about what is really happening on the ground. We are being bombarded with conflicting reports on a daily basis. We are never sure who is fighting whom, which side is committing atrocities, which side deserves the West's full support, and most important, which side we would like to have as the dominating power in the region when the fighting ends. In all my years, I've never encountered such a goddamn mess as this."

Indeed, timing was critical. Morton Riggs had been at this game long enough to know what to do next. He had been personally assigned this task by the secretary of state, and had assured his superior that he would be able to obtain Lucas's services for at least a few months. He changed gears smoothly and professionally, taking control of the conversation with an air of command that caught Lucas off guard. Pushing forward with all the subtlety of a mother grizzly protecting her young, Morton continued with manifest disregard to any opposition that Lucas might offer.

"Lucas, the secretary of state, the head of the NSA, and the president's advisory team have delegated to me the duty of bringing you to Washington, D.C. for a personal interview. Aside from the field report you so diligently wrote, there is more in-depth information that you, and you alone, can provide to us. Please understand that your background puts you in a unique position to advise us on the matter. Therefore, I have arranged a six o'clock pick-up for you tomorrow morning. You'll be shuttled from your apartment to the island's domestic airport to catch the first available flight to Bangkok. From there, you'll transfer airlines for the Bangkok to D.C. flight, which is scheduled to leave at 7:50 A.M.

your time. Two stops later and you'll arrive at Dulles around noon the next day. I will have all arrangements prepared in advance and will be personally awaiting your arrival."

Lucas's initial reaction was to stand his ground, give in to the desire to lose his temper, and get ready for verbal combat. But realizing the stakes involved, he resisted his instinct and decided to play along. *Surely,* he thought to himself, *the people in charge considered this matter important enough to make it worth my while.* He conceded nothing, but volunteered his attention long enough to hear the offer.

"So Morton, knowing what I know about these powerful people...what sort of opportunity does this present me?"

"Ah, yes, always the businessman, aren't you, Lucas? Wouldn't you prefer to help out just once for the good of humanity?" the undersecretary said with a chuckle.

"Enough of this bullshit, Morty. You called me, remember? I'm certain you want more than you're telling me over the telephone. I'm also certain you won't leave me alone until you get what you want. Why don't you pitch me your best proposal so you can stop wasting my time? I'll decide in a few seconds if this conversation continues or not. You have only one minute more. I suggest that your first offer be your best one," he snarled, leaving Morton Riggs with little room to negotiate.

"And so it must be, my friend. Here's the idea that's been circulating around the State Department water cooler. You have been chosen to be our trusted source of reliable information within the borders of ex-Yugoslavia. Bring your photography equipment and your travel kit. We'll arrange the necessary paperwork, documents and get you full access to all U.N. information and NATO command. You will be reinstated to the region as a freelance photographer for various news agencies. Your assignment will be to investigate what exactly is occurring on the ground and report rock-solid information back to us. Then we can better apply our influence in the direction we judge to be most helpful. We cannot proceed effectively in the route we've traveled thus far. We need fresh, reliable, and most important, *accurate* information in order to establish security in the region. At the same time, you'll get to see old friends, reconnect with old contacts, and maybe rekindle lost loves. Think of it as a working vacation," Morton finished. He listened delicately for any hint of success to his sales pitch.

"I'm already on vacation, Morton," Lucas answered testily. "What sort of time frame are you projecting? And what sort of risk factors have you neglected to inform me of?" Then he quickly added, "And how much compensation for my time and effort have you been authorized to pay me? This is the information I want to know about, Morton. It's your turn to give me something concrete."

"Fair enough, fair enough. Let's get right to the heart of the matter," Morton stammered, not quite sure now how best to proceed. "Lucas, we understand that this is very important, complicated work. It could be dangerous. We're prepared to pay all of your expenses and deposit ten thousand dollars, tax free, into your offshore account in the Cayman Islands for each month of your services." Morton hoped the fact that the U.S. State Department was aware of Lucas's secret banking arrangement might cause him to negotiate in distress.

"Fifty thousand a month," Lucas retaliated, convinced he was being low-balled.

"Twenty."

"Thirty and you never mention the Cayman Islands to me again."

"Twenty-five and that's as high as I'm authorized to go," the diplomat stated, matter-of-factly.

"I'll see you at the D.C. airport, Morty," Lucas answered. He smiled as he hung up the telephone.

IV

By the time the alarm clock rang at five o'clock the next morning, Lucas had already showered, dressed, and finished half a pot of coffee. Alarm clocks were strictly for backup; since the beginning of his military career thirty-five years ago, he'd been waking up before they went off. His bags had been packed and his equipment prepared the night before. His landlord had been notified and the next six months' rent paid in advance so his possessions could be safely stored while he was away. A letter enclosed in an envelope contained instructions for what to do if he did not return or establish contact exactly six months from that morning.

Lucas traveled light; anything he forgot or might need he could pick up in the States. He brought only two carry-on bags with him, one filled with Japanese cameras and photography equipment, the other with a change of clothes, a travel kit, and a few other essentials: a Swiss army knife, a Maglite flashlight, a small pair of binoculars. Tucked inside the lining of one carry-on bag was his original dossier on the Balkan crisis. A photocopy of it had been submitted to Morton Riggs four months ago. On the flight to the United States, he planned to review the original in its entirety to determine whether any of his original recommendations were flawed, and whether a better forward plan could be formulated. He was certain that diplomacy was only part of the solution and that military intervention would likely be required. In hindsight, he wondered if the subtlety of his phrasing had caused some of his advice to be overlooked. As far as who was to blame in the current disaster, he was convinced there was plenty of culpability to go around; however, he had strong suspicions about where the roots of the problem lay. Alone in his apartment, he sipped his coffee and decided against passing judgment until the details of the current situation were presented to him.

At exactly 5:45 A.M., according to his wristwatch, a white minivan pulled into the apartment building's driveway. Lucas took his bags, locked the dead bolt, and removed the key from the door. With a bag in each hand, he walked down the tiled steps to meet his chauffeur. The sun was just beginning to break through the lingering darkness, yet the morning humidity had already caused his pores to open. Before he had reached the van, his shirt was soaked with sweat.

The driver was a wiry Thai teen dressed in black slacks and a white button-down shirt. Lucas greeted him with a nod of his head, and then refused to allow the young chauffeur to load his possessions in the van's rear compartment. The youth smiled politely and pretended he understood the brief explanation Lucas gave him in English. Bags in hand, Lucas climbed in the nearest seat as the driver closed the door behind him.

The usual forty-minute commute to the airport was made in half that time, thanks to the early hour. The driver's eagerness and ingenuity intrigued Lucas, as he watched the youth weave fearlessly between taxis and motorcycles. The highway was designed for traffic to flow in two directions, but the chauffeur used the white median line as his guide to invent a makeshift third lane of traffic. Though the van's speed far exceeded all posted limits, Lucas was unafraid. He had spent too many years in too many different countries to be overly concerned. Experience had taught him to leave the driving to the locals, to wear his seat belt, and to hold on tightly. He could always close his eyes if necessary.

At exactly 6:10, the chauffeur stopped at the airport entrance. Lucas walked casually through the empty lobby on his way to check-in. By 6:35 he was waiting at his boarding gate. After settling into one of the hard plastic chairs near the gate, he picked up the early edition of an international newspaper and quickly spotted the headlines describing the catastrophe unfolding on the other side of the world. He shook his head with disgust as he surveyed the pictures of the destruction. Buildings he had walked past only months ago were now difficult to recognize. After reading the stories that accompanied the pictures, Lucas felt sick. He had witnessed this kind of destruction in Croatia, having wandered through the rubble and charred ruins of Vukovar after fighting had ended there the year before. The same year he had been in Dubrovnik, huddled with hundreds of others in a shelter during the relentless bombardment of the city from a ridge high above. When the shelling finally ceased, he had emerged from the bunker and walked around the city center to assess the damage that had just been inflicted upon one of Europe's most historic towns. It seemed to him as if there had been no attempt to take the city, only to destroy it, as if the Serbs were sending a message to the Croats that read, "If we can't have Dubrovnik, neither can you."

But in Sarajevo, Lucas knew the situation would be more complex. Sarajevo was in Bosnia, a territory altogether different from Croatia or Serbia. It was predominantly Muslim, but was home to a significant population of Croatian Catholics and Serbian Orthodox as well. At the moment, it was wedged between two warring states. Each of those countries' leaders was eager to enlarge their respective territory. Coupled with the fact that Croatia's and Serbia's leaders possessed raging nationalistic tendencies, Lucas had little doubt what results yesterday's onslaught would bring. The situation was going bad quickly, and he was certain it would soon worsen.

● ● ● ● ●

Seven years in the Balkans is a long time, Lucas mused as he waited to board his flight. *A few more months couldn't be so bad.* After all, he reasoned, he wasn't returning to the region out of curiosity, greed, or even boredom. He hoped he wasn't returning because of stupidity. What was enticing him back to the Balkans was a sense of obligation to assist in a project he had previously been committed to. From the moment of his initial assignment in Sarajevo during the 1984 Winter Olympics, he had invested too much time and effort not to see things through.

And Morton Riggs was right about him still having friends and family scattered around the region. Lucas did want to know how they were doing and how he could help. Beyond that, he shared the same DNA with the thousands fighting for survival—in a real sense, these were his people. For all these reasons, he concluded, a high-paying assignment in the middle of a war zone was a challenge he was up to.

Undoubtedly, he could endure the worst violence the war could offer. He had overcome hardships in equally dangerous situations that life had thrust upon him, first fighting for survival as a young boy during World War II, and later fighting in the American military for his adoptive country during the Vietnam War.

The depravity of war was nothing new to him. He had seen men, women, and children die many times. He himself had killed men, women, and children at times. At first he had done so simply to stay alive; then later he had done so because it was his duty. Little was left that could disturb him. Repeated overexposure to some of the most appalling conduct mankind was capable of performing had erased his ability to feel shock, horror, or anguish over such things. In a sense he had become immune.

Over time, Lucas had forgotten what it was like to feel the emotional trauma humans experience when people die. Death, it seemed, had simply become a regular happening in his life. Likewise, he was prepared to die. In fact, it was a wonder to him that he hadn't been killed already, when there had been so many opportunities. His life had begun under unimaginably violent circumstances. It seemed certain to end in similar fashion. This is what he had hoped to avoid by losing himself in another world. He had intended to leave the atrocities, the anger, the hatred, and the stupidity behind when he had bolted for the Far East. *How easy it is,* he mused, *to get involved again in the world I was trying to escape.* Something was calling him back to the very place he had fled. What was it? Money, family, duty—all these played a part. Certainly, though, there had to be a better reason. He trusted a meaningful answer would be revealed in time.

●●●●●

The boarding call came and his journey began in earnest. Forty-five minutes later, he arrived in Bangkok, where he spent his brief layover changing planes. The United Airlines flight was running behind schedule, but when he was finally allowed to board, he found himself seated in a first class seat that Morton Riggs had reserved for him. One at a time, he watched his fellow passengers board and briefly examined their facial expressions as they passed. He playfully wondered what each was thinking as they filed by on their way to the cramped space of the economy seats in back.

The flight was soon airborne and the attendants made their rounds. With nothing better to do, he watched the airline staff and contrasted their demeanors with those of the Thai attendants from the flight before. The Thais' smiles had been friendly and genuine; the Americans', on the other hand, were forced and businesslike. *It's going to be a very long flight,* he thought as he reclined in his seat. Then he closed his eyes to nap.

The first half of the six-hour flight to Tokyo passed uneventfully. Lucas slept the majority of the time, awaking twice from the jarring of air turbulence somewhere over the northern Philippine Sea.

But after the flight attendants had served a light meal of sushi and chicken teriyaki with rice and collected the trays, he took out the file tucked inside his carry-on bag. Removing it from its protective binder, Lucas began scouring the text for deficiencies. With hindsight as his guide, he found no inaccuracies.

It wasn't that the information in the document could have stopped what was happening from occurring. But a thorough analysis of it could have pointed the State Department in a better direction in how to predict Balkan trouble spots. Even more than that, a lot of flaming tensions could have been doused with some rigorous, hard-line politics. Instead, Lucas felt, U.S. policy was in line with the current American culture, applying timid, politically correct guidelines in an area of the world where political correctness could doom thousands of innocent people. Lucas had seen it countless times in the past. He had almost learned to expect it. It seemed to him to be ingrained in U.S. diplomatic policy. The refusal to understand that people in other parts of the world think, act, and desire to be different than America had led to countless poor decisions and generated substantial ill will with foreign nations. He had witnessed it when talking to U.S. embassy diplomats for years. It was his experience during the Vietnam War and during his governmental assignments in the 1970s and early 1980s, primarily in Central America and the Far East. And it was what he observed while talking with expats and tourists on his recent vacation. He was continually amazed at the stance his adopted government endorsed, regardless of the cultures these policies would affect. He hoped it arose from careless incomprehension and not from insensitive arrogance. But he could never really be sure. The political faces were always changing, but the misguided rhetoric remained the same. He had almost learned to accept it until a direct crisis within his culture of birth intervened. Now he expected more. He demanded it.

Lucas opened the dossier and began to review the executive summary he had prepared, aware that the complicated history that followed filled the pages with more tangles than the web of the most ambitious black widow spider.

• • • • •

The history of the region known today as the Balkans begins with the arrival of Slavic drifters from northeastern Europe in the late sixth century, long after the fall of the Roman empire. Eventually, the land and its inhabitants came under Byzantine rule. As the centuries progressed and the Byzantine Empire declined, the Muslim world grew and the Turks came to rule the area as a territory of the Ottoman Empire, leading directly to much of the strife happening at the moment. The Muslims fighting presently in Bosnia are the direct descendants of the Ottomans who ruled much of the Middle East, North Africa, and Eastern Europe for the bulk of the last nine centuries. The area consisting of Bosnia and Herzegovina was the last Ottoman stronghold in the seemingly never-ending battle for dominance between the region's Muslim and Europe's Christian majorities. Croatia's easternmost province, Slavonia, served as a buffer between these powers for hundreds of years. Its location divided the two dominant powers, the Austro-Hungarian Empire to the north, and the Ottoman Empire to the south. Over the centuries, countless battles were fought on this soil; both sides took turns winning new territory. In fact, the Ottoman Turks had once advanced into Hungary, conquered Budapest, and reached the gates of Vienna before being driven back to Bosnia.

At the same time, a growing Orthodox population had established a significant presence east of Bosnia. The Serbian Orthodox population was viewed as less of a threat than the Christian West and was largely left alone by the Muslim majority. Unfortunately, this indifference would prove hazardous in the coming centuries. By the 1800s, Serbian territory was expanding and its population increasing. After the crumbling Ottoman Empire finally collapsed, the Serbian presence encircled the remnants of the Muslim past, leaving the last outpost of the former isolated. The era that followed was one of turmoil and struggle for control. Ethnic tensions, which had begun centuries earlier, gradually cooked to a boil. Reports of ethnic fighting became more frequent as the decades passed.

Early in the twentieth century, one of these violent outbreaks set the world at war. In 1914, a Serbian assassin caught the visiting Archduke Franz Ferdinand of the fading Austro-Hungarian Empire unprotected. The young nationalist shot and killed him at close range. As a result of a web of national alliances already in place, the declaration of war by one country created a domino effect, bringing most of Europe into a prolonged period of conflict. Following the First World War, the region was falsely pacified like a sleeping bear; festering tensions that the war produced simmered quietly under the surface. It could only be a matter of time before they bubbled over.

When the Nazis came to power in Germany, Croatia's fascist Ustaša regime constructed an alliance with the rising European powerhouse. Together, they established supremacy in the Balkans. The Croatian regime maintained close ties to the Nazis. Their brutality soon became infamous, as they terrorized all ethnic groups in the region, including members of their own. The Serbian minority was targeted in particular, as the Ustaša attempted to drive the spreading Serbian population out of historic Croatian boundaries. When populations refused to move, genocide ensued. Minorities were shipped to concentration camps, sent on forced marches, or executed and buried. These acts of savagery left an impression that was to last for decades.

During this period, two competing forces evolved to contest the Ustaša-Nazi alliance. Josip Broz Tito's Partisans, a Communist-based army of resistance, fought the fascists from the north and east, while the Serbian Orthodox Chetniks attempted to regain regional dominance by opposing the fascists from the south.

As the Allies pushed across Europe and the Axis powers weakened, the Ustaša weakened in concert. Eventually, the Allied leaders chose to support Marshall Tito's Communist Partisans over the Serbian

Chetniks, thereby dictating who would hold power and influence in the region after the war ended. In retrospect, the Allied leaders' choice was sound, allowing for an era of peace and stability in Yugoslavia for an extraordinary period of time.

After World War II ended, Tito's communists ruled the new Federal Republic of Yugoslavia with an iron fist, but the country responded to his leadership. Ethnic rivalries were reduced to negligible levels. Six states existed within the Federation: Slovenia, Croatia, Bosnia and Herzegovina, Serbia, Montenegro, and Macedonia. Each shared Serbo-Croatian as the official language; however, the individual states' native languages were allowed to remain. The independent Yugoslav Republic was never controlled by the Soviet Union. Its citizens always enjoyed many Western-style freedoms, unlike the Soviet satellite countries where very few liberties were allowed.

Although Tito's philosophy was firmly rooted in communistic principles, he was not considered a hardliner. He worked well with the West, often to the dismay of the Soviet powers to the east. Politically, the Yugoslav leader was able to successfully manipulate East against West for decades, and was a master at improving his country's standard of living while stifling ethnic tensions. Also, he cleverly used Bosnia's Muslim population to curry favor with the Arab world. Over time, Tito became an important world figure and achieved celebrity status within his borders and beyond.

Map of Europe Pre-1990

However popular he was among his people, dissent was not tolerated and political opposition was minimized. A secret police force was established early in his rule. Reports of atrocities occurred throughout these early years, and thousands of Yugoslavians fled their homeland, fearing for their lives and their families' safety.

It was during this transitional stage, Lucas could not help remembering, when his own father disappeared. But he read on.

In retrospect, the Federal Republic of Yugoslavia was a success, much to the credit of its leader, Josip Broz Tito. But by the late 1970s, the prosperous period began to show signs of wear. In 1979, the health of Yugoslavia's illustrious leader began to fail, and the foundation for his succession was built on sand. After Tito's death in 1980, the stability of the federation was in doubt. New power struggles quickly emerged. For most of its citizens, everyday life continued as normal, but subtle signs of trouble cropped up as the years passed.

●●●●●

When the 1984 Winter Olympics arrived in Sarajevo, the U.S. State Department assigned Lucas to the region for the first time, having decommissioned him from a distinguished military career the decade before. His original assignment was not much different than the mission he had received over the telephone just hours ago. He was placed there as an observer and security specialist, to identify the up-and-coming political power players and to advise the U.S. State Department on diplomatic dealings in Yugoslavia. Because the Cold War had not officially ended, it was imperative that the Republic of Yugoslavia did not fall under Soviet control. Ironically, as time would reveal, the Soviet Union's breakup occurred sooner than that of the Republic of Yugoslavia.

●●●●●

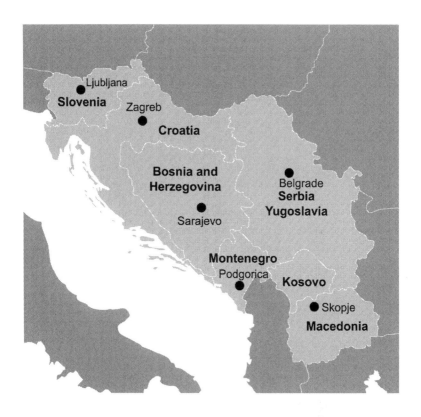

The Former Yugoslavia - Pre 1990

As the plane approached the Tokyo airport, the passengers were instructed to prepare for landing. Lucas placed the document back into its jacket and put his seat upright. Surprised at how quickly the trip's first leg had passed, he decided to finish the review somewhere over the Pacific Ocean. Obeying the flight attendant's instructions, he stowed his tray, fastened his seat belt, and prepared for landing.

V

By eleven that evening, Lucas had already spent six hours of the journey's second leg in the air. His connection was scheduled to perfection; virtually no time was lost in the Tokyo airport. The brief layover allowed just enough time for him to wash his hands and face before boarding his flight to the States. It amused him to greet the cleaning staff in decent Japanese as he entered the restroom. He had picked up the basics of the language during a brief assignment to Japan and South Korea in the late 1970s. The crew of Japanese ladies covered their mouths and giggled after he left. Lucas admired the courteousness of the Japanese and always enjoyed his time spent there.

Still, he was happy to be airborne when the flight to Chicago departed on schedule. As on the flight from Bangkok, he settled comfortably into his first-class seat, but he couldn't keep suspicious thoughts of Morton Riggs from resurfacing in his mind. Morton was never known to cater to anyone's comfort unless he needed something desperately. Lucas knew he would have to be extremely careful.

By two o'clock in the morning, the plane was halfway across the Pacific. Drowsily awaking from a nap, Lucas reopened his dossier on the Balkans, to finish the reading he had begun on his last flight.

●●●●●

The years following the 1984 Winter Olympics were ones of political squabbling and power struggle among the ethnic groups. The power-sharing agreement Tito left behind was in shambles. Because the highest percentage of the republic's population was Serbian Orthodox, the Serbs moved carefully but aggressively. The national army was systematically placed under their control, as almost all generals and high-ranking officers were Serbian.

In 1989, a ruthless and calculating political force arrived in Belgrade when a communist throwback, Slobodan Milošević, took power. The centerpiece of the new leader's inaugural address was the claim that Serbia would be the prevailing power in Yugoslavia's future, and that the process would begin with the return to Serbian control of Kosovo, an area in southwest Serbia that had been populated by an Albanian Muslim majority over the centuries.

Lucas had been present for this speech; he remembered warning the State Department through diplomatic channels to monitor the political developments in Belgrade with the utmost scrutiny. His warning had seemed to fall on deaf ears.

The Separation Of The Former Yugoslavian States - Post 1995

Later that year, a Croatian nationalist, Franjo Tudjman rose to power in Zagreb. A former general in the Yugoslav Army, he began touting Croatian separation from the republic at the same time his Serbian counterpart was promising expansion.

In 1990, Slovenia, the small, northernmost Yugoslavian state, bordering Austria, Hungary, and Italy, voted for independence. Initially, the Serbs attempted to forcefully subdue the renegade state, though it quickly pulled back and allowed Slovenia's sovereignty under the watchful eyes of the European Community. Following its neighbor's lead, Croatia also voted for partition, but could not break away as easily. Soon after Croatia's vote for independence, complete control of the Federal Republic of Yugoslavia's military was seized by the Serbs in the name of national security. In response, the Croatian nationalists confiscated all weaponry within its borders. It wasn't long before skirmishes in the villages of eastern, central, and southern Croatia broke out between Serbian citizens and the Croatian population. The Serbian civilians were armed with weaponry given to them by the still official Yugoslav National Army (JNA). Paramilitary forces were established to create disturbances serious enough to warrant JNA involvement to control regions within Croatia that the Serbian leadership considered to be of strategic importance. Belgrade's official position stated that the JNA was being used strictly to quell uprisings and to defuse the escalating civil war within official Yugoslavian borders. This ploy delayed Western intervention under the pretense that the existing republic had the situation under control.

At first, Lucas had been astonished by the Belgrade reports. Afterwards, he was almost amused by the creativity of the content.

● ● ● ● ●

In 1991, Lucas was touring eastern Croatia when full-scale war erupted after the JNA attempted to capture the cities of Osijek and Vukovar. That very summer, after having pounded both cities with heavy artillery for weeks, the Serbian-controlled military proceeded to storm Vukovar. House-to-house combat erupted inside what little of the city remained. Lucas had been tipped off about the JNA operation and had a chance to scout the area for a military buildup. Arriving just three days before the onslaught began, he was amazed at his discovery. Vukovar, a once-vibrant city that had nearly been reduced to rubble, was completely surrounded by the JNA. Most of its inhabitants had fled for their lives. Lucas watched the events transpire. With great effort, he recorded his observations and forwarded the information via a number of intelligence contacts. He escaped the Serbian onslaught by only a few hours as the remaining routes out of the city were closed off. Still, the city held on.

As the summer of 1991 ended in Vukovar, the overwhelmingly outnumbered Croatian fighters bunkered themselves down for a last stand Davy Crockett would have been proud of. Days, weeks, and months passed as attack after attack failed to thwart the city's resistance. The extended struggle demoralized the JNA, and the death toll mounted on both sides.

In September of that year, a second push to capture the city was initiated by the Serbs. This time, the JNA changed tactics and combined heavy artillery shelling with air bombardment. Nevertheless, the resistance held out, surviving on limited rations and plentiful prayers.

Croatia - Post 1995

Two months later, the JNA finally entered Vukovar's bombed-out ruins and began a cleanup operation. All remaining Croatian fighters and many civilians were gathered and massacred; their bodies were dumped into mass graves scattered throughout the countryside. Hospitals were emptied; the patients were lost and never found. Over the next several months, Lucas stayed as close to the action as possible without drawing suspicion. His contact with United Nations authorities was limited. Officially, NATO was unengaged in the matter, although unofficially Lucas knew better.

Lucas surveyed Croatia's Slavonia as thoroughly as possible without putting himself in grave danger. He regularly filed reports for the U.S. State Department at embassies in Zagreb, Ljubljana, and the consulate in Sarajevo. To obtain valid information, he established solid relationships with foreign diplomats, journalists, and villagers in the vicinity. These contacts allowed him to separate facts from propaganda and sift over the combat zone's constantly changing demographics with greater accuracy. Conflicting reports arrived almost daily. The fact-finding was painstakingly slow, deliberate, and extremely risky.

Later that same year, Lucas was reassigned to Dalmatia, the narrow strip of mountainous terrain stretching down the Adriatic coast. There, intense fighting had broken out in concert with the hostilities in Slavonia. Upon arrival, it seemed to Lucas that only the landscape and linguistic dialect had changed. The combatants' faces remained the same.

At the southernmost tip of the Dalmatian coast lay the historic city of Dubrovnik, standing out against the Adriatic Sea like a pearl in a jeweler's case. Not long after Lucas entered the city gates, JNA and Montenegrin paramilitary forces surrounded it. U.N. representatives worked desperately to spare the city from destruction, but their efforts proved unsuccessful. Mortars and artillery showered the medieval city from a ridge high above over the coming months.

Lucas was caught in the initial assault and took refuge in a bomb shelter constructed during the Cold War. For nearly six days and nights, he remained bunkered with hundreds of the city's inhabitants. Sleep was next to impossible. Food was scarce. When the shelling let up, he spent the next twelve nights helping the civilian population accumulate food and supplies under cover of darkness.

For brief periods, the bombing stopped long enough for the inhabitants to return to their homes to secure their belongings that remained intact. During these occasions, Lucas prepared his camera. He surveyed and photographed the destruction, documented dates and locations, and then forwarded the data to the U.S. State Department through intelligence alliances.

Occasionally, he was called upon to perform work of a more dubious nature. The formal policy of the U.S. government was one of non-intervention. Unofficially, the policy contained gray areas where direct involvement was permitted. Lucas was at liberty to use deadly force in certain matters that required his professional discretion. Although he had been assigned for observational purposes only, he was at liberty to lethally act in matters concerning his personal safety or in the best interest of civilians or refugees. The main difficulty for Lucas was to determine who was a noncombatant. It was not uncommon to witness citizens firing automatic weapons from their bedroom windows as the fighting spread like wildfire throughout the region. Many times neighbors turned violent against one another, sometimes after having been friends for decades.

Usually, Lucas overlooked situations where his action could not aid innocent life. As a rule, he did not act at all unless defenseless women and children were involved. He refused to choose sides, though he was not opposed to discriminating against one ethnic group or another if the circumstances dictated it. He figured that there was enough blame to go around. The majority of his time was spent photographing military buildup and documenting destruction and atrocities, which he then forwarded to his superiors.

As winter of 1991 neared, Lucas decided he had had enough. All diplomatic efforts to end the crisis had stalled and the United Nations initiatives appeared to be going nowhere, bogged down in bureaucracy. Success was unlikely within such a fragmented diplomatic framework. As the fighting continued and the European Community resisted involvement, Lucas's patience grew weary as he watched the country of his birth disintegrate into war-torn ruins.

Lucas could remember joyful festivities, where the three ethnic groups danced to accordion music and sang the same folk songs; now these same three groups were possessed with hateful rage and destroying each other with AK-47's, mortars, tanks, and landmines. Early that December Lucas requested a meeting at the U.S. embassy in Belgrade. Over the next three weeks, he drafted his conclusions and recommendations, and then submitted the dossier with his resignation to the ambassador. Upon delivery, he instructed that the document be immediately forwarded to the secretary of state. Finally, on December 19, 1991, Lucas officially retired.

VI

A powerful spring storm had passed through northern Illinois earlier that morning, delaying arrivals and departures out of O'Hare for most of the day. Air traffic controllers instructed Lucas's flight to circle for a good twenty minutes before permitting it to land; he used the extra time to look through his dossier on the Balkans to see whether any important details jumped out at him.

Lucas was anxious to disembark, stretch his legs, and move about the airport. The trip had been long and exhausting, but as he strolled down the concourse, he was surprised at how good he felt. Then again, he was proud of his physical condition and he took care of his body. He swam whenever possible and ran three miles a day; he could run as fast now at fifty-five as he could at thirty-five. In his younger days he had earned a black belt in karate, which, although he no longer practiced regularly, continued to benefit his mind and his reflexes. He found both Chinese acupuncture and chiropractic treatment helpful in staving off the other aches and pains he heard other men his age complain about. He applauded his decision not to smoke cigarettes early in life, long before the habit's health risks had been proven.

Still, nature in its cruelty was taking a toll on his physical abilities. He knew the assignment Morton Riggs had planned for him would likely require him to defend himself physically. He was confident he could handle himself with an opponent half his age, but he would have to substitute agility and finesse for brute strength and raw power.

Time was also taking a toll on his appearance. Over the last decade, noticeable wrinkles had surfaced around his eyes and nose. Pockmark scars, tracing the angle of his right jawline since puberty, stood out as his facial skin sagged with age. For the most part, his hair had maintained its coal-black color, but within the last eighteen months, with the stress from the Balkan crises taking its toll, several patches had abandoned their natural allegiance. The temples surrendered first, turning a compromising shade of silver-gray. His beard and chest hair soon followed.

What remained unchanged were his battle scars, which served as reminders of his past, but thankfully did not compromise his current physical performance. He had been shot at many times, but never shot. During his second tour of duty in Vietnam, he had suffered a fractured right ankle while being temporarily assigned to an airborne ranger unit. His final jump was a reconnaissance mission during the war's final stages that was scheduled at night and organized in haste. The selected landing zone proved to be less than adequate, and an unexpected tree snarled his parachute. After cutting himself free, a submerged rock outcropping waited for him in the undergrowth below. As he hit the ground, he heard a loud snap and instantly knew that his leg had been broken. The injury's single lasting result was that he could now feel weather changes in advance of meteorological forecasts. The damaged limb often caused him to limp on cold, rainy days. Incredibly, Lucas managed to escape the Vietnam War without sustaining any other permanent damage.

And in the early 1980s, the tip of his right index finger had been smashed by the backlash of untamed jungle as he swung a machete in Nicaragua. At the time, he was hacking his way through the underbrush to another poorly planned landing zone. The finger's main tendon was partially severed; even after surgical repair, the damaged digit never recovered its full range of motion. Instead, it remained semi-flexed, and he was unable extend the finger to point, although he could still fire a weapon effectively.

• • • • •

In 1984, the U.S. State Department assigned Lucas to the Balkans on a long-term, low-key mission of consulate security and surveillance. At first he viewed the role as a reprimand for unsatisfactory performance. Still at the peak of his career, he assumed that this latest assignment reflected his superiors' dissatisfaction. But within two weeks of arriving, he no longer resented his new position. Rather, it began to dawn on him that it was what he had subconsciously desired for years. But the assignment's full potential wasn't realized until it was forced upon him. While official business was his chief priority, Lucas spent his free time researching his past, trying to recover what little remained of his life from long ago. He was certain that within Yugoslavia there remained childhood friends and family still alive and well. Now he had the chance to explore leads that might help him relocate those people who had vanished from his life. Among these vanished people, none was as important to him as his father; Lucas was determined to discover what had happened to him and where his remains had been placed. No new information had surfaced since he went missing when Lucas was a teenager. U.S. government reports were incomplete and unconfirmed. The American ambassador in Belgrade during the 1950s was unable to press the matter because of diplomatic restrictions with the communist nation during the peak of the Cold War. His father's disappearance was never solved, leaving Lucas to suspect government involvement from the beginning. Now he was in a position to investigate the matter further. He was determined to learn the truth of his paternal loss and fulfill his personal agenda while simultaneously being paid for his official responsibilities. As a bonus, he could perform these tasks without the risk of being shot at. Perhaps he had grown wiser in his years, to perceive the benefits of his situation. Maybe fate had smiled at him. Whatever the reason, he became enthusiastic about the post and searched out ways to extend his position in Sarajevo.

• • • • •

After a short layover in Chicago, Lucas boarded another United Airlines jet bound for Washington, D.C. This one arrived at Dulles on schedule, an hour and forty-five minutes later, and although this final leg of his journey from Thailand felt almost unbelievably short, he was thrilled when the call to land was announced.

The plane landed smoothly and taxied quickly to its destination, a gate located almost mile away. After arriving at the terminal, the engines were cut and the "fasten seatbelt" lights were extinguished. The passengers rose in a herd, scrambling to retrieve their baggage from the overhead compartments as if grabbing their luggage first would mean they wouldn't have to wait their turn to exit. The first-class passengers were dismissed first, and after perfunctory goodbyes to the three flight attendants who had waited on him, Lucas stepped off the plane, minimalist luggage in hand, in search of Morton Riggs. The hunt ended nearly as soon as it began, when Morton parted a small crowd with his right hand held high in the air. With an artificial smile spread across his face, the seasoned statesman greeted Lucas effusively. After the two had shaken hands, Morton seized Lucas's left elbow and whisked him away briskly. The diplomat was accompanied by two secret service agents dressed in blue suits and dark sunglasses. Another official soon met them and joined their party, following a few steps behind. Lucas recognized him as Curtis Sheets; he held an embassy post in Belgrade. The men moved purposefully through the airport until they reached a concealed exit reserved for government officials, celebrities, and others of VIP status. At the entrance, a third secret service agent waited for the group. After Lucas and the others passed through, he locked the unmarked door behind them. Morton then directed the entourage down an iron-grate stairway and toward a limousine, which had just pulled to the curb.

Lucas was impressed with the efficiency of his reception, but wondered why all the attention was necessary. He doubted Morton Riggs often wasted energy shuttling associates to and from the airport. He presumed that Morton's schedule was tight and such precision was the result of a time constraint or a desire to avoid rush hour traffic.

The limo driver checked the traffic, turned the wheel, and veered into his selected lane. Moments later, Morton Riggs began bombarding Lucas with updates about the crisis in the Balkans, apparently oblivious to the fact that jetlag was catching up to his red-eyed conversation partner. Eventually, Lucas's monosyllabic responses must have clued him in; the State Department undersecretary shifted forward in the back seat and changed tactics.

Motioning toward the man who had joined them at the airport, Morton said, "Lucas, this is Curtis Sheets--but I think you two are already acquainted. Curtis has been brought here to update you on the latest developments in the crisis. It's his assessment that substantial changes have taken place in Belgrade since your untimely departure." Whether consciously or not, Morton was now speaking at an elevated volume, as if talking to a hard-of-hearing senior citizen. "I believe you'll find each other of considerable value in your new assignments."

Morton's style, or lack of it, finally grated on Lucas enough to rouse him from the half-sleep into which he had slipped. "Listen, Morty, I just spent over twenty-four hours traveling around the globe. Get me to a hotel, let me shower and rest for a few hours. Then, after I'm alert and prepared to participate, we can discuss matters like professionals."

"Fine," Morton sighed. "We'll drop you off at the Hyatt, get you something to eat, and give you a chance to rest. My driver, Lionel, will pick you up in the hotel lobby at seven o'clock. It is going on three P.M. now, so that gives you four hours to freshen up, gather your thoughts, and prepare any additional information. We'll meet at my office at 7:30 sharp, all right?"

Lucas ignored him. Sticking out his right hand, he aimed it toward Curtis Sheets.

"Good to see you again, Curtis. And how is the lovely Alexandra?" he asked, remembering the young Serbian trophy whose heart Curtis had captured while she worked as his translator. Curtis extended his hand and shook it robustly, demonstrating his respect for Lucas's capabilities.

"She's fine, just fine. A little irritable lately, you know how those Slavic women can get? Real firecrackers - they'll start with your fingers and take the whole hand off if you're not careful," he quipped, his British accent subtle but noticeable.

"What about Šemsa, Monika, and Mehmed? How many of the old crew are left in Sarajevo?" Lucas quizzed, feeling more alert and wanting to know the status of the most trusted consulate employees he had left behind.

"The entire team has dispersed, though the consulate still functions. Right now, it is considerably understaffed," answered Curtis.

"What changes have been made? Has everyone been evacuated? What's the infrastructure's status? Is it secure?"

"Only a skeleton crew remains. All nonessential workers were let go the day all hell broke loose. Technically, this is day number three of the siege, but by the time you get there, I'm sure much more destruction will be done. I doubt things will look the same as you remember."

Curtis then tried to create an image of the reality in Lucas's mind. "The U.S. consulate was hit the first day by some heavy artillery south of the city; howitzers, I believe. No serious damage, just a few shattered windows and a ruptured roof. No one has been able to repair the hole yet, and we're hoping that it doesn't rain. On the other hand, if it were burning, we'd be praying for a downpour. Others nearby got hammered worse than we did. I have a strong feeling the consulate will see more." Curtis waited for Lucas's follow-up questions.

"What type of fighting is going on at the moment? Has it quieted down some? Is there any encouraging dialogue taking place?"

"Oh, you know how it goes there…," Curtis said. He let Lucas contemplate his answer.

"Nothing. Not a goddamn thing," Lucas said, answering his own questions, and then turning back to Morton Riggs. "This is going bad, Morty, and it's going to get worse."

Morton drew in some air, raised his eyebrows, and then exhaled. "This is why you are here, my friend." He added nothing more, not wanting to interrupt the ongoing conversation.

Curtis picked up eagerly. "The JNA was ordered out of Bosnia weeks ago. All Bosnian-Serb nationals were allowed to stay. It's impossible to know who stayed and who didn't. We do know this: the artillery and tanks are still there. The locals, paramilitary actually, showed up well armed and looking for trouble. For a while it seemed there was very little organization, every man for himself. It may still be that way. Until we can construct some sort of organized unity, there'll be no cease-fire."

Lucas pictured a city in chaos, cars and buildings burning, citizens firing small arms from their apartment balconies, death and destruction everywhere.

"What's the casualty estimate so far?"

"Surprisingly low at the moment," Curtis replied, with a look of disbelief on his face. "The first day was the worst – that's when many civilians got caught by surprise. Snipers were shooting into crowds of unarmed protestors, for Christ's sake. Then the mortar rounds started falling. That unleashed massive panic that caused more destruction than the landing shells. By and by, the locals are taking up arms, don't ask me how. We're constantly hearing small skirmishes and occasional, larger firefights. Usually, they don't last long, but they do seem to crop up at the strangest places and at the most unusual hours; almost always in the middle of the night."

"The citizens are moving when they're least likely to be hit by sniper fire, or howitzer rounds, for that matter. It might have something to do with their drinking habits," Lucas stated. *Late-evening shots of plum brandy might give a man enough courage to risk his life by defending his home,* he considered.

"Aside from the buildings being demolished, the heavy artillery hasn't caused too many direct casualties; for now. It's the bloody snipers picking off anyone who crosses their paths that is the more immediate threat. The bastards shoot at anything that moves. Old men, women, children, they don't give a shit!" Curtis's voice became excited, his accent growing stronger with it.

The men sat and pondered these troubling facts; the mood in the limo grew somber as it approached the Hyatt. Lucas tried to assess the facts presented before him and thought hard about how best to proceed. He needed time by himself to sort through the new information. A rest, a shower, and some food awaited his attention. It was going to be another long evening.

VII

The telephone rang for almost a full minute before Lucas awoke to answer it. He had found his room quickly, and once inside, he ordered food from the service desk, showered, and then laid out the change of clothes he planned to wear to the State Department meeting. Then, exhausted from jetlag, he turned on the television and cranked up the volume so he wouldn't fall into a deep slumber. Yet as he reclined on the bed, the blaring television was no match for the devious temptations of sleep. The three hours passed in what seemed like minutes. When consciousness returned, he lay groggily on the bed and listened to the phone ring over and over before picking up the receiver.

Connected on the other end was Morton Riggs's driver, Lionel James. He was calling from the hotel lobby. James was an ex-Marine who had been awarded a Congressional Medal of Honor for his performance in the 1991 Gulf War in Kuwait. At the awards ceremony, he had made a bold move that had paid off nicely. While the medal was being pinned onto his chest, he had bluntly asked the attending congressman for a job in Washington, D.C. when his military service concluded. The congressman, who represented James's home state of Alabama, admired the twenty-four-year-old's ambition enough to promise him serious consideration. After James was honorably discharged in the summer of 1991, the congressman contacted him about the position of staff chauffeur for the U.S. State Department. James accepted the duty at once, and after a mandatory security program to qualify for the prestigious position, he was officially assigned to the State Department's limo service team and had been the undersecretary of state's driver for nearly six months.

"Mr. Martin, this is Lionel James - Mr. Riggs's chauffeur. It's exactly seven P.M., and I'm scheduled to deliver you to a meeting. Will you need a few more minutes?"

Lucas cleared his throat, attempting to hide the fact that he had been sound asleep.

"No, no, Mr. James. Just sit tight and I'll be right down." He jumped from the bed and began to dress hurriedly. Yet after a moment of mental debate, he regained his composure and intentionally slowed his pace. *No need to act like a college student who overslept for an exam. Morton called me, let him wait*, he decided.

At 7:15, the hotel lobby's elevator doors opened and Lucas stepped out. Lionel James was waiting near the front desk, standing at attention. Lucas peered through the hotel's revolving glass door and saw that the limousine's engine was still running. He left his room key with the concierge and approached the chauffeur with an expressionless face.

"Sorry to keep you waiting. Jetlag, you know?" Lucas said, as he hurriedly walked past.

"Yes, sir."

The rush hour traffic had diminished and the sleek black sedan moved confidently along the D.C. streets. Lucas assumed they were headed to the State Department headquarters, but after a short distance, he realized the limo was moving in a different direction. Curious, he chimed in on the intercom.

"Mr. James, it's been a few years since I've toured the city, but from what I remember, the State Department is in another part of town. Where are you taking me this evening?"

Lowering the glass partition, the chauffeur spoke to Lucas while looking at him through the rearview mirror.

"Mr. Riggs instructed me to take you to another location. He said there is someone he'd like you to meet before your briefing at the State Department."

"And where is that?" Lucas continued, intrigued by the altered itinerary.

"Just a few more minutes, sir, and we'll be turning in," said James.

Soon the limousine slowed and then made a left turn into a driveway that was blocked by an automated barricade. A sentry's box stood at the driveway entrance. A bronze plate on the front gate came into view as the vehicle approached. The sign read, in bold inscription, *Embassy of the Federal Republic of Yugoslavia.*

A very interesting development, Lucas thought. *I wonder what other surprises Morty has in store for me.*

The front gate guard granted Lionel James permission to proceed. A moment later, the limo slid into its designated parking place. James emerged from behind the steering wheel and circled behind to let his passenger out. Lucas hated the formality, but understood the importance of diplomatic presentation. After stepping out, he was led up the sidewalk to what appeared to be a renovated townhouse in an unassuming neighborhood. At first glance, the grounds did not appear to be protected, but on closer inspection outside surveillance could be seen. Several security cameras were strategically positioned and two armed guards dressed in plain clothes circled the perimeter. Except for the sign in front and an oversized antenna protruding from the house's roof, there was little to suggest that the dwelling was an embassy.

As they approached the entrance, another security officer opened the door and allowed them inside. They were directed into a small room to the left of the front parlor. There, they were instructed to wait. The room contained only a couch, a coffee table, and two chairs that were positioned side by side. The walls were freshly painted. Facing the couch, a painting of a fisherman bringing in his nets on the Adriatic Sea was prominently hung. A Yugoslavian flag was draped from a rod in the far corner. On the coffee table rested a vase with freshly cut flowers, two large ashtrays, and a soccer magazine in a language that used the Cyrillic script.

Within minutes, Morton Riggs and Curtis Sheets entered the room from a door on the opposite side. Morton dismissed Lionel James and the chauffeur immediately returned to the limousine. After the two diplomats were seated, Morton leaned forward and addressed Lucas in a lowered voice while looking at him directly in the eyes. Curtis sat back, crossed his legs at the ankles, and allowed Morton to explain the situation.

"Lucas, as Curtis has already told you, there have been some strategic changes made in Belgrade since you've been out of the loop. We purposely included you at this meeting so you could assess the personalities and political climate we've been dealing with."

Morton leaned back and pulled a pack of Dunhills from his suit jacket's inner pocket. He passed one to Curtis, then took out his Zippo lighter. First offering it to Curtis, he then lit his own. Again, he shifted forward.

"You're going to meet the Republic of Yugoslavia's new ambassador who was assigned here not long ago. The one you were familiar with has been recalled to Belgrade. It seems he didn't want to play the difficult hands his superiors kept dealing him. You'll be introduced as my subordinate. Speak only in English and say as little as possible. I want you to pay special attention to the ambassador's reaction when I press him on his government's position on various issues. He will meet with us for less than fifteen minutes. That is all the time we'll need. When the meeting concludes, we'll go to my office to discuss your impressions."

Just then, the ambassador's door swung open and a staff member directed the team inside. Morton introduced himself first, and then his colleagues individually. The ambassador's name was Obrad Dokić, and he had been assigned to the Washington, D.C. post only two months earlier. The young emissary presented himself professionally, dressing for the occasion in diplomatic attire, which included a finely tailored suit and freshly polished shoes. He welcomed the U.S. envoy cordially and offered them cigarettes, which Morton and Curtis accepted without delay. Plum brandy was poured into small glasses for each. They toasted the drink with a communal "Cheers!" Then, following an awkward moment of silence, Dokić rested his elbows on his desk, clasped his hands firmly together, and initiated a dialogue in exceptional English, just slightly tinted with an eastern European accent.

"And so," he started, hesitantly, "How may I help you gentlemen this evening?" Without moving his head, he cast his eyes sideways at each guest, one by one, though knowing which delegate was the group's principal.

Morton wasted no time taking the initiative.

"Mr. Dokić," started Morton, "the U.S. State Department has serious issues that need to be addressed by your government concerning Serbia's current role in the Balkan crisis and its agenda. As you know, we've been mediating the breakup of ex-Yugoslavia from the beginning. The U.S. government, along with its European allies, has presented what appeared to be a firm but flexible partition proposal that was accepted by each party from the beginning. However, now that a full-scale civil war has broken out, it appears the initial agreement has been scrapped in its entirety. We cannot seem to re-establish serious discussions with any of the warring parties, one of which is the Republic of Serbia. We are now here to learn what your government's position is and what we can do to resolve the conflict and eliminate further bloodshed."

Obrad Dokić paused in thought for what seemed like an unreasonable period of time. He sat at his desk with his hands clasped beneath his chin. His face was expressionless when he spoke.

"The position of the government in Belgrade is clear. The safety of the homes, families, and livelihoods of all Serbian citizens within the *Federal Republic of Yugoslavia* is to remain the top priority."

Morton ignored the obvious emphasis in the ambassador's words and continued. "The fighting has spread through the whole of

Bosnia and Herzegovina. It was originally agreed upon that Sarajevo was to be spared. This is no longer the case. The Serbian-controlled JNA has reneged on that agreement. The city is now under siege. What is the reason for the change in diplomacy, Mr. Dokić?"

The Serbian ambassador waited a moment longer, and then responded. "Mr. Riggs, I am sure you are aware that the Belgrade officials ordered the JNA out of Bosnia prior to the crisis in and around Sarajevo, as promised. You must also be aware that the whole of Bosnia and Herzegovina has been populated over the centuries by a large population of Serbian citizens. Surely you can understand that these citizens are seeking their safety and are defending their homes and families from outside aggressors?"

Morton pushed forward with his questioning, aware that he had been offered nothing of value.

"The United Nations has access to confirmed reports of a large JNA presence in and around Sarajevo," he repeated. "Satellite imagery confirms those reports. It is the position of the U. S. government that the Serbs are not honoring their end of the agreement. Can you give me Belgrade's official position on these accusations?"

Dokić deliberately stared into the eyes of Morton Riggs. He replied slowly and clearly.

"The Federal Republic of Yugoslavia has honored all agreements set forth by the United Nations charter. The Federal Republic of Yugoslavia is directly responsible for the protection of its citizens. The *Federal Republic of Yugoslavia* believes the *United States of America* would act the same in similar circumstances. This is my official statement and it shall conclude tonight's meeting. I enjoyed our conversation and the opportunity to have formally met with you."

The three visitors noted that the allotted time had passed and quickly finished their aperitifs. Without any new information, they graciously departed the Yugoslavian Embassy. Dramatic new insights had neither been expected nor anticipated. It was a casual meeting, designed to give Lucas a sense of Belgrade's official diplomatic stance and the direction of their future actions. Lucas was satisfied; he had heard enough.

The threesome retreated to the State Department limousine. Inside the car, the men sat quietly with their own thoughts, reserving commentary until after having reached Morton's office as originally planned. Lucas stared through the window as they moved through the city. Outside the Beltway, he noted how little Washington had changed since he last visited. Road construction was everywhere, homeless people were strewn across the sidewalks, and drug dealers and prostitutes choked many street corners. It seemed a disgrace that all of this was taking place under the noses of the nation's policymakers. Certainly some of them had to notice; or did repeated exposure eventually make them immune? Morton didn't mention it; Lionel James hadn't said anything earlier in the evening. But there it was; in the open, in front of the eyes of the world. Whatever the reason, the problem persisted and no one seemed to care.

I think it's time to leave soon, Lucas decided. While traveling throughout Southeast Asia, he had seen poverty on a daily basis and he understood the reasons for its existence in the places he had visited. In those countries, it just seemed to be natural to him. But in the United States, he never understood how crime, drugs and homelessness had so quickly plagued the nation. He felt disgusted with Washington; it didn't really matter to him that he was about to leave it for a war zone. *It can't be much worse than this*, he thought to himself, trying to ignore the unpleasant scenery outside.

Lucas turned to Curtis Sheets and inquired about what he had missed over the last few months. Curtis smiled with delight after becoming the center of attention. Lucas had many questions to ask, so many that he didn't know which ones to begin with. Primarily, he wanted to know which city Curtis had been working, what he had witnessed, and whom he had talked to and dealt with. He wanted to know who was on the diplomatic team in charge of negotiating a settlement and what progress, if any, had been made.

He asked detailed questions about the key politicians and military leaders who were responsible for the actions currently taking place. Certainly they were not of the antiquated caliber that Lucas had left behind. And finally, he wanted to know what had become of his civilian friends and contacts who, on several occasions, had risked their lives aiding him in his surveillance. In particular, he wanted to know about the condition of Edis Avdić. *May as well begin there,* he thought.

"Tell me Curtis, did you ever hear from my young Muslim friend I told you about before I left?"

"I didn't hear a word from the lad for the longest time," Curtis responded. "Then, about a week ago, I received a phone call from a man who sounded to be under a lot of stress. I couldn't understand him very well. His English wasn't terribly good and there was a lot of background noise, but he specifically asked for you. It took awhile for me to put together that it was your friend Edis."

"What was his problem?" Lucas asked.

"I couldn't be sure. We didn't speak long. I told him you might be returning soon, but I couldn't give him details. I advised him to try again in a few days, but he never called back," Curtis said. "Lucas, I really can't say for certain if he knows that you're coming."

Lucas wondered some more, but said nothing.

●●●●●

Edis Avdić was a young Bosnian Muslim whom Lucas had befriended in the early stages of the war in Slavonia, near the Croatian city of Slavonski Brod, where Lucas had been born. Edis proved to be an invaluable asset, assisting Lucas in information gathering. He put Lucas in contact with important people in the region, those with political connections, and others with military clout. Edis was well regarded by both the local Croats and Muslims. The respect was earned. He was a good soldier, a good leader, and though only twenty-four years old, Lucas told him openly that he possessed more insight than a man twice his age. It was necessary shrewdness; without it Edis would not have survived to adulthood. When the two last spoke, Edis was preparing to flee northern Bosnia to take care of his mother and younger sister in Sarajevo, a city that was, at the time, far away from the fighting. Edis knew the journey would be long and treacherous, requiring travel through hundreds of kilometers of war-ravaged countryside. Still, he considered it a trip that had to be made. There was no life for him any more in his hometown of Brčko. There, only death and destruction remained.

●●●●●

The Sava River divided northern Bosnia from the Croatian province of Slavonia; on its southern banks lay the Bosnian town of Brčko. Over the centuries the surrounding region had become home to a significant population of Serbs; now that Serbs desperately wanted to be the controlling majority, Brčko had been transformed into an ethnic hotspot. At the moment, no lives were left unscathed from the war taking place there.

Shortly after Vukovar fell in 1991, Edis's father relocated his wife to Sarajevo, where their daughter had been sent weeks earlier in anticipation of fighting that was inevitably coming. As a boy, Edis's father had witnessed the ethnic tragedies that occurred in the area during World War II. The older man predicted that hostilities would arrive before much longer in Brčko. He was correct, and he was not to survive the initial outbreak.

Almost a week before his father's death, Edis had left with a group of local men to join the Muslim militia. In the process, his group was cut off by a JNA unit and he barely escaped with his life. When he returned home six days later, he discovered his family's house burned and his father's dead body in the cellar. He had been shot, execution-style, in the back of the head. Serbian neighbors whom Edis had been close with for years refused to convey the details of what had happened. Later, a twelve-year-old Muslim boy who had been hiding in the nearby forest told Edis how he watched a local Serbian official, dressed in black commando attire, lead a group of young Serbian men to their house and instigate an argument. Edis's father was encircled; the men beat and kicked him until he fell. They carried him into his house, and then everything was quiet for about ten minutes. The Muslim boy, named Alija, said he then heard a gunshot. Alija couldn't explain further because he had run immediately after the blast, fearing they would kill him if he was discovered.

After that, Edis remained in the area despite the risk to his safety. He secretly convened some local men and formed a small pocket of resistance. It was at this time, perhaps a month after his father was killed, when he intercepted Lucas wandering in the forest, searching for traces of graves filled with murdered corpses. At first Edis's outfit surrounded Lucas and pointed their AK-47's at his head. But it soon became obvious that Lucas was not an enemy, as he was not dressed in the camouflage fatigues or military insignia Edis had become accustomed to seeing worn by the local combatants. Edis sensed there was something special about the man in the brown leather jacket, woolen pullover, khaki pants, and brown boots, whom they had found hiking alone in the woods and speaking their language without an accent. After a short conversation, Edis became Lucas's liaison. He agreed to help Lucas try to find burial sites and feed him accurate information regarding the movements of the warring parties' troops. This relationship lasted for several months, until Lucas was reassigned to Dubrovnik. They were in contact one last time before he resigned from his job in Belgrade. It was then that Edis announced to Lucas his intention of forging his way through Bosnia in order to reunite with his family in Sarajevo. He had no reason to stay in Brčko, and he had vowed never to return. Lucas understood his motives, though he strongly advised against attempting to move through such dangerous and hostile territory. Instead, Lucas recommended that his friend remain connected with the Muslim militia, which was sure to need his assistance as they fought for their survival. In the end, Edis made his final decision and Lucas could only wish him well. Before he left, he gave Edis the U.S. consulate's telephone number in Sarajevo and instructed him to search out Curtis Sheets when he got there. Now Lucas was aware of Edis's location, but his condition remained in doubt.

●●●●●

The limousine arrived at the State Department at 9:30 P.M. Morton's office was located in a secured complex near the State Department proper; the three men passed through a series of security measures before entering the building.

Morton's office was lavishly appointed. A stout walnut desk dominated the room and a burgundy leather couch with two matching chairs completed the set. An imported Turkish rug blanketed the hardwood floor. Two telephones sat on the desk and a cedar cigar box was placed between them. An obligatory but rarely used desktop computer rested in a deep sleep on the desk's right side. An American landscape painting hung above the couch and a portrait of the president was positioned on the opposite wall, just above a wet bar.

Morton seated everyone and poured drinks. He wheeled around in his leather chair, leaned back comfortably, and then raised his feet up on the desk. After removing his glasses, he rubbed his tired eyes. Lucas lifted his glass and proposed a toast commonly used in ex-Yugoslavia.

"*Živeli!*" he said, using the Serbian salutation. Next, he looked individually into the eyes of each and gently tapped the bottom of his glass to the bottoms of theirs.

Morton took a long swig of his Scotch whisky, then set his glass down in front of him. He sat in deep thought for a moment before glancing up at the faces studying his.

"What do you make of the new ambassador on the other end of town, Lucas?"

"It appears to me that the powers in Belgrade are playing for keeps," he began. "The previous ambassador came across as receptive and cooperative. Mr. Dokić presents himself as protective and defensive. I don't believe he'll be much help to us. I can't explain the sudden change in personnel. Maybe there was some internal strife, a power struggle, or some new connection that got Mr. Dokić the promotion. It's not unheard of there, you know. It is quite common for qualified workers to be demoted or replaced so that a friend or a cousin can land an influential position, regardless of whether the replacement is qualified."

Morton interjected, "I'm referring to his demeanor, Lucas. He seems obstinate as hell."

"He *is* obstinate as hell, Morty! All these young nationalists are. They truly believe in a 'Greater Serbia' and that's all they'll settle for," retorted Lucas.

"Lucas, there is something else you need to know," Curtis Sheets said, finishing the last of his whisky. "There have been many changes like this one, militarily as well as diplomatically. Almost all of the formally trained JNA leadership has been replaced with unprofessional mercenaries seeking to climb the chain of command. All of the old generals have been sent out to pasture, as it were. This new leadership can't be dealt with by using the standard methods. It's a free-for-all now."

"I have a feeling you know more than I've been told, Curtis. Don't be shy. Fill me in on the missing details."

Sheets continued, "Of course, you already know about the reports of ethnic cleansing, mass graves, and the forced relocation of civilians from areas in Slavonia and in northern Bosnia. In addition, we are now receiving unconfirmed reports of the existence of concentration camps throughout the whole of Bosnia and Herzegovina."

"Concentration camps? Jesus Christ! Morton, how long have you known about this? Curtis, are you talking about refugee camps, or more Auschwitzes, for crying out loud?" Lucas barked heatedly, having been caught by surprise.

While cutting off the tip of a cigar he was about to light up, Morton said, "Lucas, the United Nations can't get in to confirm or deny the reports. That's why we brought you back. You were the one source who can see what needs to be seen and who has reported valid information to us each and every time. We have some satellite imagery, but nothing solid to substantiate the claims. If we can get you in there to confirm, then the secretary of state can pressure NATO to take military action. Right now, we don't have the evidence or the authority to confront the Serbs with this. Until we get irrefutable proof, NATO's hands are tied and the alleged genocide continues. That's the sad truth, my friend. Due to international law, our hands, NATO's hands, and the United Nation's hands are bound until some resolutions get passed. We can't do that until we can make a legitimate case that human rights are being violated. Of course, it's too dangerous to have ambassadors, diplomats, and reporters wandering around battle zones seeking verification. We need your expertise, contacts, and skills to find the proof required for us to act."

"Lucas, these camps aren't the standard centers that the U.N. has opened to protect refugees. We are hearing rumors about 'death camps,' the elimination of all males, primarily Muslims, by mass execution," Curtis clarified. "The United Nations is receiving unconfirmed reports that the civilian refugee camps will soon be targeted as well. As it stands now, the U.N. is virtually powerless to stop this and the Serbs know it."

"Are you one hundred percent sure it is only the Serbs, Curtis? You know what kind of ramifications this will have if it spreads to all sides? The area has a long history of ethnic cleansing, you know?" Lucas was insistent. The information needed to be exact.

"For now, that's all we know and the details are sketchy at best. We've had several reports of camps existing in the east, northeast, and northwest of Bosnia and a few others in the center of the country. These are rural areas with large majorities of Serbs intertwined with Muslim minorities. Whether the Croats are involved or not is still unknown," Curtis explained, almost unnecessarily. He knew that Lucas was better aware of the demographics than anyone else seated in the room.

"And that son-of-a-bitch at the Yugoslav Embassy knows this is going on?"

"Easy, Lucas," Morton warned, "We aren't sure ourselves that this is happening, and we don't suspect that Mr. Dokić knows either. More often than not, it doesn't make good sense to have an ambassador know the full story of what's taking place at home. Sort of makes him less believable, wouldn't you agree?" He paused, took a big puff from his cigar, and then continued, "Do you now fully understand why I called you in, Lucas? If the situation was headed in a better direction and it looked like things were under control, I swear, I never would have bothered you. But things aren't going the way we want them. Now is the time to act. Any further delay and the point of no return will be crossed, if it hasn't been already"

"Okay, I get the message. But what exactly is it you think I'm capable of doing that can make a difference? Sure, I can be your eyes and ears and maybe predict a few likely scenarios to help you prevent a few disasters. But to make any real progress, you're going to have to be prepared to do more than blow cigar smoke at the problem, Morty. Military intervention is very likely the only solution if this thing worsens. You are aware of this, aren't you, Mr. Undersecretary?"

"You don't worry about what it will take on my end. I have my ass covered at all times, and I'm prepared to get done what is necessary. Until we get you in there and find out what the real situation is, I won't be doing much of anything."

The room fell silent.

Eventually, Morton spoke up again. "Well, Lucas, we discussed this in full a few days ago over the telephone, agreed on a financial arrangement, and brought you up to date as promised. Now it's time for your professional opinion. Can you deliver to us what we are asking?"

"Morty, other topics that you neglected to address, such as hazardous duties, remain unresolved. Will any damage control be required? If so, is it the standard deal? What are the conditions? What am I authorized to do, freelance-wise? And what am I restricted from doing?" Lucas fired.

"Yes, my friend, in addition to the deal stated over the telephone, all previous protocols apply. We don't anticipate any need for those kinds of 'services,' shall we say. But I can't guarantee it at this point. As usual, any unsanctioned work performed by you and at your discretion will be denied by the U.S. government. You will be left to fend for yourself. That's common knowledge and is the standard deal, Lucas. Why? You're not planning on going off the deep end, are you?"

"I just need the rules established before the game begins. I don't like surprises, remember?" Lucas added with a biting tone.

"Lucas! That was a long time ago. You promised me all had been forgotten," Morton rallied to defend himself, his face turning crimson from equal amounts of embarrassment and anger. The outburst revealed to Curtis Sheets a shelved inflammation between the two that he had not been aware of before. The dialogue left him confused and uncomfortable.

"It will never be forgotten, Morty, and it will never happen again," Lucas finished.

"Then it's settled!" Morton proclaimed, successfully changing the subject. "The plan will go like this. Lucas, you have three days to pack, prepare, review, and tie up any loose ends that need tying up. Curtis, you'll be on an early morning flight back to Belgrade tomorrow. The two of you will keep in contact via the secure lines in place in our embassy in Belgrade. Lucas, all information you gather will have to make its way to Curtis, who will then relay it to me at the State Department. There will be no other method of contact permitted. Is that completely understood?"

"Understood," they responded in unison.

"Lucas, there could be a problem getting you into Sarajevo. The airport has been shut down for days and the United Nations is working frantically to reopen enough of it to make it functional. There is no time frame on that; it could take weeks, or maybe months. In the meantime, the best we can do is to fly you into Zagreb and from there you will have to pass through areas of heavy fighting to reach Sarajevo. The alternative is for you to fly into Split on the Adriatic coast, and then hook up with a U.N. convoy that is being organized to deliver supplies to Sarajevo. Both choices run a considerable risk. You must decide now so that we can hold the convoy's departure until you get there."

"Get me into Split. I like the coast in the springtime," he said. "What then?"

"The commander of the U.N. deployment will be awaiting your arrival in Sarajevo at the airport base. You'll be assigned U.N. identification and official papers for emergency purposes. There is also a small NATO contingent already in place. You will meet with them, gather their intelligence, and be assigned to their security clearance. If you get jammed up in any way, use their resources first. There's no guarantee they'll come to your aid, but they have the most qualified allied military capability in the region. You'll have full access to any equipment and weaponry they have on hand, although I've been told that it isn't much. When you get into Sarajevo, you'll need to organize with the consulate, and check in with Curtis. The consulate will provide you with access to all the documents and information you request. The weaponry in the consulate arsenal is also at your disposal. One last detail: these are unbelievably volatile times in the area. I suggest you don't go out unarmed, and use extreme caution when you leave the consulate gates. Remember this: the snipers don't care if you're wearing U.N. blue. More than likely, it'll help put you in their crosshairs. The same goes for the U.N. marked vehicles."

"How do you suggest I get around the countryside without a U.N. escort, Morty? Do you have any idea of the terrain involved?"

"That's up to you and your resources, my friend. I'm sure you'll come up with something. There is no other way to play it." Next,

Morton added, "Lucas, you know this part of the world as well as anyone. You have friends, contacts, and family to count on. You know the language perfectly and the mentality probably better than you would like to admit. We need as much information and as many photos and hard evidence as you can get to us in the next few weeks if we're going to have any chance to shut this thing down. And even if we act immediately--and I mean today--it may still take months or years before the flames can be doused. If you discover there is something you need that we haven't supplied, let me know via Curtis, and I'll get on it at once. I've got top priority status on this, almost nothing is off limits."

After the last details were discussed, the three had very little left to say. Execution was the critical next step. Time was a commodity, and there was little of it to be wasted, so they shook hands and parted company. Morton Riggs stayed at his office and worked on logistics throughout the night. Curtis and Lucas found Lionel James waiting for them outside. The State Department limo dropped Curtis off first because it was late and he had yet to pack for the next day's flight to Europe. He and Lucas spoke little before arriving at his hotel. After reconfirming the date and time of their next contact, Lucas advised Curtis on where to gather additional materials that he wanted ready for his use once in Sarajevo. The two exchanged goodbyes before Curtis got out of the car and headed inside.

Then Lionel James shuttled Lucas to the city's other side, where his room at the Hyatt was waiting. He had many things to prepare for in the coming days. Most of all, he needed rest so he could complete the list of tasks that would require all of his energy and attention.

As they drove past the brightly lit Jefferson Memorial, Lucas recalled the first time he had seen the sight at night. It was during one of his first assignments in 1973, as he returned from a location near Morton Riggs's current office. At that time, he was undergoing an intensive course to master the French language. He had been assigned to track an Algerian-based arms dealer and the operation required him to speak and understand French as fluently as a Frenchman. The French language was not difficult for him to master because his comprehension of Italian and English guided him well. In addition, he had learned the basics of the language years earlier when he was assigned to the U.S. Embassy in Vietnam, a former French colony with many native French-speaking dignitaries. The 1973 class served to perfect his dialect and unlearn his Franco-Vietnamese accent. Similar remedial training would be required if he had originally learned to speak the language in Montreal or Quebec City. Any kind of tainted accent would have been detrimental to the success of the assignment.

It was close to one in the morning when the black limousine pulled up to the Hyatt. Lucas was exhausted. It would take a few days more before the time zone change would cease to be a problem. He knew he would have to readjust after reaching the Balkans.

Lucas bid Lionel James a quick farewell as the limo stopped in front of the hotel's revolving door. No additional comments were traded between the two before the car door slammed shut. Fighting the urge to sleep, Lucas wobbled inside and headed for bed.

VIII

By the end of the fourth day of the siege of Sarajevo, the city's inhabitants were in a constant state of shock. They were confused and angry at how their lives had deteriorated so suddenly. Just days ago, life had carried on as normal; the only noticeable hostilities came from the familiar posturing of politicians and the opinionated squabbling that was a fixture of everyday conversation. Within an extremely short period of time, these had been replaced by candid hatred and open aggression. A wheel of rage had been set into motion, and it seemed that the only possible direction was forward.

For a typical citizen in any warring nation, separation from family, hunger, and even homelessness are common. Little other than survival is important. For the most unfortunate, war means dying a premature death.

In Sarajevo's shell-shocked interior, it wasn't long before a herd mentality set in among the populace, fueling the fires of violence and rage. The political and military authorities in control of the moment were acutely aware of the emotional fervor that had overtaken the city. They used it to gain their objectives. For them, war meant opportunity, glory, and profit.

●●●●●

For the select few in control of any war machine, progress in achieving their goals can only be made if the people are convinced to participate in their grand scheme. When the population resists these objectives peacefully, they must be persuaded to comply. Of course, for most people, war means the end of life as they know it. Opposition to it is natural. That being so, the reluctant masses must be convinced that their personal sacrifices will be beneficial for the good of a worthwhile cause, whatever the controlling powers determine that cause to be. The more reactionary segment of any population need be told only that. They will not question what follows afterwards. Such individuals possess an overwhelming loyalty and passion for their nationality, ethnicity, race, religion, or political viewpoint, thereby rendering it unnecessary for them to weigh the pros and cons of what they are consenting to. Others can defy such sentiment. Their consent requires additional coaxing to permit the taking of life and the destruction of private and public property. Such resistance requires careful dilution by the authorities. From this segment of the population, the leaders must creatively entice not only approval, but also active participation. Consent is most easily attained by use of a selective and calculated propaganda campaign that strikes deep-rooted emotional chords within the citizens. This can be achieved by persuading the under-informed public to fear an unrealistic threat to their personal safety. Such disinformation reaches the population most effectively through the media. Vigorous and repeated doses of tainted news reports, received via television, radio, and print, is all that is necessary to sway public opinion from peaceful homogeny to malicious hysteria.

Psychological manipulation of the masses is not a difficult task in the hands of experts. The recipe is simple. The public's perception of the truth must be twisted to make the unfounded appear factual. Then elements of fear must be added to create panic. The people are then instructed as to how to behave in response to these manufactured conditions, and then the theme is repetitively reinforced until the illusion becomes a reality. This can be done most easily if the controlling leadership is charismatic, confident – and psychologically unstable enough to feel no guilt. Proper presentation is key. It creates the impression that the tainted information being fed to the public is irrefutable because it is being presented openly, on television or on the radio, creating a natural assumption of legitimacy. These media channels authenticate the agenda and remove any logical obstructions that remain in individuals' minds. The more animated and convincing the leadership presenting the image, the more effective the results will be. Psychologically unbalanced leaders believe the poison they spread. The more mentally unstable the leadership, the more effective the message they present. Lies become truth, and disaster follows.

●●●●●

As daylight gave way to darkness on the siege's sixth day, General Stevan Parenta was preparing to begin his operation's next phase. The heavy bombardment that had rocked the city for the past five days and nights was eased to enable the JNA to assess the city's infrastructure and its inhabitants' condition. The general trusted that such relentless shelling for such an extended period of time was certain to have taken a toll on the morale of the defenseless Muslim majority. Assuming it had, phase two could be implemented later that evening.

General Parenta had ordered his henchman, Dragoslav Obrenović, to recruit the most capable and brutal of the Serbian volunteers for a special assignment. His plan was to unleash a sniper campaign on the city. Most military targets had already been effectively destroyed; the logical next step in the process of demoralization was ready to be enacted.

Dragoslav selected a group of paramilitary assassins and armed them with the latest M-76 sniper rifles that had been recently delivered from an armament in northern Serbia. Other military-trained sharpshooters, who had been active in various parts of the city since the siege's first day, had been installed to prevent the Muslim resistance from gaining control of a larger portion of the city, as well as to protect the Serbian-occupied quarters. What General Parenta had now devised was something altogether different. He decided to increase the number of snipers significantly, and instructed them to shoot anyone who came in their sights. Muslim civilians were a top priority, and each Muslim official killed would be compensated for accordingly. Politicians, policemen, and any resistance fighters shot dead would also earn their killers bonus money. This was the phase of the operation Dragoslav Obrenović had been waiting for since the war's inception. It was his specialty. He would enjoy this enormously.

●●●●●

Dragoslav Obrenović was born in Banja Luka, a small city in north-central Bosnia, in 1950. Like most Serbs his family belonged nominally to the Orthodox Church, but they never attended services because of the negative ramifications this might have had in the newly communist country. He was aware of his Serbian heritage only because his surname was Serbian, and because his parents had told him he was a Serb. Growing up, he didn't feel like a Serb, he didn't practice the traditional Serbian religion, or associate with any Serbian organizations in particular. He did know that he was not a Muslim, but he had many good friends who were. Throughout his adolescence, he couldn't distinguish himself from a Croatian Catholic by any means other than his name. Yet this didn't matter a great deal to him; he was proud of his country, Yugoslavia, and felt he had enjoyed a wonderful childhood there.

After turning eighteen, he was called into service in the Yugoslav National Army, as all males were soon after finishing high school. Time passed quickly and the first six months of his obligation passed uneventfully. Halfway through the second stretch, however, something happened that changed his life forever.

Dragoslav was stationed far from home in Macedonia, the Republic of Yugoslavia's southernmost state. A Muslim friend in the unit invited him to play cards with a group of friends on a night before a national holiday. It was payday for the soldiers and many of those who lived in the area were allowed to go home for the long weekend. Dragoslav was unable to leave because of the travel time and distance involved. The card game progressed late into the night, and the young men drank large quantities of plum brandy, which was the drink of choice in the army barracks. In theory, the Muslim soldiers were forbidden to drink alcohol, but in reality, large amounts were consumed on most occasions.

Because the next day was a holiday, the soldiers were drinking even more than usual. Not long after the card game began, Dragoslav and the three Muslims began to gamble for money. His good friend Rasim, who had invited him to play, quickly became too drunk to continue. He left the game and lay down to sleep. One of the other players was an older, hot-tempered soldier named Mustafa. Also extremely intoxicated, he lost his entire paycheck, most of it to Dragoslav. By the early morning hours, a noticeable tension had built between the two men. Around three o'clock in the morning, tempers flared and the men came to blows in the barracks. Since all of Dragoslav's friends were gone for the weekend, he was left to fend for himself while Mustafa and the other Muslim soldier joined forces and beat him to a bloody mess. The last thing Dragoslav could recall was seeing Mustafa's army boot aiming directly at his head. Moments later, he was unconscious. He sustained irreparable neurological damage and spent the next three months recovering in the army hospital.

Dragoslav was barely fit when he returned to active duty. Mentally, he was unsound. Emotionally, he was scarred. His personality had changed completely. He became prone to aggression and violence. Physically, he had lost substantial amount of muscle mass as a result of the damage to his central nervous system; the left side of his face hung flaccid from atrophied muscles. A prominent scar, created by that final kick, snaked from the corner of his lip to the side of his left nose. He tried to keep the deformity hidden, semi-covered by a thick mustache that he was determined to wear for the rest of his life. Never again would he befriend a Muslim, and he secretly waited for the day he could avenge his aggressors.

Upon discharge from military duty, Dragoslav relocated to Sarajevo and spent the next twenty years dividing his life between the city and the open sea, where he worked as a merchant marine. His chosen profession paid well and allowed him plenty of free time. He worked sporadic stints throughout the year, usually in four month clips followed by a month or so of vacation. The day he received his first paycheck, Dragoslav started a gun collection, and his travels by sea allowed him to purchase any weapon he wanted to own and master. In the U.S., Houston, Texas, and Norfolk, Virginia, were his favorite ports. In these cities, guns were in ample supply, and the prices were affordable. He was also fond of Rotterdam, the Netherlands, and Stockholm, Sweden, where more exotic weapons could be found with enough effort.

During his month-long layovers in Sarajevo, he became an expert marksman and spent as many free hours as time allowed practicing at the shooting range. Guns and competition gradually consumed his life. Women were of no interest to him and his only friends were those he met at target practice. He became acquainted with most other local enthusiasts and competed professionally against many of them. He won almost every event, was a one-time Yugoslavian national shooting champion, and eventually became a legend to the local sharpshooters. But after his fortieth birthday, Dragoslav entered fewer contests and began drinking heavily with the men in his group. Alcohol didn't agree with his damaged brain. Often he became belligerent to the point that his friends avoided him. His shooting skills never diminished, but the satisfaction of competition faded with time, and he enjoyed competing less and less with each passing year.

When war broke out in Bosnia in 1991, Dragoslav joined the local Bosnian-Serb militia. He had no particular loyalty to his own ethnicity, but his hatred toward Muslims had not waned in the years since his injury and hospitalization. He relished the thought of revenge. He was a professional marksman; he would become a volunteer fighter, and later, a paid killer.

Once put under the control of the JNA, Dragoslav was assigned as a special assistant to the newly promoted General Parenta of the Slavonia campaign. His skills and experience propelled him to a position of authority early in the conflict. His capacity for brutal aggression and his heartless conviction gained him great respect from both his official superiors and his unofficial liaisons. It wasn't long before he was called on to lead a local paramilitary outfit that would commit the most malicious acts in Yugoslavia since the end of World War II. Dragoslav Obrenović was proud of his new stature, and he intended to carry out his duty mercilessly. Finally, his chance had come; he could make the Muslims pay.

After Vukovar finally fell, General Parenta ordered Dragoslav to return to Sarajevo for a special task that he alone would supervise from the beginning. While the general completed his objectives with the remaining inhabitants of Vukovar, Dragoslav was sent to the Bosnian capital. There, he quietly enlisted local Serbian thugs for a mission of calculated, cold-blooded murder.

Initially, Dragoslav recruited a handful of friends, local criminals, and mercenaries to serve under his command. Supplemental professionals would be added later on. For weeks, he trained each of his men individually in the art of sniper warfare, including both urban and rural settings. Professional protocol, proper techniques, ideal settings, and target isolation were coached, drilled, practiced, and learned. All men, women, and children were to be considered legitimate targets for their mission. Civilians were not to be distinguished from combatants, but they would be compensated for at lower rates. The word 'target' instead of 'person' was stressed and reinforced; it removed the human element from the act of sniper warfare. This permitted the taking of innocent life to be less psychologically taxing.

At the beginning of the siege of Sarajevo, the new recruits faced very little opposition to the constant threat that they posed. Targets were plentiful, as the unsuspecting citizens wandered freely throughout the city, refusing to believe that life as they knew it could disintegrate so easily into a murderous mayhem. But after confirmed reports spread among the people that unarmed civilians were being slaughtered by assassins hidden in burned-out buildings, they became aware of the grisly reality. Many citizens remained steadfast and refused to succumb to the terror that had encased their lives. They chose to live in dignity and take their chances. Yet many of these did not live long. For the majority of Sarajevo's inhabitants, everyday life became extraordinarily difficult. Food, water, and other necessities were in short supply. Normal daily routines were next to impossible to maintain. Coffee and cigarettes, the two commodities in highest demand, increased in price so dramatically that most people couldn't afford to buy them. The inability to satisfy their nicotine and caffeine addictions added an extra layer of misery to their already strained nervous systems. Alcohol consumption skyrocketed from already high levels. Family violence escalated, as did social aggression. Soon the quality of life in Sarajevo, a highly cultured European city, nose-dived into a struggle for mere survival.

●●●●●

"Watch how his body moves as he walks. Anticipate his movements before he makes them. Study him. Follow him. Stalk him. There is no need to hurry. Positioning and patience: these are the key components," Dragoslav preached, as he peered through a set of binoculars. "Can you see how his body rises and falls when he steps with his right foot? He carries a trace of a limp. Go with it, raise and lower the sight, ever so gently. Establish a rhythm, but don't lose your concentration on the heart. A second shot is one too many. It must be done cleanly and efficiently. You cannot make a careless mistake and risk exposing your position."

It was now day seven of the siege, and Dragoslav Obrenović had begun his mission of terrorizing the city's residents.

"What do I do if I think that the target senses me, or if I don't get the kill on the first try?" asked the sniper-in-training, a nineteen-year-old named Svetozar whose father had been longtime friends with Dragoslav.

"If the target is aware of you, you chose a poor location. Scramble immediately and reposition before those Muslim bastards hunt you down. If you don't get a first-shot kill, fire another round at the target before he realizes where you are. If you remember all that I've taught you, you won't have to go through this agony. Do not leave a maimed target to bleed to death in misery. If you don't have a guaranteed clean shot, pass on it, and then set yourself up for a better one."

The location Dragoslav had picked was a perfect one for hunting their prey. The men were perched in an abandoned apartment on the fourth floor of an eleven-story building. The shelling had destroyed the living quarters on that floor and above. All the building's tenants had been forced to take refuge in other locations. The building was situated in a Serbian neighborhood, but it overlooked a Muslim district and its main business center. The centuries-old layout of the city forced the population to pass in their direction in order to buy food or collect fresh drinking water, thereby providing the inexperienced sniper with easy targets to master his trade. The spot was secluded and provided excellent cover. It was high enough to be hidden from unsuspecting pedestrians, but in sufficiently close range for a clean shot. A howitzer round had created a hole in the apartment's wall with a circumference large enough to give a panoramic view of the street below. There was just enough space to aim a rifle without compromising their position.

"What...what happens if I know the target that I'm assigned to kill? What are my options?" Svetozar asked, his voice stammering with apprehension.

"Points are points, and money is money. These aren't times to be sentimental. All targets are anonymous: you don't know them," Obrenović answered, his voice cold.

Just then Dragoslav's eyes squinted as he looked through the binoculars.

"Well, well, what do we have here?" he asked. An armored police vehicle was slowly approaching on the street below. It stopped in front of the building adjacent to the one across from where they were hiding. Three security guards, all dressed in military police uniforms, emerged from the vehicle. Each was armed with a Russian-made AK-47. They took tactical positions between the vehicle and the building entrance. Instantly, Dragoslav perceived the significance of the structure that the guards were protecting. Apparently, it was the unofficial headquarters of a Muslim political coalition that had been organized to establish a voice for the Muslim population in any future cease-fire negotiations. A moment later, two additional individuals exited the vehicle and quickly scuttled to the safety that the entrance overhang provided. Dragoslav had switched devices to enhance his vision. Now he was watching the action through the lens of his rifle's scope. He narrated the scenario while Svetozar looked through the binoculars from behind.

A Muslim official entered first, but he was unrecognizable from the angle presented to the snipers. But Dragoslav recognized the politician's escort as Senad Begović. At one time, Begović had been Sarajevo's chief of police. Now he was an important commander of the Muslim resistance. Dragoslav knew him well; years before, they both had participated in the same shooting competitions. He and Dragoslav had been fierce competitors, but Dragoslav had always dominated the events. The competitions remained professional, but privately, Dragoslav always enjoyed extra satisfaction when he defeated a Muslim opponent.

After Begović escorted the dignitary into the building's sanctuary, the three security guards stayed outside at their posts. Two of the three were appropriately positioned, concealed and protected, revealing the professionalism of well-trained soldiers. The third guard stood out in front, exposed, away from the safety that the building provided, demonstrating an obvious lack of experience. Dragoslav recognized him as Samir Begović, Senad's youngest brother. Following him slowly with the scope of his rifle, he watched intently as Samir stopped to light a cigarette.

"About those questions you were asking, Sveto. Watch and learn. I'm only going to show you this once," he said.

Then, in a whisper, he reminded Svetozar of the escape route they had agreed on before entering the apartment. There were no neighbors on this particular floor to witness or hinder their escape. Svetozar acknowledged Dragoslav, and then quietly stood in the background, shaking nervously. He could see very little from his position and he could hear only the scraping of fallen concrete under his superior's boots as he shifted his weight to get the ideal line of fire. Dragoslav stood in a semi-erect position and took aim slowly and methodically. Simultaneously, he flexed his knees and raised and lowered his torso to achieve the proper angle.

After Samir Begović put his Zippo lighter back into his pocket, his colleagues noticed his poor placement. They called out to him to move closer to the doorway. Samir nodded in agreement, but then stubbornly decided to finish his half-smoked cigarette. Dragoslav watched the exchange through the scope. He knew the opportunity would be lost in a matter of seconds. He waited. He watched. He aimed.

After taking a final drag, Samir flicked the cigarette butt and started to retreat. As his body began to turn, the crack of a rifle rang out. The bullet's momentum lifted the policeman off his feet and spun him counterclockwise. A second later, Samir was flat on the ground. The left side of his chest was torn apart. Reflexively, he clutched at the wound while shaking uncontrollably and gasping for air. It wasn't long before he was peaceful and still.

The two other guards wanted to rush to his aid, but decided against it instinctively. They were uncertain from which direction the shot had come. It was too risky to help their friend who was laying only a few meters away. Instead, they called out for help and attempted to secure the area. Caught completely by surprise, they were clueless about where the sniper's bullet had originated.

When Senad Begović returned to the scene, he realized instantly what had happened. His younger brother was dead, killed by a precise shot to the heart. No tears fell from his eyes as he scanned the skyline. He saw only bombed-out buildings, standing as lifelessly and powerlessly as ancient ruins. Sensing that the scene was clear, Senad maintained a rigid composure and ordered the others to remove his brother's body from the sidewalk.

With the speed of an expert, Dragoslav broke down the rifle while Svetozar packed up their gear and picked up the spent shell casing. Together, they brushed over the floor where their footprints had been until no trace of their presence remained. In an orderly rush, they hurried down the nearby stairwell. Stopping on the second floor, which was left unscathed from the recent bombardment, they padded briskly down a hallway where some armed Muslim residents might still have been living. These neighbors, Dragoslav thought, would be too afraid to identify or challenge the snipers. Nevertheless, there was no reason to draw unnecessary attention. Without breaking stride, they reached a window at the far end, almost fifteen meters from where the hallway began. They climbed through the shattered pane, avoiding the jagged glass created by a mortar round's explosion. A rusty iron ladder hung outside, and they climbed down it cautiously. Once grounded, the pair darted through a series of back alleys to a rendezvous point in the Serbian-held part of the city. There, they planned to drink plum brandy and share the details of their success with the other marksmen who would gather to celebrate.

IX

The three days Lucas was allotted to prepare for his assignment passed in a blur of preparations. Before the reality of what he was doing had fully set in, Lucas once again found himself lounging in a first-class seat, this time on a jet destined for Europe.

The seven-hour Lufthansa flight to Frankfurt departed on time, and Lucas quickly settled in to rest. His career had taught him that every mission would eventually prove to be more demanding than it initially seemed. It never varied. Experience had trained him to be ready physically as well as mentally for every assignment.

After the plane had reached cruising altitude, a flight attendant delivered refreshments and a hot facial towel. Lucas accepted them, but then requested to be left in privacy. He wanted to use the time to meditate and clear his mind; it was his routine on flights en route to his assignments.

About halfway through the flight, relaxed from his meditation, Lucas fell into a state of semi-consciousness, somewhere between a light nap and a deep sleep. In this state, a replay of his Balkan childhood filled his mind, the memories as vivid as if they had happened only days ago. It was not the first time he had experienced this flashback; it came reliably every time he was on his way back to the Balkans. The first time, on his earliest assignment to Sarajevo, it had awakened him in a panic. He awoke with a sudden shriek, shaking and in a cold sweat, to the obvious irritation of the passenger next to him. After several similar incidents, Lucas learned to control these reactions.

Lucas never told anyone about these flashbacks, but the pain and fear created by his childhood trauma was always present. Eventually, he trained himself to use the images to harness clues in his search for his lost father and other relatives. The dream always started the same way, and always under the same circumstances. Its dialogue played in a combination of languages; Croatian, German, Italian, but never English. By the age of six he had mastered enough of these first three languages to converse fluently in each. Croatian was his mother tongue; German and Italian were not learned by choice, but of necessity. He had been born at a chaotic time in the world's history, in one of the most chaotic places.

The flashbacks always climaxed with the tragedy that scarred him for life. At the time, he was much too young to face such an overwhelming dilemma, and too innocent to make such a drastic decision. The memory of the first man he killed was stained in his mind forever. Other killings had happened later, each with varying degrees of complexity. But the traumatic results of his first lethal shooting left a permanent indentation on his developing psyche.

●●●●●

Luka Martinović was born in Croatia on January 2, 1937. Until age three, his family lived in Slavonski Brod, a small city on the Sava River in Slavonia. The Sava separated Croatia from Bosnia, and throughout these early years, Luka visited Bosnia often. His mother had family living in the Bosnian town of Brčko, only a few hours' journey away. On his visits to Brčko, Luka clearly sensed a change of atmosphere. The mosques and towering minarets pointed skyward like enormous spears as they traveled through the town's center. He wondered why people who lived so near spoke in such a strange dialect. Sometimes he made fun of their speech patterns. His mother always scolded him; his father usually smiled and joined in.

By early 1940, Luka's father foresaw the coming of World War II and sensed it was only a matter of time before the Nazis entered Yugoslavia. In order to protect his family, he relocated them to Samobor, a village located in the rolling hills west of Zagreb. There he had relatives who owned a farm with enough food, shelter, and work to see them through the inevitable German occupation. Luka's father wanted to be as far away from Bosnia as possible. "Nothing but trouble ever came from Bosnia," Luka remembered his father answering when he asked him why they had to move.

As he predicted, the Nazis invaded from Germany. By coincidence, they established their regional headquarters near Samobor. Soon after, an ethnic cleansing campaign began in a style that the region had never witnessed. Croatia's own fascist party, the Ustaša, expanded their powers and eagerly assisted the Nazis in completing their objectives throughout the region. Serbs, Jews, Communists, and Gypsies were expelled by whatever means possible. On several occasions Luka's father was accosted by the fascists and questioned repeatedly. Fortunately, he had learned to speak German at an early age and communicated well with the northern invaders. He displayed no bias toward any of the warring parties and prayed for the war to end so that a normal environment could exist for his family.

In Samobor, Luka spent his time helping with farm work and playing with friends. Occasionally, battles were fought so near to the farmstead that he was forced to take refuge with his family beneath the stone house for days. There they cowered until the fighting ceased.

At every opportunity, Luka's father took time to teach his son the German language. There was no way of predicting the war's outcome and his father decided it wise for his son to master the language in case the Third Reich occupied the region indefinitely. The boy learned quickly and was soon able to converse with the German soldiers on trips to town for rations.

By February 1943, after Luka had turned six, there remained no clear indication of the war's outcome. However, it had become evident to his father that the fighting was coming closer to his family, and it worried him immensely. Several times, artillery shells landed so close by that he feared they would need to flee for their lives; that to remain stationary was more dangerous than risking a daring escape. Fortunately, each crisis was avoided in the final moments.

As the time passed, the warring armies matched German infantry units against an under-supplied band of resistance fighters known as Partisans. The group was led by a Communist-minded Croat named Josip Broz. Eventually, he would become known as Marshal Tito.

In addition to fighting for their homeland's liberation, the Partisans were fighting for control of Yugoslavia once the fascist occupiers were driven away. The resistance was ruthless and relentless. Luka's father had heard rumors that the Partisans were collecting the region's native German-speaking civilians and executing them as spies. He was aware that many locals knew of his German-language capability and was afraid he would be reported. Many nights, he laid awake worrying for his own and his family's safety. Later that same spring, as the fighting intensified and the war closed in, Luka's father made a decision that altered his son's life forever.

●●●●●

Luka's father traveled to Samobor on Saturdays in search of rations that were in short supply. He hitched together the horse and wagon, journeyed alone, and tried to remain a safe distance from any perceived danger. As he passed through town one particular Saturday, he became aware of several unfamiliar men. They were not the usual faces of the townsmen he had seen regularly during the past year. Their faces were hardened and expressionless, their bodies thin and malnourished. On this visit, he had an uneasy feeling that he was being followed, almost stalked. Nothing else seemed remarkable or out of place, so he ignored the stares and dutifully finished obtaining the rations his family needed. As Luka's father was filling the cart with boxes of canned goods and other supplies, a smaller, spindly man of about his own age approached him from behind. Calmly, he began to help fill the wagon. In Croatian, he spoke casually, as if the two had known each other for many years. Unable to assess the man's motives, Luka's father played along warily. Experience had taught him not to panic in such situations, to speak slowly, and to think quickly. The newcomer kept the conversation short and wasted little time making his point known.

"Hello, my friend. Are you Mr. Ivan Martinović?" he asked.

"Yes."

"Please, carry on naturally. There is something important I must tell you."

"I presumed so. What do you want?" Martinović replied, lifting a box onto the wagon. From the corner of his eye, he peered around the town for signs of trouble.

"There is a man who would very much like to meet you. He is an important man who is in need of your service. He will be waiting for you on the edge of the small village near the farm where you live. When you leave Samobor, return the same way in which you came. Don't look for him, he will find you. Do not fear for your safety. That has been assured." And with that the conversation ended.

Luka's father did as he was instructed. There was little else he could do. The resulting suspense was not as dramatic as perhaps it should have been. It was an unpredictable time in the region, and he adjusted to surprises quickly. He finished his task and headed home along the same route which had taken him to town. When he was not far from his destination, perhaps fewer than two kilometers, a group of well-armed men emerged from the surroundings dressed in slipshod military attire. Each had a small red star displayed upon his uniform. They took the reins of his horse and led his wagon through the war-ravaged village's stone buildings. Ivan Martinović was taken to a secluded location, hidden from the main road and out of view from the immediate countryside. He stepped down from the wagon and was escorted into a sunlit barn that had been holding livestock. The air reeked of manure. The mud floor was covered with hay and animal waste. From the shadows in the barn's backside, a man emerged dressed in full military attire. His voice called out and invited Luka's father to join him. In an instant, Ivan Martinović realized the significance of the meeting. He was in the midst of the Partisan fighters. He had been delivered to a meeting with Tito's regional commander.

An informal introduction was made, and a handshake was exchanged. A cigarette was offered and accepted.

The uniformed officer sat down easily at a wooden table in the rear, inviting Luka's father to join him. Two subordinates paced near the front entrance, on guard for signs of the enemy. The entire village, consisting of fewer than twenty houses, was under the continuous surveillance of a war-hardened unit of Partisan fighters. It was not uncommon for German panzer tanks to pass by on regular patrols.

Tito's officer spoke first. He inquired about Ivan Martinović's family. To Luka's father, it seemed as though the Partisan officer had substantial prior knowledge of his personal history, so much so that it made him uncomfortable. The Partisan commander repeatedly mentioned his German-speaking ability. He questioned how and why it came to be. Soon it dawned on Luka's father that he was undergoing a background check. Two possible explanations were considered. He feared the end result that both of them presented. His first inclination was that the rumors of the German-speaking civilian executions were true. Gradually, the interrogation focused on his personal loyalties. Sensing he was being recruited, he hoped privately that this was the second possibility. Simultaneously, he worried this choice would also lead to his early demise. His voice began to quiver as he spoke; his hands shook inside his coat pockets. The war was now being pushed onto him. Further evasion was impossible.

After several minutes of astute interrogation, Tito's officer was satisfied with the answers to the questions that he posed. Confident of Ivan Martinović's honesty, he explained the current Partisan military situation to Luka's father in as complete detail as prudent. Ivan believed the information to be accurate. He appreciated knowing enough of the facts to evaluate his situation.

The scenario the officer described was grave. A major offensive by the resistance, in combination with British air support, was being planned for the area in the coming days. The Partisan commander predicted the region would suffer massive destruction and promised that the local farmsteads would be looted for supplies and destroyed. There was no guarantee of civilian safety. Life for the surviving noncombatants was predicted to be harsh and unforgiving.

When the Partisan leader felt the time to be appropriate, the conversation's main purpose took place. He did not mince words. He told Luka's father that he had lived in Russia for several years during World War I. He had mastered the Russian language, but was not fluent in German. A week earlier, the last fluent German-speaking officer under his command had been killed in action, leaving a void that desperately needed to be filled. His Partisan unit had a few soldiers with German-speaking skills, but their knowledge was inadequate. It was imperative that the commander have a subordinate proficient in German to interpret and translate for him to achieve his military goals. Captured German soldiers needed to be interrogated; intercepted messages and communications needed to be understood with full comprehension of all inferences.

Ivan Martinović was fluent in the Low German dialect and could make a significant contribution to Partisan efforts. It was well known that he had no direct ties to either the Ustaša or the Nazi Party. He possessed a desirably untainted political past. In essence, he had something the Partisans wanted, something the commander urgently needed. On that basis, the resistance leader made Luka's father a proposition he could hardly refuse. His family would be spared the hardship to follow. But in return for the consideration, something vital was expected of him. Ivan Martinović realized that the information concerning the region's coming destruction was offered in good faith. In the end, there was little to debate.

The commander informed him of his army's extent. Over the last twelve months, the Partisan army had grown exponentially. Insurgent fighters were now organized from western Hungary to the Adriatic coast, though most of the Adriatic archipelago remained under Axis control. Soon a large portion of Bosnia and sections of Slovenia would be firmly in Partisan control.

The regional commander offered Ivan Martinović's wife and son safe passage through central Croatia to the Adriatic Sea. From there, they would be sent to a sparsely populated island named Lošinj. There, they could wait out the remainder of the war under the protection of Partisan sympathizers. In return, Luka's father was to become the officer's German interpreter and translator until the war's conclusion. Ivan Martinović would be given six hours to prepare his family before departing and a full day to report for his assignment. With this, the conversation ended.

● ● ● ● ●

Before reaching home, Luka's father rehearsed how he would present what had just happened – and what was about to happen – to his family. Timing was critical, but he had so little of it. After returning, he gathered his wife and trembled as he spoke. He was uncertain what would become of him in the days and months to come, but his family's safety took precedence. Husband and wife agreed with little deliberation. In any case, a debate would not have been tolerated. The mother and child were packed at once, and Luka's relatives were forewarned of the impending dangers. They had just enough time to pack what valuables they could carry and bury those they could not bring along. Then, the family dispersed to the sanctuary offered by friends across the Croatian countryside.

The mother and son left just before sunset that evening. Luka kissed his father's unshaven cheek when he said goodbye. He noticed his father's sunken eyes and the subtle look of fear on his face as he tried to appear brave in front of his son. Even as a grown man years later, he never forgot how his father squeezed him tightly, held his hand, and told him to behave for his mother until they saw each other again.

"Why aren't you coming? Where will you be?" the boy asked his father.

"Papa has a business trip with some very important people, Luka. It cannot be avoided," his mother answered for her husband.

With tears streaming down his cheeks, Luka questioned, "When will I see you again, Papa?"

"It won't be too long, son," his father answered. He gave the boy one last kiss and lifted him to his mother, who was already seated on the wagon.

A tentative plan formed to meet on the island exactly one month after the war's official end. This was the best possible arrangement for such unpredictable times. The driver snapped the whip and the three abandoned the farm; Luka looked back and waved.

The wagon moved slowly in the day's twilight hours. It was driven by an old farmer named Branko who lived in a neighboring village. Luka recalled setting out bundled in a bulky woolen coat, two pairs of pants, and three pairs of heavy socks - fully prepared for the multi-day trip through the cold air of the mountainous Gorski Kotar region. They soon reached Branko's house and went inside to warm themselves and to collect supplies for the treacherous journey ahead. Winter travel was hazardous in Gorski Kotar, even for the most experienced local travelers; there was never absolute certainty that the mountain passes would be open. Traveling by train was the ideal method of winter travel, but in this case, it was deemed unsafe because the Nazis and Ustaša remained in control of the railway.

Early the next morning, Branko filled the rickety carriage with blankets, food, water, and plum brandy before setting off on the excursion. He would take them across the Gorski Kotar mountains as far as the village of Ravna Gora. In Ravna Gora, Luka and his mother would spend the night in the house of another contact and be prepped for the journey's next leg, possibly its most dangerous.

As they progressed, Branko felt relatively safe from attack by the warring parties, but the threat of an accident because of thick fog or an unexpected blizzard was always present. The capricious weather made night travel ill-advised. Fortunately, decent conditions prevailed and discomfort from the cold air was all they had to endure until they neared their destination. Luka slept most of the way, buried under a pile of thick woolen blankets.

Branko, Luka, and his mother arrived in Ravna Gora on schedule. They were welcomed into a two-room stone cottage at the edge of the village, owned by a broad-shouldered elderly woman dressed in layers and layers of clothes. It was impossible to tell her age. Luka's mother deduced that she was a widow because of the traditional black clothing that she wore. The lady was the mother of a high-ranking member of Tito's army. She fed the refugees broth, cooked cabbage, and boiled potatoes. She gave them hot tea to drink. The cottage owner moved slowly about. She spoke little, but maintained a sympathetic look in her eyes.

In the morning they rose early to begin the journey's next stage. If the agreeable weather continued, they would arrive that afternoon in a village named Grobnik, just east of the Italian city of Fiume.

As they approached the Adriatic coast, new dangers would arise. The coastline was still under Axis control, and Fiume was infested with military personnel. Luka and his mother had no documents granting them permission to move freely through the region. Great care would be necessary to avoid border patrols. In addition, the six-year-old boy was the only one in their group with any knowledge of German. Any confrontation with the border guards would mean immediate arrest. Deportation to the Ustaša would undoubtedly follow.

Before World War II had begun, Fiume was the designated border between Italy and the Slavic state. The city was still under fascist control, but recently the Partisan army had become better represented on the Yugoslavian side. Even so, extra caution was required. Their wagon skirted the city and rolled down the rocky terrain out of sight via a little-used gravel road that terminated at the Adriatic Sea. As they descended, the three could feel the temperature rise as they neared sea level. The smell of salt air filled their nostrils.

They wasted no time at the coast. When the wagon stopped, they were swiftly transferred aboard a small fishing vessel that was preparing to leave on an evening run. The old captain and his burly daughter served as the crew. Using the fisherman's years of experience, the pair could navigate the Kvarner Gulf nimbly enough to deliver their human cargo to Lošinj before any suspicion arose. The father and daughter were accustomed to dealing with frequent naval patrols and their presence rarely attracted attention.

Luka and his mother were guided into the boat's hull and hidden under a pile of blankets. The bundle was topped with a mound of fishing nets. The fisherman instructed them not to make any noise if the boat were stopped. He gave them a little food and drinking water for the long, uncomfortable journey, then returned above deck.

The boat's floor was covered with bilge water and diesel fuel. The odor from the fishing nets choked the air. Luka soon became sick. As the motor turned over and the craft left the marina, he began to vomit profusely. At the journey's halfway point, he developed a high fever and vomited some more. His mother held him close and tried to fill his stomach with fresh water. It was Luka's first time at sea and years would pass before he would willingly leave land again.

Though the trip seemed unending, in fact it took most of an evening. Fortunately, the sea was calm, sparing the mother and son an even more horrendous journey. When the boat slowed, it cautiously approached a little-known harbor on the island's southeast corner. Through the dark, an islander and the captain's daughter exchanged flashlight signals announcing that the coast was clear. The boat pulled in smoothly and moored at the tiny fishing village named Veli Lošinj. Inside the boat, the mother and son could hear the captain speaking to people on shore, first in Italian, and then in Croatian. Suddenly, the hull door opened and Luka and his mother gasped for fresh air. They emerged wet and soiled, but safe and sound.

Next, introductions were made and the two refugees were put in the custody of Rudi and Stella Kraljić. An older couple, they were sympathetic to the ragged condition of the newcomers and took them in quickly but casually. They took care not to appear suspicious. They offered their charges a change of clothes and several extra blankets to keep them warm for a night hike across several kilometers of rugged landscape. A biting, late-winter wind awaited them.

The Kraljić family had lived in this remote location for many generations. They were familiar with every part of the island and knew each of its permanent inhabitants. They also knew the whereabouts of the occupying forces at all times. At the war's onset, their only son had left the island to join the original Partisan army. He had climbed the ranks and earned Tito's highest respect. It was through this connection that Luka and his mother were able to spend the war years in relative security, in exchange for his father's German-language expertise.

Lucas and his mother now inhabited a small bungalow tucked away in the south of the island, about three kilometers from the nearest village. This arrangement was not to last forever, but the privacy was necessary until Rudi Kraljić felt comfortable integrating them into the village population. The stone house offered two cots and a wood-burning stove. It had been used primarily as a shepherds' shelter before the war had begun. The Kraljić family had owned the property for generations, and Rudi used to keep beehives on the premises as a hobby. More recently, it was used for Partisan purposes whenever the need arose. Rudi's son stayed there on his brief visits. Sometimes it was used to temporarily house intelligence officials or downed Allied airmen fleeing enemy capture.

The mother and son adapted easily to the quiet island lifestyle. Luka spent two hours a day learning to speak Italian and helping his mother around the house; beyond that, he had free rein of the area and spent his unsupervised free time exploring the surrounding landscape. By the end of the first month, he knew every rock and tree within a three-kilometer radius.

Provisions were limited. During the first weeks of their stay, Rudi Kraljić was able to visit with meager rations only occasionally. Later, Luka and his mother were brought to the island's main village every so often to obtain supplies. They used the time to practice speaking Italian with the locals. Luka picked up the language quickly and was fluent in a few months. His mother struggled for much longer, but with practice improved in proficiency. Luka coached her when he had to. For her part, his mother was amazed at her son's linguistic talents and openly proud of his fluency in three languages at only six and a half years of age.

•••••

The island's occupying forces varied in number. One Italian platoon and a small number of German soldiers were permanently stationed there in order to maintain security and track Allied ship movement. Also, six German specialists were assigned to the island to operate radar and record ship traffic throughout the upper Adriatic. Several German officers roamed the nearby islands at random. Two of them appeared consistently, usually together, but sometimes alone, to supervise the troops under their command. Oftentimes, and without notice, they would disappear for weeks at a time.

Luka maintained a safe distance from the German soldiers. He noticed how tension throughout village increased when they were present. He often saw the Italian soldiers kicking soccer balls with local children in an open field near the village center. The Germans, by contrast, would sit alone at the nearby café, drinking wine and smoking. They looked on with disgust and held the Italians in contempt for their lack of seriousness in the war effort. For their part, the Italian troops largely ignored the Germans. By spring 1943, it had become obvious that the Italian army would soon capitulate.

• • • • •

That summer passed uneventfully. Mother and son had established a steady routine. Luka adapted gloriously to island life and took advantage of all it afforded a six-year-old boy. He had no friends and spent much of his time alone, but he rarely tired of exploring, swimming, and spying. He gradually became aware of the island's occupying troop positions and learned their scheduled maneuvers. It was easy because island life was so compact, and village life was even more so. The Italian troops were rarely rotated and became familiar with most of the inhabitants, but recently arrived replacements were singled out and treated with distrust until having been permanently assigned. Sometimes months would pass before they were welcomed by the locals. The Germans were never accepted.

One morning during mid-summer in 1943, Luka greeted Rudi Kraljić at the hidden cottage's front door. Rudi, a fast-moving man who spoke softly and never wasted words, took Luka to his old beekeeping facility and announced his plan to re-establish the hive. Luka looked on with delight and was thrilled when Rudi invited him to help. Over time, the older man gave him more and more responsibility for the bees. It was slow and deliberate work, but he was allowed ample time to learn its intricacies. Soon the hive was thriving. One day toward the summer's end, Rudi Kraljić brought Luka some fishing tackle that had been stored in his cellar for the last several years. It was a gift, he said, to show his appreciation for the hard work that the boy had contributed toward the beehive's success. Luka accepted the gear excitedly. That day, Rudi escorted him to the rock-lined coast and taught him the tricks of coastline fishing. He promised to take the boy out to sea in his dry-docked fishing boat when the war ended. Luka rapidly became an adept fisherman. It consumed much of his free time, but he never neglected his daily beehive responsibilities. While fishing, his whereabouts were not a concern and his mother never feared for his safety.

●●●●●

On the morning of August 29, 1943, Luka awoke early, packed a basket of fruit, a bottle of water, and his fishing gear, and walked alone to Lošinj's southwest shoreline. The sky was clear and the grass was wet as he meandered carelessly down the familiar footpath. He scaled a wall of loosely stacked rocks before bouncing down a limestone embankment to the edge of the sea. That day, the water was so clear that he could see schools of sardines swimming several meters beneath the surface. The island's southern side had only one road and was mostly uninhabited. Luka felt as though he could hide there and not be discovered for weeks. Before casting his line, he watched as several seagulls swirled above and occasionally swooped down toward the water. He studied a cormorant, a black, duck-like bird, as it paddled on the surface. Luka watched with amazement as it dipped beneath the sea and swam in a fishlike manner for almost a full minute before surfacing with its beak full of sardines.

He had not been fishing for long when a noise seeped into the background that contrasted with the crashing waves and seagull screeches. The unusual hum was soon accompanied by a sight so strange that it was almost beyond belief. An object materialized from the northern skyline; it resembled nothing he had ever seen. The thing roared and sputtered. As it neared, the racket's source was identified. Luka recognized it as an airplane, though one unlike any he had ever set eyes on before. At first, the plane blended with the sky and was almost invisible. Eventually, its position was made obvious by a stream of black smoke that poured from its nose. The clatter it gave off grew less fearsome the closer it came. Soon the sound resembled that of an injured animal crying out for help. The plane was painted silver and flaunted a bright red tail. Its fuselage was tilted to the right and its nose was slightly elevated. All of a sudden, it dropped in altitude and fell quickly toward the sea.

Luka stood still in disbelief. He watched in awe as the spectacle progressed, soon reaching its climax in full view, only a few hundred meters away. When the plane collided with the water, a second, identical plane dove from above at maximum speed. It flew past the crash site, rose speedily, and then circled again. The first plane, its cry for help going unanswered, skimmed violently across the waves until the water's drag killed its progress. The downed aircraft continued floating. Luka continued watching with heightened interest.

A lone man emerged from the floating airplane. Straddling the cockpit, he waved his right arm as the second plane dove low on another approach. Once again, the accompanying plane flew near, dropped in altitude, and then lifted a wingtip before ascending in a blaze. Just as quickly, it disappeared in the direction of the Italian coast.

The pilot now stood on the plane's wing and moved slowly about. Gradually, he lowered his body into the water. Once immersed, a life jacket inflated around his neck. Then the downed airman directed himself toward the rocky shore and began swimming. After a long struggle, he arrived at a large slab of limestone and pulled himself up before collapsing on the beach. From where Luka was standing, the pilot was barely visible, but he could see that the man was lying motionless. Minutes later, his airplane turned sideways, bellowed a short moan, and then gave in to nature's demand. After the saltwater had swallowed it, it came to rest on the Adriatic floor, forty meters beneath the surface.

Luka was unsure what to do. He was overcome with anxiety. His first inclination was to run to his mother and report what had happened. But soon another impulse overtook him, and instead he left his belongings and darted curiously toward the location where the man was lying. Gaining courage with each step, he scaled large boulders and climbed over the smaller rocks until he found the injured pilot.

Luka's first impression of the downed airman was one of shock. Blood was flowing down his torso; his breathing was heavy and irregular. The boy's astonishment, however, did not result from the man's physical state. Nor did it come from the moans of pain escaping from his swollen lips. The feature that stunned Luka most of all was the color of his skin. It was totally black. Luka first imagined that he had caught on fire and was burned like charcoal. Yet upon closer inspection, he saw that this was not the case. All of his clothing was intact. The pilot was wearing a tan jumpsuit and brown boots. His head was covered with a leather cap. A pair of goggles dangled loosely against his chest and a holstered pistol was strapped to his waist. The aviator was bleeding from wounds around the neck and shoulder and his shirt collar was stained with blood. Luka was sure he was part of the war.

The pilot gradually opened his eyes and spotted the boy staring down from the rocks above. When he tried to speak, Luka froze from fear, still unable to comprehend the man's black skin.

"Water...water," the pilot said.

Luka stood bewildered for a moment. He soon realized that an unfamiliar language was involved. Still confused, he did not respond, but continued staring at the dark skin.

"Water," the soldier repeated, this time more powerfully.

Grasping the word's similarity to its German equivalent, *wasser*, Luka sprang into action. He ran back to his fishing spot to retrieve his supplies. In minutes, he reappeared, startled to see that the pilot had managed to change positions. The man was now sitting upright, pistol in hand. The more Luka studied him, the more serious his injuries looked.

Luka offered his bottle of water to the soldier. The black man scanned the landscape with his eyes and tried to assess his situation. As the boy spoke to him in Italian, the aviator smiled, interpreting it as a sign that he was not in German-held territory. When Luka tried to explain to the soldier that his airplane was under the sea, the wounded pilot stopped him and then concentrated in silence for a few seconds.

"*Non parlo italiano*," he said. He could see the look of understanding in the boy's eyes. "*Io parlo inglese. Io sono Americano.*" The U.S. airman had learned only these phrases in the short time he had been stationed in Italy.

Luka continued staring at the man as he drank from the water bottle. When the pilot tilted his head to swallow, he saw the source from which the blood was leaking. A large fragment of glass was lodged in the muscle to the left of his throat. The pilot could not rotate his head, nor raise it upward. He had little use of his left arm and a throbbing numbness shot into the fingertips.

As the man tried to quench his thirst, Luka recalled how in Samobor he had heard the German soldiers talk about the *African schwarzer*, and how there were many such people in America. But he had never seen a black man before, nor any other American, nor had he ever heard English spoken. He wondered what he should do next.

The two stared at each other for a while longer. Luka watched as the soldier regained some strength. He soon tired of looking at the American's face. Out of curiosity, his eyes dropped to the gun he held in his hand.

"*Pistola*," Lucas said, pointing at the deadly chunk of metal.

"Yes, yes, pistol. It's a Colt forty-five," the soldier stated.

"Colt forty-five," Luka repeated, holding out his hand.

After scanning the coastline with his eyes, the American ejected the chamber's loaded round and removed the clip. Wincing from pain, he passed the gun to the boy who held it with pride. Luka lifted it, pointed it at a rock, and then closed his left eye as he pretended to shoot. "Peschew! Peschew!"

"Okay, okay – there's enough of the real thing happening these days - that's not for you," the fighter pilot said. He held out his right hand and repeatedly pulled his fingers toward his palm, demanding the gun to be returned.

Luka gave back the pistol and looked again at the man's black face. The pistol was reloaded and the clip inserted. Luka watched interestedly as the pilot concealed it in a crevice behind the boulder he was resting against.

Luka pointed at the man's neck and said, "*Sangue.*"

The American's eyelids squinted as he tried to decipher the boy's message. Luka pointed at his own neck, and then repeated, "*Sangue.*"

The airman reached up and felt a sharp sting as his fingers brushed over the piece of broken windshield embedded in his flesh. He lowered his right hand and glared at his fingers, now covered with blood.

"Oh, Lordy, Lordy, Luther P. Hayes, what have you gotten yourself into?"

Until that morning, Second Lieutenant Luther P. Hayes had an unblemished flight record and was the pride of the American 332 fighter group out of Tuskegee, Alabama. He was the latest addition to the squadron but had already achieved notoriety by shooting down six German fighters in only nine missions. This morning's mission was supposed to be easy, and many pilots had hoped to be assigned to it. His ninety-ninth squad was assigned to escort a bombing run over a munitions factory near Trieste, Italy. Resistance was predicted to be light. Upon arrival, the squad encountered no German fighter opposition, but cloudy conditions and heavier than expected anti-aircraft fire scuttled the mission. As the group circled to return home, a large explosion of flak blasted through Lt. Hayes's plane. Shrapnel crashed through the windshield and damaged the engine. The concussion left him disorientated for several minutes. He lost contact with the group and headed southeast over the Istrian peninsula in a P-51 Mustang that refused to obey his commands. A plane from his squad trailed him across the peninsula and followed him along the Adriatic archipelago to its point of impact. Lt. Hayes was aware he had been pursued, but was unsure who had tailed him. The plane's radio had been destroyed, and his vision was limited because of blood that had sprayed into his eyes. His goggles had not been in their proper position, breaking a cardinal rule taught in flight school. He was sure that one of his squad members had recorded his position and would report his whereabouts to his commanders. The lieutenant was confident that a rescue operation would begin, yet, doubtful thoughts persisted.

"Looter P. Hayes," Luka mimicked.

The downed pilot smiled. "Luther P. Hayes - that's it. *Io sono* Luther P. Hayes."

"Looter P. Hayes," Luka happily repeated. He had been unexposed to the English sound 'th,' making him unable to pronounce the name correctly. "*Io sono* Luka."

"It's nice to meet you, Luka."

Lt. Hayes looked at the blood on his hand and closed his eyes in frustration. He was cold and feared going into shock. Luka jumped down from his perch and helped the soldier move to a spot in the sun. He took the pilot by his good arm and pulled him a few meters to the right. The young officer had just enough strength to make the move. Suddenly, an idea struck the boy. In a flash, he decided to run to his cottage and come back with supplies. He knew that if he hurried, he could return in less than an hour. There was no way the American could walk so far over such grueling landscape. He tried to explain his idea to the soldier, but stopped after realizing the effort was futile. Using his hands, he demonstrated his intent, and then quickly left, not completely sure if the airman understood his message.

●●●●●

The boy ran as fast as his short legs allowed and he was home in record time.

He called out immediately for his mother, but there was no response. He wanted to tell her about what had happened and bring her along to help fix the soldier. Calling again, he heard no reply. It dawned on him that his mother had gone to the village to get supplies for the week ahead. There was no way for him to know when she would return, so he searched the cabin and collected items that he thought would be useful. He took a blanket, a small knife, a needle and thread, and an extra bottle of fresh water. Also, he brought a bottle of *grappa*, a distilled alcoholic drink made from grapes. After putting these items into a basket, he returned down the path, still short of breath from the trip uphill. He was determined to return as quickly as possible and after slamming the door shut, he sprinted through the pine trees, unaware of his mother calling out his name as she approached. When her son did not respond, Luka's mother decided to put away the supplies and search for him afterwards, like she had done so many times before. It wouldn't take long.

●●●●●

Captain Hans Krieger had returned to Lošinj the previous night from a routine inspection of the islands under his command. A six-man crew, working in rotating shifts, was in charge of the surveillance stationed at Osor, a small village on the adjoining island of Cres's southern tip. A few weeks earlier, the majority of the German army had been redeployed further down the Dalmatian coast. Intelligence reports indicated that the allies were planning a large-scale invasion in the Partisan-controlled area of Yugoslavia.

Osor's strategic location was indisputable. The village was situated near a canal that separated Cres's southern tip from Lošinj's northernmost edge. A short bridge, less than thirty meters in length, connected the islands together. From Osor, the whole northeast section of the Adriatic could be monitored for ship traffic and bombing raids.

That morning, the captain woke early and walked into the station's control room deliberately and unexpectedly. A brief equipment inspection preceded his survey of the previous week's log. Upon this task's satisfactory completion, he remained with the soldiers on duty to critique their performance.

On each inspection over the recent weeks, he had noted that the Italian soldiers had been of little assistance to the Germans. He knew that the Italians knew that a large portion of Italy was now under Allied control. It was only a matter of time before they were no longer aligned with the Third Reich. The captain was certain that the Italians could not be counted on.

It was between 8:20 and 8:30 A.M. when two specks appeared on the screen of the rudimentary radar equipment. Over the next few minutes, one dot repeatedly appeared and disappeared, while a second one stayed constant nearby the flickering first one. This lasted for a short time until only a single anomaly remained. Soon the steady dot reversed course and disappeared heading west. Not long after, the screen was empty. Although little information could be gleaned with certainty from what the radar had captured, such an oddity was not to go unchecked. Coordinates of the first speck's last location were taken and Captain Krieger set out alone to Lošinj's southern fringe. About an hour later, he arrived near the calculated coordinates.

Stepping out of his military vehicle, the German officer breathed in the salt air. A light breeze had picked up, causing waves on the sea's surface to break. The captain walked down an old sheep trail which forged a path through pine trees and along rock-stacked walls in the direction of the sea. Once near the sea, the beaches were few and typical of the region, consisting of open strips of almond-sized stones and larger rocks, which periodically emerged between massive sheets of limestone that sprawled into the water. As he moved, he looked into the sea and noticed with approval the clarity of the water. He wanted to remember the location for future reference; perhaps he would bring his family here for a vacation after the war had ended. Yet he quickly dismissed such ponderings and continued his duty. There was a war to be won. It was no time for daydreaming.

Instinctively, the German captain engineered an efficient, one-man patrol to cover an estimated four kilometer stretch of coastline. He hopped from boulder to boulder while the midmorning sun beat down on him. It wasn't long before he stopped in the shade to remove his gray SS jacket. Now the officer stood motionless in a sleeveless white undershirt. A black iron cross dangled from a red and black striped band that hung around his neck. During the break, he lifted his head and once again breathed in the salt air. After he exhaled, alarm surged throughout his body as enormous amounts of adrenalin flooded into his bloodstream. The captain's gaze had fixed on an unexpected sight. In a sheltered clearing, about thirty meters ahead, two legs clad in heavy brown boots stuck out from a rocky den. The German officer withdrew his holstered P-38 Walther and clicked a round into the chamber. Moving quietly forward, he approached the site cautiously.

●●●●●

As Luka galloped down the trail, a million thoughts raced through his mind. *Who was this strange man? Why wasn't he afraid of him? Should he be afraid of him? What should he do about him? When would he tell his mother? What would she say?* He knew the pilot's injuries were serious, but calling in the island's doctor was sure to alert the German soldiers. *Maybe he didn't need a doctor at all? Maybe his condition wasn't so bad?* He no longer feared the Italian troops. He saw them drunk and out of uniform almost every time he went to town. He had overheard the Italians say that, for them, the war was over. Luka decided he would try to stop the soldier's bleeding, and then let his mother make the final decision.

Time raced by as he ran. He reached the end of the tree line in full stride, but completely out of breath. Under the last bit of shade, he stopped to rest. He set the basket down, took a drink of water, and caught his breath before returning to the sun-drenched landscape. There were still about two hundred additional meters left to run. A few minutes later, he was again moving toward the downed American.

●●●●●

Luka had missed his mother's return by only minutes. She left in pursuit of him. She knew the path he had taken very well; she had come looking for him at his fishing spot countless times before. In all the previous instances, she had called out his name after reaching the beach and then made a short search in either direction before her son always appeared, running toward her from a distance.

●●●●●

As Luka moved steadily ahead, he climbed over the rocks and boulders with a mountain goat's precision. He knew exactly when to jump, when to push, pull, and slide. His approach was smooth, graceful, and silent as he pressed onward. But when he was less than fifty meters away from his destination, he froze. He heard a voice: a loud, demanding, angry voice. It was speaking German.

Luka crouched out of instinct. He set the basket down and crept forward in search of a better place to see. He sneaked around large rocks and crawled through hidden passages that were a natural fit for his undersized frame. He moved closer until he was in full view of the transpiring commotion.

The German officer from the village, the one of the two that was not often there, had discovered his secret. The officer had his pistol pointed at the American pilot's head and was cursing him in German. Luka understood perfectly.

"*Schwarzer!* Get up, you nigger! Get up!" he hollered, before kicking Luther P. Hayes in the ribs. Luka didn't understand the English words the German officer barked, but their intent sounded evil.

"Second Lieutenant Luther P. Hayes, United States Air Force, serial number 332...," the American said, and then stopped after receiving a second, brutal kick.

"Get up! Get up!" bellowed the Nazi. Grabbing the wounded airman by the right arm, he yanked him to his feet, never letting his pistol veer from his prisoner's head.

The fighter pilot managed to stand and stagger a few steps before stopping. Before he could continue, he bent forward at the waist and gasped for air. Another kick to the stomach dropped him to his knees.

Luka watched in horror and began to shake from fear. He knew about the sufferings of war, but had never seen such an atrocity. The pilot was injured and defenseless. Luka sensed no reason to kick him. It sickened him. He felt weak, and then he grew angry.

The American stood up again and advanced a few meters more. As they progressed, the men flanked Luka's position by fifteen meters to the left. The pilot wobbled a bit further before stopping again. This time, the kick came from behind and caused him to lurch forward. Lt. Hayes landed against a large rock, but stayed upright by using his uninjured arm to brace himself. The airman's nose gushed with blood. Luka was sure he could not take much more. The American pilot dropped to his knees and looked around defiantly as the German shouted and waved his P-38. In a moment of fate, the aviator's brown eyes passed Luka's hidden position. Their eyes locked. The pilot thought for a second and then looked down at his empty holster. Again, his raised eyes met Luka's squarely. The airman nodded his head and gave a final glance in the boy's direction as he stood back up. Luka nodded in return. It was his only chance. Now noticeably swaying, the black man was barely able to maintain his balance. He needed to advance at least thirty meters more to give the boy time to put their plan into action.

After the two soldiers passed, Luka sprang to his feet. The distance to the pistol was short, but he had to stay quiet and keep out of sight. He dashed to the den where the pilot had been resting. It wasn't difficult for him to find as fresh blood was still pooled in the spot where he had been sitting. Luka remembered the crevice where the pistol was hidden, and he reached for it carefully. It seemed much heavier to him now, and his hands shook as he held it. He thought to practice his aim, but resisted the temptation. Creeping back, he followed the pair as they moved along the rocky path.

The pilot stumbled forward reluctantly. With his right hand, he kept his left elbow pinned close to his body. Every step produced an agonizing jolt of pain that surged down his arm and into his fingertips. His entire left hand was swollen and difficult to move because his wrist had been fractured from the impact of his plane hitting the sea. The German pursued in a relentless, hawk-like manner. Every so often, he seized the American's shirt collar and jerked, all the while barking obscenities in German, and keeping his pistol trained on his prisoner.

●●●●●

Luka's mother gained momentum and quickly reached the point where her son could usually be found. Twice, she called out and waited. When there was no reply, she made her way over some bigger rocks in the direction where she thought he might be. Her first guess was wrong and she searched for ten minutes in vain. Retracing her path, she headed in the opposite direction, stepping carefully along the choppy trail and devoting her full attention to maintaining her balance. If she had looked up for just one moment, she would have witnessed the full drama unfold. She did not.

●●●●●

Shortly after Luka freed the pistol from its hiding place, he caught up to the two soldiers as they slowly moved ahead. He wasn't sure what to do next, but he was determined to save his new friend, and he was unafraid of the consequences. He crept up to a point five meters behind the pair. Digging deeply for courage, he called out in

German and aimed the heavy pistol. Startled, the two men turned around, little by little, just as Luka had ordered.

The German captain stood perplexed. He had, in fact, never shot anyone, certainly not a young boy, but under no circumstances was he going to forfeit the recognition the captured pilot would provide. A promotion was a certain result of his actions. He did, however, admire the boy's valor. He spoke softly to him in German while the two pointed their pistols at one another. Slowly, the American began to inch away. Captain Krieger noticed and instantly retrained his weapon on the wounded airman. At the same time, he continued speaking to Luka.

"Little boy, don't you know we are at war and that this man is the enemy?" he asked in a friendly tone.

"He's not the enemy," Luka answered.

"Sure, he is; look at him. He doesn't look like us. He doesn't speak the same language as us. He would hurt us if he wasn't injured. Just put down the gun, young man, and I'll take care of this," the Nazi officer said.

"*Neću*," Luka refused in his native Croatian language. He distrusted the German.

The German officer rolled his eyes while calculating how to resolve the unlikely standoff. He tried again, this time pleadingly, "My young friend, I need your help against *our* enemy. Will you please put down that pistol?"

The American pilot looked sternly into Luka's eyes, encouraging him not to give in. Once more, he nodded his head up and down. He was certain the German would not wait much longer.

"I won't. You put your pistol down!" poured out of Luka's mouth.

Captain Krieger assessed the situation hastily. It would be best, he decided, to shoot near the boy to frighten him and then make a dash for the fallen pistol. The injured American would not be able to escape. It would all be finished shortly.

●●●●●

That next second, Luka's mother stepped around the final rock that was blocking her view. Instantly, she let out a shriek.

"Luka, no!" she shouted, just as the German officer whirled his gun toward the boy and squeezed the trigger. He did not have time to accurately aim before a blast rang out from between the Luka's hands. The loud crack was followed by a malicious discharge from the Colt 45. The German spun reflexively. His body jerked backwards and fell against some limestone boulders that kept him standing. Grimacing with pain, he attempted to re-aim the nine-millimeter Parabellum, but Lt. Hayes, foreseeing his enemy's intent, managed two steps before lunging forward in an attempt to deflect the German's aim. The injured men fell and thrashed about on the ground before the German captain rolled out from under and lifted his weapon to fire. Again a loud crack exploded from between Luka's hands. This time Captain Krieger's body froze before falling limply against the rocks. Using his good arm, Lt. Hayes pulled himself up. He reached out and pried the P-38 from the dead German's grip. Then he passed out.

Luka's mother charged to the scene and snatched the gun from her son. Hurrying over to the injured pilot, she took the weapon from him as well. She ordered her son to her side. Luka ran to his mother and started to try to explain what had happened. He started to cry. Then they cried together as she held him close. *How brave he was. How bold. And how naïve*, she thought.

She knew they were not safe now. The German officer would be missed. Others would come searching. Maybe they were already alerted.

"Oh, what has my Luka done?" she cried aloud.

Luka pulled away from his mother and kneeled down next to the American. The pilot was breathing heavily through his open mouth. His nostrils were clogged by dried blood. The boy ran back for the water bottle and brought it to his lips. He handed the bottle of grappa to his mother and she took a big drink. After a while, the pilot regained consciousness, sat up, and smiled. He looked gratefully at the boy and said, *"Bene, bene, bravo."* The words did not precisely express what he wanted to communicate, but it was suitable for the moment. He could see that Luka had understood his message.

•••••

It was at this point that Lucas Martin woke up in a cold sweat the first time the dream had occurred. Other times it lasted longer, making him relive how the Partisan network arranged for a boat to deliver them to an Allied submarine in the Adriatic Sea. The airman and two refugees were then transferred to a U.S. military base in Italy where they remained until the end of the war. From there, Luka and his mother were relocated to the United States, where they lived in New Jersey in a neighborhood of Yugoslavian refugees. It was in New Jersey that Luka Martinović adopted the more American-sounding name of Lucas Martin.

Two years after the war ended, Ivan Martinović was reunited with his family in the United States. Six months after that, he was recalled to Yugoslavia on official business. Lucas never saw him again.

Lucas remained in contact with the American pilot after the war. By the time World War II had ended, Lt. Luther P. Hayes had been promoted to the rank of captain. He went on to serve two tours of duty in Korea before being honorably discharged as a major. His recommendation helped Lucas get accepted into the West Point Academy on his eighteenth birthday.

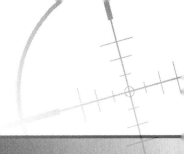

The captain lowered the landing gear. His aircraft had been given clearance to land ahead of other scheduled arrivals. One of his passengers had to be transferred immediately to a U.N. cargo plane that was carrying relief supplies destined for Sarajevo by way of Split, Croatia, where a convoy was stalled, awaiting his arrival. After touching down, the airliner taxied pompously in front of a line of departures that had been halted by the air traffic controllers. Inside the cockpit, the crew commented to one another about the influential strings that must have been pulled to ensure the expedient transfer of Mr. Lucas Martin.

Lucas quickly disembarked and was shuttled to another concourse where the relief plane was waiting with it engines running and its crew ready. The flight staff welcomed him aboard, and minutes later, the plane was airborne.

Lucas didn't feel the need to sleep; time zone changes had been such a common occurrence during his career that he rarely experienced jet lag on flights shorter than twelve hours. He relaxed in the pilot's cabin and said little to the small crew. He was not allowed to discuss his assignment with anyone, of course. The crew was fully aware, however, that an entire United Nations relief effort was being stalled for his delivery, and they made their own guesses.

The uneventful two-hour flight ended on a note of excitement when the plane bounced thunderously down the runway's entire length after landing. Excess momentum created by the heavy freight made it difficult for the cargo plane to stop, despite the pilot's efforts. The captain fought ferociously to steady the rolling beast and bring it under control. After successfully doing so, the skipper turned the tamed plane around and offered Lucas a teasing smile.

"I hope you enjoyed your flight," he said.

Returning the smile, Lucas noted the beads of sweat that had collected above the pilot's brow.

A fleet of supply trucks was waiting at the Split airport for the plane's arrival. Most of them were painted white and had large U.N. emblems displayed on each side. A U.N. support team, dressed in military fatigues and wearing blue berets, manned the trucks. Approximately twenty loaded trailers were parked in formation a short distance from some empty ones which were scheduled to be filled with cargo from the transport plane. This latest delivery would require several hours of transfer time before the convoy could depart.

Lucas checked in with the operation's Dutch commander. His name was Robbert de Graaf, and like most Dutch Lucas had met over the years, he spoke English well. Colonel de Graaf was a career military man who had worked for the U.N. since his retirement from NATO forces in the late 1980s. Lucas knew of him by reputation, but the two had never met. He estimated the colonel and himself to be around the same age. After an informal introduction, Lucas was briefed on the mission's objective and timeframe.

"Mr. Martin, the trucks will be fully loaded over the next several hours. When the task has been completed, I'll lead the convoy out of Split and through the Dalmatian countryside until we reach Imotski. Soon after, we'll cross into Herzegovina. We've been cleared for travel by the Croatian military authorities. I don't expect any trouble with them, but the situation will get a bit sketchy after we enter Herzegovina. There, we could run into anything from mafia bandits to Serbian paramilitaries wanting to add to their caches. Some Croatian units and the Muslim militia might like to have a piece of the cake, also. Unfortunately, we aren't very well armed, and I was unable to attain a proper defense escort," the Dutch colonel cautioned.

Lucas listened respectfully while de Graaf spoke; he knew that his presence was of minimal importance to the colonel's assignment, that to him he was just along for the ride. But after the Dutchman finished, Lucas said, "If you don't mind, Colonel, I would like to ride with you in your vehicle. If there is any communication breakdown, perhaps I can assist you on the spot?"

"Excellent. We should be set to depart shortly. There is a hotel near the airport to which we have access. Why don't you go get some sleep and freshen up?" the colonel suggested. "I'll have my assistant retrieve you when it's time to leave."

Lucas accepted the offer and left to rest for the journey ahead. He appreciated the professionalism and efficiency of Colonel de Graaf, which seemed to him to be an attribute of the Dutch in general.

Almost five hours later, around two o'clock that afternoon, Lucas was awakened by the colonel's second-in-command, another Dutchman named Captain Klaas van den Berg. Lucas leapt into action and made his way to the hotel lobby to meet his escort. The two climbed into a four-wheel-drive vehicle and joined the U.N. convoy that was ready to deploy.

At the column's lead were three Croatian police vehicles. A single blue light flashed on top of each car's rooftop. In the line of trucks that followed, every driver was expected to keep in contact via radio and walkie-talkie. Regular reports to the commander were required.

A short distance outside Split, the caravan climbed above sea level and lumbered toward the valleys inland from the Adriatic coast. Every few kilometers of their ascent, hidden sheep pastures popped out from between rock walls. It wasn't long before they reached the sun-scorched mountaintops that had looked like lifeless mounds from hundreds of meters below. The elements had polished the crests smooth over time, and all vegetation stopped well below their limestone peaks. Along the roadside, random cypress trees stood in defiance of incessant winds that doggedly attempted to break their pose.

Lucas turned his head and looked in the direction from which they had come. Far in the distance he could see the coastline and its jagged rocks that disappeared into the sea. To his surprise, the view reminded him of the opening scene in the movie *Planet of the Apes*. He recalled watching the film in a bar during his third tour in Vietnam in early 1970. Amused, Lucas attempted his best Charlton Heston imitation, just loud enough for his escorts to overhear.

"Take your stinking paws off me, you damn, dirty ape!"

"Ya, ya, we were thinking of that, too!" the colonel said, smiling at Lucas through the review mirror. Soon the captain joined in and said, "You maniacs! You blew it up! Ah, damn you! Goddamn you all to hell!" Then all three men shared a good laugh.

The convoy progressed steadily and soon reached the Croatian-Bosnian border, just past Imotski, where the police escort halted the line and approached their border's heavily guarded gates. While smoking cigarettes, two of the policemen spoke at length with the border patrol guards before waving the convoy through. A short distance further, the trucks were stopped a second time at the entrance to Bosnia and Herzegovina.

There, a different team of armed guards walked slowly toward the lead vehicle with annoyed expressions on their faces. Their hands were fixed firmly to the AK-47s that dangled from their shoulders. The ranking guard approached the lead U.N. vehicle and spoke harshly in the local dialect. The colonel flashed his credentials and replied in German. The guard gave no response. He stared down through the window, a scowl on his war-worn face. The U.N. official responded again, this time in English, and received an identical sneer. Yet from a slight change in his eyes, Lucas recognized that the Bosnian had understood the Dutchman's second attempt.

Six additional armed guards walked alongside the row of trucks, suspiciously snooping for clues of the contents inside.

The Dutch leader snapped angrily at the border guard and demanded to know the reason for the delay. Again, he received no response. Without explanation, the head guard turned his back and briskly walked away. In response, the U.N. colonel sat seething, expecting him to return. A few minutes passed before Lucas leaned forward and asked if he could assist. Permission was granted.

Lucas exited the vehicle and carefully moved toward the small shack used by the border police. After clearing his throat, he stepped inside, and then spoke in his best attempt at the local dialect.

"Excuse me, sir, but my colleague has sent me to find out what the delay is about."

"There is no delay," the guard answered, mockingly. "This is standard procedure. The trucks will have to be completely emptied and searched to see if they contain any prohibited materials," he said, as he extinguished a cigarette. The guard had a crazy gleam in his eyes, as if he had been exposed to the stresses of war for too long. His hair was coarse, curly, and prematurely gray. In a half ring around his upper lip, a thick salt-and-pepper mustache was stained yellowish-brown from the tar of thousands of cigarettes. His fingers trembled as he spoke. Flippantly, he lit another cigarette and turned away.

"But your men haven't begun to search anything. This could take hours, and we are expected in Sarajevo as soon as possible."

As if on cue, the policeman faced Lucas, lifted his hands palm side up and shrugged his shoulders. There was a look of contempt on his face. Again, he puffed at his cigarette. He added, "This could take *weeks*. But my men have a job to do. Their orders are clear. They must eat also, you know?"

Lucas's eyes opened a little wider as he realized a shakedown was underway. Once again reminded that he was in the Balkans, he turned his back subtly and removed his wallet from a pocket in his jacket's lining. He took out a thousand Deutschmarks, and rolled the bills tightly into a tube. Reaching across the desk, Lucas slid the bribe into the guard's shirt pocket.

"I think you and your men should go have a cup of coffee or something," he suggested.

The policeman glanced down at the roll of money nestled against his chest. He exhaled the last drag from his cigarette, and then pressed out the butt in an overflowing ashtray. Shaking his head in agreement, he left the hut and gathered his subordinates. Lucas returned to the colonel's vehicle and slid into his seat. Outside, the temperature had quickly dropped. A light drizzle began to fall.

The U.N. commander looked on as the barricade was lifted. He turned to Lucas with puzzlement on his face.

"And so, my new friend, please tell me. What were the magic words that you dispensed?" he asked.

"The magic didn't come from my mouth, Colonel. It came from my wallet. Always remember, cash speaks the loudest in the Balkans. The United Nations owes me a thousand Deutschmarks."

"No problem, Mr. Martin. You'll be reimbursed immediately upon our arrival in Sarajevo."

"The question that remains, Colonel, is 'How much more will we need to be reimbursed?' There is still a long journey ahead. The final tally could rise significantly."

"We'll manage, Mr. Martin. Perhaps better than you think," the colonel added confidently.

Lucas smiled cynically. *He's definitely new around here,* he thought to himself.

XI

As the convoy progressed into Herzegovina, the wind-worn mountaintops of Croatia gave way to low-lying bluffs and narrow, sunken valleys. A few of these valleys concealed hidden treasures, secluded villages that had been left undisturbed by the ravages of war. Most did not. It wasn't long before evidence of recent combat surfaced. The supply trucks had traveled only eight kilometers inside the border before the frames of burned-out houses came into view. The war's frontlines were constantly changing. It wasn't uncommon for the warring parties to exchange territory several times in the same day, leaving national and ethnic control confused and uncertain. At the moment, all historic boundaries were no more than obsolete lines drawn on outdated maps.

After seeing this initial devastation, the supply convoy prepared for the worst, but it advanced an additional thirty kilometers inland along the tapered, twisting roads without witnessing any similar destruction.

"Mr. Martin, we've passed through six villages since entering Herzegovina. The first three were leveled and the last three were completely intact. How do you explain that?" asked Colonel de Graaf.

Lucas quickly briefed his U.N. chauffeurs on the region's ethnic differences, and added, "In this particular part of Herzegovina, there are some villages that are mostly if not exclusively populated by Croatian Catholics, and located far enough away from Muslim and Serbian populations, to survive unscathed." No one could be sure for how long.

As his Dutch colleagues thanked him for sharing his expertise, it began to dawn on them how unprepared the world was in dealing with this man-made catastrophe.

"Things will change for the worse the closer we get to Mostar," Lucas continued. "There is a majority Muslim population there, remnants of the Ottoman Empire from centuries past. These days, the Croatian Catholics and the Serbian Orthodox are better represented."

As the relief column moved along the winding highway leading to the historic city of Mostar, the road grew narrower and less even. Heavy tank and personnel carrier usage had wreaked havoc on the pavement. The asphalt was rutted and chewed from abuse and neglect, and potholes dotted its surface, often forcing the convoy to slow to a crawl.

Mostar is perched like a bird on the banks of the Neretva River. As they approached, plumes of black smoke shimmied upward over its horizon. The column stopped when it reached a checkpoint manned by the Croatian Army. A small outfit of soldiers, each holding an automatic weapon, was resting and smoking at the side of the road. Lucas and the colonel stepped out of their vehicle and walked toward them openly, yet cautiously. The beleaguered troops studied the line of trucks with suspicion. In Croatian, Lucas asked to speak to the unit commander.

"The commander's at the front line," the nearest soldier explained.

"Do you have contact with him, a radio maybe?"

Two other soldiers, sitting on a concrete embankment and smoking black-market cigarettes, looked at one another in disbelief. At first, they laughed. A second elapsed before the sarcastic smiles turned into irritated glares. "The officers are busy at the moment. Why don't you come back a little later?" one shouted, with a raspy voice.

Lucas ignored him and maintained eye contact with the soldier who had originally answered. "Do you have an idea what the situation is in Mostar? Will we make it through the city without being fired on?"

"I doubt that. At the moment, Serbian irregulars are involved in a heated battle with the Muslim resistance. We're watching it play out. You might be able to skirt the heavy stuff if you take the secondary road around the perimeter, just above the city. But that isn't for sure," answered the young, unshaven warrior. He was wearing grimy fatigues, as if he had been in combat earlier that day. He was nervous and twitched agitatedly. A red and white checkered crest was stitched onto his uniform's shoulder. "What are you hauling, anyway?" he asked, taking a drag from his cigarette.

Lucas knew better than to answer the question. He ignored that it was asked, and thanked the soldier. Then he and Colonel de Graaf turned and walked away.

Re-entering the commander's jeep, Lucas asked to see a map.

"What are we in for?" asked the colonel.

"From the looks of the horizon, we'll need to bypass the city. The main highway passes through the city center. It's unusable because of the fighting. Instead, we can detour around Mostar via a secondary road. He advised us to take this route," Lucas said, pointing at the Croatian soldier. "But he doubted our safe passage would be guaranteed. What kind of defense capabilities have you been issued?"

"Less than we need, I'm sure," the colonel responded. "We have two personnel carriers with small caliber weaponry and two platoons of lightly armed infantry - nothing that could withstand artillery or a full-scale attack, mind you. I was promised that the safety of the convoy would not be in question. Are you expecting trouble?" the colonel asked. His face had lost its usual red hue.

"Are you in contact with NATO forces through the U.N.?" Lucas questioned.

"My orders come directly from the U.N.-NATO joint command at the Sarajevo airport. They are awaiting our arrival. If we get hung up, we can count on them for assistance, but I'm unsure of how much."

"It may not require much, just a show of support to get us through the rough spots," said Lucas. "I doubt they will provide airstrikes, but I think a jet fighter flyover might be valuable."

The colonel agreed and ordered his radioman to keep an open channel with headquarters in Sarajevo.

The convoy pushed ahead toward Mostar. Along the way, it passed dozens of concrete houses that had been riddled by shrapnel and bullets. Charred automobiles littered the roadsides. The military checkpoints increased as they approached the embattled city.

"So, exactly who is fighting whom today?" asked the colonel.

"From the insignia on the uniforms of the soldiers we just passed, I think it's the Croats and the Muslims against the Serbs, at least for the moment. I expect the alliances to break in the near future," Lucas answered. "Colonel, you aren't transporting any military supplies, are you?"

"I believe not, but that's all I'm allowed to tell you," he answered.

"Fair enough, I know the game. The reason I ask is because, as you know, the Serbs are well supplied militarily. The Croats are also, but less so. The Muslims, however, are more desperate. As we pass through territories held by them...well...you never know what to expect. Just keep your eyes and that radio frequency open," Lucas advised.

"I hear you," agreed the colonel.

The trucks closed in on Mostar's periphery sooner than expected. After climbing a hilltop overlooking the city, the colonel ordered the fleet to stop to assess their position. The officers and Lucas got out of their jeep and looked below through binoculars. Several buildings were on fire, and the shelling continued as they watched. While they were discussing their options, local residents sped past the stalled convoy headed for safety, away from the embattled city. Scores of cars were streaming by. Some were newer sedans, but most of the others were subcompact ones in various conditions. Lucas saw several vintage Volkswagen Golfs, Yugoslavian-made Fiat Zastavas, Renault R4s, and Serbian-made Yugos, and each were stuffed to their rooftops with supplies and personal belongings. Many of the drivers honked their horns and shouted obscenities in the local dialect at the foreigners as they passed.

"Get the hell out of the way!" bellowed an angry driver, his right hand gesturing wildly.

"*U pićku materinu!*" shouted the next one.

"What did the last one say?" the colonel asked Lucas.

"Well…he told you to go back to where you came from inside your mother," Lucas replied with a smile. "Colonel, look down along the river, and then a little bit up. Do you see the bridge sticking out from between those two buildings?"

The two Dutchmen replied in the affirmative.

"That's an artifact of the Ottoman Empire, built by the Turks. It must be four hundred years old. I doubt it will survive this war. Now look east and a little higher up. That's a shelled mosque and the stump of a minaret."

"They mean business, then?" the colonel asked knowingly.

"Uh-hmm."

The three pulled away and returned to the convoy. Just as the colonel reached his vehicle's door, an artillery shell was heard whistling in their direction.

"Incoming!" someone shouted from behind.

"Let's get a move on before they get us in range!" the colonel ordered. The driver hit the gas and the trucks followed them over the slender road in the opposite direction of the civilian traffic. Automobile horns continued to sound irately, but the colonel pressed forward and forced the traffic out of the way. He opened radio contact to his men and ordered them to advance at all cost. No civilian obstruction was to be tolerated.

Artillery shell explosions sounded with varying degrees of intensity as the convoy climbed the mountainside. The trucks coughed and churned as their diesel engines pushed forward in an effort to escape their hemmed-in position. Flying shrapnel, rocks, and clods of sod pelted the trailers as the artillery rounds closed in. One by one, the supply rigs rolled over the hilltop and out of range. Only a few in the rear received any damage; the final one being hit hardest when a shrieking mortar shell exploded less than two meters from its trailer. The fiery hunks of metal destroyed several tires and broke loose the trailer's rear hinges. A third of its contents were spilled onto the road before the driver was permitted to stop and investigate the damage.

Colonel de Graaf guided the group to a point of safety, then ordered an immediate inspection and assessment. Several trailers had suffered severe damage, making them unusable until repairs could be made. No casualties were reported, but the thought of leading an unarmed convoy through a battle zone heightened the colonel's concern for his men.

"What is the convoy's status, Colonel?" Lucas asked after the commotion had settled.

"It's not good. We have five trucks with enough damage to delay us at least a full day. I've been on the radio to headquarters. They're sending men and equipment at first light tomorrow. We'll have to camp here for the night," replied the colonel.

"I think that's wise. Keep an armed patrol posted on guard duty. By now, everybody knows we're here. I don't expect any trouble, but I wouldn't rule out possible raids on the supplies. If I may, I suggest having your men repack all the cargo that fell out of the last trailer as soon as possible. There is no sense leaving a trail to the cache. And keep the unit away from the roadsides; there may be land mines already in place."

"It's being done right now. It will be completed within the hour," the colonel said.

Lucas was quiet for a moment, then spoke again. "Colonel, it looks as though you're fixed here for the night and probably a full day longer. My orders are to get to Sarajevo as soon as possible. I have a contact that lives not far from here. With your permission, I would like to have your captain deliver me to him so I can arrange for transportation into Sarajevo on my own. I will inform the U.N. command of your situation in detail after I get there."

"Can you ensure the safety of my officer?" the colonel asked.

"No, but I can assure you that it is not far. If we leave soon, he should easily return before darkness sets in. I believe the risks to be limited."

"Captain van den Berg, do you consent to this?"

"It should be no problem, sir," the captain responded.

"Take two men and some weapons. Avoid all dangerous situations. Remember, you're under my command and not Mr. Martin's. Any sign of trouble and you make double-time back here. Understood?'

"Loud and clear, sir," the captain answered.

"Get going and be back here before dark. Don't make me regret this decision."

"Yes, sir," the captain answered. The jeep was promptly loaded, and they sped away at once.

The captain drove at breakneck speed through the surrounding terrain. The landscape was rugged and navigation difficult. Jagged mountain peaks and slim gorges were mixed among the rolling hills and rock-filled pastures. Dusk was approaching in the early summer evening, the air was cool, and a light fog crept in, limiting visibility. Military activity was only one of many dangers present while driving at high speeds in such uncertain terrain. The local drivers were aggressive and frequently made daring passes around wicked curves. Sheep, full after a day of grazing, often darted clumsily onto the pavement from the overgrown roadsides and into the paths of unsuspecting drivers.

But Lucas had a plan. He was a longtime acquaintance of a local politician who was partial to the Croatian cause. More importantly, Lucas knew, this individual was sympathetic to the cause of his own personal gain. The war was proving to be profitable to the well-connected, and he supposed his associate to be very important among the region's businessmen and black marketers. Complicating matters, however, was that Lucas was uncertain if his contact would help him or how much his assistance would cost. The two had not spoken since Lucas left the Balkans the previous December, and he had reservations regarding his acquaintance's reliability for the challenge ahead - the task of delivering him safely into the world's most dangerous city.

●●●●●

Lucas's associate was named Ante Boban. The two had met several years earlier when Lucas was first-assigned to the Sarajevo consulate. At that time, 'Mr. Ante,' as Lucas called him, was an entrepreneur in the making. He was a pure high-pressure salesman who wouldn't take no for an answer. Ante Boban had started as an ambitious capitalist when the concept in Yugoslavia was in its early stages, long before the fall of communism. Ante's lack of tact was disturbing. In fact, during their initial meeting, Lucas could hardly tolerate the man and his methods. Slowly, though, he came to appreciate his persistency; he predicted that Ante's knack for capitalism would make him very successful. Everything was for sale with 'Mr. Ante,' and even committing fraud was considered good business. Lucas suspected that if Ante Boban had been born in the United States, he would have gravitated toward the used-car industry, or perhaps been an unscrupulous insurance salesman, or possibly the kind of lawyer who chased ambulances.

Their first meeting was particularly extraordinary, and it happened not long after the 1984 Winter Olympics. Soon after Lucas had been assigned as security chief of the U.S. embassy and consulates in Yugoslavia, Ante Boban began arriving daily at the consulate in Sarajevo insisting on an audience with the consulate's U.S. trade liaison. After repeated warnings and several threats of arrest, which were required to ensure the consulate's integrity, Lucas took the time to listen to what he had to say. Ante Boban's business idea intrigued him enough to arrange a meeting with a consulate department head. Shortly thereafter, a business arrangement was struck with an American tobacco company, elevating Ante's status within the region. Eventually, he became involved in the local government and emerged as a powerful figure in the dodgy world of Balkan politics. Ante never forgot Lucas Martin for his original assistance, and actively sought out his friendship. Lucas, by contrast, knew enough to keep a certain distance from such a shady character, but the two spoke occasionally and always with the best intent. Now Lucas needed him. Ante Boban would never have been his first choice, but Lucas was in no position to choose.

●●●●●

The Dutch captain, Lucas, and the two armed escorts raced along the backroads of Herzegovina, past tiny villages whose names were vaguely familiar to Lucas - Potoci, Čitluk, and Čehari, Konjic, Bradina. After about two hours of driving, they passed through some of the area's heaviest fighting. Their progress was often slowed because of potential dangers like land mines, overturned vehicles, fallen rocks, trees, and other road debris. In the passenger seat, Lucas studied a map and directed the captain toward the quiet village of Nevenski Most, nestled in a scenic valley along the Višnja River. The destination was well outside Sarajevo's outskirts, and he felt confident the fighting had not reached Ante Boban's home. Thirty kilometers before reaching Sarajevo, Lucas instructed the captain to exit the main highway.

After turning, the jeep followed a side road that decreased in size the farther they advanced. It was not long before it became a one-way lane, barely wide enough for the U.N. jeep to pass. Eventually, the lane morphed into the private driveway leading to Ante Boban's villa.

They appeared to be interrupting festivities of some kind. A crowd was gathered at the rear of the house; Lucas could see a group of men and women sitting around a picnic table that was covered with food and large jugs of wine. Three other men were standing near a brick grill turning a lamb on a spit. A few more were casually kicking a soccer ball around the yard. As the four-wheel drive vehicle closed in, someone sounded a call of alarm and several men dashed forward armed with AK-47s. Startled by the commotion, Ante Boban emerged from the house, unsure of what to think. The war still seemed too many kilometers away for this to be a military assault. Seeing the black U.N. symbol painted on the sides of the jeep, he quickly assessed that trouble would not develop and called for his security to set aside their guns. A few minutes later, the mystery was solved when Lucas stepped out of the vehicle. A large smile, revealing crooked teeth permanently stained from heavy cigarette and coffee consumption, spread across Ante's face. In time, his forearms opened wide while his elbows stayed drawn firmly against his ribs.

"Ooohhh! Lucas, my oldest friend! How are you?" Ante bellowed, in what Lucas considered a classic Balkan style. Ante skipped gracefully down a short flight of steps while balancing a glass of wine in his right hand and holding a burning cigarette in his left one. He was dressed in a white, button-down shirt under a black vest. His matching black slacks, his favorite pair, were faded with overuse and longevity. His outfit was completed with white socks and black slip-on shoes. Lucas smiled. Ante hadn't changed a bit.

"I'm fine, Ante. Thank you. I hope you are as well?"

"Never better, Lucas, never better. There's a war on, you know? There's money to be made! Yes, money to be made!"

"I see the cruelty of war hasn't changed your attitude, Ante."

"Only for the better!" Ante proclaimed. "Lucas, what can I do for you, my old friend?"

Lucas met Ante at the villa's bottom step. He pointed at his military escorts as he spoke.

"Ante, these men can't stay here. Their unit is waiting for them near Mostar. I want to send them off, but first, I'm going to ask a favor from you. Can we talk in private?"

"Lucas, of course we can!" he responded energetically, as if this was the business deal he had been waiting for all day. The two always spoke in English. Ante was aware of Lucas's fluency in Croatian, but speaking in English satisfied his ego and made him feel more important in front of his companions. "How can I assist my old friend, Lucas Martin?"

Lucas led Ante out of earshot of his guests. "Ante, I'm due, no, I'm past due in Sarajevo and I need to get there as soon as possible. And I don't mean to the fringe. I need to get to the U.N. headquarters, inside the airport, *tonight*."

"Impossible!" Ante fired back. "Do you have any idea of what lies ahead after this point?" he asked. His use of English grammar had suffered from lack of practice. "The more closer we get to Sarajevo, the more destroyed is everything. The more increased is the Serbian military and their checkpoints. It will be dark soon, my friend, there is no chance tonight."

Lucas suspected that Ante was overstating the situation and didn't want to leave his party. He pressed on. "Look, Ante, it's not as if I have other options. And it's not as if you won't be well compensated for your efforts, or *abilities*, shall I say?"

Ante delayed his response until the meaning of Lucas's last statement had been fully absorbed. He began to speak, stopped, and calculated. With a cigarette wedged between his lips, he fidgeted with his shirtsleeves, shifted his weight some more, and then replied, "Lucas…what sort of proposition do you have in mind?"

Lucas answered, "Look, Ante, I know what is racing through your head. Don't get too greedy; I'm only asking for a forty-minute ride." Lucas thought for a moment longer and added, "And the way you drive, it will be more like fifteen minutes!"

"Lucas, please don't be so modest. Do you realize exactly what you're asking of me? This is a suicide mission of the grandest proportions, and I'm hoping to survive this war to see the end. There is no way through the Serbian blockade, not even for me."

"Ante, don't tell me your connections don't reach all the way to the top. If you wanted to, you could stop the shelling, or at least delay it, for a day or two. I'm sure you're strongly connected to the players on all sides - because they all want what you have."

"Okay, Lucas, so I am an equal opportunity businessman. Certainly you would agree that cash has no ethnic favoritism. This war has created the world's largest duty-free zone. What do I care if a few nationalistic maniacs want to rearrange the borders? Profit without borders, that's what I always say. But even still, I'm not willing to risk my life for…how do you Americans say…peanut money!"

Ante scratched at his close-cropped hair, then lit another cigarette. He nervously shifted his weight from one leg to the other and repeated the motion in a restless fashion. He was a tall, hyperactive man with very little body fat. His head was large and his facial features were prominent, with a protruding brow line and a jaw that jetted outward from his thin, wrinkled face. His heavy eyes were cold, black, and deep-set. They shifted from side to side at an unpredictable rate. His buzzed hairline grew in a widow's peak, and since childhood, his left temple had sported a one-inch scar.

"But, in the event that I *could* satisfy your needs, what is being offered in return?" he asked.

This was the opening Lucas had been hoping for. He knew he had to make the offer attractive or Ante would end the conversation on the spot.

"It's only a forty-minute ride, Ante. Three thousand Deutschmarks. You'll be there and back before the lamb gets cold. But we must leave at once."

"Lucas, please, allow me four or five hours to make some telephone calls. I need time to clear a path. I think we should wait until tomorrow."

"No deal. We leave immediately. I'm nearly a day behind schedule as it is," Lucas said. Then he pulled out his money belt and began counting off Deutschmarks, one hundred at a time. "Stop stalling, Ante. You'll be back in an hour or so."

Ante stared hungrily at the easy money. Lucas imagined it was a stare like a lioness would give an infant wildebeest that had strayed from its mother.

"Okay, okay," he answered. "But I must warn you, I've had a bit to drink."

"Of course you have, Ante. Of course you have," Lucas replied.

He returned to the U.N. vehicle and relayed the results to Captain van den Berg. Then he gave directions back to the convoy and sent them on their way. Before parting, he assured them that he would personally advise the relief team in the morning. A few last words of encouragement were exchanged before the jeep was off.

As Lucas bid them farewell, Ante gathered two bodyguards and informed them of the plan. The pair collected their weapons and waited in front while Ante scurried behind the house. A few moments later, a faded silver Mercedes-Benz barreled out from around the villa's back side. A thick cloud of dust rose from the gravel driveway when Ante slammed on the brakes, bringing the car to a halt a few meters from the waiting passengers. The driver introduced Lucas to his security team and directed them to get in. Lucas chose to sit behind Ante. The bodyguards climbed into their seats and rested their AK-47s between their knees. When everyone was settled, Ante wheeled the car around and pressed hard on the gas. He was not one to waste time when money was involved. The car quickly pulled into the nearby village, and then screeched out a turn as the Mercedes headed in the direction of Sarajevo.

Behind the steering wheel, Ante smoked a cigarette and repeated his reservations about the journey. Simultaneously, he floored the accelerator and pushed the car onward.

"I swear to you, Lucas, this is a bad idea. I've had no time to prepare my contacts and right now is a delicate time for such boldness. Everyone is a target, and I don't know how much clout I have with the forces in place, especially with the Serbs. If things go bad at the checkpoints, I'm holding you accountable."

Lucas sensed this was not so much a threat as it was a subtle test for more money.

"We'll be fine. Just stay calm and use that little bit of charm you keep reserved for these difficult moments," Lucas advised.

Darkness had set in. There was little traffic on the road. Most of the area's electricity had been shut down for days. They passed several military convoys along the way. Lucas identified them as belonging to the JNA. The closer they got to Sarajevo's outskirts, the more military traffic they encountered. Their automobile was stopped several times, but they were not harassed at the checkpoints. Ante had dealt with this situation often. He knew the right things to say and the right names to drop at the right moments. This is what Lucas had been counting on. All four travelers were astonished at how smoothly the journey passed. Before reaching the airport, they came to a final checkpoint, one that Ante considered to be impenetrable. Lucas reassured him and coached him on what to say. They had to pass through this final obstacle in order to reach the U.N. headquarters, which was near the suburb of Illidža. Once inside, Lucas could advise the base commanders on the condition of the stuck convoy and contact the U.S. consulate before attempting to enter the city the next day.

"Keep your head up, Ante. Establish eye contact with the patrol. Tell the guard your name and where you intend to go. Speak with authority. If he tells you it's not possible, assure him that you have clearance, but you're not allowed to elaborate. Tell him that you have just returned from Montenegro on official business straight from

Belgrade. If he attempts to question you, control the conversation. Raise your voice and tell him to stand aside, so that he and the rest of the Serbian army can be smoking American cigarettes until the end of the war. He'll get the picture," Lucas said.

Ante grimaced and repeated his reservations. At the barricade, the military policeman approached the Benz with an air of insolence and a strut of arrogance. He tapped three times on the driver's side window, each time stronger than necessary.

"Give me your identification card," he demanded. After snatching the card from Ante's hand, he stood puzzled at the position he had put himself in. Lucas was aware the Serbian soldier had recognized Ante's name. The guard's disposition weakened slightly. "What can I help you with this evening?" he asked, taking care not to back down completely. He avoided eye contact.

"I've been directed by some important people in Belgrade to continue through to the airport. I was told that my car had been cleared to pass, and that the shelling would temporarily cease. I will need about an hour – not longer. I am in a hurry," Ante said. Then he waited for a reply.

"I must clear this with my superior," the guard responded, and began to turn away.

"This has already been cleared to the top, because it came from the top. I am not asking, I am telling. Repeat this to your superiors. Also, tell them to stop the shelling around the airport for the next one hour," Ante barked, hoping to put the guard on the defensive.

Lucas cringed in the backseat, worrying that Ante had pushed too strongly. He began having private doubts about how much influence Ante really wielded at the moment. A drawn-out verbal conflict was not in their best interest.

"I will return soon. Relax for a moment," the checkpoint guard ordered. Then he walked away.

The inside of the Mercedes 300 was silent. Ante tapped fretfully on the steering wheel while his bodyguards clenched their weapons. Their nervous hands were positioned for action; their palms were soaked wet with perspiration. Ante lit a cigarette and passed the pack to the others. Lucas opened his window and listened for signs of trouble. He could hear nothing outside.

The checkpoint guard disappeared into a portable control cabin. It was dimly lit on the inside by a single bulb hanging from a wire that was connected to a generator outside. The surrounding area was brightly lit by spotlights attached to an additional row of generators. Several well-armed soldiers patrolled the area. Each smoked continuously.

Lucas watched as the guard in the booth contacted his superior via a handheld radio. The conversation grew more heated the longer it lasted until finally the soldier slammed the receiver down in frustration. After the guard exited the booth, he summoned three lower-ranking soldiers. The four conferred, and then slowly closed in on the silver Mercedes. As they neared, they fanned out around the vehicle and waited for their superior to speak. The ranking guard put his hands on the driver's side door and leaned through the opened window. He rotated his head and examined each passenger. Finishing that, he spoke gruffly to Ante. His breath reeked of cigarettes and coffee.

"You have been given clearance to pass through at my discretion. Your safety from a temporary cease-fire is also at my command. However, I haven't yet been persuaded that your intentions are in the Republic of Yugoslavia's best interest."

Again, Lucas recognized that a shake-down was underway. He nudged Ante from behind the driver seat. Undoubtedly, Ante knew best how to handle the situation. The businessman wasted no time and began direct negotiations. He felt compelled to offer little and hoped Lucas would remain patient in the backseat.

"Sir, I am here on the orders of your superiors. I shall be out before I'm in. Really, absolutely less than one hour. This is not much to ask?" Ante spouted, with his palms facing the heavens.

"I am not at liberty to delay the war effort for even one minute, not even for the best of motives. We will have to work out an arrangement, or it will be impossible for you to pass without significant risk to your safety," the soldier said.

Ante balked at the last statement. He was certain the Serbian guard was not posturing.

"May I step from the car, then? There is something I would like to show you."

"Yes, but slowly and with care to avoid any accidents," the guard answered.

Ante pressed the trunk lid release, opened the door, and turned in his seat. He stood up slowly and joined the men at the rear of the car. Along the way, Ante stretched his arms and spoke amiably with the soldiers. After reaching the trunk, he lifted the lid and removed a heavy duffel bag. Then he slammed the trunk shut and, in dramatic fashion, placed the bag on the Benz before opening its zipper. One by one, Ante pulled out eight cartons of American cigarettes and three bottles of Scotch whisky. For effect, he set the items down on the metallic surface harder than necessary. With a showman's flair, he pressed his hand on top of the cigarette boxes and gradually faced the patrol.

"Do you think that now we may pass unmolested for a short time?" he asked.

The highest-ranking guard looked each subordinate in the eye and smiled. The smile was returned by each.

"I think that can be arranged. Put your car into low gear and don't stray too close to the sides of the road. They are heavily mined. The shelling will resume in exactly one hour. I expect you to be back before then. I repeat…in exactly sixty minutes, the bombardment will begin again whether you have returned or not. Don't lose your way," the head Serbian checkpoint guard said, while lifting the cigarettes off the trunk. Using his free hand, he waved up the barricade and returned to the control booth.

After Ante put the duffle bag back into the trunk, he got into the car and began to drive. Once they were clear of the checkpoint, he spoke to Lucas while looking through the rearview mirror. "You can add another thousand Deutschmarks to my account, Lucas. Black market rates have created enormous inflationary pressures, shall we say?"

"No problem, Ante. You did a wonderful job. You're a real service to your countrymen!"

With that, Ante's bodyguards chuckled in delight.

"I do the best I can in these very trying times, my friend," Ante added, contributing to the jovial atmosphere.

The aged Mercedes angled its way down the mountain slope and slowed to a prowl as it neared the airport. Night had set in and it was impossible to tell the extent of the destruction created by the recent shelling. Several buildings and houses, now nothing more than burned-out casings, could be seen standing in ruin. Machine gun fire was audible in the distance, but the artillery shelling had stopped. For how long remained unknown. Lucas's concern grew internally, Ante's surfaced outwardly. He did not trust the Serbs. Not in business and definitely not in war. Before the hostilities had started, he had made little distinction between his country's ethnic groups. National cooperation was all he had ever known. Things had changed overnight. The Serbian population had been whipped into a frenzy. He succeeded in business with the Serbian authorities based solely on cigarettes - something they craved. But he trusted no one. And they did not trust him. Few people trusted Ante Boban. He had earned his reputation not as a tough businessman who crushed his competition with effective marketing strategies, but as a greedy entrepreneur who left no stone unturned in his pursuit of profit. He was viewed as a swindler who succeeded where all others had failed. But because of this success, he had achieved a great deal of wealth, much more than men better than himself.

When the Mercedes reached the Sarajevo airport, Ante felt a sense of relief as the car stopped at the U.N. checkpoint. As he steered the Benz toward the French soldiers manning the barricade, Lucas prepared his documents and identity card. Ante let the car idle, and Lucas stepped out and made his presence known. The

French guard informed Lucas that they had been expecting him and that an escort was prepared to take him to the camp commander.

Lucas returned at once to give Ante the bribe money. He included some extra, assuming it would be needed to renegotiate his way out of the encircled airport. Ante, always formal and disgustingly likeable to Lucas, bid him farewell extravagantly. It was established that the two would meet again, preferably under better circumstances. Then Ante turned the Mercedes and pointed it in the opposite direction. He stepped on the gas and the taillights quickly disappeared.

Lucas entered the compound and was shown his sleeping quarters and a place to clean up. The camp commander was waiting to be informed about the stalled convoy's status. Lucas was to be briefed on the ongoing diplomatic negotiations and on the course of the fighting. Their meeting was kept short. Overcome by exhaustion, Lucas returned to his cot as soon as possible. This day had been grueling, and he was certain there would be many more ahead. Tomorrow's itinerary included devising a way into Sarajevo and re-establishing contact with the U.S. consulate in the city center. From there, he would contact Curtis Sheets in Belgrade to begin the mission's next phase.

XII

General Parenta was on his cellular phone listening raptly to a progress report from an artillery unit leader on the city's opposite side while Dragoslav Obrenović stood nearby. Until a few minutes ago, he had been leaning across his vehicle and staring into a pair of binoculars, assessing the results of the day's assault. When the shells had suddenly stopped falling around the Sarajevo airport, he was livid. He had not ordered a cease-fire, and all his artillery unit's efforts were now at risk of being wasted. He hated waste. As the report drew to a close, he stood bewildered with his mouth half open.

"Goddamn it, Dragoslav! Get your ass to Mt. Igman and find out why the shelling has stopped!" he ordered. He slammed his hand down on the vehicle's hood in a fit of rage. "I want someone's head handed to me. Do you understand? We had the entire Muslim resistance in the western suburbs pinned down, and now a corridor has opened up near the airport. We don't have the necessary forces in place, and the enemy is clearing out. *U pičku materinu!*" he roared. "It was a matter of a day or so to their surrender, and the whole strategy has just been ruined!" Still incensed, General Parenta pounded the hood several more times with a clenched fist.

Dragoslav Obrenović stood passively, while thinking how to deflect his superior's wrath. Trying to remain calm on the outside, his mind raced frantically, searching for another culprit on whom to place the blame. Only he possessed enough authority to order the temporary cease-fire. But when the checkpoint guard had contacted him, he was dying for a cigarette. They had become scarce, and he hadn't smoked in several days. At the moment he received the call from the checkpoint guard, he would have given anything for a full carton. No time was taken to consider the consequences of his decision. Just the same, he neither accepted nor denied responsibility for the command, but assured the general that the situation would be taken care of.

Dragoslav wasn't slow in finding an opportunity to escape his angry superior. He desperately needed to control the damage that he had created. He started his vehicle and sped toward the Mt. Igman checkpoint, just above the airport. Arriving in record time, he entered the communications booth, grabbed the radio, and ordered the artillery units to resume shelling. Within minutes, dozens of 82-millimeter mortar rounds began falling at a fast and furious pace.

●●●●●

Ante Boban's Mercedes-Benz had made it less than halfway up the mountainside when the first shells poured down around it. Ante was shocked but not surprised by the Serbian double-cross. He floored the accelerator and tried to steer clear of the sides of the road. Every so often, he turned off the headlights in an attempt to avoid detection. The Benz was a moving target on a curvy road. Aided by darkness, Ante knew the mortar rounds would have a difficult time finding their mark. Stealth was their only chance of escape.

The speeding car swerved and veered as its driver steered for survival. Eventually, a number of rounds closed in, hurling chunks of shrapnel against its body. All at once, a rear passenger-side window caved in when a golf ball-sized piece of metal crashed against its reinforced glass. The bodyguard in back was spared only because of his fortunate position: he had been lying face down across the seat, praying to make it out alive.

Ante shifted into a higher gear as the car closed in on the JNA checkpoint. He did not need to rethink his plan of action. To stop meant certain death. He had no intention of reducing his speed until the Serbian blockade had been cleared. Without hesitation, he stomped on the gas, pushing his car to top speed. By now, his bodyguards had recovered and readied their weapons. Each was prepared to fire. As the car came close, they conspired to wait until the last moment in an effort to delay drawing incoming fire.

●●●●●

When the Mercedes neared the checkpoint, the mortar rounds stopped falling. The Serbian platoon was positioned and waiting. Dragoslav Obrenović commanded the unit with skill and precision. It was his reputation that was on the line. He ordered the ranking guard to halt the advancing car, then waited anxiously to see what would happen.

Ante revved the six-cylinder engine to its maximum capacity and pointed the car at the barricade. Just in front, the guard strutted several meters toward the approaching Benz waving a portable stop sign in his right hand and carrying his weapon in his left one. Ante aimed the blazing Benz at his legs, intent on taking him out first.

The smell of fear and perspiration inside the Mercedes was strong. Adrenaline caused sweat to stream from the men's pores. Even with the shattered back window, the air was thick from labored breathing and spent oxygen. Moisture condensed on the windshield's inner surface.

Charging forward, the car rammed through the guard's pelvis and crushed his legs. His red lamp was flung airborne as his body bounced to the side of the road.

Dragoslav Obrenović had predicted the driver's intentions and called out for his men to open fire on the renegade automobile. Tracer lights filled the night sky as rifle round after rifle round burst toward the car.

Ante hollered to his companions to return fire. They had decided that if they were going to die, then they would take out as many of the Serbian soldiers as possible. As his companions opened fire with their AK-47s, Ante steered the car toward the wooden obstacle blocking their path. Incoming rifle rounds riddled the heavy-plated Mercedes from all directions. Ante fought tenaciously to maintain control of the car. He cursed the position that his greed had put him in.

Obrenović watched the action unfold from behind the scenes and decided that he would be the last line of defense that the Mercedes would need to overcome. The source of his problems had to be stopped so his reputation as General Parenta's second-in-command could be restored. He could not bear the thought of falling out of favor with the general or losing the perks his favoritism provided. He would not fail.

Ante weaved his way through the onslaught. A large gap in the battle line opened, and it suddenly appeared that there was a chance of escape. The extra expense of the Benz's armor was more than worth the price now. Ante had begrudgingly invested in the added protection many years ago.

The Serbian soldiers were unprepared for the battle they were fighting. They had become complacent from the daily routine of lobbing shells on defenseless civilians. The prospect of close-quarter combat with an enemy who was returning fire caused many soldiers to scramble and take cover. Dragoslav watched the unit's performance with disgust. He became certain that his presence would be required.

When the Benz smashed through it, the barricade arm collapsed with little resistance. Large splinters of painted wood fluttered skyward from the force of the impact. Only thirty-five meters more and their survival was virtually assured.

Additional Serbian soldiers appeared and opened fire on the racing Mercedes with their automatic rifles. Suddenly, a daring young irregular appeared in the road and began firing his pistol into the car's windshield. Ante spun the wheel madly and drove through the youth's frozen body. A great thud echoed as his corpse was tossed aside. Instinctively, Ante searched for others to ram.

Dragoslav sensed the momentum shifting. A few more seconds and his quarry would escape. It was now time for him to act. Reaching to his left, he lifted the unit's grenade launcher up to his right shoulder. As the Benz sped past, he knew there would be only one chance. As he took aim, he calculated the lead with a marksman's skill. With nothing to obstruct his view, the shot would be an easy one. He estimated the distance, and then pulled back on the trigger. A burst of bright light sizzled toward the fleeing Mercedes.

A second later, the projectile reached its target and crashed through the passenger side door. A magnificent explosion flipped the car end over end until it came to rest on its top. Then everything was quiet. Dragoslav walked toward the car carrying a 30-caliber Tokarev pistol in his right hand. The car's engine was engulfed in a heavy black smoke. The rear tires continued spinning.

Peering through the back window, Dragoslav spotted the bodyguards' distorted bodies inside. They were lying listlessly and bleeding. He searched for signs of life. There were none. Unwilling to take chances, he fired a round from his pistol into each of their foreheads. Then he circled the car and approached the driver's side. The door was ajar and filled with bullet holes. Ante's mangled body hung limply out of the side. His face was disfigured; his right ear was gone. The hair on the right side of his head had been singed off from the explosion. Barely conscious, he struggled to breathe. Lying on his left shoulder, Ante looked up with his right eye. Dragoslav bent over him and stared down ruthlessly. Squatting next to the twisted figure, he reached inside Ante's jacket and removed his wallet and a wad of cash. This hurt Ante more than the physical injuries he had suffered. With disdain, he could only grunt in response.

"Yes, yes, Mr. Smuggler. I know all about it," Drago said mockingly, as he popped the car's trunk release. Moving behind the overturned Benz, the paramilitary leader pulled out the duffle bag filled with black-market cigarettes and Scotch whisky. Then he returned to the car's owner.

"Well, it looks like you won't need this stuff anymore," Dragoslav taunted. The Serbian soldiers, who had surrounded their leader, smiled with amusement.

Ante inhaled slowly, gathering the last of his strength. Staring up with his right eye, his glare of hatred was obvious. "Fuck you, Chetnik!" he murmured, with the last of his power.

"I see. So this is how you want the end to be? Then this is how you shall have it," Dragoslav said. He stood abruptly, and lifted his weapon from his side. He did not look to the others for approval. He did not want to show hesitation, mercy, or weakness. A statement was being made to those under his command. In one fluid motion, Dragoslav filled his weapon's chamber and cocked back the hammer. Stepping a meter away, he fired a round into Ante's right temple. Ante's body jerked violently, relaxed, and soon was completely still.

"You two: take the bodies from the car and bury them together over in that ravine," Dragoslav ordered, pointing at two idle soldiers. "And you two, push the car over that hillside and set it ablaze. Don't just stand there. Get it done now! We don't have all night."

After these tasks were completed, Dragoslav returned to the general with a carton of cigarettes, a bottle of whisky, and a satisfactory report. General Parenta was pleased. Dragoslav Obrenović had retained his powerful position.

XIII

The next morning, Lucas woke early at the U.N. compound which had been constructed in haste along an airport tarmac shortly after the conflict began. At the moment, the airport still wasn't fully functional, nor was it totally secure. Definitive control was still being negotiated between the United Nations and the Serbian military authority.

Before going to bed the night before, Lucas had spent almost an hour with the camp commanders, briefing them on the convoy's position and condition. He gave the officers suggestions on how to remedy the caravan's plight, and informed them of the equipment that would be needed to get the stranded trucks to safety. In return, the U.N. commanders provided Lucas with the most current information about the fighting at their disposal and issued him every document that he requested. The material, however, was hardly enough. There were large gaps in the details and many questions - questions which he alone would have to answer, using his own methods and resources. This, as Morton Riggs had repeatedly reminded him, was the reason why he was recalled – it was his specialty.

●●●●●

At daybreak, Lucas rose from his bunk still groggy, but he felt better after a shower and shave. As he looked out the bathroom window, he could see very little. The sky was overcast, and it looked as though it would rain. After dressing, he headed directly to the camp's kitchen. The cook had been working for nearly an hour, but Lucas was the first to appear. He was famished and the breakfast, consisting of cold cereal, bacon and eggs and a glass of orange juice, was appreciated. After eating, he sat alone and sipped a cup of coffee. Soon he had recovered enough energy to study the details he had received the night before and plan his mission ahead. Today his top priority was to reach the U.S. consulate, where the staff was awaiting his arrival. From there, communication would be restored with Curtis Sheets in Belgrade, and his fact-finding duties could begin.

Lucas's main challenge was to enter Sarajevo without becoming the victim of an early-bird sniper. He was aware that the city's inhabitants usually came out at dawn to collect food and water before the snipers had readied their rifles. By mid-morning, roads could not be crossed and pedestrians were unable to walk safely in the open. A full sprint in a zigzag pattern was necessary to avoid becoming an easy target. Life expectancy depended on agility. Some people could not adjust to this new threat. Many were killed while trying to cling to their crumbling routines. For many others, the sheer horror of living under such circumstances was unbearable. The suicide rate had skyrocketed, and this was only the beginning of a conflict that showed no signs of stopping.

Lucas could well imagine the population's daily struggle for survival, yet he had not experienced the reality firsthand. When he had left Sarajevo several months ago, it remained untouched by war, and the citizens were optimistic that their homes and lives could be spared. At that time, it was still one of the prize cities of ex-Yugoslavia - and indeed of all Eastern Europe. What he expected to find now would be only a broken reflection of what he remembered. It sickened him to think about it.

To Lucas, the Serbian military's strategy for Sarajevo's population was painfully obvious. He couldn't believe that such heinous tactics were actually being deployed. He was beginning to think there could be no reasoning with this kind of mentality, that there was no hope of a peaceful resolution, and that military intervention would be required. Early on, when the fighting had first erupted in the countryside, he had refrained from drawing such conclusions. But after months of exposure to the unrelenting aggression, lies, and corruption, he felt certain where the major blame rested. And after learning of the reports of ongoing atrocities committed by the Serbian forces, his opinion had solidified. Now only physical proof was needed to confirm to the rest to the world what he suspected to be true.

The Bosnian-Serb leadership excelled at hiding the truth and covering their tracks. Lucas hoped that a more expedient ending to the conflict might result if he acted quickly and successfully. He knew that if his mission failed, tens or hundreds of thousands of people could be displaced, uprooted, or killed in the meantime. Delay in his assignment's start was unacceptable; even if his mission was a success, the fighting was likely to continue for weeks, months, or perhaps years to come. Already, too many innocent lives had already been lost; others were physically alive, yet dead inside. Their exhausted minds were simply unaware of the fact.

●●●●●

In a little while, the camp officers entered the dining area. They poured themselves cups of coffee, then sat down with Lucas. The mood in the room was tense as they informed him of the latest developments. At first light, the stranded convoy had come under attack, and the rescue team was just now starting out. Neither unit was authorized to engage in battle, leaving the commanders in significant distress. NATO had ordered an F-15 flyover that halted the Muslim militia's attack temporarily, but it could not be known for how long. The base commanders had been on the telephone ever since, trying to secure permission for their soldiers to defend themselves and protect the relief supplies they were transporting. Once again, it seemed that the U.N. bureaucracy was on the verge of getting innocent people killed.

Lucas cleared his throat.

"Gentlemen, I don't mean to interrupt at such a critical moment, but I would like to change the subject if I may."

They consented.

He continued, "As we discussed last night, it is imperative that I get into the city center and reach the U.S. consulate today - alive. I am already behind schedule. Important officials in Washington are anxiously awaiting my contact. If a plan can be devised to get me to my destination as soon as possible, I will be in communication with some high-ranking U.S. government officials. Perhaps then I can do something about your bureaucratic problems with the U.N."

The group's ranking officers glanced at one another. Then they nodded in agreement. The commanding colonel promptly asked, "Mr. Martin, do you really have Washington's ear?" A second later, he clarified his question, "More importantly, do you have the capability to expedite the assistance we seek?"

Lucas considered his response before answering.

"I'll just say that I've been promised any assistance from the U.S. State Department deemed helpful to my mission, which is now in your mission's best interest."

"Then it's settled," the French colonel said. He barked at a Canadian subordinate, "Major, I authorize you to mobilize the armored personnel carrier and deliver Mr. Martin into the city. Take command of the project and get this done as soon as possible."

"Immediately, sir!" the major answered.

"Mr. Martin, if there is something we have that you're in need of...speak up. Does anything come to mind?" asked the colonel.

"How well-equipped is your arsenal?"

"Limited; what do you want?"

"I think a pistol will do. Once the armored vehicle drops me off, I'll likely have to make my way to the consulate on foot. No one can know what to expect inside the city center."

Just then, a massive explosion rocked the neighboring village of Ilidža, shaking the makeshift buildings inside the compound. Early-morning battles were already raging, and Lucas had yet to study the surrounding layout.

"Colonel...is this base secure?" Lucas asked. "That explosion sounded awfully close."

"No, our safety is not guaranteed. We've negotiated with the Serbs, and they have agreed to allow us free access into and out of the city for humanitarian efforts, but every day we're finding this to be less so. In fact, the immediate area around this compound has taken some malicious artillery hits, but the Serbs always deny responsibility or play it off as a stray round or a misfire. I don't trust them, and they know it. After entering the city, watch your back. When you are on your own, trust no one," the colonel warned.

"I imagine a nine-millimeter from the armory should suit my needs. I can upgrade once I reach the consulate."

At the colonel's command, the major escorted Lucas to the weapons cache. As Lucas looked through the locker, he reserved commentary so as not to alarm the major. He was amazed at the inadequacy of the weaponry the base had for its protection. The armory was lacking in firepower, and the compound could be easily overrun if the fighting drew closer.

Lucas chose a freshly oiled Berretta and took plenty of ammunition. He also took some other equipment he thought might be useful: a small set of binoculars, two smoke canisters, a compass, and a flashlight. He also snatched a pair of Gore-Tex boots and a rain poncho. He decided to wear the boots, and packed the rest into a waterproof rucksack, which he slung over his shoulder. He fastened the loaded pistol to his belt.

Lucas was dressed in khaki commando pants and an olive green turtleneck sweater. A black windbreaker hung unzipped on top. Around his waist, his cash and documents fit neatly into a thin belt that could not be seen under his shirt. Inside of the belt, Lucas also kept personal papers which never left his possession while he was in the Balkans. In a separate sleeve, he stored a tattered, yellow envelope that contained the last letter his father had ever written to his family and a worn, black and white photo of Lucas sitting on his father's lap when he was still a small child. On its backside, in faded ink, his mother had written: Ivan and Luka Martinović, Slavonski Brod, Croatia -1939. Lucas intended to use these items to help determine what had become of his father whenever the circumstances allowed.

He left the barracks and headed to the base control center where the camp commanders were waiting. They had maps of the known strongholds of the warring parties, and they studied them closely. The situation looked grim for Sarajevo's civilians. The Muslim resistance was outnumbered and poorly armed. They were fighting with limited provisions and using ineffective weaponry. It would not be easy for them to upgrade their arsenal; U.N. sanctions had made arms-dealing impossible. Nonetheless, the Muslims were making great efforts to improve their armaments via the black market and by other means. For now, what existed was a collective army of shoddily trained, under-equipped civilians fighting for their survival.

Lucas had known Sarajevo by heart before the siege had begun, but the city's infrastructure had changed dramatically since his departure. Roads and bridges had been closed and entire buildings had been demolished in his absence. Looking over a map, the officer proposed how Lucas might reach his destination. A single main artery split Sarajevo down the middle. To use this road, an armored vehicle would be required. Lucas didn't like this prospect. The vehicle would be exposed to sniper fire and artillery shelling from every angle. The commander insisted that a U.N.-marked transporter would not be fired on, but Lucas suspected otherwise. Still, no better alternative existed. It was decided that he would be dropped near the city's main post office, and then advance on foot. After reaching the relative safety of the post office, Lucas planned to consult with locals to learn how to best maneuver the rest of the way. From that point onward, the risk of being targeted by a sniper's rifle would increase dramatically.

By eight o'clock, the armored vehicle was prepared and waiting to leave. Lucas set in his gear, and then scanned the horizon with binoculars. While searching the surroundings, he spotted several JNA tanks positioned along the wooded hillsides and howitzers poised on the adjacent mountains. The Serbian ambassador in Washington had obviously been lying – less than a week had passed since Lucas had attended the meeting at the Yugoslavian embassy in D.C.

It wasn't long before shots rang out and shells rained down east of the compound as fighting began in earnest. Lucas consulted with the major, and they decided to leave immediately rather than risk being mistaken as a legitimate target. The driver navigated the cumbersome transport as fast as it would go. His orders were not to return until Lucas had been safely delivered.

The armored vehicle chugged out of the compound exit with authority. It was painted white and bore a large U.N. insignia on each side. Diesel fumes from its engine wafted insidiously into the riding compartment; Lucas's memory immediately made a connection to his childhood boat ride to Lošinj Island. A feeling of nausea began to creep over him. He knew this journey would be a short one, but he worried that it might be hours before the nausea left him. He couldn't afford to feel sick now.

After the transport left Ilidža, it turned right onto the main thoroughfare leading into the city center. As they progressed, the apartment towers that flanked Sarajevo's various neighborhoods came into view. Some of the neighborhoods were primarily populated by Serbs, and others were home to Muslim majorities. All the buildings showed considerable destruction, and some were still burning from recent shelling. When Lucas looked out a porthole, he could see fire-damaged structures in every direction. Decades had passed since he had witnessed such devastation.

The main thoroughfare consisted of four lanes, two identical paths running in opposite directions. The lanes were separated by an above-ground tram system that had been one of the city's most popular modes of transportation before the fighting had started. Now it was unusable. The multicolored trolleys had first been abandoned because of the power outage. More recently, they had been used for Serbian artillery target practice. Lucas saw several tramcars lying on their sides, torched and ruined.

When the road reached the business district, it narrowed in width, bringing the city's infrastructure closer together. As the U.N. transporter rolled past some of the tallest buildings, Lucas felt a tap on the shoulder. It was the Canadian major, seated to his right.

"Welcome to 'Sniper Alley,' Mr. Martin.," he said. "Things have changed a lot since you were last here - even the street names!"

Lucas returned the Canadian's rueful smile.

"We're approaching the Holiday Inn now. Most of the international press and TV crews are staying there. Don't ask me why. It's taking as many incoming rounds as the competition. It's not safe anywhere."

"Are you in contact with many of the foreign journalists?" asked Lucas.

"We try to be. They are a good source of information. We trade intelligence with the dependable ones and stay away from the leeches. Everybody is after something in this place...watch your back."

Lucas nodded.

The U.N. personnel carrier moved steadily and was spared from attack. As it reached the post office, it began to slow. A wind-whipped drizzle began to fall. The personnel carrier was now only two kilometers from the U.S. consulate, but the route there was blocked by rubble and debris, the result of multiple direct hits by howitzer rounds into various eighteenth-century structures.

Fallen bricks and mortar spilled onto the street. No one had been ambitious, brave, or stupid enough to attempt to clear a path.

"It looks like this is the end of the line, Mr. Martin. From here, you're on your own. Once you are out of this vehicle, consider yourself a legitimate target. About a hundred and fifty meters remains before the first point of cover. The rain will make you less visible, but it will also slow you down. You can take refuge in the entryway of the post office. To get there safely, I advise you to run like the wind. Once you're in the doorway, you can catch your breath, but stay out of sight. From then on, press yourself alongside the concrete walls and try to stay hidden. When you need to cross a street, make a run for it. Do not walk, and do not dawdle."

Lucas smiled at the major's simplistic advice, though he appreciated his concern. He was certain the major was unaware of his credentials in such matters. He shook the Canadian's hand and wished him well. Then the transport's door opened, and he burst out and into hell's fire.

Lucas bolted in the direction of Sarajevo's main post office. Along the way, he was forced to scale mounds of glass, steel, and concrete. In midstride, he hoisted himself over a fractured utility pole, and then scurried for shelter. The dash was less eventful than anticipated, yet an ample amount of fear played havoc with his adrenal glands. When he reached the building's entrance unharmed, he took a moment to relax and assess his situation. Very few pedestrians could be seen moving outside.

In the distance, he spotted an old man hustling out of one structure and into another. All was quiet except for the light rain caressing the pavement. Suddenly, he was startled to find another man standing in a darkened corridor, sharing the sanctuary that the doorway provided.

Undaunted, Lucas turned to him and asked, "Has there been much sniper fire this morning?"

The stranger emerged from the darkness and walked slowly toward Lucas. He had an unnerving, glossy look in his eyes. He answered, "My friend, there has been much sniper fire in the last one hour, one day, and one week. A sniper fired at me as I ran here. My brother-in-law was killed two days ago while trying to collect fresh water." His voice trailed off and a tear fell from his right eye. Just as quickly, he collected himself. Soon a look of hatred dominated his face. He added, "Those fucking Chetniks will kill us all!"

Lucas stared at the ground, regretting that he had asked. The response was not what he expected.

"I need to make my way to the U.S. consulate. Do you have any suggestions about how I can get there safely?"

The man considered the possibilities for a moment. His eyes had cleared. Then he answered, "You are about a kilometer and a half away from where you want to go. You'll have to cross plenty of open ground. I can show you a shortcut that will get you started, but I advise you to find somewhere to wait until darkness can cover your final crossing."

The suggestion was rejected in Lucas's mind as soon as he heard it. He was almost a day behind schedule; he couldn't spare another eight hours.

"If you could take me to the nearest crossing point, I would appreciate it very much. From there, I'll be on my own."

"I have time for that. That's the only thing I have plenty of anymore," the man said. "We should leave right away. We've been in here long enough and those Serbian bastards might start lobbing shells on us," he added. The man extended his right hand and introduced himself, "My name is Mirsad Sulejmanović. It's good to meet you."

"I'm Lucas Martin - the same to you."

The strangers left together immediately. Mirsad led the way, with Lucas following in his footsteps. At a nearby doorway, the Muslim man peered up at the surrounding tenements and searched for movement. There was none. Outside, a few other people were cautiously moving about. All of them carried empty plastic containers in the hope of collecting rain water. Everyone knew that daylight was the worst time to be outdoors, but the people were thirsty and dirty. Many were attempting to catch the water as it trickled slowly from rooftop drainpipes, leaving them exposed and stationary - easy targets for hidden assassins.

"Fools!" Mirsad exclaimed, "They're going to get themselves killed!"

The next instant, just as Lucas peeked out of the doorway to examine Mirsad's statement, a loud crack rang out from an adjacent building. Not far away, a middle-aged man doubled over and collapsed on the damp pavement. The lanky figure lay motionless next to the two full water canisters that he had been carrying.

Instinctively, Lucas and the Muslim withdrew back into the building. They were less than fifty meters from where the civilian was laying. They studied the body for movement.

Lucas spoke first, "Shall we go get him? He may still be alive."

"Leave him - he's dead. He was stupid, and there is no reason to get ourselves killed for the sake of a dead fool. His family will come and take him after dark. Let's go."

Mirsad directed Lucas in the opposite direction. They were still inside the post office, passing down a long, windowless corridor that ran the length of the city block. Where it ended, they entered a secluded courtyard through a broken door. The courtyard reeked of mildew and urine. Dozens of homeless people had taken refuge there.

Sarajevo's post office had been considered the pride of the city's Austrian-Hungarian Empire architecture. It was built in grand style with thick walls of limestone blocks and concrete. The structure would be able to withstand considerable shelling before meeting its demise.

The pair treaded gently through the occupied square. With his pistol drawn, Lucas stopped every so often to look and listen for snipers who might have taken a position in the bombed-out structure. He was prepared to kill any threat he encountered. Mirsad pretended not to notice. After reaching the courtyard's opposite side, they stepped through an artificial exit, a large hole that had been created by an artillery round several days earlier. Some of the city inhabitants had settled near the opening and appeared content with the shelter that the thick walls provided. As the pair moved among the scattered crowd, Lucas briefly studied some of the faces. Fear and confusion dominated their shell-shocked expressions. He had observed the syndrome countless times throughout his lifetime and could diagnose the condition more quickly than any Ivy League-schooled psychiatrist. The men moved past the slouched bodies to the exit. From there, they scuttled a dozen meters outside to the end of a brick wall extending from the post office exit. The barrier stopped at a major intersection. It was the last place they could move unthreatened.

"Mr. Martin, this is as far as I dare to go. From here, you are on your own. Do you see those three buildings standing at the end of the parkway and a little bit to the right?" Mirsad asked, pointing into the distance. "The one in the center is the U.S. consulate that you seek."

From an angle previously unseen, Lucas recognized the consulate with some difficulty. The difference between his memory and reality was startling. He was grateful for his escort's help.

"There is a lot of open space between here and there. I think it will be wise for you to go back inside and wait for darkness to set in," the Muslim repeated. "Then you should be able to reach your goal with less risk."

Lucas pretended to agree, then waited for Mirsad to leave before continuing his plan. Sensing that his assistance was no longer required, the Muslim man reached out and shook Lucas's hand a final time. Lucas thanked him and the two parted company.

On his own again, Lucas calculated the best routes of travel and considered all possible alternatives. None of his options were appealing. In order to reach the consulate, he would need to cross a large, open intersection and run almost a full kilometer along an unprotected parkway.

He squatted and shuffled his feet a bit further along the brick wall. Where it ended, he took out his binoculars and scoured the horizon. Reaching his destination appeared difficult, if not impossible. The remaining distance was well over eight hundred meters of open ground. Even if he were lucky enough to survive a sniper attack, there would be nowhere for him to hide if he were wounded. Most of the trees were leafless, and many others had been chopped for firewood. His instincts warned him that snipers were active in the vicinity, stalking their next careless victims. The unobstructed field of fire where Lucas intended to run was too obvious. Yet awaiting nightfall was impossible.

He studied the gray horizon for several minutes, seeing no signs of hidden marksmen. He checked his watch and contemplated the consequences of an additional delay. Then he rescanned the parkway meticulously and debated the best routes to run. His intuition warned him against moving too soon, but his desire not to lose any more time insisted on immediate action. A battle raged inside his head.

"This is crazy!" he mumbled to himself, over and over. *I need to cross nearly a kilometer of open terrain, all the while being exposed to multi-angle kill shots by trained snipers. I must be out of my mind!*

He continued scanning the neighborhood buildings while contemplating a choice path to run. Every so often, he looked down and checked his watch.

It would have to happen soon, he thought.

As the minutes passed, the sky darkened and the earlier threat of a downpour became a reality. The light drizzle quickly transformed into a mass of large, heavy drops. Lucas retreated along the brick wall and re-entered the post office. He opened his rucksack and put on the rain poncho. It completely covered his torso and supplies. Drawing its hood up tightly over his head, he prepared to wait in the rain for the perfect moment to make his move.

With a growing uneasiness, he returned to the end of the wall and rechecked his plan with his binoculars. With each passing minute, the rain fell harder. Before long, he was crouched in the middle of a robust cloudburst. The water pounded against the cobblestones and danced over the parkway pavement. A charged mist rose up from the heated concrete, creating a hazy fog above the surface.

It must be now! he thought. His heart pounded wildly. Quickly, he secured his stuff and tightened his bootstraps. Then he inhaled three times to relax his muscles. An instant later, he was gone.

XIV

Dragoslav Obrenović waited patiently for something to happen. He had recovered from a small celebration the night before and was still glowing inside from the praise and approval General Parenta had given him for taking out the smuggler in the Mercedes-Benz who had been trying to escape the city. Before the evening was over, the two had polished off a bottle of Scotch whisky and vowed to elevate the sniper presence within the city. The Serbian authorities in Belgrade, sensing that the Muslim resistance was beginning to crumble, had ordered increased military pressure. Both men were happy to provide it.

Early that morning, Dragoslav re-entered the city and spread the word to his subordinates that their campaign had been elevated to top priority. All sniper activity was to be intensified. Dragoslav was to lead the efforts. His first order of business was to prepare for duty, mapping out prime locations and narrowing down choice areas for kill shots. His men welcomed the new orders and held an impromptu celebration, passing a carton of cigarettes and a bottle of whisky around. It was a rare opportunity to earn a promotion and a bonus. Cash rewards for each kill were now almost double the original payouts. Dragoslav led by example, boasting his intention of killing at least three targets that day.

●●●●●

When rain began falling at midmorning, Dragoslav grimaced with disgust. Afternoon targets had become scarce, and bad weather was sure to keep the population indoors. He instructed his team to take positions that would allow easy access to citizens desperate enough to venture out to collect the fresh water that nature was providing that day. He ordered his men to be cold, cunning, and heartless. Sympathy equaled weakness and would not be tolerated.

Dragoslav chose a position near the city center, just north of the Austrian-built post office. The spot was on the third floor of a ten-story apartment building that had stood vacant since the first night of shelling. The location offered an ideal view and granted unobstructed access to targets arriving from several directions. In addition, it provided numerous escape routes into nearby, Serbian-held neighborhoods. Methodically, Dragoslav prepared his equipment, loaded his gun, and adjusted the site. Then he waited.

By late morning, however, Dragoslav had accomplished little in the ruthless art of sniper warfare. Because of the frequent showers, most of his time was spent smoking cigarettes and searching obsessively through his binoculars. His M-76 sniper rifle rested on top of its case near his feet.

"Fucking rain!" he muttered.

As time passed, the moisture absorbed into the atmosphere. The air grew thick, and it became difficult to breathe. Around one o'clock, a much heavier downpour began to fall. Out of boredom, Dragoslav put down the binoculars and picked up his rifle. He stared through the weapon's scope in disbelief. A heavy fog now hovered above the ground, limiting visibility in all directions. The rain fell harder, and it appeared that no let-up would occur.

"This is no goddamn good," he growled, taking a drag from a cigarette. Moments later, he decided to abandon his hideout for the day. His services would be of better use with an artillery unit, propped on a bluff, overlooking the city. From his current perch, he had observed several potential targets that the howitzers had failed to destroy.

Flexing his knees, he bent forward at the waist to examine the conditions through the rifle's scope a final time. As he did, a sight appeared that caught him completely by surprise. A lone man, draped in a hooded poncho, had burst into the open and was sprinting in an erratic, zigzag pattern. The figure dashed across the main thoroughfare, the street named Maršal Tito, and then headed daringly through an open parkway running parallel with a sixteenth-century mosque built by the Turks. Dragoslav watched as the man maneuvered evasively. He scurried over the cobblestone surface, hurdled over piled debris, and dodged between several leafless trees. Standing water splashed as he galloped. The runner's pace varied from an all-out sprint, to staggered leaps and bounds, making the target difficult for Dragoslav to isolate in his scope's crosshairs. The man's rain poncho was spread wide and hung loosely, concealing the precise location of his vital organs. The target's hood was pulled tightly around his head. His face was completely hidden from the assassin's view; only a gap for his eyes was visible.

Very clever, Mr. Mystery Man, Dragoslav thought. He adjusted the rifle continuously in an attempt to keep the moving target in sight. Every few meters, a sizeable cloud of fog obscured Obrenović's view and gave the runner another chance to escape.

"Oh...what is this?" Dragoslav muttered aloud. "This guy is good. He can't be from around here." He fell silent in concentration.

Dragoslav's trigger finger waited patiently for a command that did not come. Unable to draw a clean shot on the target, he refrained from firing and studied his opponent's running pattern and covered facial features.

I need to know who this well-trained adversary is, he thought. The lost prey safely ran out of rifle range, and then disappeared down an alleyway separating the U.S. consulate from its neighboring buildings. Dragoslav continued watching in disbelief.

It looks as if we have a new player in town, he mused, silently. *And I think we shall meet again.*

Then, unwilling to admit defeat, he said smugly, "I think I'll save him for next time." Dragoslav's dissatisfaction lingered a short time longer as he hastily broke down the rifle and collected his possessions. The day's task was a wash, so he finished it begrudgingly. The results of his efforts were unacceptable. Then he remembered that another bottle of Scotch whisky was waiting for him back where he stayed, so he decided to sample a little of it to help forget the miserable conditions.

Maybe the day isn't entirely ruined, he considered in anticipation. Without delay, he left the city center and made his way to an abandoned apartment that he had seized in the outlying suburbs. It was a three-room flat, confiscated from a Muslim family that had fled for their lives. First, he would have a drink; afterwards, he could easily reach the artillery unit under his command to advise on the evening's bombardment.

In less than an hour, Dragoslav was again alone, comfortable and dry, in his newly acquired lodgings.

"Maybe something good can be salvaged from this day after all," he mumbled, with morbid contempt. Then he poured his first glass of whisky.

XV

Lucas stopped to catch his breath and evaluate his progress. His last sprint had lasted no more than three minutes, but it had seemed like an Olympic marathon. The U.S. consulate was now within walking distance. How safe of a walk, he could not know. Now that he was secluded, he pulled out his pistol, then pressed his back against a brick wall and scanned the skyline for movement. There was none. Sweat mixed with rain trickled down the sides of his face. His chest wall expanded and contracted as his heart pumped vigorously. Under an overhang, he hid to shelter his body from falling elements, whether weather-related or man-made. He did not expect to reach his position without being fired on at least once.

The threat of instant execution surrounded him and paranoia played havoc with his senses. It was impossible to know when, or from which direction, a sniper round might come. Over the course of his career, he had fought in numerous battles and countless firefights, but had always maintained confidence in his ability to outmaneuver his opponent. This was different. Now he had no control and no way to know which maneuvers would be successful and which would bring him into harm's way. He wondered how the city's civilians managed to function, knowing that death from a hidden assassin could come at any moment.

After getting his bearings, Lucas plotted his next moves. About fifty meters stood between him and where he intended to go.

From a distance, he tried to determine whether the consulate was even occupied at the moment. He could detect no signs of inside activity. All the windows had been boarded shut since the initial bombardment had rained down.

Even assuming the building was occupied, he knew there could be no guarantee that he would be instantly recognized. He had to make sure his approach would not be perceived as threatening to the security staff inside. Lucas knew that unexpected intruders made the U.S. Marine Corps protectorates irrational and aggressive. He had little choice but to gamble that the security team was prepared for his coming and that they would recognize him. He waited a little longer for the right moment. The rain began to fall harder. This reassured him. He credited the bad weather with ensuring his safety on the treacherous run to his present position.

After holstering his pistol, Lucas stepped out from under the overhang. The only sound came from the water pounding against the pavement. His apprehension lessened and his confidence grew with each step. It was unlikely that even an experienced marksman could accurately aim through several hundred meters of pouring rain. Any persisting threats would likely come from the buildings adjacent to the consulate. He walked warily to the rear of each structure and peered into the openings for signs of life inside. Only stillness presented. He now believed them to be unoccupied and harmless.

In time, he returned to the alley entrance. Poking his head around a corner, he scouted the panorama. At ground level, many civilians could now be seen scurrying in the parkway where he had recently passed. Each carried plastic containers, and all were set on collecting rain water. Lucas reasoned that the locals knew best when it was safe to move about in the open. He stepped out from between the buildings and darted over to the consulate.

At the consulate entrance, he buzzed the intercom and waited for the security camera to clear his identity. A stern military voice barked instructions through the speaker. On a numbered panel

Lucas punched in a clearance code. A second later, the gate latch clicked open, and he was instructed to enter. But before he could do so, twin mortar rounds were heard whistling in his direction. The sound was too familiar. Reflexively, he crouched down into a defensive position. The next instant, successive explosions erupted in the nearby parkway, spraying chips of searing metal into the air. Time once again started to pass in slow motion. When the havoc ended, Lucas stood from his crumpled posture and looked toward the area of impact. Several bodies, chewed and mangled by the shrapnel, were sprawled across the pavement only a short distance from where he had been running a little earlier. Blood flowed freely over the cobblestones. There was nothing he could do to help. The next moment, a burly Marine grabbed him and pulled him in.

Safely inside, Lucas was swarmed by greetings and salutations. The facility was not large. The staff was a fraction of what it once was, and even at peak capacity, it had employed only a dozen full-time workers. At the moment, only three Americans maintained its daily functions alongside a couple of locals and a few Marines.

The consulate's importance had diminished over the last six years. In fact, until war had broken out in Bosnia, it was targeted to be disbanded by the U.S. State Department. Hosting international dignitaries during the 1984 Winter Olympics had been its major glory. Since then, it had done little more than issue tourist and work visas, facilitate the development of regional business interests between the United States and local partners, and serve U.S. passport holders who lived nearby or were visiting the area.

Lucas toured the building and examined the structural damage it had suffered in his absence. The tile roof had been clipped by a mortar round and the bricks supporting it had caved in on one side. All electrical and telephone connections had been temporarily replaced and the reliability of those services remained in question. Luckily, the consulate had backup generators in case of power outages and a state-of-the-art satellite telephone system should basic communications be lost.

The tour lasted fewer than ten minutes; then Lucas was directed to a private room with a secure telephone line. It was long past time to establish contact with Curtis Sheets. In Belgrade, Curtis was impatiently waiting to be informed of the events which had transpired in the last seventy-two hours. His own update to the State Department concerning Lucas's status was already overdue.

●●●●●

"Lucas, what the hell happened to you? You're nearly a full day late. I thought maybe one of the Serbian sharpshooters used you for target practice."

"It's not so easy to hit a moving target, Curtis. My legs have never felt better."

"Ah...then the legend lives on? I see. Very well; maybe I can put you to good use."

"What have you got for me, Curtis? Any developments or confirmations since we last talked?"

"There are new reports coming in almost daily. Here in Belgrade, I'm still getting the runaround from the heads of state. They continually deny everything, always passing blame and pointing fingers at the Muslims or the Croats. They expect me to believe that the Muslims are building the bloody detention centers to detain Muslim refugees!" Curtis exclaimed.

"Curtis, I need the most solid leads you've got: locations, a trusted eyewitness account, a low-quality photograph...something to start with," Lucas stated.

"We're working on it. Later today, Morton will fax me some new satellite photos that he wants checked out first. A description of the area and its coordinates will be attached to the fax that I'll send to you. Several unverified camp sightings have been reported in the eastern and northern sectors. It will be tough going; gaining access to the area may take some time. We need the confirmation as soon as possible, but don't get killed in the process."

"What time frame am I looking at, Curtis? Have I got enough time to re-establish contact with my old sources? Some trustworthy support would be useful."

"Morton didn't give me specifics. I'm estimating a few weeks, even a month if it's necessary. You know what is required for verification. Get it done right the first time and leave no room for debate. All evidence must be irrefutable if we're going to present it to the United Nations. We'll arrange for our next conversation a week from today. If you run into problems or need anything out of Washington, call me before then, and don't be shy. Do you need anything off the bat?"

Lucas gave Curtis the full account of the U.N. convoy bogged down in Herzegovina. He forwarded the names and contact numbers of the base commanders at the U.N. headquarters inside the airport. Curtis affirmed that he would personally cut through the bureaucratic red tape. Lucas didn't doubt his colleague's word for a moment. He had the utmost respect for Curtis's ability to deliver prompt results. He was extremely efficient. The two men finalized the details, and then Lucas's mission was officially underway.

XVI

After that, several weeks went by in which Lucas made very little progress. Almost daily the Serbian military increased its presence around the city and applied invigorated pressure within it. The leaders of the JNA calculated that the civilian population would grow desperate enough to force the Muslim resistance to surrender and accept the fate they had designed for the Bosnian capital. Meanwhile, Lucas grew more and more impatient.

Inside Sarajevo, sniper fire had escalated to extreme levels. Life was at a virtual standstill during the daylight hours. It was unsafe for anyone to be outdoors before nightfall. Even brief exposure in an apartment window could result in sudden death. After dark, movement became possible, but the city could hardly be considered safe. Crime was rampant. Rape, murder, and theft were all becoming commonplace as city leaders and government officials grew ever more powerless to protect the population.

When Lucas called Curtis Sheets for the next scheduled update, he had little information to divulge. He insisted that Curtis relay to Morton Riggs the restrictive conditions entangling him – that movement inside the city was severely limited, and that travel outside the periphery was virtually impossible. Several times Lucas had ventured out to the suburbs during the late-night hours, but each time he was forced to retreat because of heavy fighting that erupted close by. The Serbian military gripped the city like a vise, and its leaders were tightening the clamps every day.

Lucas continued to hope that he would soon be able to gain passage into the Bosnian countryside. In the meantime, he focused on establishing relationships with journalists, reporters, and television correspondents and their crews. Somehow, the press managed to remain an ongoing source of accurate information. He was at liberty to share pieces of information with select contacts that he trusted, so long as they reciprocated and didn't expose his cover. It was his intention to develop a network of media resources with whom to swap leads. Irrefutable information was a hot commodity. Journalists had deadlines to meet. Editors were paying inflated prices to keep their correspondents located close to newsworthy stories. Underworked reporters, idled by sniper fire, were costing their newspapers dearly. Everyone was under intense pressure to obtain breaking leads.

●●●●●

On the last day of his first month in Sarajevo, Lucas ventured out to an underground café that the foreign media and aid workers frequented. Just a few minutes' walk from the Holiday Inn, the bar had become a hangout for the English-speaking journalists after hours. Lucas hoped the unpretentious atmosphere might be congenial to his recruiting additional sources of information.

The café bar was originally named Bistro Olimpijada, in reference to the Sarajevo Winter Olympics, but it had recently been renamed. Now it was called Sklonište - "Bomb Shelter." The prices for drinks were exorbitantly high, but the beleaguered foreigners seemed happy to pay. For reasons unknown, it was one of the few establishments that never ran out of Scotch whisky or cold beer.

That particular late summer night, it had been dark for nearly an hour before Lucas dared to cross Sniper Alley. He sprinted across the infamous thoroughfare, then hurried down the concrete steps leading to its submerged entrance. With a wry smile, he noticed a sign someone had sarcastically hung above the arched doorway. It read, "*Pazi, Snajper*" - beware of snipers. As he was about to open the door, it swung toward him, opened from the other side by a man exiting. A thick cloud of cigarette smoke rolled out with him.

This should be interesting, Lucas thought. He squinted his eyes and walked in. Inside, a blast of hot air laden with tar and nicotine greeted him like a punch in the nose. When the initial shock wore off, he forced his way through the crowd, surveying the clientele as he moved. Before long, he stood alone at one end of the bar. Catching the bartender's attention, he ordered a Heineken, and then eavesdropped randomly, searching out conversations in English. While sifting through the banter, he began to home in on a high-pitched ranting. Trying to match a face with the familiar voice, Lucas peered around the shoulders of a Bosnian man standing to his left who was chain-smoking and drinking plum brandy. Inconspicuously, Lucas glanced toward the commotion. An argument was growing louder above the chatter at the opposite end of the bar. Soon he spied the source of the trouble. A group of five news correspondents were involved in a heated discussion. In the middle of the fray stood an American reporter whom Lucas recognized as Forrest Stevens; he used to report for the *Washington Post*. Lucas had heard that Forrest had been fired from the paper a few years earlier, but had never confirmed the account. One thing was certain: Forrest had not changed a bit. It appeared to Lucas that the American had instigated a senseless debate with a group of British and Canadian journalists. As Lucas listened, Forrest did most of the talking while the group ganged up against their American colleague.

●●●●●

"I'm telling you...*this* is a civil war and nothing less! Get that Northern Ireland shit out of here right now!" Forrest shouted, louder than necessary. "You can't even compare the two. This is a war among nationalities, religions, and ethnic groups. Yeah, ethnic groups! That's why they call it *ethnic cleansing*, you stupid limey."

To Lucas, it seemed that Forrest wasn't arguing so strongly out of passion for his position, but simply because he was trying to provoke a fight. He was a self-righteous loudmouth, exactly the kind of character Lucas detested.

One of the Brits, a bearded, heavyset man with a thick Cockney accent, added fuel to the fire.

"Listen, you illiterate Yank, I've been covering Northern Ireland for decades, so don't you tell me that's not a civil war. People have been getting killed for years, and some are probably dying now while you're running off your mouth."

"War? *War*? You call that a war? It's a bunch of cat-and-mouse bullshit performed by a group of sissy terrorists who set off bombs to kill innocent bystanders. And that is *if* they don't first call the police and tell them where the bomb is hidden. Explain to me why they don't just get on with it like these people and have it out like men? Jesus Christ, the fucking Irish say they want a free Northern Ireland, but they don't want to fight for it with honor! And you Brits are afraid to go in there and defend what you claim as your own - kick some ass and clean house!"

The two Brits sat speechless with disbelief. Lucas sensed a rage building inside them. The Canadians sat quietly, looking uncomfortable.

Forrest continued, "This is a war. This is a primitive, bare-knuckles, fight-to-the-end, winner-take-all, battle for independence. No...you can get that Northern Ireland shit out of here right this second!" Saliva sprayed from the American's lips as he ranted. His balding scalp had turned a crimson red.

Lucas sensed that punches would soon be thrown. Under different circumstances, he might try to defuse the situation. Not this time. He did not want to be discovered by Forrest Stevens. Privately, he hoped that one of the Brits would lose control and take a swing at the insufferable American. In the end, neither desire was fulfilled. After a few moments of tense silence, one of the Brits said, "Oh, fuck it. I have better things to be doing...like taking a stroll down Sniper Alley," and he and his compatriot walked away. In an act of moral support, the Canadians followed and left Forrest alone in search of another English-speaker to pester. It didn't take him long to approach Lucas from behind.

"Well...who do I see here? Is it my favorite spook? Or rather, maybe I should ask, what brings you here? Or, better yet...*who* brings you here?" Forrest asked. His East Coast accent was obvious.

"Perhaps you shouldn't, Forrest. Perhaps you should sit the fuck down and lower your voice," Lucas responded tersely, taking control of the conversation.

"Take it easy, Mr. Secret Agent Man. I'm just putting a little life into the party," Forrest squawked.

Lucas's temper burned. He had to use maximum constraint to not grab the obnoxious journalist by the throat and crack him hard in the face.

"Besides, one day soon you might need me," the journalist added. "So tell me, what's a heavyweight like you doing in a place like this?"

Lucas debated whether to respond. Then he answered, "I was just about to ask you the same question. I thought the *Post* tossed you off their payroll?"

"Oh, they did. But this is a funny business, you know? This war broke out, and they couldn't find a qualified war correspondent with experience like mine, so they called me back with an apology. They actually doubled my salary!" Forrest boasted. He followed his statement with an exaggerated bellow of laughter.

"Maybe they were hoping a sniper might finish you off?"

Forrest ignored Lucas's remark and continued. "So, I will presume that you're here on Uncle Sam's payroll. What gives?"

"You're not to presume anything. As a matter of fact, you're not to acknowledge having seen me, having spoken to me, or even to knowing me. Not because of any government assignment, but because I don't like you," Lucas answered.

"Take it easy, Mr. Bond. I'm serious, you may need me more than you think. For example, tomorrow I have an opportunity to visit the neighboring villages on a tour organized for foreign press. I'm allowed to bring a photographer along, but the *Post* didn't assign one to me. Did you bring your cameras?"

"And what do you expect in return?" Lucas quizzed, suspiciously.

"Nothing, and that's the beauty of it! I don't want anything other than some good company and personal protection if things don't turn out as peacefully as planned."

"Then what would I owe you...professionally?" Lucas asked.

"Same deal as you would make with any of the others, I'm sure. I want to be in the immediate loop on any valuable information you uncover. And no holding back – I want the good stuff. And I expect to be the first to know. What do you say?" Forrest arrogantly asked.

Lucas contemplated the offer momentarily. Then he said, "In addition to tomorrow's excursion, I want first dibs on all other, similar tours that you're invited to take while you're here. I also want it known that I am to be used as your personal photographer on every assignment. But I am strictly freelance. I can accept or decline your invitation at will or depending on my availability. I will notify you when you can use somebody else."

"No deal! Jesus, you don't want much, do you? This is a one shot deal, partner. Any additional gigs that come my way will have to be renegotiated. You're not the only game in town and this is a seller's market. So...how do you like me now? Are you in for tomorrow or not?"

Lucas weighed his options. Progress had been so slow getting out of the city that it left him with little bargaining power.

"What's the itinerary, the departure and arrival times? And what are the designated destinations?

Forrest answered, "We leave at eight A.M. on a Serbian-chaperoned tour bus through the neighboring villages to the north and to the east. Half the bus will be filled with international aid workers, and the other half with journalists. We're scheduled to visit three nearby Muslim villages to witness the civilian population's condition. After that, we'll tour some Serbian villages to observe the destruction committed by the Muslim resistance. I doubt we'll be shown the truth, but our safety has been guaranteed. We'll return at four P.M.. Now what do you say? Is it a deal?"

While Lucas was considering the proposition, his attention was diverted by the profile of a person seated at the café bar's far end.

"Just sit tight here a minute," he said to Forrest. Standing up, Lucas managed to slip through the crowd without losing sight of the man. Still unsure about the identity of the face with the familiar features, Lucas approached him cautiously from the side. As he moved nearer, he became certain.

"Excuse me, is this seat taken?" he asked. He did not want to surprise the young man, who was nervously sitting and smoking. Lucas's companion looked up slowly and exhaled cigarette smoke from the left corner of his mouth. Soon a broad smile stretched out across his worried face. All at once, he stood up and the friends shook hands.

"Lucas Martin, I thought I might find you here! I was hoping that you didn't leave for good. How are you?" said Edis Avdić.

"I'm fine, Edis, just fine. But I've seen you look better. My God! What have you been through? I almost didn't recognize you."

"I should have taken your advice, Lucas. Going to Sarajevo was the worst mistake I could have made at that particular moment. I almost didn't survive."

"What happened?" Lucas asked, pulling up a chair in anticipation of a long story. Months had passed since he had seen his young friend.

Edis launched into his story. "I left Brčko and headed for Sarajevo with two friends a few days after I last saw you. We started out at four in the morning and made good progress without any problems. We traveled by foot and hitched rides every chance we got. Nearing Tuzla, we saw areas of very heavy fighting. We decided not to continue in that direction, so we skirted the city and detoured toward another village farther west. Even heavier fighting had taken place there. Dead human and animal corpses were scattered everywhere. The entire area reeked of rotting flesh. We passed through the village and continued southward, forced to stay along the main roads because we had been warned that the shortcuts through the hills were mined. Whenever we could, we rested during the day and traveled at night. We didn't feel safe anywhere and didn't want to be spotted by the villagers. If they were Serbs, they surely would have reported us. From time to time, we stopped at houses we knew to be Muslim-owned. Usually, the families fed us and offered us a place to sleep. You could sense the distrust in people. Everyone was paranoid and scared. They were afraid to leave their homes, and they were afraid to stay. Despite all of that, by the sixth day of our journey, we felt confident that we would reach Sarajevo safely."

Lucas sipped his bottle of beer as he listened.

Edis continued, "On the seventh night, we approached a village named Kladanj. Along the way, we saw a lot of farm houses that had been destroyed. Some were still smoldering. My friends intended to reach Sarajevo at first light and insisted on pushing forward, but I refused to go with them. I stood firmly that it would be better to set up camp, and then leave at sunset the following night. There was too much JNA activity going on, and the situation needed to be better evaluated. They disagreed and left without me. Before parting, we arranged a place and time to rendezvous just outside of Sarajevo. I knew it was a bad idea for them to go at that time, but the war hadn't reached Sarajevo yet, and they were desperate to reunite with their families. They wouldn't listen to me. It was a really dumb idea."

Lucas studied Edis's face as he spoke. The young man had aged considerably since they were last together. He was much thinner now; his cheekbones protruded and his jaw line was sharp where baby fat had been before. His eyes seemed deeper and were set heavier. Strands of silver had appeared in his naturally dark hair.

"And then - what happened next?" Lucas asked.

"The next morning, I awoke at dawn to scout the area. I followed the path my friends had taken. As I reached the village outskirts, I witnessed something that I could hardly believe. I heard voices shouting military commands and ethnic slurs. I took cover in the nearest ditch and crawled forward to see what was happening. I maneuvered to within thirty meters of a burned-out building. Outside, there were about twenty JNA-uniformed soldiers. Most of them were heavily armed and they were yelling at a group of Muslim men they had rounded up. The soldiers marched them to the back of the building. My two friends were in the front of the line. They could not see me. Their faces were white with fear. I didn't know what to do. I thought that they would be put on a bus that was parked nearby, and then transported to one of the camps holding captured Muslim soldiers. A few minutes passed before they were all out of sight behind the building. And then...and then, I heard it," Edis paused, his voice started to quiver. "It happened so fast. The shots rang out from their automatic weapons. Only the Serbian bastards returned. They fucking killed them!"

When Edis had calmed down, Lucas asked, "Did anyone survive?"

"Well, you know how it goes. Dead men tell no tales. The Serbs took no chances. As soon as I could, I moved around to the back. I saw most of the rest. After the AK-47s stopped, the unit leader walked from body to body and put a round from his pistol into each head."

Lucas deliberately changed the subject.

"You mentioned camps. Do you know for certain that these exist?"

"I haven't seen any personally, but their existence is common knowledge. Every Muslim man talks about them. They say it is better to die fighting than to be rounded up and wait to be slaughtered."

"If I could get us out of Sarajevo, do you think you could take me to one?" Lucas asked, searching Edis's hollowed eyes.

"Lucas, I would like very much to help. But…it seems that I have bigger problems to worry about at the moment."

"What is it?"

"It's the Serbs, here in Sarajevo. Word is spreading that they are rounding up Muslim women and holding them," Edis said. As he continued, he became noticeably agitated. "My younger sister, Amra…she has been missing for over a week."

"That explains why you look so distraught."

"That, and lack of sleep and food," Edis responded, managing a humorless smile.

"Do you have any idea where she could be?"

"I've heard about some apartment buildings in Grbavica, the Serbian district, filled with Muslim girls. It could be one of them, I don't know. They are only rumors, but I believe them to be true."

"Listen, Edis, for now let's concentrate on finding your sister. Then we'll explore the countryside in search of those camps. Agreed?"

"Sure."

"Tomorrow I'll be gone on a tour organized for journalists. When I return in the evening, we'll meet here again to discuss what can be done."

"Lucas, watch your back. There are snipers everywhere. They do not discriminate if you're a foreigner. And trust nobody. These are desperate times."

"Thanks for the advice, my friend. I'll see you here tomorrow night," Lucas said. They shook hands before parting.

Lucas strolled casually back to where Forrest Stevens was waiting impatiently. Sensing his annoyance, Lucas sat down casually and reopened the topic they had been discussing before.

"So, are we on for tomorrow, bright and early?" Lucas asked.

"Bring your photography equipment and anything else you think will be useful. We'll meet in the lobby of the Holiday Inn. The bus leaves at eight A.M. sharp, so don't be late," Forrest said.

"See you then," Lucas replied. Then he stood up and left.

XVII

The tour group returned to Sarajevo later than scheduled. Lucas was glad to be out of the cramped bus and even happier to be rid of Forrest Stevens. The trip had been a disappointment from the outset. Forrest had collected no newsworthy information, and Lucas was unable to photograph anything of significance. As expected, the JNA sponsors had filled the day with propaganda showcasing their own stellar behavior while exaggerating the abuses the Serbian population had suffered as a result of Muslim aggression. The trip was a waste of time, and Lucas's frustration was mounting.

As soon as he could, Lucas ditched Forrest at the Holiday Inn and returned to the U.S. consulate. Along the way, he saw evidence of fresh shelling that had taken place in his absence. A large, star-shaped imprint scarred the pavement right in front of the consulate gates. Fist-sized chips were missing from the building's concrete walls, the result of shrapnel that had sprayed from a mortar round explosion. The threat of additional mayhem lingered in the atmosphere.

Once he was inside, Lucas checked in with Curtis Sheets and relayed the unsatisfactory results of his efforts that day. Reluctantly, Curtis passed along a rebuke from Morton Riggs to the effect that Lucas needed to start earning his keep. Lucas was unfazed. Morton was in no position to give reprimands, and everyone knew it. He interpreted it as a sign that the statesman was under heightened pressure from Washington's chain of command. Probably Morton was being prodded to push Lucas into producing evidence that could give his superiors a justifiable reason to intervene. For the moment, there was none.

Lucas washed his face with water from a large cistern that was located under the building. Running water within Sarajevo had been unavailable for weeks. The building's reservoir was the consulate staff's only guaranteed supply of water. After washing up, he changed clothes; he then felt ready to continue with the day's plan.

On his way to meet Edis Avdić, Lucas exercised extra caution. Enough daylight remained to make the short journey deadly. Snipers were likely to be scattered throughout the neighborhood. He hustled across the main thoroughfare to the underground café. Though he had crossed the street many times since his arrival in Sarajevo, it was still several minutes before his heart rate and adrenalin levels dropped back into a normal range.

Lucas scanned the room vigilantly. At this hour, the Bomb Shelter was still half empty, and it was easy to find a seat at the bar. Lucas sat and watched as international journalists gradually wandered inside and filled the place with the sound of English being spoken in varying degrees of fluency. Across the room Lucas spotted Forrest Stevens, holding a beer and harassing a group of German reporters. Forrest was energetically embellishing the adventures that he had experienced earlier in the day. Avoiding attention, Lucas waited patiently for Edis to arrive.

When Edis Avdić walked into the bar, he stood near the entrance and looked for his colleague. When the two established eye contact, they exchanged nods of the head and searched out a table where they could talk without interruption. By now tables had grown scarce, but Lucas spotted one in a rear corner. He ordered two coffees and they sat down.

●●●●●

"The tour today was a disaster. We didn't see anything that could be considered reportable news. The whole trip was useless."

"Don't waste your time with Serbian-sponsored propaganda trips," Edis said. He scoffed as he lit a cigarette, and then slowly sucked the smoke into his lungs. "You'll see nothing they don't want you to see. And anything that is reportable will be used to their advantage...maybe to buy them more time."

Not wanting the conversation to turn into a rant, however justified Edis's anger was, Lucas steered it back on course.

"I need verifiable proof, Edis. Hearsay and rumors won't get the United Nations and NATO to act. If I can't get out of the city, I can't get the proof needed for them to intervene," he said. "And I can't get much accomplished within the city limits. The goddamn snipers have all movement pinned down."

"On that point, perhaps I can help," Edis said, tapping his cigarette into an ashtray. "Today I had a chance to scout the buildings I told you about yesterday. After doing so, I was in contact with some of the Muslim resistance. My sources were generous with information concerning the most recent sniper activity. I have recorded peak times and approximate locations of the latest shootings. There is no set pattern, which stands to reason, but pieces of a system are falling into place. Maybe we can break that system and go on the offensive?"

"We? As in you *and me*?" Lucas asked.

"Lucas, I intend to do it alone, but I believe you to be more qualified at this sort of thing than I. Isn't that so? I could sure use your expertise with this."

"Fair enough. I'll advise you. But any dirty work that needs to be done, you'll be doing alone. Understood?"

Edis agreed. He suspected that Lucas would assist him if his help was needed. It was taken for granted that he would not have consented without realizing the full obligation.

"What details do you have for me?" Lucas asked.

Edis answered, "I've mapped out the locations where the snipers have been most active. They are spread out in a half-ring along the edge of the Miljacka River. That is very consistent with the Serbian-held parts of the city. But the latest shootings have come from a surprising location - an isolated high-rise. Its use as a sniper base is relatively new. From there, a lot of civilians have been killed in the past few days."

"I heard that a kid on a bicycle was killed today. Was that from the same building?"

"The shooter took his head off, Lucas. A ten-year-old boy! And yesterday, a twelve-year-old was shot in the spine and left to die. An hour passed before his family could retrieve him under the cover of darkness. Now he's paralyzed from the waist down. He'll never walk again."

"Fucking amateurs! No professional soldier would leave such a mess!" Lucas flared. "Anyway, have you been able to calculate the times or identify the floors the shooter is using?"

"I'm sixty percent sure of the location used by the sniper today. But get this…the pattern is mixed, so there could be more than one. And even more unbelievable, they're holed up in a building on the Muslim-dominated side of the river. It's the last in a row of three abandoned apartment tenements, just on the fringe of the Muslim-held line. The shooters don't have very good protection from the main Serbian forces. And they don't seem overly concerned with concealing their presence. They've been using the same two floors!"

"Psychopaths," Lucas snapped.

"What do you mean?"

"These have to be untrained maniacs with very poor sniper skills. They could be bounty hunters or mercenaries. Whatever they are, they are unprofessional and much too reckless. I doubt they have the support of the JNA command," Lucas said. "It sounds like they're killing for fun rather than following orders. That building is where we'll begin. Before daylight tomorrow morning, let's meet and scout out the situation. If we can narrow down their positions, maybe we can turn the tables and let the predators become the prey."

Edis unfolded a hand-drawn map and gave it to Lucas. They scheduled a 5:30 A.M. meeting the next day. The men planned to strategically position themselves in spots offering good views of the building Edis suspected was being used as a sniper base. After studying the building, they would wait until something happened, hoping to zero in on the gunmen's whereabouts before other victims could be killed or maimed.

Lucas realized that the plan's chances of success were low and that the risks were high. He had never before participated in such a surveillance scheme. He calculated that with patience, combined with the snipers' apparent carelessness, their position could be discovered and their threat eliminated.

When no questions remained, the two parted company.

Lucas retraced the path across Sniper Alley that he had taken several times before. A certain confidence surfaced from his previous successful crossings. There were no automobiles on the street to delay his progress, only pieces of broken glass and the remnants of demolished trolley cars. Distant rumbles of artillery fire shattered the evening silence. The nearby hilltops were briefly illuminated by exploding shells. Small arms fire riddled the night air, echoing against the desecrated, empty buildings. Aware of the pending dangers, he wasted no time crossing the street.

Lucas passed swiftly through the consulate security, still in a state of deep concentration about the next day's plan. Once inside, he collected the gear he wanted to take with him and prepared himself mentally for the day ahead. Before long, he was bunkered in for the night.

XVIII

Twenty-four hours later, Lucas and Edis met at the Bomb Shelter in the same manner as the night before. Their plan this night was to compare notes on the day's observations and decide what to do next. Once again, Lucas showed up first and grabbed a table in a quiet corner of the bar. Even more so than the previous evening, they had to sit somewhere where they wouldn't be distracted. The slightest oversight in detail could result in dire consequences. After Edis arrived, they ordered Turkish coffees and began the conversation before the waiter returned.

"This isn't going to be easy," Lucas stated. A look of deep concern shrouded his face.

"I was just thinking how everything appeared better than expected," Edis said, with an expressionless face. Lucas studied his demeanor more closely and attempted to gauge his level of sincerity. After a moment, Edis winked and cracked a subtle smile.

Lucas continued, "Did you see the sentry planted in the main lobby? How do you propose we get past him? Also, I'm now certain there are two shooters, and that each is working on a different floor. I think I spotted one on the third and sensed another on the fifth floor today. But that could change tomorrow."

"It won't," Edis followed. "I know the mentality here. You said yourself that they are amateurs. Man, did you see the madman on the third floor open fire on that U.N. motorcade? It was impossible for him to hit anything from that range. And he left himself daringly exposed. Why not just hang a flag out the window!" he ranted. "And the shooter on the fifth floor fired twice at a target. Talk about guts!"

"Don't confuse bravery with stupidity, Edis. That kind of recklessness will do them in, even if we don't."

The duo talked about the tenement's design and security, and how they might breach it. The snipers had to be eliminated. Both men realized, however, that the human catastrophe happening around them would be little changed by their efforts. It didn't matter. The notion of stopping some of those who were taking innocent life appealed to their strained senses of morality. More importantly, the action would be the first step in finding Edis's disappeared sister. The area near that apartment tower was the last place she had been seen. He clung to a slim hope that she was alive.

"So how do you plan to get past the Chetnik in the lobby?" Edis asked, hoping Lucas would have a plan – and want to take the lead role in executing it.

Lucas sighed. "It won't be easy. We could storm the entrance together, but if we take the sentry out first, we risk drawing attention. The element of surprise will be lost, and we'll never reach the shooters upstairs. Besides, we don't know who may be covering him from the adjacent buildings. No...somehow we need to bypass the lookout on the way up and deal with him afterward. We'll need some major distraction."

"Too risky," Edis replied. "Any disturbance big enough to draw his attention would likely alert every sniper in the area."

The men pondered the problem for a little while. There were no alternative elevators to consider, nor fire escapes or other points of entry into the ancient apartment block. Edis spoke next. "What would serve us better is the opposite of a diversion. What we should consider is life as usual."

"What do you mean?" Lucas asked.

"Regardless of the shelling and snipers, basic needs are forcing people to be more active during the day than you'd imagine. While it's true that all civilians are potential victims, I suspect some to be

185

less so. You need to be in the 'less so' category. Then you can just walk into the building nonchalantly."

"Which ones are those...the ones in the 'less so' category?" Lucas wondered.

"Everyone can be a sniper target, and mortar rounds don't discriminate, but I believe some targets are more desirable than others. Young people are seen as better than old ones, and men as better than women. You should enter as part of the scenery; as an old woman returning with a loaf of bread."

Lucas considered the possibility.

"That's not bad, Edis. I used a similar tactic by dressing in a traditional Bedouin garment in Algeria several years ago." Lucas confided to Edis how he entered a regional government building unnoticed wrapped in a burnous to steal some documents earlier in his career. "The disguise only needs to be convincing for a little while. If we get the timing right, the sentry won't be paying much attention. I'd need about forty seconds - enough time to get past him and up the first flight of steps. It won't matter what I appear like on the way back down – the only thing he'll notice is my gun pointing at his head. I'll get my hands on the weaponry tonight. If this thing goes wrong, I'll need to shoot my way out, and you'll be my only backup. You find the costume. And try to make it convincing. If everything goes smoothly, I'll be out before I'm in and no one will be any wiser."

Lucas thought a moment longer. "But still, there's too much ground to cover on foot. It'll be impossible to outrun trouble if we're discovered. Can you find a vehicle that can get us out of the area, in case the plan goes awry?"

"I was afraid you were going to ask me that. Even if I could get hold of a car that runs, it will be just as difficult finding gasoline. I'll make some stops tonight to see what is available."

"Do your best. Any old, battered one will do. It only has to start, run, and get us out the range of fire. And don't forget to bring a shopping bag filled with the largest loaf of bread in the city," said

Lucas. "I have the operation's design in my head. I'm going back to the consulate now to rummage through the arsenal. We will need more than the Berretta under my belt. Let's meet again tomorrow, same time, same place, and go over the final details. If you think of any last questions, ask them then. The sooner we get this over with the better."

Edis looked at his partner sternly in the eyes. He reached across the table and shook Lucas's hand.

"Lucas, I want you to know you have been a great friend and that I really appreciate what you're doing for me. I hope I haven't asked too much from you. There is a chance that this may not end well. If anything goes wrong, I'll never forgive myself."

"Relax, Edis. I'm not doing this entirely for you. I've been boxed up here for weeks, and I haven't done anything to help these people. I'm capable of contributing much more. Go take care of your business. Then try to get some sleep."

Edis got up and left. Lucas settled the bill at the bar. As he paid the tab, an open hand firmly gripped his left shoulder. Without flinching, Lucas prepared to pummel the owner of the hand that was accosting him. As he slowly rotated his head left, he clenched his right hand into a rock-hard fist.

"Lucas, old buddy!" roared the voice of a drunken Forrest Stevens. "What have you been up to? You've been having some serious pow-wows these past few nights. Are you holding out on me? You better fill me in!"

"There's no news for now, Forrest. We'll sit down tomorrow evening. Then I'll tell you all that I know." With that, he brushed passed Forrest and pushed his way through the crowded bar toward the exit.

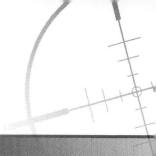

XIX

The next morning was eerily quiet considering the battles that had raged in the surrounding suburbs the night before. Lucas had slept little as the explosions from artillery shells, rocket launchers, and mortar rounds shook the hillsides in all directions.

As the resistance within Sarajevo grew, the fighting around the city intensified. The Muslim forces, now better equipped, were being supplied with black market weaponry and reinforced with imported fighters from Muslim countries to the east. The day before, Edis had pointed out to Lucas a bearded Middle Eastern soldier who had been smuggled into the city to support the Muslim cause. Now dozens of these mercenaries were in almost every unit. Edis was not impressed with this outside influence. He worried about what would become of his Bosnia after the fighting ended. For his part, Lucas was concerned about the arrival of fundamentalism into what was once ethnic stability. Certainly, it was something worth bringing to Morton Riggs's attention at the U.S. State Department.

•••••

Edis arrived at the rendezvous point first. Alone in the deserted building, he smoked cigarettes while waiting for Lucas to show. From a shadowy corner, he peered out at the city through a gaping hole in a concrete wall. As the sun slowly rose over the eastern mountains, daylight filtered through Sarajevo's fragmented infrastructure. Piles of wreckage, scattered garbage, and smoldering mounds of charred ruins revealed evidence of war in every part of the besieged Bosnian capital. A dusty smoke polluted the atmosphere.

From where he was hidden, Edis could clearly see the remains of two minarets that had once towered over the city. The nearest was lying on its side, broken into pieces. The second, still upright, was missing its upper third. Pieces of its mid-section had been chipped away, the result of artillery rounds that had exploded around it. From the nearby hillsides, the Serbian paramilitaries had used it as a target to calibrate their weapons' sights. The segment left intact was so pitiful it made Edis smirk in spite of himself.

The moment's peacefulness was interrupted by footsteps. Edis stepped out of his hideout just long enough to pull Lucas into his sanctuary.

●●●●●

"There. He's in the same place we spotted him in yesterday," Edis whispered. He pointed out a sentry near the front door of the building Lucas intended to enter.

"It looks like he hasn't been awake long," Lucas answered, spying through binoculars. "Let's get a better idea of the layout before we make our move. Did you get a car?"

"I came up with something. It's parked around back. Your disguise is inside, under the hatch."

"We should study the scene a while longer," Lucas said to his friend. "The sniper holes need to be identified before we can refine the plan. Also, we need to devise an escape route in case problems pop up." Lowering the binoculars, Lucas faced Edis and looked squarely at him. "But I'd prefer to get this done right on the first try," he added.

"Yeah, me too," Edis agreed.

The men took opposing positions and studied the building entrance. An hour later, they relocated to examine the other nearby tenements for signs of danger. None were discovered. It was about 8:30 when a crisp crack rang out from the first building they had scouted. The pair scrambled back to their original positions.

"It's them! They're at it again!" Edis said excitedly.

"It's definitely one of them. The shot's report sounded like a Crvena Zastava rifle. The other will probably be at it soon. Let's go over the plan once more. Then we'll go to work," said Lucas.

Lucas hustled to the back of the building and retrieved a duffel bag he had stashed on his way in. When he returned, the pair headed to the structure's far end, a section left mostly undamaged by the recent shelling. A hidden passage under a buckled wall led them to a sheltered clearing. In the middle of the makeshift garage, Edis had parked the automobile.

"So, how did I do?" asked Edis, unsure of his achievement.

"It's perfect," Lucas proclaimed.

The car was a worn-out Renault 4, a model that had dominated the city in numbers rivaled only by the Yugo before the siege had begun. This one, built in the 1960s, was cream-white and heavily spotted by surface rust. Every tire was bald. The glass in three of the four windows had been knocked out. At the moment, the hood was raised; the battery cables were disconnected.

"Once she's started, she works fine," Edis explained. "But after I drop you off, the engine must continue running. The electrical wiring is rigged, so if the ignition gets turned off, even for a few seconds, the battery will quickly drain and die. It won't restart, so it will have to be abandoned at the first sign of trouble. A friend of mine bartered for a few liters of gasoline; just enough to get us out of the vicinity, but not much further. If you have to drive, don't be shy with the accelerator."

"No need to worry about that. What did you come up with for a disguise? Will it do the job?"

Edis pulled some silk material from a canvas bag. "Take off your boots and socks, and then roll up your pant legs. You can drape this over your clothes," he said, tossing the garment at his friend. "You'll need to wear sandals. I think these will fit."

Lucas secured his documents inside the nylon pouch he had taken from the U.N. base at the airport and fastened it around his abdomen. Then he followed Edis's instructions verbatim. The results proved satisfactory. The colorful fabric hung loosely over his clothes and made him appear ten kilograms heavier. Around his head, a silk scarf was wrapped just loose enough to conceal his face. Glancing downward, Lucas remarked with a smile, "Do I need to shave my legs above the ankle?"

"Lucas, you're trying to appear as an old Bosnian woman. I worry that your legs aren't hairy enough," Edis answered with a grin.

Reaching into his duffel bag, Lucas pulled out a sawed-off shotgun that he had taken from the consulate arsenal. It was already loaded and ready to use.

"This is for you. Use it in case I'm pursued as I leave the building. It's not effective from a long range, so don't fire unless the target's torso is exposed. If you come under attack from above, take the gun and run for cover. Got it?"

"Got it," Edis answered.

"How's your financial situation?" Lucas asked.

"It could be better."

Again Lucas reached into the bag and removed a roll of bills. He tossed it to Edis.

"Here are five thousand Deutschmarks. If our plan isn't successful, go underground and stay there until the fighting stops. This mess won't last forever."

From his rucksack, Lucas pulled out his semiautomatic Berretta and slid it into a holster that was strapped around his shoulder. The combination fit nicely under his new attire. Last, he produced the weapon with which he intended to use during the assault - a German-made MP5. Its grip molded to his hand as if the weapon were an extension of his arm. From under the Renault's rear hatch, Edis removed a large loaf of bread. Using his Swiss Army knife,

Lucas carved out its underside deep enough to embed the MP5's top half. On the bottom of the cloth bag, the spare clip and sound suppressor were set inside first. Both were covered by Lucas's sock-filled boots. The stuffed loaf of bread was placed on top, allowing easy access to the weapon if it was needed fast. A hunch told Lucas it would be.

The plan of attack was kept simple: Edis would drive the disguised Lucas to within ten meters of the apartment block entrance. When the timing was right, Lucas would emerge disguised an old Muslim woman. From there, he would penetrate the building incognito, advancing past the Serbian sentry to proceed up the steps. The elevator, presumably out of service because of lack of electricity, would be ignored. Once safely away from the guard, Lucas would search the suspected floors until the sniper holes were discovered. After killing each, he would shed his costume and retrace his path to the lobby. There, Lucas would shoot the guard before being chauffeured away in the beat-up Renault. The entire operation was calculated to last twenty-five minutes or fewer. No time was allowed for delays.

An even simpler contingency plan was formulated on the spot. If their plot was uncovered, the mission would be aborted. The pair would separate, cover each other when possible, and regroup at the garage where they were now. If they made it that far, Edis had contacts in the local resistance who could help them escape.

Although neither mentioned it, both realized that the mission's success depended on a large amount of luck. Yet they were undeterred. The plan would go forward.

●●●●●

At about 9:30, Edis started the car while Lucas made final checks of his weaponry and costume. The scheme started without a hitch. The sunny streets were traffic-free; very few pedestrians were in sight. Miraculously, the previous night's bombardment had left the roads unobstructed. In the distance, a commotion at a nearby outdoor market created a welcome distraction. From a tactical standpoint, the disruption pleased Lucas a great deal.

Edis circled the block once before stopping the car short of the building's doorway. From there, one of the mission's most dangerous segments would begin. During this ten-meter stretch, Lucas would be required to walk slowly within the range of fire of multiple snipers. He could not move fast and risk revealing his true identity before the lobby had been entered. In order to make the plan convincing, a certain amount of time would be necessary to deceive the guard inside before reaching the stairwell. While Lucas was doing this, Edis was obligated to sit, watch, and wait in the open - a task as daunting as what his friend was attempting to pull off.

As the car slowed to a stop, Lucas repeated final instructions to his accomplice.

"Remember, Edis...keep the engine running the whole time. No matter what the outcome, we'll need to make a fast getaway. Give me exactly twenty-five minutes and then bolt. If I get pinned down - don't wait," he directed.

Edis agreed with a nod of his head.

With a look of confidence forced upon his face, Lucas stepped from the car, shopping bag in hand. Edis lit a cigarette and watched him hobble away. It was now 9:40 A.M.

• • • • •

Lucas humped his spine and shuffled his feet as he moved toward the building's entrance. The guard had to be tricked for as long as possible. If questioned, Lucas had decided not to respond. Instead, he would lower his head further and continue walking in the direction he was going. If physically confronted, he would draw his Berretta and shoot the Serbian soldier at once, aborting the mission while there was still time.

• • • • •

Lucas arrived at the front door undisturbed. He saw that a cloud of cigarette smoke filled the lobby and a half-finished bottle of plum brandy stood ready on the sentry's makeshift desk. Once inside, Lucas walked forward until the guard's attention became directed toward him.

The civilian soldier was a middle-aged man with tired-looking eyes. He had an oversized head propped up on sloped, muscular shoulders. A bushy mustache and a scruffy beard covered his thick lips. He stared spitefully at the Muslim woman as she passed. From the corner of his eye Lucas spied an AK-47 assault rifle standing near the guard's chair.

Already half-drunk, the sentinel tossed a few slurs in the old woman's direction, but she ignored them and shuffled forward, her head hung low.

Those will be the last insults you ever spew, Lucas thought with satisfaction.

After reaching the staircase, Lucas climbed the steps one at a time, taking extra care not to give up his disguise prematurely. After reaching the second floor landing, he took a moment to catch his breath. Just one floor remained before the level of the first known sniper hole would be reached. Lucas considered the lack of escape routes in the lightless corridor and elected to climb to the fifth floor to eliminate that shooter first, if he could be quickly found. Then he could come back down and repeat the process.

He encountered no one on the stairs, and on the fifth floor landing, he stopped to calm his nerves and reassess the situation. Within moments, he heard the sound of boots trampling over loose tiles. The footsteps came from an apartment that Edis had suspected to be a sniper's lair the day before. Seconds later, the scraping of plaster chips confirmed the existence of an unseen person. Lucas waited a moment longer. Then, out of the blue, the crack of a rifle resonated from the suspicious flat. Now he was certain.

Without a sound, he removed the MP5 from its camouflage and quickly attached the silencer and inserted the clip. The chamber's first round had been loaded before exiting the Renault. It was time to act.

Lucas stashed his bag in the stairwell. Silently, he walked down the darkened hallway. He was well aware that the corridor was littered with broken pipes and shattered glass; he had considered using a flashlight, but decided against it on second thought. Instead, he ran his free hand along the wall for guidance, aware that the slightest misstep could announce his presence, alter the mission's outcome, and possibly bring his life to a premature end.

As he closed in on his destination, Lucas saw that the apartment door was ajar. From the slight crevice, a thin strip of sunshine beamed into the corridor. The smell of cigarette smoke, combined with gunpowder, crept out. The stench was surprisingly strong, and its potency briefly halted Lucas's advance. At the moment, the shooter's exact location was unknown. Nearing the door, Lucas listened closely, trying to get a better idea of his target's position. Soon a muffled grunt, followed by the gurgle of a bottle of liquid being upturned, broke the silence inside. Lucas was patient. He concentrated intently and allowed his eyes to adjust to the change in lighting. Sweat dripped from his brow as he mentally prepared for battle.

Twenty seconds later, his veiled head was poking through the apartment doorway. Lucas held his weapon tightly and craned his neck to scan the interior. His head rotated diligently; first left and then to the right. Halfway through right rotation, his eyes suddenly stopped. He was stunned by what he saw.

A man - rather, a boy of about sixteen-years-old, was standing near the window and aiming a scoped rifle at a civilian below. The youth, dressed in semi-military attire, wore an olive-green shirt with a red star printed over the heart. Nearby, his camouflaged jacket hung from a nail in the wall. His weapon was about to be fired when the apartment door burst open.

Still incognito, Lucas entered boldly, pointing the MP5 at the boy's head. He raised his voice and barked commands, determined to surprise the youth into passive compliance. But the boy's lack of experience caused him to use poor judgment. Confused and excited, he reacted reflexively. Before Lucas had the situation under control, the boy wheeled his rifle, planning to kill the masked intruder. Lucas squeezed his MP5's trigger once, sending a muffled bullet toward the teen's skull. Instantly, his head jerked upward and his body was thrown back until his shoulders collided with a concrete wall. In one fluid motion, his knees buckled, leaving his immature frame heaped on the floor.

Feeling no remorse, Lucas quickly searched the flat for other assassins. None were found. With his mission half-complete, he left the dingy apartment in haste. Back in the stairwell, he retrieved his bag before heading to the first sniper's position. On the third floor landing, he reinspected his costume, determined to repeat the same technique he had just successfully used. Once again, he checked his watch. There was precious little time to waste. Only fourteen minutes remained before Edis would leave without him.

Lucas entered the hallway and walked warily down its center. As he moved, he felt different sensations than what he had experienced before. This time, a feeling that he was being watched from the shadows was present. Lucas maintained his charade, hunching his posture and imitating the gait of an old woman. Guided by experience and intuition, he moved forward with all of his senses on high alert.

Halfway down the twenty-meter corridor, the faint noise of an opening door sounded from behind. Caught by surprise, Lucas stopped in his tracks, aware of the vulnerable position he was in. At the moment, he was defenseless from a rear attack. His pulse shot upward; perspiration drained from his pores. Panic was not an option. What he heard next surprised him more than the young sniper two floors above. It was a stifled sob; the delicate whimper of a female's cry. Lucas stood frozen.

"Old lady, old lady, go back! They'll kill you if you go on!" warned the voice of a young woman.

Lucas did not move. Slowly, he turned his head to confront the faceless voice. After his vision adjusted, the shape of a female head appeared, peering out from behind a cracked door. Lucas's disguise remained intact, so he moved closer to her position. Little by little, he raised an index finger to his lips, signaling the young woman to be quiet. Just as slowly, he removed the scarf from his head and revealed to her his true identity. Tears filled her swollen eyes as fear overtook her. Previously trembling, she now shook uncontrollably. Lucas drew nearer. Through the faint light, he could see bruises covering her face and arms. Both wrists were scarred with rope burns. The girl's face was pale; her hair was uncombed. All of her clothing was torn and stained. Lucas whispered to calm her down.

"How many are there?" he asked.

She lifted a thumb and index finger, indicating there were two.

"Which apartment are they in?" he followed.

She pointed at a door at the hallway's far end.

With her attention distracted, Lucas pushed open the door and forced himself into the apartment in which she was being held. Impulsively, the young lady tried to scream. Before she could, Lucas clasped his hand over her mouth. Applying firm pressure, he felt her cheeks wither in his hold. Her nerves were hanging by a thread.

"Ssshhh. It's alright...everything will be okay," he said. "I'm not going to hurt you. Please, don't scream. If you promise to be quiet, I'll remove my hand. Can you be silent?"

The girl looked up and nodded. Teardrops rolled down her cheeks. Looking around the room, Lucas saw signs that the girl had not been alone. Blankets and pillows were scattered on the floor and shoes and other articles of clothing were piled nearby.

"Listen. I'm going to relax my grip. You and I are going to talk, okay?" he asked.

The weakened girl looked into his eyes. Lucas released his clutch.

"Are you alone?"

She nodded in the affirmative.

"Where are the others?"

The girl then mumbled something about the others being taken away earlier in the day.

"Can you walk?"

Her answer was barely coherent. Lucas sat her on the couch and then shed his costume. Reaching into the bag, he kicked off his sandals and replaced them with his socks and boots. Finally, he rechecked the weapons in preparation for a final assault.

Lucas instructed the girl to prepare for escape. Still sobbing, she stopped crying long enough to agree to follow him when he returned. Before leaving, he assured her she would be safe and made her close the door after he went back into the hall.

Cat-like, Lucas moved down the darkened passageway. Timing was crucial. Just nine minutes remained. After he neared the apartment, he pressed his ear to the outside wall. Inside, the voices of two men could be heard talking and swearing.

●●●●●

"Come on, you Muslim bastard. That's it…just a little further - *jebo te*. It's time to fall down on your knees to pray!" said one. Soon after, a rifle fired. The duo privately rejoiced.

"Your aim is still too high…and too far too left - *u pičku materinu!*" reported his colleague, who was watching the spectacle through binoculars. "Now finish him. Shoot him in the belly. Let him bleed awhile!"

The rest of the conversation was indecipherable. Lucas gripped his weapon firmly and reached for the door. He pleaded for it to be unlocked. It was. Once in position, he forced his left shoulder against the metallic surface and applied downward pressure on the handle. The door opened simply, smoothly, and silently.

The intruder entered the apartment before the snipers could react. Caught off guard, the Serb who had been critiquing the shooter's accuracy dropped his binoculars on the floor. With panic-stricken eyes, he reached awkwardly for his sidearm. The weapon had barely been unholstered before Lucas sent a round through his head, killing him at once. The dead man's partner reacted differently. Seeing his disadvantage, he began trying to talk his way out of his death sentence.

"Who are you? I can see that you are no Muslim. What are you doing here!" the Serbian paramilitary demanded.

"Never mind who I am. Lower your rifle and sit down. Your orders have just changed," Lucas said.

The civilian soldier pointed his weapon toward the floor, but defiantly stayed standing.

"Look, Mister. I have very important connections across the river. I can make your life in Sarajevo very comfortable, or extremely unpleasant. Do you understand? Now get out of here! Forget about this business and leave me alone," he said, reaching for a bottle of plum brandy that stood near the window. A look of worry began to show on his face.

"No. It's too late now," Lucas said calmly.

The sniper was struck with an increasing level of frustration.

"What is it you want? Money? I have plenty. How much do you want?" he asked, trying to mask his unease.

"I don't want your money. I want your rifle. We are going to leave here together, right now. It's your lucky day…for you, the war has just ended. You should be happy," Lucas said.

The Serb's frustration morphed into despair. He lifted his head upward and contemplated his options. Then he took an extra large drink of plum brandy. Sensing defeat, he calculated that additional negotiation was pointless. With a burst of drunken courage, he lifted the rifle that rested at his side. Before it could be accurately aimed, Lucas sent two muted bullets through his chest. The assassin dropped to the floor. Blood flowed from his mouth as he clung to the last moments of life. A few seconds passed before he rolled from his side onto his back. Gasping for air, he stared up from below. Near the end, he collected the strength to curse his opponent.

"*Ma jebi se, Hrvatino! Pička ti materina!*"

Lucas got the message. Without delay, he removed his Beretta and pointed it at the fallen sniper. Then he finished the job he had started.

Once again, Lucas checked the time. Just minutes remained before Edis would leave, so he abandoned the apartment and hurried to where the young woman waited. There, he knocked hard on the door to announce his return. After hearing the deadbolt slide free, he pushed the door open and grabbed her arm.

"If you want to live, do exactly as I say! What's your name?"

The girl did not respond. She looked as if she had been drugged. Lucas shook her hard and asked again. This time, she managed to reply.

"Amra...Amra Avdić," she said in a shaky voice.

Lucas was dazed by the revelation. But time was running out. Vital questions that needed answering would have to wait. He pulled the young lady's elbow and half-dragged, half-carried her into the hall. Next, he guided her lethargic body down the blackened stairwell. As they reached the bottom step, the startled sentry jumped for his AK-47. Lucas shot him before his weapon had been lifted.

Now...take a moment and regain your composure, Lucas thought to himself. He was breathing heavily. The girl had not been factored into the plan. Before leaving the building's protection, he had to consider if any adjustments needed to be made. Under grueling pressure, he couldn't think of any. Again, he checked his watch. They were right on schedule.

Edis, you had better be there and that car had better be running!, screamed inside his mind.

XX

From the moment Lucas left the car, Edis felt an uneasy stirring in the bottom of his stomach. He lit a cigarette, hoping the nicotine would calm his nerves. Then he had another. After finishing the second smoke, his queasiness only seemed to worsen.

Twenty-five minutes was a daring – many would say foolish – length of time to remain an open target. His uneasiness, however, was not from lack of courage; he had been in equally dangerous positions many times over the last year and survived them all. Rather, it was because he now had the unsettling sensation that he was being watched, or *studied*, by someone. The longer he waited, the more intense his anxiety became.

Edis fidgeted inside the automobile. He scanned the neighboring buildings for danger, for some signal that might convince him to abort the mission ahead of schedule. He could pinpoint nothing specific, yet he realized that a professional sniper would never let his presence be known. He felt like a trapped rabbit sensing that an unseen hawk had it in its sight.

As the minutes ticked by, Edis hummed tunelessly and tapped his fingers on the steering wheel's bottom rim. He checked his watch often, noting the irony of how slowly time passed when he wanted it to pass quickly. At the ten-minute mark, Edis caught a glimpse of a sudden flash in a building located to the south, toward the Miljacka River. Something shiny in a third-floor window frame snared his interest. He looked over, taking care not to seem obvious.

The window was glassless; its outside edges were scorched black as a result of a fire earlier in the week. Edis could not be sure what he had seen inside; the flash had lasted only for a second. But what he saw in the glimmer's absence concerned him a great deal more. It appeared to be the shape of a man; a silhouette leaning forward, watching him through binoculars. Edis tried to appear oblivious to the undesired attention. In reality, the circumstance brought him to the brink of terror. His casual demeanor abandoned him involuntarily. Nonchalant movements became impossible. Curiosity and fear overwhelmed him. He had to know.

Ever so slowly, Edis cast his glance upward and singled out the window in question. Again he saw the silhouette of a man. He turned away abruptly and started to tremble. A flurry of thoughts raced through his mind, temporarily immobilizing him. In order to resist sheer panic, he reviewed Lucas's final instructions. After regaining his composure, he checked his watch. Still five minutes remained.

"Oh, shit! What should I do? What should I do?" he muttered aloud. *Leave the car running!* was the last order he remembered Lucas giving.

Once more Edis looked toward the suspicious window. This time, he focused blatantly without trying to conceal his distress. To his surprise, nothing was visible except a black, featureless void. The human form had vanished. He was about to breathe a sigh of relief when the shape resurfaced, this time in an altered position. The alarm of self-preservation sounded. Edis had only moments to make a life or death decision. One last glance confirmed his fears. The man in the window had changed optical devices. Now a scoped rifle was being aimed at him by a crouched assailant. He had only seconds to flee.

Forcing open the rickety car door with his left elbow, Edis snatched the shotgun with his right hand. In one smooth motion, he thrust his body out of the car and sprinted for cover, pressing the weapon to his side as he ran. Not far away, a burned-out café, decimated by the recent bombardment, provided him refuge. Crouching down and out of breath, he gasped for oxygen. Amazingly, not a single round had been fired during his flight.

Now almost fifty meters from where Lucas was scheduled to emerge, Edis knew that his friend was unaware of the attention that had been attracted. As a warning, he had intentionally left the car door open in hopes of signaling to his friend before he came out into the open. Lucas's only chance of escape would be to race to the Renault's protection and flee before the gas ran out. To do this, he would have to be alerted in advance to the danger above. Edis wondered if his warning was clear. There was no better alternative; there had been no time to come up with a plan.

For now, Edis realized he could do nothing more than wait, watch, and prepare. He was certain that his assistance would be required for Lucas to escape the threat. When that moment came, he needed to be ready to act.

The aged Renault continued idling in neutral with its headlights turned on, their power fading by the minute. Edis estimated the sniper to be a little more than a hundred meters from where the car was parked. The shooter had an unobstructed view of the path Lucas would take. It would be a long, difficult shot at a moving target, but one that could be made by an expert marksman.

Edis figured that the sniper was working alone, that no reinforcements were nearby to assist. He had heard rumors of snipers working in teams to isolate potential victims. Yet he doubted the rumors were true. Until now, the Serbian irregulars were unorganized and indiscriminately placed. Most were rogue mercenaries who preferred to work alone. If this was the case, Lucas still had a decent chance of escape.

Creeping forward, Lucas's protégé maneuvered to a better point of observation. In front of the café, he crawled along a series of concrete planters that had contained chest-high shrubs around its terrace before the siege began. At the moment, they were still filled with soil, but barren on top. Stopping beside the last safe barrier, he pointed the shotgun in the direction of the automobile that he had just deserted.

His plan was to wait for Lucas as he exited the high-rise's front door. When his partner appeared, Edis planned to empty his shotgun's chamber to warn him of the impending danger. While he waited, he tried to think of a better plan. None came to mind. It was Lucas's only chance.

XXI

The event unraveling caught Dragoslav Obrenović by surprise. It was early in the day and his senses were not yet sharp. The paramilitary leader had been up late the night before, reformulating tactics with General Parenta. The two had consumed large amounts of alcohol while evaluating reports of the battles being fought in the nearby villages. It appeared to them that the Muslim resistance was growing stronger outside Sarajevo. In reaction, the intoxicated general demanded that the sniper pressure within the city be increased to unprecedented levels. It had become clear to the Serbian authorities that more extreme measures would be needed to break the city's morale. With drunken enthusiasm, Dragoslav vowed to stain the streets with Muslim blood.

• • • • •

Dragoslav rose early the next morning, organized his men, and gave them their updated orders. He prepared maps of the city center and deployed his teams into new districts. Neighborhoods previously untouched by their malicious tactics would be given special attention.

Dragoslav's personal unit planned to advance beyond the neighborhood of Grbavica, crossing the Miljacka River to strike at the heart of the Muslim population. Just days before, a few novice snipers had been sent there to test the resistance. The amateurs had killed several civilians without opposition. Now Dragoslav and his men would expand on those efforts.

●●●●●

Just before daybreak, Dragoslav met with two of his top subordinates. Three scoped rifles and a Zolja rocket launcher were distributed among them. Then, as a group, they singled out a prime location for another day of killing.

They selected an uninhabited building on the edge of a Muslim neighborhood. Once inside the apartment block, the three marksmen spread out in classic form, choosing positions that would maximize their range and allow them to cover one another.

On the third floor, Dragoslav chose a fire-scorched apartment for his lair. It had been abandoned by its owners long ago, making it unlikely that he would be discovered. It offered a panoramic view and quick access to an enclosed stairwell to the street below. From this perch, he could survey the adjacent buildings and scan an area of over a hundred meters with his rifle. As the sun rose in the eastern sky, he felt confident that the day's mission would be successful.

The first part of the morning was uneventful. But as the sun grew brighter and the day grew warmer, Dragoslav began suffering the consequences of the previous night's drinking binge. It was around 9:30 when he finally had to abandon his post to relieve himself. A short while after returning, he noticed that a change in scenery had taken place in his absence. On the street below, a battered, cream-colored Renault 4 was now parked a little more than a hundred meters from his hideout. While studying this peculiarity through his binoculars, he saw that the driver was still inside. Equally interesting, the car's engine continued running. This oddity further aroused his curiosity and prompted him to analyze the scene more thoroughly. Moments later, Dragoslav realized that his presence had been discovered when the driver began to fidget. Attempting to ignore the undesired attention, the wheelman remained in place, a point that raised the sniper's suspicion even more. Through his rifle's scope he inspected the scene more closely.

Seconds later, the driver made a hurried escape and Dragoslav was convinced that some kind of plan was underway. The shotgun concealed at the fleeing man's side confirmed his hunch. His blood pressure shot up in response. Fueled by adrenalin, he sprang into action and dashed toward the stairwell with weapons dangling from both shoulders. Reaching the steps, he lunged down them two at a time, stopping briefly on the two lower floors to collect his team. Calling out frantically, he instructed both to meet him below with their rifles ready. The squad leader anticipated trouble ahead; backup would surely be useful.

By the time the team had assembled to assess the situation, the car's driver had disappeared into the protection of a burned-out café, almost a hundred and fifty meters away. Still unaware of an accomplice, a plan formed for Dragoslav's subordinates to search the deserted vehicle while he covered them from behind with his rifle.

The Serbian paramilitaries strutted cautiously toward the car with their rifles ready. There was no pedestrian traffic; the main thoroughfare was empty. As they closed in on the sputtering Renault, chaos erupted.

Across the street from the abandoned automobile, a series of shotgun blasts disrupted the tense silence, causing the Serbs to crash to the ground. Recovering quickly, they were relieved to see that none of their company was injured. Still mildly confused, they separated and searched out positions of safety. Only one would find shelter alive.

●●●●●

Like an enraged bull, Lucas charged into the open with his MP5 spewing eight hundred rounds per minute in the direction of the two Serbian snipers. The nearer one was killed instantly, struck in the head by successive nine-millimeter rounds. His companion managed to dive over a mound of fallen concrete just as the fury of Lucas's weapon was unleashed.

Wasting no time, Lucas pulled the frightened girl to the car's passenger-side. Squeezing her arm firmly, he opened the door with his other, and then shoved her inside. Circling around back, he approached the driver's door with a gasp of relief. Luckily, it had been left open.

Before entering, Lucas peppered with gunfire the last known position of the surviving sniper. He hoped this would make the gunman stay down long enough for them to escape. Then he tossed his weapon in back and jumped behind the wheel. Unwilling to tempt fate, he slammed the door shut and stomped on the accelerator. The Renault's horsepower was lacking, but it provided enough thrust for the tires to scream out with zeal. Lucas cranked hard on the steering wheel and pushed in the dash-mounted gearshift, eager to flee the deadly circumstances.

●●●●●

Slow to react, Dragoslav Obrenović watched the action unfold. Slightly dumbfounded, he had been caught off-guard for the second time in a few weeks. He was livid: his head filled with anger, his neck burned from a combination of embarrassment and rage. As the seconds ticked by, he regained his composure, but remained puzzled about how to resolve the crisis. On the verge of losing his self-control, he tossed aside his rifle and lifted the rocket launcher off the ground.

He quickly sprinted to a better position, knowing he had only one chance to redeem himself. For this drama to end favorably, his aim would have to be exact. With just seconds to spare, he propped the weapon onto his shoulder and directed the sight toward the screeching car.

●●●●●

Lucas spun the steering wheel hard to the left before returning the tires to a forward alignment. Cursing the engine's performance, he pleaded aloud for more power. The Renault's top-heavy frame was unsteady and vulnerable to attack. He knew it could not withstand incoming fire. A single direct hit would be catastrophic. In moments his fate and the girl's would be decided. Distance was not yet an ally.

● ● ● ● ●

Dragoslav inhaled deeply and then exhaled while concentrating on the racing Renault. Its back hatch was narrow and would be difficult to hit. The rocket's placement would have to be perfect. Once more, he took a deep breath and relaxed. With a surgeon's steadiness, he pulled the trigger.

The miniature missile erupted from the casing and spiraled toward the car. At first it appeared as if the grenade would punch directly through the back window. A split second before contact, however, the round curled down and to the right, barely nicking the rusty metal bumper sticking out beneath the hatch. A powerful blast sounded on impact. The rear tires disintegrated at once; the car's chassis separated from its snail-shaped body, causing it to spin out of control.

The Renault skidded and swerved like a drunk on an icy street. Lucas's driving ability was no match for the force of gravity. With a vise-like grip, he cranked the wheel, barely missing an overturned tram car lying at the side of the road. An instant later, the out-of-control automobile ran over a section of trolley track that warped upward from its bed. The protruding steel lanced the car's undercarriage and, combined with its momentum, lifted it from its natural position. The Renault turned abruptly before flipping end over end and coming to a shrieking halt. When the commotion had ended, the car was laying flat on one side, distorted and smashed. Soon everything was still.

Inside the Renault's mangled frame, Amra Avdić lay motionless, unconscious from a blow to her head. Lucas had been thrown from the front seat during the upheaval and had landed about ten meters from the wreckage, where he lay in a fetal position.

Tenaciously, he tried to raise himself. Lucas's face was bloodied and his mind unclear. He knew that only moments remained before their capture - or worse. Climbing to his knees, he managed to crawl a short distance before his strength failed him. Each attempt to stand was aborted when his weakened legs crumbled under his weight. After exhausting his energy reserves, he collapsed on the cobblestone road. As he lay silent, laboring to breathe, he sensed the approach of an unwanted visitor. It was a man dressed in commando apparel.

"Oh...you again?" Dragoslav growled with contempt. "I thought I might see you another time."

Now nearly in shock, Lucas wondered what would happen next. He lay still and concentrated on taking in air. Deep respiration was impossible. He was certain that several ribs had been broken. With his vision obscured, Lucas looked at the figure standing over him. He glared at the man's scarred face and was barely able to interpret his vindictive taunts. Then all words faded as he fell into unconsciousness.

●●●●●

Edis watched the events play out. When the dust had cleared, he assessed the situation and simultaneously planned his escape. For the time being, the Serbian reinforcements had not discovered his position, but he was sure they were aware of his presence. Crawling backwards, he returned to the shot-up cafe to study the scene from a safer distance.

Edis watched as a group of paramilitaries carried the bodies of Lucas and what appeared to be that of a young woman. For a moment he swore that the woman could have been his missing sister, but he was certain that could only be wishful thinking. Edis rubbed his tired eyes and squinted in an attempt to improve his vision, but before his focus could adjust, the pair had vanished into a nearby building surrounded by a crowd of Serbian militia.

When additional soldiers began to arrive, he decided to leave or risk being captured or killed. Ignoring Lucas's final orders, Edis vowed to return, better prepared, and with a strategy of his own. Then he fled.

XXII

"It seems that your associate is behind schedule this evening, Stevan. Is there something I should be worried about?"

"Relax, Goran. He'll be here. It's a long journey from eastern Bosnia. Extra precautions had to be arranged to ensure his safe travel," General Parenta replied, exhaling smoke from a hand-rolled cigarette. "Try to have some patience, my friend. These are delicate times," he added.

The Serbian general outranked the Croatian colonel, but there was no tone of authority in his voice. In their business dealings, they always addressed each other by their first names, dispensing with military formalities. Besides, the men had known each other for years before the war had begun. At the moment, the two of them were awaiting the arrival of an important Bosnian-Serb political leader.

The men stood outdoors as they chatted. The ethnic Serb officer, dressed in freshly pressed military attire, leaned against his car with hands at his sides. His left hand was clenched into a fist with the thumb inserted into the waistline of his pants, under the belt. His right hand held the cigarette between the index and middle fingers; its palm rested on the wooden handle of a polished revolver that he wore holstered on his right hip. The general's Croatian companion circled restlessly. He, too, wore a military uniform, camouflage fatigues that were dirty from a full day of leading his troops in battle. A red and white checkered crest was prominently displayed on his sleeve.

Almost ten minutes earlier, each officer's Mercedes-Benz had pulled into the parking lot of an isolated factory just outside of Mostar. It was a bauxite processing plant, built during the Tito years, which now stood unused next to railway tracks that had been derelict since the beginning of the war. The facility and its environs were deserted. It was the perfect setting for a private meeting.

The air was cool and crisp. The cloudless night sky was alive, sparkling with millions of stars. No electricity was connected on the premises; the only man-made light came from the cars. Parked thirty meters apart, the automobiles were pointed toward one another with their headlights beaming and their motors running.

The entrance to the factory grounds was a little-traveled road that ended at the main highway a hundred meters away. At the junction, a cast-iron gate regulated traffic. The perimeter was wooded. The quarry grounds were encircled by a chain-link fence that was rusted and decayed to the point of uselessness.

On the site, each Mercedes owner was accompanied by a single bodyguard. The armed escorts were familiar with one another. A precedent had been established at their first meeting several months earlier, and every subsequent reunion followed the same routine. Their superiors met together near one parked car, while the two bodyguards waited by the other, which was parked well beyond earshot. There, they passed the time until being called away. Little was said between them, but both carried submachine guns and smoked cigarettes. The general's bodyguard, Dragoslav Obrenović, was dressed in a brown and green camouflage combination. He stood with a slouched posture and behind his snarled mustache his face seemed to wear a permanent sneer. Snug against his hip rested a 7.65-millimeter Scorpion; its 'automatic' setting selected. The other guard wore dark green fatigues and carried a nine-millimeter ERO, a Croatian copy of an Israeli Uzi, from a strap slung over his right shoulder. Both men realized that their presence here was unnecessary, that that their roles were trivial. They passed the time by pacing, smoking, and thinking.

Soon the glow of another automobile's headlights came into view. This one, a BMW, moved smoothly over the road's rutted surface, winding and weaving until its headlights glared in the direction of the two waiting Benzes. At the lot entrance, the BMW's progress was delayed while its driver tried to determine which Mercedes to approach. After realizing the cause of the confusion, General Parenta stepped between his car's headlights and waved his outstretched arms. The BMW pulled forward before stopping at the Benz's front end. A brawny thug stepped from the front passenger door. He walked around the vehicle and opened the door for the occupant in back. After completing the delivery, the car jolted forward and parked beside the second Mercedes where the two bored bodyguards were waiting. The civilian's security force did not join the others.

The tardy associate, a stocky, well-fed, middle-aged politician, was formally greeted by the military officers. With sweaty palms, the newcomer shook each participant's hand. He was dressed in an Italian-made suit, with his shirt collar unbuttoned and his tie loosened at the throat. His hair was long, gray, and thinning on top. A strong smell of alcohol accompanied his labored exhalations.

●●●●●

"Well, gentlemen, how are the profits progressing?" he began, glancing smugly at the Croat for the initial reply.

The Croatian colonel's response was evasive. He was unwilling to divulge too much information at the meeting's onset, knowing the gravity of the discussion to follow. As quickly as he could, he deferred to General Parenta.

The general cleared his throat. He answered the politician's question vaguely, then steered the conversation elsewhere. "Boss, the news is mostly good. Consumption is increasing daily; revenues, likewise. Herein lies the problem, the reason that this meeting was called. The supply channels throughout Bosnia are being squeezed.

It is getting harder to deliver the goods to the areas of highest profit margin. For now, the cigarettes are not a problem, but the weapons and landmines require special precautions. The international sanctions are beginning to take affect. We are going to need some support from Belgrade to get the U.N. to ease its pressure."

"Uh-huh," replied the party member, who was already braced for bad news. "Stevan, I believe that you persuaded me, or rather, you *convinced* me that these sanctions would not affect the trade routes. It was *your* testimony that swayed my decision to pursue these objectives! Until now, my faith in your professional judgment has been unwavering. Indeed, my influence has made you a very wealthy man. Why do you now inform me of this bullshit?"

General Parenta responded, "I assure you, everything is going according to plan. My calculations show that just six months, perhaps a year more, of uninterrupted operations will allow our families to prosper for generations to come. I am simply requesting help for the delay, not the elimination, of sanctions that are inevitably coming."

"Stevan, your request is not so simple," the politician flared, "there are always complications, *outside pressures* to be dealt with. For example, getting the European countries to retract their positions was not so difficult. But this time, the Americans are the ones applying the pressure. It has been progressing for months. Deflection is not so easy. Getting them to back off, less so. Do you now fully understand the magnitude of your request?"

Sensing potential easy money slipping away, the Croat re-entered the discussion. "Look, these are trying times for all of us, but we've come too far to withdraw."

The intoxicated politician eyed the Croatian officer with contempt. His tolerance for the enemy was noticeably less than that of the Serbian general. "You're not so quiet anymore, eh? Okay, speak up. Tell us your solution!"

Promptly, General Parenta intervened. Moving between the two, he nodded to his Croatian colleague and requested some privacy. The colonel gladly consented. Next, the general wrapped his right arm over the politician's shoulders and led him twenty meters into the darkness.

In a hushed tone, General Parenta addressed his civilian superior. "In case you are unaware, we now have a pawn with which to manipulate - some collateral that we can use to adjust our position in the eyes of the West. I insist that we take full advantage of what fortune has given us," he added.

"Are you referring to the American in Sarajevo? What is his condition? Is he still alive?" the Bosnian-Serb politician questioned.

"According to the documents he was carrying, he is a *Croatian-American*. The difference deserves distinction. He's alive and unaccounted for. He will surely be missed."

"But will he survive?"

"It's hard to say," answered the general. "He suffered considerable head injuries; multiple, deep concussions. The doctor said there is a lot of swelling around his brain. At the moment, he is unconscious. He may never wake up," the general stated.

"What about the girl who was with him? Will she live?"

"Oh, you know how Bosnian-Muslim girls are...pretty thick-headed," General Parenta answered. "The doctor says that her unfortunate emotional state is the result of previous stressful conditions, not from her recent trauma. However, I'm not entirely certain of the doctor's mental capacity either. He's been under a lot of strain lately." The two chuckled lightly.

The politician quickly grew serious again. Speaking through tightened lips, he asked, "What is it that you have devised? It better be good. I can't meet with our business partners without giving them a full report. These are very powerful people, Stevan - both of your heads are on the line!"

General Parenta answered, "I have just received new orders from my military commanders in Belgrade, bold, innovative thinking coming straight from the top. I'm to carry out these orders in the coming weeks. It's a risky plan, but the strategy is sound."

"Go on, elaborate. What are you getting at?" the bureaucrat scowled. "And how will this improve our troubles in private business?"

"The official objective of these military orders is twofold. First, and most important, is to divert attention away from the JNA and Serbian ambitions. The second priority is to put the spotlight on Croatian culpabilities. The new orders will support Serbia's claims of Croatian destabilization in its attempts to salvage the Federal Republic of Yugoslavia. I plan to fulfill Belgrade's demands by completing both objectives at once. Simultaneously, I've devised a way of accomplishing a third objective of my own - the easing of U.S. pressure and the delay of U.N. intervention. This should allow our business operation to continue and permit our profits to soar."

The politician's face signaled equal amounts of interest and skepticism. The need for further explanation was obvious.

"From its developmental stages until now, only one major complication for my assignment's success stood out," the general continued. "To achieve the desired results, my superiors have deemed it essential to have this plot carried out by a foreign entity in order to minimize suspicion of Serbian involvement, should it fail. Moreover, they wish to establish evidence of Croatian instigation, or even better, Croatian *incrimination*, no matter what the outcome. For this reason, I think our new captive will prove to be very useful. Problem solved."

The politician remained confused and General Parenta sensed it immediately. Before he could begin asking questions, the general started in again.

"Look, at the moment, the balance of world opinion is tipping in favor of Croatia's position in the war. Up until now, and with diminishing enthusiasm, mind you, the West has tolerated Serbia's assertion of securing the Federal Republic of Yugoslavia. Since the strategy has produced very little progress so far and the destabilization worsens daily, world opinion is clearly shifting as a result of the pressure the Americans are applying. The plan I have devised will once again tip the scale in Serbia's favor."

The general stopped to collect his thoughts. Misspeaking now could derail his entire plan. After a moment he whispered, "To successfully complete my third objective, a simple bait-and-switch ploy will be used, along with some espionage, extortion, and an assassination. Of course, a possible international crisis could result if the plan goes awry, but if everything goes according to the script, the latter need not happen. The Croatian-American agent is the key."

General Parenta then looked over his shoulder to make sure his military adversary was out of earshot.

"What is it? Can he not be trusted?" the Bosnian-Serb politician asked.

The general snickered. "He cares only for the money. The single thing I trust about my Croatian colleague is his sense of greed. He does not realize what is at stake."

The general checked again before resuming, "If my plan is successful, enough time will pass, at least six months to a year, for the JNA to gain complete control of Bosnia and the Dalmatian coast. This time span will also provide an additional six months to profit from the supply routes already in place. When the West finally does intervene, Serbia will be better positioned to negotiate a favorable settlement. To achieve this postponement, Belgrade must prove to the world that illegal interference in the Federal Republic of Yugoslavia's internal affairs is coming from Croatia. By adding our new prisoner into the mix, this can also be twisted so as to be construed as U.S. collusion. The international community will have to speak out in our defense. The Americans will be forced to back off. When that happens, we will be the ones applying the political pressure."

● ● ● ● ●

Moments later, the two rejoined the Croatian colonel near the general's Mercedes. As they approached, General Parenta announced genially that the two had reached an understanding. Then, without warning, he spoke to the Croatian officer with a tone of intimidation in his voice.

"Goran, in order to firm up the supply channels, I've got a task to ask of you," he said.

"What is it?" the Croat asked.

"For our profits to grow, I have some cargo that needs to be safely delivered across the border into Croatia. It is a man in an unconscious state. This might be difficult, but not impossible for a person with your status."

"It can be arranged. No problem," the Croat offered proudly.

"There are always problems," the drunken politician warned.

Suddenly, as the general explained the situation, the snap of a broken branch and the rattle of a rolling rock sounded from inside the nearby forest. Unable to see through the moonless night, the men dispersed and the bodyguards were summoned. They paced the tree line with their weapons drawn. In the distance, fading footsteps could be heard rustling through the underbrush. The source's origin remained unknown. In a burst of frustration, Dragoslav Obrenović sprayed the landscape with his automatic weapon. Not to be outdone, the Croatian bodyguard opened fire as well. After a half a minute or so of random gunfire, General Parenta ordered the guards to hold their fire.

"It was probably a cat or a dog. Maybe a deer," the drunken politician said.

The Croatian colonel ordered both bodyguards to return to their Mercedes. Spitefully, Dragoslav looked to General Parenta, who followed the Croat's order with an identical order of his own. Smirking at the Croatian officer, Dragoslav turned his back and walked away.

Over the next few minutes, an abbreviated version of the general's conspiracy was retold to the Croat, minus the details of the political double-cross. After the general had finished, the three were in agreement. They would tell no one of their plan, and as soon as the fine points could be worked out, it would go forward. The timetable and intricacies could be quickly calculated. The next morning, the comatose American agent would be moved in preparation for the operation to begin.

After settling some logistical matters, the group separated. The politician left first because another business meeting required his attendance. Minutes later, General Parenta and the Croatian colonel disappeared from the scene. There was a war to be fought, work to be done, and money to be made.

PART II

XXIII

The salty scent of sea air saturated the room where Lucas lay. At first, he thought it was impossible, but he knew that smell, and it flooded his mind with childhood memories. He had just regained consciousness; he knew right away that he was too weak to lift his head from the pillow. For now, his environment had to be evaluated from the sides of his eyes.

Lucas figured he was in a bedroom of a private home, or perhaps a villa, somewhere near the Adriatic Sea. The room was small and minimally furnished. It contained a bed, a nightstand, a hardwood armoire and two matching chairs, all typical in appearance and commonly found in homes along the Dalmatian coast. The plaster walls were sanded smooth and painted white. A watercolor of a fisherman mending his nets beside a dry-docked boat hung on the wall above his head. The window frame was barred and padlocked. Its glass pane was half-open. He could hear voices outside. Soon he would get up and investigate, but first he had to rest a bit longer.

After another hour, he felt strong enough to sit upright. He examined his body for signs of injury. Remarkably, there were few. He looked into a hand-held mirror that lay on the nightstand. The image he saw perplexed him. His face had been cleaned and his beard was smoothly shaven. The reflection revealed traces of multiple, half-healed bruises above the right temple which were now yellowish-brown in color. The remnant of a one-inch gash, which had been previously sutured, was visible on his forehead. He calculated he had been unconscious for several days, if not weeks.

Shifting toward the foot of the bed, Lucas leaned forward and rested both elbows on his knees. He put his head in his hands and strained with all his might to remember what had happened and how he had gotten here. He could recall little. His long-term memory was intact; he knew who he was, what he had been doing, and where he had been doing it. But his short-term memory failed him; the when, why, and how of his present condition were a mystery.

After a few more minutes, Lucas collected the necessary stamina to dress. The clothes he remembered last wearing were nowhere to be found. Instead, another outfit was waiting for him. The garments were neatly folded and laid out on the chairs – and, he noted, were exactly his size. He put the new attire on methodically, taking care not to move his head suddenly. Every change in position triggered an episode of vertigo and ignited a throbbing pain in the back of his skull. There was no doubt that he had recently suffered a severe concussion.

The clothing fit well, though it certainly represented someone else's sense of style. Lucas was now clad mostly in black. He wore a pullover, jeans, and black leather shoes and leather jacket. At the head of the bed, a pair of Italian-made sunglasses rested in a nightstand tray, along with the watch he recognized as his own.

After regaining sufficient power, he decided to locate the voices he could hear outside and try to determine the seriousness of his quandary. He opened the bedroom door and shuffled down a short, empty hallway. The main living room was on his right. Inside, an outdated set of furniture faced a television set. The villa's front door was nearby and closed. Coming to the kitchen, he peered out through a large, open window. Only blue water could be seen to his left and straight ahead. To his right, where the island bowed out toward the open sea, a village was visible in the distance. Several white houses with orange-tiled rooftops were grouped together, perched along the water's edge. There were no villagers in sight.

A cool breeze entered the window and the salt air stung his still-sensitive face. Moving over to the back doorway, he looked out and saw a group of men gathered on the terrace drinking wine. At the moment, a heated discussion was underway. Lucas could not follow the argument in detail as multiple disputes were occurring at once. He cleared his throat to announce his presence. Instantly, a half dozen faces stared back at his, each expressing varying degrees of surprise. All at once, the six raised their wine glasses into the air and toasted a collective "*Živjeli!*" - "Live long!" - in salutation to the risen warrior.

Lucas scanned the participants' faces one by one, trying to identify them and determine their significance. Only one seemed familiar, the face of the man with the crooked lip and twisted mustache who had towered over him after the Sarajevo crash. Instantly, his forgotten past replayed in his mind, though in an off-tint color. But the scenario didn't make sense. It was obvious that he was no longer in Sarajevo, and equally as evident that he was on a Croatian island in the Adriatic. His puzzlement resulted from the fact that so few of the men gathered around the table were Croatian.

The bright sun beat down forcing his eyes to squint as he passed through the door. The sunglasses lessened the glare minimally. It was a warm day, but a steady breeze kept the temperature at a comfortable level.

Almost mechanically, Lucas walked across the terrace tiles. His blood pressure increased with each step, causing his head to pound viciously. As he moved, he noted how the men crowded around the table seemed to be enjoying themselves. At the same time, he sensed that the cheerful mood was a facade.

"Come, sit, Mr. Martin! Have a glass of wine – it will help your head feel better," proclaimed the man in the center, who had been dominating the debates that Lucas had been listening in on from his room. Lucas knew that he was the principal of the group. A decorated .357 magnum revolver rested on the table in front of him, having recently been passed around for each man to admire. The others sat quietly and conceded to his lead.

"It seems I'm at a disadvantage," Lucas said. "You know my name, but I don't know yours."

"Yes, of course! Please, let me introduce myself. I am General Stevan Parenta of the Federal Republic of Yugoslavia's National Army. These are my colleagues, bodyguards, and business associates, but their identities are not important."

Lucas sat down and studied each attendee more thoroughly. He thought he recognized at least one other member of the group, but could not be one hundred percent certain.

"Where am I?" Lucas asked, accepting a glass of wine that was served to him.

"You are enjoying the island of Korčula's splendid beauty in the magnificent Adriatic Sea!" the general answered grandiosely. Then he turned his head and gazed over the railing to watch a distant sailboat. "Life doesn't get any better than this!" he declared, before taking a large drink from his wineglass.

"How is this possible?" Lucas queried. "You, and at least one other of these men, are Serbian nationals. I cannot imagine that your presence in Croatia is welcome."

"Oh, by and large, it is not. But JNA generals need relaxing weekends too…and as you are aware, these are the Balkans. Here, everything is possible!" the JNA officer boasted. The others sitting around him laughed. "Of course, it helps to have influential contacts on 'both sides of the fence,' as the saying goes."

"I see," Lucas said. "So what am I doing here? I am not an influential contact."

"Oh, but you are," General Parenta returned. "Everyone has a role in the grand scheme of things. You just don't know it yet."

Lucas examined each face in more detail. At last, it struck him. The Serb with the crooked moustache was indeed the final face he had seen in Sarajevo. Across the table from him sat a Croat, a high-ranking officer he remembered seeing in Dubrovnik almost a year earlier.

"So…fill me in, General. What is my part in the grand scheme of things?"

With that question, the Croatian officer and his bodyguard got up to leave. The general refrained from answering until they were gone.

Lucas sensed that another hidden presence was observing the meeting from a distance. Of this he could not be certain, but he had experienced a similar sensation too many times before to question it. At no point did he feel threatened, so he ignored the feeling and continued the conversation with the JNA general.

"Well, my new friend, I have an assignment for you," the general said. "I shall not refer to it as an *order*, but rather, as a very strong proposal. Do you feel fit for active duty?"

"Duty?" Lucas asked with surprise. "It depends, General. What exactly are you proposing?" As if on cue, two of the remaining four associates stood and went inside the villa.

General Parenta paused a moment to analyze how best to present the scheme he was about to deliver. Turning abruptly in his chair, he leaned forward and began to speak with a tone of authority. The welcoming politeness that had been present earlier in the conversation disappeared.

"An opportunity has been offered to me – a private job that holds no direct bearing on the war in Bosnia. It is, however, a task that will pay me handsomely when it is completed. You see, like you, I am also in a position to accept freelance work when the financial incentives are appealing to my personal interests."

"What does any of this have to do with me?" Lucas responded.

"This particular enterprise, upon its completion, will pay you handsomely, too, Mr. Martin …because it will be performed by you. And be assured, you will be well compensated for your efforts. As always, I am willing to pay, as they say, 'big bucks' for successful results. I promise to make it financially worthwhile for your time and troubles," the general added. Then he sat back in his chair. Folding his arms, he studied Lucas's face for some sign of interest.

"General, I don't have any idea what you're getting at. And I have no patience for games - my head hurts too badly. Why don't you just get to the point?" Lucas fired back.

"Very well, and I appreciate your candor, Mr. Martin," the general replied with a grin. "I like your style immensely."

Lucas resisted the urge to roll his eyes at the obvious flattery.

Again, General Parenta leaned forward. "I have been contacted by some very high officials in Croatia. It seems our Catholic adversaries have a private job that needs to be performed on their behalf. This vital task cannot be done internally without jeopardizing the political power that these officials currently wield. Therefore, they have decided to hire me to complete this mission for them. Of course, if the price is right, and in this case it is, I am willing to overlook my political and religious differences to help them in their time of need."

"What sort of business are you talking about, General?"

General Parenta stared coldly at Lucas. "Assassination."

"What?" Lucas questioned.

The JNA general continued, "As I am sure you are aware, there is a peninsula in Croatia's northwest corner named Istria. This province was once in the possession of the Italians. Upon the dissolution of our beloved Republic of Yugoslavia, a sort of free-for-all has developed, with every province wanting to go its own way for what each feels is in its own best interest. Istria is no different. The inhabitants there are overwhelmingly in favor of breaking away and returning to the Italian state. Zagreb will not allow this dissent to continue."

"Where do I fit into this? This does not concern me."

"Slowly, Mr. Martin; I'm getting to the point. It seems that Zagreb has isolated the source of the current commotion. It revolves around a popular politician named Renato Angelli who has acquired the ear of the people. He is lobbying for a referendum that would allow the citizens to vote on secession in the next few months, likely before winter begins. The Zagreb officials do not want to see this vote happen. That can be guaranteed in only one way: the elimination of this instigator."

"I still don't understand why you are telling me this," Lucas insisted.

"It is quite simple, Mr. Martin. I have achieved my present stature by making quick, courageous decisions and by using effective, talented people. I am a good judge of character, and I consider you to be highly competent in your field."

"What field is that?" Lucas said.

The general chuckled a little and said, "Tell me, Mr. Martin, what organization are you affiliated with? The CIA? NSA? A U.S. Defense Department black-op outfit?"

Lucas did not answer. He had heard rumors that the CIA had been dabbling in ex-Yugoslavia's affairs since its breakup; apparently the general had heard them as well. "I am simply an observer, General. A freelance photographer wanting to get the story straight," he said.

"Come now, Mr. Martin. I have personal knowledge of your performance in Sarajevo. I understand that you are proficient with more than just a camera. And that is exactly what I am looking for. I am offering you the possibility to earn a million dollars, cash, which will be deposited into the foreign bank account of your choice. All you must do to procure payment is to travel to Istria, isolate Mr. Angelli, kill him, and bury his body at sea. The operation's details have nearly been finalized. It could not be easier. You will be paid after I am paid - immediately after the mission's completion. And after all this unfortunate business is finished, I will be happy, you will be happy, and when this war has ended, we'll all be a lot better off."

"Why don't you use one of your own associates, General?" Lucas asked, shooting a glance toward Dragoslav Obrenović.

"As you can well imagine, Mr. Martin, it would not look good having a Serbian assassin running around a Croatian stronghold killing politicians. In addition, our workers are often incompetent and lack attention to detail. No, I prefer to work with an outsider in a critical mission such as this."

Lucas believed otherwise, but declined to debate the bogus reasoning. Confronting the general at this point was hardly in his best interest.

"And if I refuse?"

"Ah, yes, refusal…I considered that you might not be enticed by the money. Greed doesn't rule everybody, does it, Mr. Martin? In that case, if the money isn't incentive enough, then you should know that the Muslim girl whom you were trying to rescue is still in our possession. At the moment, she is being treated rather well… better than any Muslim deserves, in my opinion. If you decline my generous offer, then I will have no choice but to repeal the order ensuring her safety."

Lucas was caught off guard by the unexpected blackmail. The concussion had temporarily erased Edis's sister from his mind. Now the events that had brought him here were returning in vivid detail. As Lucas considered how to counter the general's offensive maneuver, a sinking feeling overcame him. His blood pressure jumped in response. He hoped the flush in his face was not visible.

"I remember the girl looking as if she had suffered enough because of your orders, General. Why don't you leave her out of this?"

"Then you have accepted my generous offer! Excellent, Mr. Martin - I was hoping that you would make the logical decision," he replied boldly.

"Not so fast, General Parenta," Lucas said, trying to stall for time to think through his options. "What guarantee do I have of the girl's safety? Is she here? Can I check her condition?"

"No, she is not here. No, you cannot see her. As for a guarantee, you have my word as a distinguished officer of the Federal Republic of Yugoslavia's National Army."

Lucas changed directions, intentionally placing less importance on the girl's well-being.

"Then never mind her. If you're offering me a million dollars, I presume there is at least twice that amount in it for you. I suspect much more. If I'm providing the labor, why should you receive anything more than a finder's fee?"

As the negotiations intensified, the general's bodyguard sat entranced. Dragoslav had developed an acute interest in how his commander delegated the terms of the deal.

"Ah! So there is a greedy streak running through your veins, Mr. Martin. Excellent! Do not feel ashamed, it exists in all of us. I respect a man who is passionate about money because I understand him. You see, I also have an enormous desire for money. More precisely, I crave *cash* - hard currency. Now do you understand? We are not so different. We share the same values. Did I tell you that before the war I used to be a banker?"

"Then you can understand my intention to reconfigure the provisions of your proposal. If I perform more than half of the operation, then I demand more than half of the payout. These are my professional rates. They are non-negotiable."

"Please, Mr. Martin, do not be ridiculous. You are in no position to dictate terms. The deal stands as-is, no changes. A million dollars and you and the girl will be released on my personal guarantee. If you refuse, then I will not be able to find a use for either of you. Do you now fully grasp the stipulations?"

"Clearly," Lucas responded.

Again, General Parenta leaned back in his chair. He had aged significantly since the war's onset and dramatically since the siege of Sarajevo had begun. Not long after the shells started falling on the Bosnian capital, his hair had turned much whiter. Of the jet-black hair that had once covered his head, only a few stubborn strands remained. He had lost weight and his frame showed obvious signs of fatigue. Emotionally, an egotistical confidence masked an underlying sense of disgrace. The general's smoking habit had shot up and he now consumed more than two packs a day. It was his secret desire for the war to end quickly, so he could retire a wealthy man. He tried to convince himself that the blood on his hands would wash away over time; that a life of luxury would clear his tarnished conscience. His body, however, was refusing to accept the tale that his mind was spinning.

"So, when is the deed to be done?" Lucas asked.

"You will have time to make a full recovery. I am expected in Sarajevo soon. I shall return with a detailed account describing exactly how the mission shall be carried out. The dossier will list the times, places, and logistics - everything necessary to guarantee success. You will remain here, under the supervision of my associates, of course. Think of it as being my personal guest rather than being my prisoner. A medical specialist will check on you periodically. I promise you that your health will be as good when you leave my control as it was before your unfortunate accident. Please, make yourself comfortable; take every opportunity to rest and regain your strength. It will be needed soon. You may walk down to the private beach and swim daily. Help yourself to the spectacular wine and abundant seafood. Remember, when you finish this assignment, you can live out the rest of your life in a paradise such as this."

"That's what I thought before I returned to the Balkans," Lucas answered, wondering how he became entangled in this insane situation.

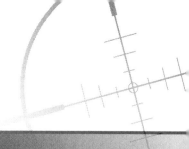

XXIV

In the weeks following the general's departure, Lucas used his time wisely. With each passing day, he could feel his strength returning and his wounds healing satisfactorily. His mind churned constantly, plotting how to escape the situation that had been forced upon him. When no clear-cut solution was forthcoming, he began to believe that the general's scheme would have to be fulfilled in order to save the young woman's life. There was little other choice.

To Lucas, the concept of killing one innocent victim to save another was more unsettling than inconceivable. Killing wasn't the problem. Killing for money wasn't even the problem. He had killed countless times for money, for payment that he accepted without guilt. The money was never an issue. He was simply collecting resources for his livelihood, compensation for professional services rendered to his government and ordered by his government. Yet he had never faced a situation like this. The act of taking an innocent life was not in his repertoire of expertise. Always before, orders to kill had been issued by his superiors, whose judgment he could not question. He was never personally familiar with the victims, and he was never forced to choose between two individuals whose existence inflicted little harm on others. He had always killed willfully and deliberately, but he had never been blackmailed into committing murder.

● ● ● ● ●

As the sunny skies of summer gave way to autumn, the weather became less predictable. In late September, a string of cloudy days lowered the sea's temperature, making it too cold to swim in comfortably. Now Lucas spent most days in his room, recuperating and implementing an improvised rehabilitation routine. Eventually, all the joints that had been damaged in the crash recovered full motion and most of the injured muscles had been reconditioned to their previous levels of strength. Time passed quickly. Soon, he was certain, the call for him to begin General Parenta's mission would come. Still unable to figure a way out of the predicament, Lucas decided that the only thing to do was to proceed cautiously and seize any opportunity that presented itself to save the girl's life. In the meantime, it was crucial to be in top physical and mental condition.

By mid-October, the days had grown shorter and darkness set in around six o'clock. The tourist season had ended several weeks ago, though Lucas knew that this was an almost irrelevant fact; the war had decimated the industry to a fraction of what it had been in the prewar years. A handful of foreigners did visit the Dalmatian coast despite the hostilities, but by now, most of those had vanished. At present, the island was generally deserted except for the permanent inhabitants who lived the winter months in isolation. Their time was spent fishing, gardening, and drinking the wine they produced in their personal vineyards.

Weeks had passed since Lucas had talked with anyone other than the two guards who were detaining him. Every so often, a cranky, retired gynecologist stopped by to check on his health. Two days earlier, she had proclaimed him fit to leave the island. Lucas correctly predicted the general would arrive soon after. There was too much money waiting to be made.

On the fourth day after his final physical exam, Lucas awoke to the sound of two cars idling in the villa's private entrance. Peeking through the shuttered windows, he could see the general leaning against his Mercedes-Benz. He was engaged in a serious conversation with two companions. The first was the man with the mustache and the permanent sneer. With his head flexed forward, he was listening attentively as if trying to absorb every detail of the general's spoken words. Lucas could tell critical orders were being assigned. More frequently than necessary, the general's lackey nodded his head up and down, attempting to demonstrate thorough understanding of the instructions the general was giving.

The second participant, the Croatian officer Lucas had recognized on the terrace after rising from his coma, stood nearby with his arms folded. Every so often, he interrupted the general to clarify details for the other man's benefit. The Croat spoke quickly and always used both hands to accentuate his message. Upon making his point, he instantly surrendered the conversation's control back to the general. In return for the respect, General Parenta seemed to be allowing extra opportunity for the Croat to inject his expertise throughout the conference. The man with the mustache contributed little to the dialogue. Instead, he repeatedly shook his head in the affirmative and maintained a look of uncertainty on his face. Lucas had seen the exact expression on the faces of hundreds of people during his years in the Balkans. He perceived that the fellow was acknowledging full comprehension of instructions that he did not fully grasp. Focusing in on this weakness, Lucas hoped to use any potential confusion to his advantage.

Before long, the three men dispersed. The two Serbs walked up the concrete driveway toward the villa. The Croat, meanwhile, moved the general's Mercedes to another location, then sped away in his own.

Lucas dressed hurriedly, then moved to the kitchen to prepare coffee. Not yet fully awake, he self-prescribed a high dose of caffeine to ensure his alertness. He wanted to be at full attention in order to absorb the general's objectives and gauge his demeanor. He intended to commit the entire conversation to memory so that the pending scheme could be dissected later. Then any flaws the plan provided could be uncovered. Somehow, someway, he was determined to derail the general's plans.

Be smart and wait. Patience and intelligence, he repeated over and again in his mind.

Before the general reached the villa, Dragoslav Obrenović had moved ahead and gathered the two bodyguards. The three retreated onto the terrace so that the general and his prisoner could talk privately about the assassination. Lucas sat at the kitchen table and waited for the general to enter.

"Ah, General, welcome back," he said, standing up to shake his adversary's hand. Lucas was experienced enough to conceal his disdain for the man and his methods. "Please sit down. From your timely return, I presume that you are keen to get started on the task you previously told me about. Have I been declared physically fit?"

"Yes, Mr. Martin, I am satisfied with your progress report. I am also happy to announce that the Muslim girl is improving each day; an achievement I am particularly proud of, considering the sorry state in which we received her. Does that answer your next question?"

The general was brief and purposely vague. The fact that Amra Avdić was alive was the message he sought to convey. Lucas knew that the status of Edis's sister would not be discussed in more detail; this was a business conversation.

"Of course, it answers the very next question I had."

"I thought so. Good. Now we can move on to other matters of importance. I have been briefed, and I have issued orders to my team. The deal stands as previously stated - one million U.S. dollars, *cash*, deposited into the foreign bank account of your choice after the execution of Renato Angelli – the Croatian politician from Istria. This *is* what was agreed on? Correct?"

"And then the girl and I go free, unharmed, and never to be heard from or seen by you again?"

"Exactly, Mr. Martin. Now you are speaking my language. Money and young ladies - a beautiful combination!" the general said, briefly attempting to bring a bit of lightness into the conversation.

"So...I can't just show up and kill a man. What is the plan that you have designed?"

"Slowly, Mr. Martin, everything has been arranged. I will go over the details with you shortly. For the moment, enjoy your coffee. Tell me, how are you feeling?"

The general turned casually in his chair as he talked. He picked up his briefcase and placed it on his lap. Reaching inside, he removed his revolver and placed it in front of him on the table.

"Thanks for your concern, General. I am back to normal, but I feel as if your interest lies more with the profit you seek rather than my well-being."

"Mr. Martin, I know what you are thinking. Please understand that I am not some beast from below. This is just a typical business proposition – *Balkan business,* if you will. It is how things are done here. Many times, death is fairer than life. This is one of those instances. It is the purest form of survival of the fittest, or to put it another way, it is a normal procession of the Balkan food chain. In order for the strong to thrive, the weak must be sacrificed. Fortunately, I...*we,* I shall remind you, just so happen to be in a position of strength. Try not to burden your conscience with the morality of the matter. Rather, close your mind to the reality, execute the mission precisely, and collect your reward. The past will be quickly forgotten. Do not struggle with circumstances that are beyond your control. Only then can you, and the girl, continue enjoying long and healthy lives. I give myself the same advice every morning when I get up from bed."

"Thanks for the guidance, General. My coffee is almost finished. Can we go over the mission's details now?"

"Of course we can, Mr. Martin. You Americans are always in such a hurry to discuss business, aren't you? Or shall I say, you *Croatian-Americans*?" the general added. A wry smile stretched across his face. He removed some papers from his briefcase and shuffled them around.

"And so...let us begin. The political movement is based in the Istrian city of Pula. Today is Friday. Two days from now, Renato Angelli is planning a major rally in a hotel ballroom in the city of

Opatija. Opatija is the dividing line between the Istrian peninsula and the Croatian mainland. The powers in Zagreb fear that if the public support for partition is achieved in Opatija, there will be no stopping the success of his campaign. The disappearance of Mr. Angelli must take place on Sunday, the day of the rally."

"So the rally never takes place?"

"No, Mr. Martin, the rally does take place. It *must* take place. Only after the event shall you perform the task," said the general. "You see, it is a classic example of cause and effect. The people will know what happened. Indirectly, they *must* know. They are like sheep; once their shepherd has been removed, they will follow the first authoritative figure who takes the lead. That leadership will be imposed by Zagreb."

"What about inquiry into Mr. Angelli's disappearance?" Lucas asked. "Surely he'll be missed."

"That also will be handled by Zagreb. Steps to control the press and public outcry are already underway. People have short memories in the Balkans. Troublemakers usually don't last long."

"This means I have just two days to prepare for a mission in an unfamiliar city and in an unknown setting?"

"Relax, Mr. Martin, everything is under control. The rough edges are being polished as we speak. You will have two relaxing days ahead of you. Think of this as a paid vacation."

"What plans are being made? How is this to be handled? Who is the handler that I will be dealing with?"

"The plan will go like this. Today, an anonymous associate in Opatija, unknown even by me, is making final preparations. You will leave tomorrow afternoon on the overnight ferry to Rijeka, which will deliver you early Sunday morning. The anonymous associate will be awaiting your arrival. After establishing contact with you, he will take you on a tour of Sunday evening's events in Opatija. By then, the plot's full itinerary will have been prepared to the last detail. You will listen carefully to his instructions and obey his directions as given. Do exactly what you are told, when you are told to do it, and you will be back on the ferry to this private paradise before you know it. Upon your return, a money transfer will take place from a bank in Europe to a bank in the Caribbean, which will then relay it to a bank account in Cyprus. From there, as you and I sit comfortably on the terrace sharing a bottle of fine French cognac, a telephone call shall be placed to this bank. At that point, one million dollars will be wired electronically to your account. How does that sound, Mr. Martin?"

"What about the girl? When do I see her?"

"Ah, yes, the girl. She will be waiting here with me. She can have the pleasure of listening to the telephone call that we place. Immediately after our business has concluded, all of your clothing, documents, and possessions will be returned. Then you will both be escorted, via sailboat, to any port in the Adriatic Sea that you choose. No one will have the slightest idea of your involvement, nor mine. After we part company, we shall both continue enjoying robust lives. Are there any other questions, Mr. Martin?"

"What happens if the plans change? What if the rally gets canceled, or if Angelli reschedules for another day?"

"Don't worry so much about circumstances that are out of your control, Mr. Martin. Things don't change so quickly here. This event has been planned for weeks, perhaps months. Just do whatever your handler tells you to do. Leave any alterations for him to deal with."

By now, Lucas had tired of the general calling him 'Mr. Martin.' Wanting desperately to draw the conversation to a close, he finished his coffee and announced his intention of preparing for the next day's trip. Feeling almost physically sickened by the meeting's outcome, he tried not to let his frustration show. It was clear now that he was dealing with professionals and that escaping the jam was unlikely.

There has to be a moment of vulnerability, he told himself. When that time came, he would need to strike instinctively, aggressively, and without hesitation.

As the conversation ended, General Parenta stood up from the table with a look of self-importance. Raising his revolver, he waved its barrel from side to side to capture Lucas's attention. Then he uttered a final warning.

"Don't do anything stupid, Mr. Martin. Just do what you are told and everything will go as planned. You have my word on it," said General Parenta. Then he turned his back and walked away.

Lucas went back to the room he had been living in for the last several weeks. Needing distraction, he outlined the itinerary the general had described and searched out the plot's weaknesses. Moments later, he noticed the general through the shuttered window, retracing his path down the driveway. As if on cue, one of the Serbian bodyguards chauffeured his Mercedes from its parked position to a spot at the driveway's edge. On the walk toward the waiting car, an animated conversation again developed between the general and his right-hand man. When the men disappeared, Lucas closed the window and resumed his preparations. The prospects of the next forty-eight hours spun around in his head, making him feel physically and mentally exhausted. He took a short break to concentrate and rest.

•••••

Moving toward the car, General Parenta felt compelled to make sure that Dragoslav had absorbed every aspect of his assignment. He fired off a series of questions, quizzing his subordinate on the scheme's design. The end result was too important and there was no margin for error. Miscalculations that might lead to failure could not be tolerated. The general had to be certain that Dragoslav was in control of the situation. His fortune depended on it.

Together, they rehashed every aspect of the plan. Nothing was omitted. Upon Dragoslav's successful completion of the evaluation, one additional aspect, purposely withheld before, was put into place. At that point, General Parenta stopped walking and took hold of his companion's shoulder. He pulled him closer and lowered the volume of his voice. Speaking slightly above a whisper, the general asked Dragoslav what his exact intentions were with Lucas Martin after Angelli's assassination had been completed.

Obrenović delayed his response, wondering if a trick question had just been served to him. He decided to answer logically, reluctant to question the general's integrity.

"After witnessing the mission's completion and seeing Angelli's corpse dumped into the sea, I will pay off our contact in Opatija and escort Lucas Martin back here…to you?" he answered, with an intonation that was more of a question than a statement.

The general squeezed his cohort's shoulder tighter. Glaring directly into his eyes; he lowered his voice still further.

"No, Dragoslav, absolutely incorrect. You are going to kill Mr. Martin and leave his body *inside* the boat next to Renato Angelli's. Their corpses do not get dumped into the sea. The craft needs to be discovered by the Croatian authorities with both bodies found together. Lucas Martin's pistol, documents, and identification *must* be included. And Dragoslav, before you leave Opatija, eliminate our contact. Never leave witnesses, Dragoslav. Never."

The two men continued walking to where the Mercedes was waiting. They got in and were driven away.

XXV

The drive to Korčula's western side was enhanced by the comfort of the general's Mercedes. Along the way, the late afternoon sun accentuated several stunning views from the island's highest points.

As they traveled, Lucas studied the terrain, which consisted mostly of sloping hills separated by wide, spacious valleys. Near the crest of each bluff, cypress trees pierced the skyline in all directions. Further below, massive vineyards carpeted the valley floors. On both sides of the road, trees bearing figs, olives, and other fruits grew in abundance. Because of the splendid scenery, the nearly half-hour journey passed in what seemed like minutes.

As the car neared the sea, the early evening sunlight reflected off the water's surface, coating everything with cobalt light. The display succeeded in soothing Lucas's frazzled nerves. As the Benz coasted down the final bluff, Vela Luka, a well-known fishing village and one of the island's main ports, came into view.

Lucas noticed how the village setting came alive the closer they got. The village panorama was complimented by the sea's blue backdrop. To the left, a white ferryboat was moored to the harbor wall. From a distance it had seemed tiny, but it dominated the scene on closer approach. As they drove alongside it, the ferry stood out magnificently, like the tip of an iceberg in arctic waters.

Lucas had made this same trip several years ago, and if not for the dreadful circumstances involved with this venture, he would have been happy to be making it again. This time, however, he was anxious and preoccupied with the mission ahead.

By the time the general's car had passed through the harbor gates, several others were already lined up waiting to be driven aboard. The ferry was now undergoing preparations for a trip that it had made a thousand times before. While its engine churned, the smokestack puffed black clouds of exhaust into the air. Scheduled to leave at six o'clock that evening, the ship was expected to arrive in Rijeka at seven the next morning. During this period, Lucas hoped to devise a way out of his desperate situation.

General Parenta's chauffeur steered the Mercedes past the waiting cars before slowing its speed. Under strict orders, the driver shunned pedestrian traffic. He strayed to the lot's far end and parked beneath a palm tree; one of many lining the marina.

At the ticket office, Lucas's escort bought him a one-way fare. There was still an hour before departure, so Lucas and the general walked to the village center where they stopped at an empty cafe for something to drink. Under a sprawled awning advertising a beer company, the rivals sat opposite one another and sipped coffee. Not a word was spoken between them. This suited Lucas fine, as he had no interest engaging in conversation anyway. Instead, he ignored the general and daydreamed in silence.

Scanning his eyes across the 'L'-shaped marina, Lucas did his best to enjoy the moment. A gentle wind was blowing. The cool breeze contrasted nicely with the daytime heat that was still rising from the terrace's asphalt surface. As he looked around, the layout of the palm trees caught his attention. Each stood tall and grandly. Most were decades old. Some, he imagined, had been there for centuries. To pass the time, he studied their tactical placement around the waterfront.

Branching off the main street, thousands of brick-sized, limestone rocks spun a web of walkways throughout the village center. Its dwellings had been built close together; some were painted in bright colors, others were left their natural, concrete gray. All of their windows had wooden shutters that were painted white, green, or brown. Most properties had fruit trees full of maturing mandarins or lemons. Others had large shrubs laden with purple flowers.

Inside the marina, fishing boats were tethered to the bulwark at the opposite end of where the ferry waited in anchor. Scores of small boats, schooners, and rubber dinghies buoyed peacefully in the late afternoon sun; their reflections were cast upward by the crystalline sea. A few seagulls circled overhead. Occasionally, one would plunge headfirst into the water in pursuit of small fish swimming in the shallows.

As he sat, Lucas again felt a peculiar sensation that he was being watched, or stalked, by a hidden person. He examined the surrounding landscape, the dwelling rooftops, and every window for evidence that might justify his unease. Nothing could be seen.

Seated to his right, General Parenta chain-smoked cigarettes while waiting for the mission to begin. Discreetly, Lucas looked him over. He noticed how unhealthy the general now appeared compared to their first meeting several weeks before. His face was sunken and withdrawn; its skin was dry and weathered. New wrinkles had surfaced around his eyes and lips. Once, after the general had lit consecutive cigarettes, Lucas saw that his right thumb and index finger were stained brown from constant exposure to tobacco tar. A gentle tremor showed whenever his fingers were fully extended. General Parenta took great lengths to conceal his unsteadiness by keeping his hands semi-clenched, but his secret was revealed every time he took a drag or lifted his coffee cup. Lucas also noted the efforts his rival made to hide his overstressed nerves. It was the general's intention to appear as always being in complete control. His stressed body, however, was unable to obey the commands that his mind was ordering.

When the ferry horn sounded for the passengers to board, a hint of relief flashed across the general's face. Without haste, he gladly paid the waitress before he and Lucas returned to the car where Lucas's duffel bag was being stored. For security reasons, General

Parenta did not approach the ferry. He chose to stay inconspicuous, unwilling to risk being identified by an informed passenger. He was well aware that at the moment he was unprotected from any threat posed by Croatian nationals who might learn of his presence.

Without saying a word, Lucas turned his back to him and took a few steps toward the waiting transport. Before he was out of earshot, General Parenta decided to issue a final warning to him.

"Remember, Mr. Martin, the girl and I will be here awaiting your return. I expect nothing less than the highest professional results."

Lucas grinned to himself from the thoughts running through his mind. He stopped, turned slowly, and dropped his bag on the concrete.

"And remember, Mr. Martin. Don't lose your concentration, and…" the general began.

Lucas halted the lecture with a scowling face. He raised his right hand and waved his index finger from side to side, stopping the general in midsentence.

"That's enough from you, General. You've said enough. You only need to be concerned with delivering the girl to me and getting me my money. There will be no more commands given to me by you. Understood?"

Smiling broadly, General Parenta leaned backwards with his hands on his hips. "Of course, Mr. Martin! Please, excuse me. I'm afraid that giving orders has been habit-forming. From now on, I shall treat you as a colleague, or better yet, a business partner!"

Lucas did not return the general's smile. With disdain, he jerked the duffel bag over his right shoulder and whirled his body. Then he walked in the direction of the waiting ferry.

●●●●●

The cumbersome passenger ship bellowed a final boarding call before its gangway was retrieved. Twilight overtook the autumn sky as the ferry headed to open sea. Lucas quickly found his cabin, but resisted the urge to remain confined. He dropped off his bag, returned to the open upper deck, and leaned across the port side rail. There he stayed until the sun disappeared over the western horizon.

After the sunset was spent, he moved to the ship's opposite side and faced the Croatian mainland and the Dalmatian archipelago. Enough daylight lingered to reveal the splendor of the mountainous coastline. In solitude, he listened to a lingering group of German tourists who had gathered to marvel at the beauty of the scenery. Wanting to take his mind off his predicament, Lucas gladly conceded his privacy to the troop of retirees who had been enjoying the season's final days basking in the sun. He eavesdropped on their conversations in the German language, and to his surprise, understood everything they said. He was impressed that he had not lost the language skills he had acquired so early in his childhood.

After darkness set in, the wind picked up. Fleeing the blustery gusts, the tourists took refuge inside the climate-controlled lounge. Lucas took advantage of the privacy. He retrieved his leather jacket from his cabin and bought a few cans of pilsner at the bar. Returning to the deserted deck, he found a plastic chair sitting by itself. He pulled his jacket collar snugly around his neck and sat in defiance of the unfavorable conditions.

Looking out above the sea, he studied the village lights of each island as they continued up the chain. There were hundreds of islands in all; each differing in size, shape, and ecology, in spite of their proximity. Lucas knew the largest ones and had visited most of them on various occasions throughout his life. Deep into the night, he identified each by name as the ship lumbered ahead. During the first half of the cruise, the ferry passed Vis, Pašman, and Dugi Otok. Eventually, it chugged passed Silba before reaching Lošinj, where the best and the worst days of his childhood were spent.

As Lucas stared at Lošinj's silhouette, the thought occurred to him that the life and death situation he now faced was, in reality, less dire than his tragic childhood experiences. In fact, over his lifetime, he had survived many tight spots worse than the one he was currently in, and prevailed unharmed under more dangerous circumstances. Surely he could find the fortitude to make it through this crisis. The thought boosted his spirits. For the first time in several days, a latent sense of resilience was aroused in him. It gave a reinvigorating jolt to his fatigued psyche. Almost instantly, he felt stronger and less trapped in General Parenta's web. Still uncertain as to how, every instinct told him that it was possible to escape. He sat still for a while longer and pondered, hoping it was not the alcohol that had given him the sudden burst of confidence.

As the ferry sailed alongside Lošinj, his mind continued to wander. Lucas knew that Goli Island was less than sixty kilometers from Lošinj's opposite shore. A chill ran up his spine at the thought. For decades, Goli had been the home of a Yugoslavian detention center. It had imprisoned hundreds of dissidents, criminals, and political foes during Tito's reign. During the 1980s, Lucas had received reports that his father had finished his life breaking rocks at the facility's labor camp. He tried desperately to confirm the allegations, but official prison records never concurred with the reports of its former inmates. Just before the republic had dissolved, Lucas had gained access to the deserted island by using his State Department connections at the U.S. Embassy. Before his visit, he sifted through all old prison documents he had accumulated. To his dissatisfaction, no evidence that his father had been imprisoned there was ever found. When his investigation ended, he was disgusted by the thought of human life that had wasted away on that desolate rock. He left disappointed and vowed never to return.

As the ferry neared its final destination, the moonlit sky vanished behind heavy, dark clouds. The southerly wind increased in strength until the sea started to swell and the ferry began to sway. Before long, black sheets of rain were slamming across the open deck as if an omen had arrived in anticipation of the next day's affair. Lucas felt queasy.

Soon the island of Cres, the last to be circumnavigated, would come into view. Lucas returned to his cabin and tried to sleep for the remainder of the trip. In three hours, the ferry was scheduled to arrive in the Rijeka port where the anonymous contact would meet him to begin the despicable endeavor.

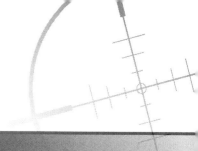

XXVI

In the years before the war, the city of Rijeka had thrived as an industrial port. Now its future was in limbo; all freight traffic had stopped as a direct result of the conflict. Just a few kilometers west along the coast, however, the city of Opatija managed to maintain its stature as a popular resort town, renowned for its Austrian-Hungarian Empire-era architecture, grand villas, and nightlife. Despite their proximity to each other, the two cities seemed to share little more than the erratic weather patterns common to the region of the north Adriatic.

As the ferry entered Rijeka's harbor early Sunday morning, heavy rain was pouring from the turbulent sky. Lucas was aware that Mt. Učka, a long, sloping mountain which towers over Opatija from behind, often holds weather fronts at a standstill. This rainy spell, he knew, could last for days, or weeks. He hoped to be able to use it to his advantage.

Lucas stalked hurriedly down the ferry's exit ramp. On purpose, he was the final passenger to disembark. Earlier, as the vessel came into port, he spied his contact, whom he identified by the car the general said he would be driving. After taking his final step downward, Lucas headed in the man's direction.

The stranger held an umbrella in his left hand and beckoned Lucas with his right one. He stood next to a white Audi. Its engine was running and the windshield wipers worked busily to scrape the constant flow of water from the glass.

Lucas sprinted for the car and plunged into the front passenger seat completely soaked. His contact slid in on the driver's side in similar fashion, slamming his door behind him. Once inside, he collapsed his soggy umbrella and tossed it onto the back floor without saying a word. Both men breathed heavily; a thick condensation accumulated on the windshield. The car's interior reeked of stale cigarette smoke. In time, the driver turned and extended his right hand for his passenger to shake.

"Welcome to Rijeka," he said, grinning casually. "My name is Borislav."

Lucas didn't believe him. He ignored the hand gesture and beamed his eyes directly into those of the driver. "Let's just get this over with, shall we?"

"Yes, of course, Mr. Martin. You are correct - enough with the small talk," the stranger said in English. "Let's get the job started."

Lucas studied the man's characteristics, accent, and apparel, trying to determine his Croatian or Serbian allegiance. He estimated his age to be about fifty. Borislav was a broad, barrel-chested man with muscular shoulders and a pot-belly in its early stages. His legs were short and stump-like. His hair was cropped short; a thick moustache was trimmed closely against his upper lip. His mannerisms suggested that he had been militarily trained, yet his unmanaged physique indicated that it was unlikely that he was an active participant in the ongoing war. Based on his initial impression, Lucas suspected the man to be aligned with General Parenta rather than with the Croatian authorities. He presumed that his handler was well-connected, and likely supported by a powerful network of Serbian civilians living in the vicinity. Lucas caught a glimpse of a nine-millimeter pistol holstered against his left flank, under his raincoat. Lucas speculated that he was carrying additional firepower.

"Here's the program," Borislav said, "Right now, we're going to Opatija. There, we'll inspect the layout of this evening's event. You'll need to be familiarized with the city and the general area.

I'll describe to you the design of tonight's operation at once. We'll rehearse the mission later this afternoon. My associates and I have determined this plan to be the best way of assuring success. It is non-negotiable. You are not allowed to improvise or veer from the given commands. Do you understand, Mr. Martin?"

"I'm positive I already agreed to this a few days ago. Don't repeat it again. If you want to work with a professional, *Borislav*, then act like a professional," Lucas sneered.

The control didn't take Lucas's terse reply as an insult. In reaction, he reached inside his jacket and gripped his pistol's handle. "Just so we understand one another," he said, with a self-satisfied grin on his face.

The Audi cruised through the Rijeka streets in the direction of Opatija. The unrelenting rain eliminated almost all road traffic. Even fewer pedestrians were out at the early hour, except for an occasional old woman, covered in black, en route to Mass at a nearby church.

The car wound and weaved along the rocky coastline. Within fifteen minutes, they were in Opatija, where Borislav guided them through the city center. The town's architecture was genuinely brilliant, but even when his vision was not obscured by the frequent cloudbursts; Lucas was in no mood to appreciate it. From time to time, his handler interrupted Lucas's thoughts to point out landmarks that would be significant for the night's agenda.

"There! Just around this corner is the hotel where the rally will be held. By six o'clock, the place will be packed with people, all pilgrims coming to get guidance from the soon-to-be late Renato Angelli. The gathering is scheduled to last three hours. Afterwards, my sources have confirmed that the politician will be driven to a local restaurant, the Konoba Marun, in the nearby fishing village, Lovran. A private celebration will follow. These festivities usually turn into big, drunken bashes. Security will be lax or minimal. It is there that you will strike. We'll go there next."

"*Security*? Nobody said anything about security. What kind of security? How big of a force? What type of weaponry?

These are questions that I need answers to, Borislav. Don't just brush over details that are vital to the mission's success!" Lucas spouted.

"Don't worry; the situation is completely under control. You don't need to be concerned about a thing," the escort promised.

Lucas had been in the Balkans long enough to know that the words *don't worry* were generally a reliable reason to worry. He continued his interrogation.

"What has been the security's past protocol? What is my escape plan in case of trouble? What are my alternatives, you know, plans B and C? Is there a contingency plan?" Lucas fired, confusing the driver with his intensity.

"Mr. Martin, this celebration will not be the type of organized affair that you are accustomed to. If Angelli has any protection at all, it never amounts to anything more than an over-the-hill bodybuilder who likely won't be armed. All the skilled, able men have been recalled to Slavonia and Lika to fight my Serbian brothers," Boris said, confirming his ethnic loyalty. Spontaneously, he broke into hysterical laughter.

Lucas drew a deep breath. With his right hand, he rubbed his tired eyes. He had been hoping he might be able to alert Angelli's security force, to warn them of the impending plot before it became a reality. Unbelievably, security would be almost nonexistent. There could be no excuse for a failed attempt on an unprotected target. For the moment, his options remained limited, so he decided to play along; to advance the mission's course while at the same time searching for an exit point.

Borislav's wild laughter continued until Lucas couldn't help himself. "I see it doesn't bother you that thousands of innocent people are having their lives destroyed because of a few power-hungry, money-grubbing politicians and professional soldiers. Your commanding general is a fine example," he snapped. "And you think it's funny that civilians on all sides are getting killed and families are being torn apart for their self-serving motives?"

"Mr. Martin...I do what I am told, and that is all. Do you understand? It is not up to me to decide policy or to philosophize about morality. There are only two kinds of warriors in this world: those who fight to win; right or wrong, and those who fight for right; live or die. I choose the best of all options; to win and to live."

Lucas turned his head away. In silence, he stared out the passenger window as the car glided through the villages lining the coast on the way to Lovran. Studying Borislav's demeanor had become less interesting. The man's name wasn't the only thing that Lucas distrusted. Something in his character signaled Lucas to be careful. Maybe it was his tiresome, stupid smile or his attempt at appearing indifferent that warned him of a camouflaged competence.

"We are almost there. Mr. Martin, I advise you to change your train of thought in preparation for the mission ahead. From now on, things will move fast. The young lady's life and your bank account depend upon it," Borislav said, acknowledging his awareness of Lucas's business arrangement.

After entering Lovran, Borislav steered the Audi through the village center before turning into an empty parking lot adjoining its marina.

"We are now within walking distance of the restaurant where the task shall be completed. The mission will be carried out in darkness, most likely in the rain - ideal conditions for success. If you are as good as I think you are, the job shall be accomplished without difficulty. Of this, we are counting on."

The men walked to the back of the car. Borislav took with him a leather attaché case from the back seat and placed it inside the trunk before pulling out two fresh umbrellas. Handing one to Lucas, he slammed the trunk lid closed. A cold, sporadic drizzle fell from the sky. It was impossible to know when the next downpour would begin.

Leaving the car, the men crossed the empty lot on foot. At the fringe of the vacant space, an asphalt footpath that followed the coast began. Two seafood restaurants were positioned on opposing sides of the walkway entrance. As they advanced along the path, they became hidden from the restaurant views. Moving forward, the walkway led them to two separate flights of steps clinging to the limestone ledge. One flight led down toward the sea where a cement dock extended into the water. On the footpath's other side, an identical staircase ascended ten meters to the road above. Rusted, iron railings guarded both of the stairways' edges. Lucas didn't need the scheme to be explained to him in better detail. It was too easy to envision. A more perfect setting for the assassination could not have been selected. There would be no excuse for failure.

"At the bottom of the steps leading down to the sea, a covered boat will be moored, ready for your return after you finish the job. I will be waiting at the street above, prepared to help you carry Mr. Angelli down. After reaching the dock, we'll reboard the boat and weigh down the corpse. Then we'll head a few kilometers out and dump his body overboard. The waves promise to be choppy, I hope you have your sea legs," Borislav added, smiling sarcastically. Shifting his body and attention, he continued. "Up the stairs and across the road is the restaurant where the agitator will be celebrating after the rally ends. The only challenges to the mission's success will lie in your ability to single Angelli out of the crowd long enough to put a bullet through his head, and to carry him here unnoticed. Fortunately for you, there will be lots of laughter, singing, and dancing for distraction. Also, plenty of wine will be flowing, and ample accordion music will cover your actions. A professional of your caliber should have little trouble, I would imagine," the general's agent added. There was obvious spite in his voice and Borislav now seemed to be enjoying the position of dominance that he held.

Next, the men climbed up the steps to scout the restaurant grounds. The structure was well sheltered, easy to access, and without surveillance. Aside from the task of isolating his target, Lucas could see no reason to fail. It would be too simple.

"What about the house on the restaurant's right side?" Lucas queried.

"My sources tell me it's inhabited by an old lady who goes to bed early and always closes the windows because of the music. The shutters will be drawn if the rain continues falling throughout the night. She has no dog, but the neighbor on her left owns a German shepherd. It is always chained."

Lucas studied the layout some more. He gauged the distance from the restaurant to the old lady's house to be less than thirty meters. Both buildings were made of stone and none of the house's windows faced the restaurant. Around back, one large window was placed near a closed door. The entire backside was blocked from the restaurant's view by a towering stack of chopped wood that served the old lady as her winter source of heat.

The men moved about the grounds, taking care not to draw attention. When Borislav stopped to light a cigarette, Lucas escaped his companion's supervision and wandered toward the old lady's house. From a distance, he spied an axe tucked within a crevice of the woodpile. The tool was rusted from exposure to the elements and looked to have been little used. Wanting not to raise suspicion, he quickly returned and drifted toward the restaurant's rear entrance. Along the way, he noted all its windows, but was unable to locate the one he was searching for, the window to the men's room. As he crept around the backside, a cook bounded out from the kitchen door. Lucas reacted at once. He pressed himself to the wall and backpedaled vigilantly, taking care not to lose his balance as he moved. Unsatisfied with his findings, he nevertheless returned to Borislav's side. Then both men nonchalantly returned to the seaside walkway.

"It will be next to impossible getting the politician alone inside the restaurant,' Lucas explained as they walked. "If the target cannot be separated from the crowd, then the job will have to be performed behind the neighbor's house. Even if I can succeed in luring him away, the oldest of ladies will be awakened by a gunshot."

Instantly, Lucas's handler reached into his jacket and removed a metallic, tube-shaped object. At first, he cupped it protectively in his palm, and then slowly revealed it for Lucas to see. "We thought of that also. It's nice to know that we are all in agreement," he said, now displaying a pistol's sound suppressor in his opened hand. "It's by no coincidence that this one works well with a nine-millimeter Berretta," Borislav added. Then he lifted his jacket and showed Lucas his lost pistol. "Compliments of General Parenta," he added.

"Here is a recap," Borislav went on, pointing at the concrete dock below. "We will approach that landing by sea at ten P.M. You will scale the steps and stake out the restaurant, carrying with you a plastic tarp and enough duct tape to seal Angelli's dead body. Between ten P.M. and two A.M., you will stalk the politician until the ideal moment arrives. After getting him alone, you will fire a single round into the back of his head. There may be only one chance at success, so you better make it count. Afterwards, you will wrap his body and bring him across the road to where I'll be waiting. Together, we'll carry the politician down and lift him into the boat. Once that's done, we'll head out to sea to dump him. When we return to the marina, I'll call to inform the general. As soon as I hang up the phone, we'll leave for Dalmatia to complete your business agreement. It is as easy as that. Any questions?"

Lucas had none. In theory, the simple, well-organized plan was sure to succeed. The lack of security would make it an easy job to carry out. In fact, the operation could have been successfully performed by someone much less experienced than he was. After further contemplation, Lucas began to question the necessity of his involvement. The general's story didn't add up. There was no reason that his top man, Dragoslav Obrenović, couldn't execute such a basic procedure. There had to be another reason for his presence. The more he thought about it, the more concerned he became. He decided to go forward, using his utmost caution, and vowing not to take his eyes from Borislav for the rest of the day.

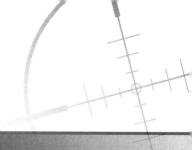

XXVII

The autumn day succumbed to night prematurely, pressured by the relentless, rain-filled sky. By six o'clock, all lingering daylight had changed to darkness, and every streetlamp glowed accordingly. The wind, which was growing stronger as the evening progressed, exacerbated the misery that the frequent downpours created. The disagreeable weather confined most of the village residents to the comfort of their homes. Except for a handful of passing cars on route to Opatija, there was little sign of life to impede Lucas from completing his assignment.

At 9:40 that evening, a small boat was crashing over choppy waves along the Adriatic coast. Battling the treacherous sea, the schooner motored through a blanket of gloom. Inside its cabin, Lucas sat blindfolded, dressed in black and covered in raingear. As he held tightly to the wall, he mentally reviewed that afternoon's events while the vessel chugged ahead.

●●●●●

Almost five hours earlier, Lucas and Borislav had rehearsed the mission a final time. Afterwards, they drove to a nearby village named Medveja, where they sat in a private corner of a seafood restaurant and ate fish caught in the day's earliest hours, just before the weather had turned for the worse. Lucas devoured his food ravenously. He had not eaten in the last eighteen hours. Borislav, by contrast, ate with relish. He happily gorged on grilled whitefish and gulped glassfuls of wine between bites. The spectacle disgusted Lucas. Had it not been for his demanding hunger pangs, he would have boycotted the meal in protest of the upcoming adventure. Yet he needed the energy; he had to eat if he wanted the stamina to defeat his adversaries and escape his dilemma.

"That's it, Mr. Martin. Eat! The sea is rough. Some pasta will help to keep your stomach calm," Borislav bellowed, his mouth full of fish. Smiling condescendingly, he continued chewing loudly before taking another big swig of wine.

Lucas drank only water, but he took every opportunity to refill Borislav's emptied wineglass. *Like a college student trying to get his date drunk*, he thought sardonically to himself. Yet he was aware of an advantage he might have if his chaperon became intoxicated.

After the meal, the men sat and said little to one another. Borislav relaxed in the solitude, swilling wine and smoking American cigarettes. Only the sound of large raindrops, pounding against the windows nearest their table, broke the silence.

Lucas hated every moment of that afternoon. His mind stirred impatiently in anticipation of the task ahead. The wait was almost unbearable. The wasted time tested his resolve and ate at his conscience. At the moment, evading the coming tragedy seemed unlikely; preventing it appeared to be impossible. Soon the nightmare would be over, at least. Lucas's options were few, and the situation was out of his control. He would eventually have to choose a course of action, and then act upon his decision. The safety of his friend's younger sister, whom he barely knew, troubled him deeply and elevated his anxieties.

As afternoon turned to evening, the men continued to dawdle. Lucas was unclear of the immediate plan. He presumed that his companion was expecting a colleague who would assist in the caper. After a long period of lost time, Borislav checked his watch, and then got up and walked to the restaurant's reception area, displaying a noticeably drunken swagger.

Standing in the doorway, another man greeted him with a handshake. Lucas watched with interest as they talked. He studied their mannerisms as their conversation progressed. When the pair parted company, Borislav returned in different character. He had sobered; his demeanor was businesslike. Now he engaged Lucas with the facial expression of a boxing trainer lecturing his fighter between rounds of a bout. Lucas knew the moment had come.

"It is time to put you to work, Mr. Martin. We are set to move within the hour," the Serbian operative said. "My associate is accumulating the proper attire right now. We are exactly on schedule, and everything is proceeding as planned. The routine will go just as we drilled this afternoon. This will be the easiest money that you have ever made," he quipped. A fiery glaze had surfaced in Borislav's bloodshot eyes.

Ten minutes later, Lucas was ushered out of the restaurant and into the backseat of Borislav's car. Before he could evaluate the dynamics of the moment, he had changed his clothes and covered himself with drab, insulated rainwear. The apparel would undoubtedly serve him well; as it was impossible to know how long he would be forced to wait in the rain for his target to appear. Soon the Audi was put into gear. Time now raced by.

Borislav put basic security precautions into place. Lucas was blindfolded, rendering him unable to recognize which marina the boat would leave from. Undeterred, Lucas counted the turns and calculated the direction and distance driven in an effort to estimate the marina's location. It was only a short drive before the car rolled to a stop. A few seconds later, Lucas was led outside and guided aboard a small boat that was immediately put to sea.

After the schooner left the marina's protection, it bounced over the rough water toward its destination. Lucas sat opposite of Borislav while a third man commandeered the helm. During the trip, he replayed the mission's details in his mind's eye. As the boat neared the concrete landing at the bottom of the rock wall scouted earlier that day, his blindfold was removed. It was now 9:50.

● ● ● ● ●

The tiny cabin provided barely enough room for the three men to move around. As they approached the shore, the foul weather caused the small craft to rock and roll, making it difficult for Borislav's associate to lower anchor and moor to the dock. Lucas offered his assistance, but was reprimanded on the spot.

"Let him do his job, Mr. Martin. You have more important things to consider," his handler growled. Before long, Lucas sensed the presence of another accomplice helping out on shore.

From the briefcase resting on his lap, Borislav took out Lucas's nine-millimeter Beretta. For effect, he waved it around his captive's face.

"You'll need this," he said. Twirling the weapon once, he lowered it callously. "And this, as well," he added, while pulling the silencer from the satchel. With a few quick twists, he screwed it into place. Finally, the attaché was stowed inside a locked compartment.

Lucas said nothing; he could think of no useful reply.

Borislav continued, "Do you recall the covered bus stop at the top of the steps? It has total visibility of the area in which you will be working. I will be waiting there, watching your every move. After you finish the job, bring the body down to the road. Now listen carefully: you will not transfer Angelli's corpse across the main street until after I signal that the coast is clear. When I wave, you move across as fast as you can. After you reach my position, I'll help you to lug him down the steps. After that, we'll be out to sea to feed him to the fish. Once that's done, your duty is finished; the girl's safety is guaranteed."

At exactly ten o'clock, the boat was securely tied. No one had noticed its presence. The nameless third man was dismissed. Two at a time, he scaled the stairs upward before disappearing over the top. In the distance, Lucas faintly heard a car door slam shut and an automobile's engine start up. A second more passed before the vehicle sped away.

Borislav and Lucas were now alone inside the cabin. Wind-whipped rain pelted against its Plexiglas windows while unruly waves sprayed over its hull and the vessel shook violently in response. From his shirt pocket, Borislav removed one nine-millimeter round and inserted it into the Beretta's chamber with a sudden, angry click.

"Remember, Mr. Martin, you'll probably have only one chance at success. Make it count. One bullet into the back of the head," the Serb repeated. Leaning forward, he dug his right thumbnail deep into the back of Lucas's skull. "I'm sure that you're aware of the vital area at the base of the brainstem. It's a guaranteed kill point," he said. Then he passed the weapon to Lucas, handle first. "And Mr. Martin..." Boris started, before stopping himself from repeating another warning. Instead, he lifted his plastic rain poncho and exposed a fully-loaded automatic pistol strapped to his waist.

Lucas looked away contemptuously. He got the message. Like a bolt of lightning he was out of the boat and up the steps outside. The air was cold, heavy, and damp. As he breathed, each exhalation ejected a warm mist that vanished into the night. He wished that he could do the same.

After reaching the top step, Lucas glanced at the bus stop where Borislav would be waiting. He stood still momentarily to check the area for unexpected activity. There was none, so he crossed the road and hustled over to the restaurant's far side.

Lucas peered through a window on the building's west end. It was open at the top and located not far from the chimney of a well-lit fireplace. He could feel the heat it emitted through his insulated clothing, and a trace of steam was released whenever the wind gusted and slapped cold droplets of rain against its warm bricks. Inside, a party was in its early stages. It appeared to be growing by the minute. Lucas was sure he could not be seen.

As he watched the celebration develop, his target was identified. Renato Angelli stood in the center of the dining room, proudly greeting well-wishers who were congratulating him on the speech he had given earlier that evening. At that moment, the master of ceremonies appeared to be unprotected.

Italian was the dominant language in the room. Lucas listened closely and tried to follow the conversations. He could tell that Renato Angelli was held in high regard. The politician presented himself as a professional, natural leader who was fighting for his people, much to the disapproval of the authorities in Zagreb. Now the motives brewing in the Croatian capital had become clearer to Lucas. It was a dastardly deed that he was being forced to commit, yet he could still see no way out. Before long, it would be time to act.

The restaurant's interior was cozy and welcoming. Oaken tables and chairs stood on a floor of polished tile; large oak panels covered the lower two thirds of the plaster walls. The upper third was painted white and decorated with seascape paintings. Shelves with antiques decorated the room's periphery. Several miniature Italian flags in red, white, and green were dispersed throughout the restaurant. A large banner proclaiming *"Viva L'Italia"* was boldly draped across the main dining room wall. As the room swelled with people, accordion music began to play, enhancing the festive mood.

Against the wall opposite the fireplace, Lucas saw a buffet table laden with sliced prosciutto, salami, and bread. Cheese and olives were set out on other trays. Several metal canisters filled with *Fuži*, a type of pasta popular in Istria, were surrounded by others containing assorted sauces. A handful of waiters carried out countless flasks of red and white wine and systematically placed them at the guests' tables. Gradually, the whole restaurant filled with a cheerful atmosphere. Singing, laughing, and dancing soon erupted. A steady stream of cigarette smoke rolled out of the vented window along with increasing levels of noise. The ideal moment was drawing near.

Initially, Lucas decided that the men's room would be the ideal spot to isolate his target. He guided his hand along the stucco wall and hunted for the restroom whose location he had been unable to pinpoint earlier in the day. He found it, but was quickly disappointed. After locating the window, he discovered it to be too high to look through and too narrow to enter. The back door connecting to the kitchen was equally inadequate. It was in constant use by the busy kitchen staff. He would be unable to enter unseen. For obvious reasons, the front door was not an option. An alternative solution would need to be found in the coming hours; when the party was in full swing, so that Renato Angelli would not be immediately missed. He would have to find some way in.

Lucas relocated to the yard of the neighboring house, where Borislav had told him the old lady lived. He walked softly and took a position that allowed him to observe the restaurant out of sight. The rain began to fall harder, so he drew his hood tightly over his head. Glancing toward the bus stop, he spotted his Serbian chaperon perched like a hawk surveying the terrain. He could clearly see the glow of Borislav's cigarette cherry betraying his shadow. Phantom-like, Lucas leaned against the woodpile and monitored the party's traffic while the raindrops dripped from his brow.

After almost two hours of waiting, Lucas noticed that a pattern had developed. Many partygoers chose to escape the crowd and cool off on the restaurant's covered terrace. Usually, they smoked cigarettes under the canopy before returning to the festivities inside. It was Lucas's hope that Renato Angelli would take such a break. As the very thought disappeared in his mind, an unexpected event occurred. Alone and unguarded, Angelli emerged through the doorway.

Seconds later, the politician was holding a lit cigarette. Under the restaurant awning, the guest of honor stood alone and smoked. Lucas froze momentarily. His heart raced in anticipation. Considering his choices, he quickly formed a plan of action. A steady drizzle continued falling. Lucas was certain that Borislav was watching the drama unfold.

Once the first cigarette had been extinguished, the politician reached for another. As he lit the second, the rain let up in intensity. During the lapse, Angelli looked in all directions before climbing down the terrace steps. Unexpectedly, he hurried through the mist in the direction of the neighbor's woodpile, taking quick drags from his cigarette as he walked. Lucas leaned backwards and tried to remain invisible. Without a sound, he retreated and took refuge in a blind spot further behind the house. If Renato Angelli appeared around the corner, he would have to strike. He prepared his pistol and waited. He heard footsteps sloshing through the soggy grass. It had to be him, it could be no other.

Just one bullet...better make it count, Lucas remembered.

Taking one last look around, he spotted the rusted axe left abandoned in the rain. An idea struck him. He lowered the pistol and slid it under his belt. Grabbing the neglected tool, he squeezed its handle firmly and rotated the blade away from the point of impact. Lucas stalked his victim some more.

It wasn't long before the scent of cigarette smoke filled the damp air. Lucas waited a bit longer and listened carefully, trying to learn what the politician was doing. A moment later he heard it. Mixed with the patter of the light rain was the familiar echo of a man relieving himself, less than two meters away. Both men were hidden from all views. Lucas had only seconds to act. Raising the makeshift club, he glided into place.

This is going to hurt, but maybe you'll have a chance to live, he thought before attacking.

When he heard the distinctive metallic sound of a lifted zipper, Lucas pounced with a lion's quickness. In an instant, it was over. The club's head landed squarely in the back of Angelli's head. The blow jarred the politician's cerebellum causing his knees to buckle. He staggered a few steps until his body collapsed facedown in the mud. Angelli convulsed briefly before relaxing. It was a clean concussion. Soon the politician was perfectly still.

Again the rain picked up. There was no time to waste, so Lucas unfolded the tarp and wrapped the bureaucrat's body from head to toe. He predicted that Borislav would be too drunk, wet, and lazy to check for the bullet's entry wound. Using his Swiss Army knife, he cut several slits in the plastic to allow Angelli access to fresh oxygen. Then, with all his might, he heaved his victim over his shoulder and carried him toward the sea. A few minutes more and it would all be over.

"Just one bullet…better make it count," Lucas mumbled to himself as he moved. One by one, he shuffled his tired legs forward in the direction of the waiting Serbian agent.

Borislav flicked out his half-smoked cigarette when he saw Lucas coming. Timing was crucial. At any moment, someone could emerge from the restaurant and witness what was going on. He readied his weapon and prepared to kill anyone who stumbled upon them.

In spite of Angelli's awkward frame, Lucas made good progress. His feet splashed through puddles as he scurried over the rain-soaked pavement. As planned, Borislav helped carry the cumbersome load down the steps. As they neared the side of the boat, a heavier downpour began to fall. Lightning filled the night sky.

Lucas boarded first and took hold of Angelli's limp legs. A flurry of impulses poured through his brain. Pretending to hoist the unconscious man, he positioned himself to perform a scheme that had been brewing in his mind. Seconds before, he had decided to wait until Borislav's hands were full and his attention was distracted by the matter at hand. Then, when his adversary was unprepared, Lucas was going to drop Angelli's legs, pull the Berretta from his waist, and shoot Borislav in the heart.

But the opportunity never came. As another lightning bolt illuminated the night sky, Lucas looked up to an unexpected sight. Borislav remained standing with his pistol pointed at him. Surprised by the double-cross, he stood dumbfounded. He had nowhere to run and no leverage with which to negotiate. Saying nothing, he awaited his fate. Borislav began to speak, but his words were drowned out by the rumbling thunder. Lucas assumed his end was near.

"You have been a good accomplice, Mr. Martin…!" Boris shouted, before being muted by a loud thunderclap. The Serbian agent took aim.

A brief moment passed before more lightning lit up the sky, followed by another roar of thunder from above. This time, an additional blast boomed in concert with the storm. It was the roar of a gunshot fired from nearby. When it ended, Borislav's body lurched forward and crashed into the boat. Lucas was knocked off balance by the sudden sway. Both men landed on the deck, with Borislav's heavy mass on top. Some time passed before Lucas was able to breathe. Borislav did not.

As Lucas regained his senses, he could see blood mixing with the rainwater on the vessel's floorboards. He was unsure if any of it was his own. Still pinned on his back, he wrenched his neck to view the landing, far too confused to know what had just happened. Then suddenly, between waves, he felt the boat tilt unnaturally. Lucas sensed that another person had boarded. He struggled to free the weapon that was still under his belt, but the weight of Borislav's body made it impossible. When Lucas looked up again, he saw that another man had indeed boarded the boat. It wasn't long before the familiar face with the twisted lip was staring down at him from above. In his right hand, Dragoslav Obrenović held a Scorpion submachine gun that was pointed at Lucas's face.

"I should have done this a couple of months ago," Obrenović scowled. Lucas squinted, returning a cold stare into the assassin's icy eyes. Beneath Borislav's girth, he searched madly for his pistol. A few more seconds ticked by before another explosion ignited through the storm. This blast was louder than the first, though it originated from further away. Instantly, the machine gun fell from Dragoslav's hand and slammed into Lucas's forehead. Like falling timber, the Serbian assassin landed on top of the pile of bodies. Smothered by the extra weight, Lucas struggled for air, kicking and squirming to receive oxygen. Now even more blood was flowing in the boat. With one massive thrust, Lucas freed the pistol from his belt just as the latest gunman rushed down the concrete steps. The unknown assailant held the metal rail with his right hand and wielded a sawed-off shotgun in his left one. Urgently, Lucas took aim with the pistol, but balked from firing at the sound of the stranger's pleading voice.

"Lucas, *stop*! Don't shoot. It's me, Edis! Don't shoot!"

XXVIII

"**W**here the hell did you come from?" Lucas asked as his head began to clear. He was elated to see his friend. The timing could not have been better.

Edis reached out his hand and helped Lucas to his feet.

"It looks like I arrived in the nick of time. Just like in a Hollywood movie, eh?" his young companion joked. "How did you get into this fix?"

Still dazed, Lucas did not answer. The men looked around to assess the extent of their troubles. The crash of thunder had disguised the gun blasts. No one else was in sight; for the moment, they remained undiscovered. But there wasn't much time.

"It's a long story, although I suppose you'll need to hear it," Lucas finally replied. "How did you get here?"

"I borrowed an ancient Fiat Zastava from a sleeping family in Dalmatia. It is slow, unsteady, and hell to drive in the rain. I barely made it to Rijeka before your ferry arrived," Edis said.

"You've been following me since Korčula?"

"My friend, I've been following you since the Serbian militia carried you and the girl off the Sarajevo cobblestones," Edis said. "It is a good thing you left me the money. You can always get what you need as long as you have plenty of cash."

"God, Edis, the girl! There's something you need to know..." Lucas said. He stopped to catch his breath.

"What? What is it?" Edis asked.

"The girl...she's...your sister. She's alive," Lucas finished. He inhaled deeply. "But I'm afraid not for much longer if we don't hurry. We need to clean up this mess and get back to Dalmatia on the double!"

Lucas rummaged through Boris's many pockets. After several tries, he found what he was looking for: the keys to the white Audi.

"Help me get the wrapped body back on shore. That man is alive and needs to be taken someplace safe. I think there's a hospital nearby. Right after that, we'll get on the road," Lucas ordered. "Somewhere around here is a car that can get us there in good time. We have to be on the first ferry from Split to Korčula in the morning or your sister will be killed."

The fact that his sister was alive was slow to be grasped by Edis. Shocked by the revelation, he stood rigid with a confused look upon his face. Lucas moved over to him, grabbed his shoulders, and shook hard twice.

"Edis, you need to be alert and ready to act! We have very little time to save her life," he barked.

The men lifted Renato Angelli and carried him back up the stairs. At the top step, Lucas kept the body hidden while Edis retrieved the old Fiat. After parking curbside, they took turns stuffing the comatose politician in. Once out of the rain, Lucas peeled the plastic back to check his condition. Renato Angelli was definitely alive. His respiration was faint, but a pulse was palpable over both carotid arteries. Lucas smiled with relief.

"He'll be okay, but I'm sure his head will ache for a while. He may have to take a month or so away from politicking," he said to Edis. *I probably did him a favor,* he thought to himself.

Lucas climbed back down the steps and reboarded the boat. With one swift kick, he opened the compartment where Borislav had stowed his briefcase. He pulled it out and set it aside. Then he searched the corpses for anything useful. He took Borislav's watch and also his wallet. Counting the cash inside, he was satisfied with the number of Deutschmarks it contained. Dragoslav Obrenović was next. A packet of papers, snugly wrapped in plastic, was hidden in his raincoat's lining. Lucas removed it and slipped it into his jacket as the rain pounded against the cabin. From one of Dragoslav's outer pockets Lucas took a black leather case that held a rectangular device inside. Unable to ascertain its function in the downpour, he stuck it in the briefcase before passing it to Edis, who was now standing on the dock alongside the boat. Finally, he searched the floor for other items of importance. Dragoslav Obrenović's submachine gun was quickly located and passed to Edis. With a little more effort, Lucas found Borislav's nine-millimeter pistol hidden under his torso.

The men dashed up the concrete steps and put the supplies into the Fiat. Before leaving, they returned to the schooner a final time. With perfect teamwork, Edis unfastened the lines while his partner hoisted the anchor. Once the boat had been freed, Edis secured it while Lucas tied the steering mechanism. Next, Edis pointed the bow to the open sea while Lucas started its engine and pushed the throttle forward. There was just enough time for Lucas to jump safely from the craft as Edis released his hold.

The boat bobbed blindly out to sea. The men were certain that days would pass before the dead Serb agents would be discovered lying in a pool of crimson water. Lucas didn't give the matter another thought.

With no time to waste, they rushed back up the steps. The storm's intensity began to diminish. Across the road, the celebration had not yet ended, though some people were using the break in the rain as an excuse to leave. Several partygoers could be seen in the distance, dashing toward their cars under their umbrellas' cover. For the moment, it appeared that Renato Angelli's absence remained unnoticed. There would be just enough time for Lucas and Edis to make their escape.

The overloaded Fiat labored toward the Lovran hospital. En route, they decided it would be too risky to deliver Angelli to the hospital entrance. Instead, they schemed to drop him where he could be quickly found by the emergency staff. When the Fiat had pulled to the front gate, they lifted the politician out of the car. Lucas rechecked his vital signs. This time, his pulse had stabilized and his breathing was stronger. Every so often, he mumbled words in Italian. Soon he would regain full consciousness.

Edis helped Lucas prop Renato Angelli against the perimeter wall. Lucas then blasted the car's horn for nearly a minute. Eventually, the hospital's outdoor lighting switched on. Both men shouted out, attempting to attract aid that was slow in coming. Finally, an ambulance sped near as the old Fiat pulled away. Watching through the car's mirrors, they confirmed that help had arrived. Lucas was confident that Renato Angelli would recover without any problems.

From Lovran, they drove toward Opatija. It was now 12:40 in the morning. The men desperately needed to find the faster Audi in order to reach Split before the morning ferry left for Korčula. On a hunch, Lucas instructed Edis to turn into the marina in Ičići; a fishing village located about five kilometers away. To their immense relief, the car sat alone in a corner space.

"Thank God for this," Lucas said to Edis, "Your sister may have a chance."

"We've got a lot of catching up to do while we're on the road," Edis said.

"Just get in the car. You can talk first while I drive," Lucas ordered.

XXIX

The men transferred their things into the Audi without delay. Just as they finished, another hard rain began to fall.

Lucas slid behind the steering wheel and hid the weapons under his seat. Then he took the pouch he found in Dragoslav Obrenović's raincoat, opened it, and examined its contents. Edis, who had Borislav's briefcase resting on his lap, waited before opening it.

"What's in the packet?" Edis asked his friend.

A satisfied look appeared on Lucas's face. Wrapped tightly inside were his passport, U.N. identification, and NATO authorization. The letter from his father and the picture from his childhood were also enclosed. Each had been safely preserved; dry from the rain, and spared from the fatal gun blast. Now various obstacles which might impede their return down the mainland might be avoided. The documents would grant them passage through roadblocks and expedite the proceedings at military checkpoints. Even with these new aids, however, travel through the war-infested Lika region, their most direct option, was certain to be dangerous. Battles were flaring daily - sometimes by the hour. Fortunately, an alternate route came to Lucas's mind; a safer option. For now, all signs suggested that Edis's sister could be saved.

Feeling almost gleeful, Lucas set the documents aside and quickly familiarized himself with the car's dashboard controls. While he did, Edis sifted through Borislav's satchel's contents. He quickly found something that reaffirmed the seriousness of their situation.

Assorted items and bundles of papers filled the briefcase. After picking through a random stack, Edis found the hard leather case that Lucas had put inside while still in the boat's cabin. The case held an electronic gadget resembling a telephone, though unlike one that Edis had ever seen before. He strained his eyes examining it in the poor lighting. It was obviously some kind of communications device, but he was unable to determine exactly how it might be used, so he referred it to Lucas.

"How do you think this works?" he asked, passing it over.

An expression of grave concern wiped away his partner's approving smile. Lucas postponed his reply until he had studied the object more closely. After raising it to the dome light, he became noticeably agitated. He contemplated a bit longer before answering, "This could be big trouble. It may just be the device that gets your sister killed."

Edis snatched it away and held it to the light. "*Jebote!*" he swore, "What is it?"

"It's a cellular telephone. It can be used from anywhere, and at any time. I saw a demonstration of one at a technology show in Bangkok. If I'm correct, it will be ringing soon. A certain general will want to know the status of his business deal."

"Oh, shit! Lucas, what are we going to do?"

"Nothing. If it rings, don't answer it. Better yet, let's remove the battery. The general will be informed that the signal has been lost, but won't be given an explanation why. We don't have much time. It's almost one o'clock now...with a little luck, he won't overreact until tomorrow morning. Let's get on the road."

Lucas started the car and pressed hard on the accelerator. In minutes, they had left Opatija behind and were racing through the heart of Rijeka. As they exited the port city, their speeding auto was waved over by a policeman on late night patrol. Lucas didn't consider stopping, or even slowing. Rather, he deliberately hit the gas and blazed past the drenched civil servant. A quick glimpse into the rearview mirror showed that the policeman was unresponsive to his defiance of the law. He stood passively, holding his miniature stop sign high above his head with a mixed expression of surprise and disbelief showing on his face. The Audi rolled forward, the officer giving its unlawful occupants no threat of delay.

"Oh, my Croatia!" Lucas said, chuckling lightly. Edis joined with a grin of his own.

The next forty minutes passed in silence. To drive at high speeds along this curving costal road demanded complete attention and absolute precision. Lucas kept his eyes glued to the road as the sedan whipped past towns whose names he recognized: Bakarac, Crikvenica, Senj.

After breezing through Senj, the men debated the best choice of travel routes. Lucas opposed taking the more direct path through Lika. He was extremely wary of driving through the region's war-torn mountains, despite his recovered credentials. Heavy fighting was underway, and their way was sure to be obstructed by several Serbian militias that were trying to secure dominance in the region. Edis, who had journeyed north just two days before, was able to confirm his suspicions. On his drive to Rijeka, he had witnessed the exodus of some villagers who were left homeless as a result of the fighting. Once, when he stopped for directions, one of them told him that Serbian paramilitaries were accosting the people from his village who refused to leave. As a result, many had fled their homes out of fear for their lives. And further south, several JNA units had the Croatian coastal city of Zadar surrounded in a classic attempt to divide the new republic in half and gain access to the sea. Getting past Zadar to reach Split was going to be tricky. If they could penetrate Zadar, a thin strip of safe travel along the Dalmatian coast still remained.

As the Audi pressed onward, slow-moving military convoys appeared and stalled their progress. At several points, Lucas was forced to perform terrifying passes around hairpin turns. Edis clung tightly to the car's interior, not saying anything. He was eager to tell Lucas the saga of his past few months, but now was hardly the time.

"Slow down here," Edis cautioned. "The ferry landing turnoff is a poorly-marked crossroad. In the dark, it will be easy to miss. I hope the ferry is running at this late hour."

"It should be. Since the war started, they've been operating at night with their lights off to avoid detection. It's safer that way - the JNA has a very capable air force," Lucas replied.

Just as he finished his sentence, Lucas left the main highway and steered down the winding road leading to a village named Prizna. On the village outskirts, a lonesome ferry floated dockside in the dark. The Audi took a position behind a line of three automobiles and a longer chain of military vehicles all waiting to cross the channel. There would be no problem finding space on the next crossing.

Less than thirty minutes later, the ferry had docked at the island of Pag. As soon as its metal platform was lowered, the Audi bounced off it and onto the island's north shore. The instant all four tires had touched land, Lucas stomped on the gas and swerved around the lumbering military convoy. Now there was traffic-free travel to the island's southern tip, where a short bridge reconnected it to the Croatian mainland.

They reached the link in record time. While driving over it, Lucas turned off the headlights until they were safely across. Back on the mainland, a twenty-minute drive through the Poljica region was necessary before Zadar came into view.

Blockades manned by the Croatian military surrounded Zadar. The municipality was blackened; all power was out. Fires burned in the distance. Nevertheless, many civilians were moving about freely under the cover of night. Surprisingly, the Audi breezed through the city's war-torn interior without any problems. Lucas picked a cautious path through the city center before abandoning it in a thankless haste. The pair wondered aloud when the next round of artillery shells would again start falling from the sky.

After Zadar, the road straightened considerably. As the car raced down the coast, Lucas glanced at Edis and nodded his head, acknowledging that it was a suitable time to hear his account. At last, the overdue conversation began.

"Let's hear it, young man. Tell me the tale. How long have you been following me? How did you handle yourself?"

Edis started hesitantly. "Lucas, I saw the car get hit in Sarajevo. Believe me; I did the best I could. I swear that if I had known that the girl was my sister, I would have shown no mercy on those Serbian bastards!"

"Don't worry about it. You responded properly. You did what you were told to do. Besides, you were outnumbered and too far out of range to help. We were up against real professionals. I'm lucky to be alive. You did a fine job," Lucas said. "After they took us, what happened next?"

"I followed the paramilitary unit to where they held you. I was certain they wouldn't stay in that neighborhood for long – as you were in the middle of a combat zone!" Edis said. "Mortars, artillery shells, and rockets were landing all around the building you were in - most of it was JNA fire. I ran back, organized the money and gear you left, and prepared to follow you on a moment's notice. I found a spot where I could monitor your movement; a hideout that provided me with instant mobility," he added, excitedly. "Getting out of Sarajevo was the hardest part. Luckily, I was able to stay in contact with the Muslim resistance. Some friends of some friends arranged for me to buy my way out of the city."

"How? There hasn't been access out of the city since the siege began," Lucas said. "I tried every possible way to get out!"

"The Muslims have constructed a tunnel under the airport. It connects the city to the western suburbs. Few people have access to it, but with the right connections and a sufficient amount of cash, passage can be obtained," Edis answered.

"That tunnel could save the city! But..."

Edis interrupted, "At first I wasn't sure if you were even alive. But early the next morning, I saw you bandaged and I knew that your injuries had been treated. Later that day, some Serbian militia took you and the girl - I mean, my sister - away in a Mercedes. The resistance kept me informed of your position. A short time later, I made my way out and into the hills. I was able to acquire a car with enough gasoline to follow you to the border. Along the way, I got lost for a while. By chance, I guessed correctly at the destination the Mercedes was headed and was able to catch up. I saw it stop before a Croatian military checkpoint near Mostar. There, they moved you into another vehicle where they kept you under guard. From then on, things got weirder," Edis said. Before continuing, he stopped to gather his thoughts.

Lucas was intrigued. He waited impatiently for his friend to continue.

"After a while, a second Mercedes joined the first. This one had a Croatian officer in it; I could tell by his uniform. From a distance, I followed those cars to an abandoned factory outside the city limits. It was after nightfall, so I climbed through the woods in the dark to where I saw their headlight's shining. I managed to reach a spot near where the Serbian general was parked. A meeting took place between him, the Croatian officer, and a Bosnian-Serb politician. I got close enough to hear some of their conversation. They had some kind of scheme to use you as a tool to implicate the U.S. government with tampering in the Republic of Yugoslavia's national affairs. That's when I almost got discovered. I barely escaped through the brush, dodging automatic weapon fire the entire time!"

"Of course!" Lucas exclaimed, pounding the steering wheel with his right palm. "There had to be a better reason why General Parenta insisted that I carry out the assassination since his own men could have easily done the job."

"But why? What difference does your involvement make? Everyone knows that the West will intervene eventually."

"The question isn't why, Edis, but when? If two Serbian officials met with a Croat, then some dirty business is taking place. It must be profitable because they don't want to shut the operation down yet," Lucas said. "Listen, the U.S. State Department has been applying heavy pressure on all sides to end the fighting - especially on the Serbs. My involvement in the assassination of a political official in ex-Yugoslavia would link me to the U.S. government. That connection could force the pressure valve to be released. And it also explains the dual-party meeting on the island of Korčula I walked in on unexpectedly."

"My God, everything is for sale in this place. Imagine that, a Serbian general vacationing with the enemy in the middle of the war!"

"Edis, it's no secret that wars are extremely profitable. It's been proven throughout history. It is big business for those in control at the expense of the masses. I've witnessed it too many times," Lucas said.

"Speaking of expenses, I had to pay a healthy price to cross the Croatian border without a hassle. I hope you don't mind my liberal use of your money."

Lucas exhaled sarcastically. Then a broad smile came to his face. "Not at all. That's why I gave it to you. Sometimes it's good that everything is for sale around here."

"Lucas, there's something else you should know about when I was lost outside of Sarajevo. While trying to find my way, I believe I stumbled across two of the detention camps that you were seeking. The first wasn't far away from the city. It was well guarded, so I couldn't get too close. Nonetheless, I studied it for a short time through my binoculars. I'm certain of its purpose. After I got my bearings, I estimated the coordinates and copied down the names of nearby villages and landmarks. A similar situation happened further south in Herzegovina, close to Kalinovik."

Lucas sat up straight, delighted with the information that had been delivered to him. Finally, his original mission was progressing - some critical intelligence he had been hired to find had been discovered.

"When we get to Split, I'll contact the U.S. consulate in Sarajevo and arrange a conversation through proper channels. Maybe the

State Department can get the U.N. to move and NATO to intervene. Don't lose those coordinates!" Lucas pleaded. "For now, let's concentrate on getting us, and your sister, out of this mess alive."

The car rolled on. Edis continued his story. He became energized. Lucas could see a transformation take place in him as he spoke. His spirit had returned after learning that his sister was alive, and the fight had returned to his spirit.

"Early the next morning, I caught the Mercedes as it waited to enter Croatia. The Croatian officer had everything prearranged. I doubt the border guards knew of your presence. I crossed the border and followed them down the coast. Before long, they drove up the Pelješac peninsula to Orebić from where a ferry carried you away. After confirming its destination to be Korčula, I placed a call to a friend's cousin who lives on the island. Then I waited. When your ferry arrived, he followed the cars to the villa where they held you. That afternoon, I took a later transfer. Ever since then, I've been scouting your position and watching for changes in your status. I spent a lot of my time sleeping in a cramped car, surveying the villa, and studying the general's schedule. Many powerful people visited that house on different occasions," Edis said. "After you regained consciousness, when you walked in on the meeting between the general and his cronies, I presumed that something big would follow. I was prepared in advance for your excursion to Rijeka."

"I'm very impressed, Edis. I couldn't have done a better job myself."

"Thanks. Did I mention to you that I spent a lot of time sleeping in a cramped car? You can owe me for that," Edis joked, rubbing the side of his neck.

"You know the layout of the general's villa better than I do. If you want, you can direct your sister's rescue later today," Lucas offered.

"I'm ready right now," Edis answered.

As the Audi hummed down the Dalmatian coast, the road became more twisted the farther they traveled. In several places, their path drifted inland and cut across more war-ravaged countryside. When dawn finally broke, Lucas saw the remnants of dozens of bombed-out homes still stubbornly standing in ruin.

Eventually, the road reconnected with the Adriatic coast. As the day's early hours passed, the morning sunshine revealed seascape scenery that no camera could capture and no artist could ever replicate. In all his travels, Lucas could not recall having seen such extreme beauty and wretched ugliness positioned so closely together.

As the journey progressed, Lucas reviewed the last forty-eight hours in his head. The information Edis had enlightened him with brought somber questions to his mind.

What if I had assassinated the politician from Istria? The negative ramifications would have been endless. If I had been killed, what would have been the position of the U.S. government after having been implicated in the conspiracy? Certainly Morton Riggs's pressure-producing abilities would have been drastically weakened within the United Nations. How long of a delay would have resulted? How many hundreds of thousands of lives would have been lost or destroyed in the meantime? These thoughts caused his stomach to knot. Now more than ever he was determined to stop General Parenta.

One by one, the speeding Audi left the coastal cities and villages behind. The pair raced past Biograd na Moru, charged through Vodice, and blazed by Šibenik. In time, they whizzed around Primošten and Trogir before finally reaching Split. As they drove through the center of the city, the scent of salt air filled the car, rousing Edis from a short, energizing nap. Once alert, he helped guide his partner through Croatia's second-largest metropolis.

In Split, the heavy morning traffic created jams on the main thoroughfare. Lucas swore as he swerved among the Dalmatian drivers. After reaching the harbor, he parked the Audi in a string of cars awaiting transfer to Korčula.

When the car's engine had been killed, the men hurried to the ticket office. Imperative tasks now needed to be completed. Edis confirmed the departure time and purchased tickets while Lucas searched out a public phone. It was critical that Edis's information be relayed to Curtis Sheets while it was still of value.

The reaction Lucas would receive from Curtis was unknown. Almost two months had passed since their last contact. At the moment, he was unaware of any changes that had developed in his assignment. But for that matter, he was uncertain if his mission was still active.

A predesigned protocol was in place in which Lucas was obliged to follow. Such procedures had been established since unexpected changes could be handled in no other way. First, he was required to confirm his identity with the consulate in Sarajevo. At that point, officials there would launch secondary communications with the U.S. Embassy in Belgrade.

The relay went smoothly. The satellite signal was weak, but without a transmission delay. However, discretion was compromised on several instances when Lucas was forced to raise his voice in order to be heard on the receiving end.

●●●●●

"Jesus Christ, Lucas! Where the hell have you been? I have to say…I feared for the worst. Morton has all but written you off. Are you okay?"

"I'm alive and well, Curtis, but I'm not in the clear yet. All said, I'm in the middle of a dangerous game right now. I expect the next six to eight hours to be dicey; possibly lethal."

"I'll send in the cavalry at once! Just tell me the where, when, and how I can help," Curtis offered.

"For now that won't be necessary. I already have my backup, and we'll have to handle the situation alone. Curtis, I need you to listen carefully. I have gathered some credible intelligence from a reliable source. It's dated, and there are no photos or hardcopy, but I believe it to be exactly the information that Morton is after.

The specifics must be received by you precisely. I have the names of villages, descriptions of landmarks and the estimated coordinates of other locations in Bosnia that need to be investigated. All of this data needs to be verified, but I think the content will prove more than satisfactory. I believe that this will be enough evidence to get the U.N. and NATO to act."

"Bravo, Lucas! Good work, old boy. I'll transcribe it immediately. Now how can I help you in your current crisis?"

"There is nothing you can do, Curtis, really. Our timeframe is limited. Maybe you can arrange to have a med-evac helicopter on one of the aircraft carriers in the Adriatic Sea to be on 'stand-by' over the next eight hours. Otherwise, just sit tight. I'll deliver my status to you as soon as I get the chance. And Curtis...I may have to break protocol in the coming hours," Lucas said, apprehensively. He waited for a response. None came, so he added, "Don't worry, my friend, only in an extreme emergency."

"Lucas, be assured that I trust your judgment unquestioningly. But it'll be my arse if you break protocol. Please...only in a 'life or death' crisis, understood?" Curtis pleaded.

"You have my word on it, Curtis."

The conversation continued. The details of Edis's findings were relayed. Curtis was impressed by the information's accuracy. The orbiting satellites would have little trouble isolating the suspected coordinates. He congratulated Lucas and wished him well before the discussion ended. Lucas knew that it was not yet the time to revel in a job well done.

XXX

By the time Lucas's telephone conversation with Curtis Sheets had ended, Edis was waiting to his right and a little behind. The young Bosnian leaned against the nearest wall, holding the ferry tickets in his right hand and a lit cigarette in his left. He twitched and fidgeted anxiously. Small beads of sweat were beginning to collect at his brow and temples. While the unseasonably muggy Dalmatian weather was noticeably warmer than what they had left behind in Rijeka, the increased perspiration was not a result of the weather. Rather, it was a physiological response to his soaring adrenalin level. He took off his jacket and folded it over his arm.

Warm as well, Lucas followed suit. After removing his own jacket, he was surprised to find it soiled with the boat's motor oil and stained with Serbian blood.

Their tickets in hand and Lucas's telephone conversation complete, the pair maneuvered their way out into the bright morning sunlight. With each passing second, time was becoming more of a factor. Once they were a safe distance from the ferry's other passengers, Lucas shared the highlights of his talk with Edis.

Lucas trusted Edis unequivocally, yet he had to exercise discretion. Only facts that were crucial to their survival and their plan's success could be shared. Edis understood this; he did not press for additional details.

Lucas felt it was essential for his partner to be aware of all the possible adverse consequences of their forthcoming adventure.

Edis needed to know that the assault they were planning would be performed alone, unsanctioned, and at their own risk. If the rescue attempt ended in their capture, injury, or worse, neither support nor assistance from the U.S. government or military could be expected. Despite this revelation, Edis didn't hesitate. For his part, Lucas preferred it this way - he liked working without restrictions. *Besides*, he thought to himself, *we're the good guys here. Right is on our side.*

Before long, Edis drove the Audi onto the ferry. While waiting for it to depart, the pair scanned the parking deck for agents General Parenta may have stationed aboard. They spotted none.

Seeking privacy, they climbed the staircase leading to the upper deck. Once topside, they found seats in an empty corner. There, the men reviewed the layout of the general's villa. Lucas described the structure's interior and Edis detailed the nearby terrain. The villa's current security situation was unknown; until they made an on-site assessment, they would not be able to predict what weaknesses they could exploit. Nevertheless, they developed a plan to save Edis's sister. The strategy was rudimentary, yet practical in theory. The tactics were conventional, but they left room for improvisation as needed. After the property had been surveyed in person, any remaining questions could be answered.

The ferry chugged ahead. During the trip, time passed at a snail's pace. Both men realized the odds of their plan's success were lessening with each tick of the clock. In any case, the three hour voyage to Korčula could not be rushed.

It was now 8:30 on Monday morning. Edis had rested little in the last thirty-six hours and Lucas even less. Amazingly, both warriors felt fresh. The boat ride seemed to produce a peculiar, hypnotic state that rejuvenated their exhausted bodies. The calm sea created a sense of well-being in spite of their heightened states of alertness. A cautious confidence overtook them. Soon this ordeal would be over.

When the ferry docked a few hours later, Lucas lingered topside while Edis hustled below. As his partner scoured the island landing for signs of trouble, Edis prepared the car to go ashore. Minutes later, Lucas appeared at the passenger side door and quickly got in.

"It's all clear for now, but there are several spots for an ambush inland. If the general has been tipped off, I expect they'll be waiting for us somewhere along the way. The rocky hillsides will provide plenty of vantage points for them to strike. Let's ready the weapons, just in case. Once we get on the road, push the engine to its limit. Don't stop for anyone or anything."

"No need to worry about that," said Edis. "I know the road, and I know the way. Just be prepared for any surprises."

"Count on it. Let's go!"

Lucas took out the weapons and inserted the clips into each. Their firepower was limited, but it would suffice if they managed to catch the general's security team unprepared. They knew the Serbian officer was vulnerable on the Croatian island. Lucas doubted that his protection had been increased. The villa could ill afford to have extra attention drawn to it. He expected to have only the general and the two guards to deal with. Edis pressed down hard on the gas pedal.

After a fifteen-minute drive through the heart of the island, the car stopped at an unmarked crossroad. In the distance, the Adriatic Sea reappeared. They were now less than three kilometers from the general's hideaway.

The villa's location was remote; only a distant village and a few lonely cottages had been passed along the way. Edis pulled the Audi to the side of the road and put it in neutral. He knew the surroundings intimately, so Lucas had him review the landscape leading down to the general's house in better detail.

"I'll park in that ravine filled with rocks and shrubs," Edis said, pointing with his right index finger. "I used that spot all last month. The car will be well hidden from the road and visible to only a few grazing sheep. Once we're ready, we'll have to scramble through some heavy brush and crawl down a vineyard to reach the house. Where the grapevines end, there's a spot with good cover and a perfect view of the property. From there, we can better define the security situation." Then he added, "If everything checks out, we can advance even further without being seen until the road adjoining the driveway must be crossed. To do so undetected, our timing will need to be perfect. If successful, we can approach the villa's front door without a problem - close enough to listen for any conversation inside. I made it that far a few times when you were lying in bed," Edis said. "Maybe we'll be able to hear my sister's voice as well."

Lucas nodded in the affirmative. Edis pulled ahead, parked, and then turned off the engine. Wasting no time, they got out and prepared for battle. All unnecessary clothing was discarded. Mobility was essential. They pressed on.

Leading the way down the familiar path, Edis guided Lucas over jagged rocks and through tangled shrubbery. As they neared the edge of the ravine, a rock-pile wall, built to fence sheep, blocked their path. It appeared to be several decades old. Edis scaled it first, crossing with unexpected difficulty. After completing the feat, he suggested that Lucas try a better spot, further down the line. Ignoring the advice, Lucas chose the nearest point of negotiation. As he hoisted himself above the chest-high barrier, several low-placed rocks shuffled loose under his weight, throwing him off balance. In an instant, he lost his grip and flailed wildly into a hip deep patch of brier growing below. The serious expression on Edis's face was replaced by a devilish grin. The smirk continued as he watched his friend wander to safety through the spiny thorns. Seconds later, when the spectacle had ended, Edis's smile disappeared. His attention instantly refocused on the task at hand. He and Lucas continued forward.

When the men reached the vineyard, the villa's orange clay-tile roof came into view. Now only seventy meters stood between them and Edis's sister. Yet the scenario waiting for them below remained unclear. The security situation would remain a concern until they took their final position.

While still out of earshot, the men checked their weapons. A round was inserted into each chamber. Lucas held the silenced Berretta; Edis carried Dragoslav Obrenović's Scorpion submachine gun. If necessary, it was Lucas's intention to shoot first with the silenced pistol in order to maintain their secrecy. Edis elected to cover his back and repel any threat that surfaced. After his sister had been rescued, he volunteered to defend their retreat from behind – possibly the most dangerous part of the operation. If their plan worked perfectly, no shots would need to be fired at all - and no more killing would occur. This outcome, unfortunately, was idealistic and one neither man expected. There was too much at stake.

At the top of the vineyard, they dropped to their knees and crawled to where the main road separated them from the villa. Near the roadside, the view was unobstructed. Staying hidden, they studied the scene before them, now only twenty meters from their final destination.

●●●●●

Dressed in a thick robe and rubber sandals, General Parenta paced hysterically over the ceramic tiles on his back terrace. He looked beleaguered, as if he hadn't slept in days. Another man, a bodyguard, sat at the terrace table drinking coffee. He was dressed in casual clothing and had a semiautomatic pistol strapped to his shoulder. Over and over, the general dialed his cellular phone and fired obscenities at the underworked guard. A briefcase, which was pushed snugly against the table, sat on a chair between the two.

"Where the fuck is Dragoslav? He was supposed to check in with me hours ago!" General Parenta snapped, while forking his fingers through his uncombed hair. When the phone's mouthpiece failed to respond, he slammed the device down on the tabletop. The bodyguard's coffee spilled in response.

"I know Dragoslav well, General. He's the best there is. Everything will be fine," the guard declared.

"Then why doesn't he answer? The job was supposed to have been completed hours ago!" his superior roared.

General Parenta paced some more and redialed the cellular phone. Again, there was no answer. In a huff, he turned his back to the villa and leaned over the terrace railing with his hands outstretched. Silently, he glared out over the sea. His respiration was heavy; his body rigid. Lifting his head skyward, the general's eyes beamed up in frustration. A short time later, he took in a deep breath, then exhaled with a disgusted hiss.

"*Jebo te! U pičku materinu!*" the general cursed out over the water. Several seconds later, when his mind had calmed, he spun to face the villa. The bodyguard, still seated, seemed oblivious to the general's conduct. Saying nothing, he sipped at his coffee.

"Saša, I need to cool off. I'm going for a swim. You stay here and manage the phone. Keep trying until that son-of-a-bitch answers. When you reach him, you come and get me. You don't walk: you run! Understand?" General Parenta ordered.

"Of course, sir," the subordinate answered.

With that, the JNA general turned and trudged down the stairway leading to the beach. When he was out of sight, Lucas glanced at Edis. Both men knew that now was the time to act. They studied the bodyguard sitting in view a while longer. His back was turned, ignorant of their presence. The useless cell phone occupied his attention.

Quietly, the pair got up and moved to the front of the villa. The general's Mercedes-Benz was parked in the driveway. Alone, Lucas moved toward it and felt its hood. It was cold and clearly hadn't been driven that morning. It was doubtful that anyone else had come so early in the day. Lucas returned and whispered the information to Edis. The notion that only two guards were securing the villa remained unchallenged. Even though Edis's sister and the second guard's location remained unknown, their plan moved forward.

Lucas darted to the far end of the house - the side that both men were only vaguely familiar with. Edis stayed hidden and covered the front door. As Lucas peered around the corner, his instincts told him it was where he had been kept during his recovery. The sound, smell, and limited view were hauntingly familiar. From where he now stood, a portion of driveway, half of a palm tree, and the remainder of a sprawling bush, which were previously hidden while he was in captivity, could now be seen in full.

Lucas knew the villa's interior by heart. From the outside, he searched for the window of the bedroom where he had been held, deducing it to be where Edis's sister would also be kept. It was unlikely that the guards had changed tactics in the past few days.

After reaching the correct windowsill, he quietly pulled himself above the marble ledge. The outside shutters were closed and bolted. Nothing could be seen, so Lucas retraced his path to the front of the house, holding his pistol as if he expected trouble.

Next, he climbed the steps leading up to the front door. Surprisingly, it was unlocked. When he peered inside, Lucas saw that the television was turned on and a Formula One race was blaring from it. He could smell food cooking. The kitchen, which was hidden by a concrete wall, was still out of sight. Lucas signaled for Edis to come closer. In a heartbeat, Edis had scaled the steps and was leaning over his partner's right shoulder.

Lucas placed his thumb to his chest and nodded toward the kitchen, indicating he intended to go there first. Next, he directed Edis's attention to a room at the hallway's opposite end. Explaining with hand signals, he instructed Edis to go there next. Message received, Edis headed in that direction, hoping to find his sister inside.

Now alone, Lucas moved quietly over the hardwood floor, and then glided smoothly over a Persian runner leading to the kitchen. Where the rug ended, he stopped and peeked around the corner. Instantly, the scene became clearer, and he was optimistic about what he saw. The second bodyguard was standing by himself at the stove; his attention was diverted by the food he was preparing. The guard's automatic weapon sat on the kitchen table, almost a meter and a half away. It was a careless mistake for a professional to make. In order to subdue him, Lucas knew he had to be fully separated from his pistol, and that only seconds remained to avoid more killing. Once this was done, the fate of the others could be decided, but only after Edis's sister had been freed.

●●●●●

Edis hurried toward the closed bedroom door. With his left hand, he turned the handle slowly, squeezing the Scorpion firmly in his right one as he did so. He was ready to kill anyone blocking him from his sister. Still unsure of her whereabouts, he could feel her presence inside.

She had to be there. Where else could she be? he thought.

The door opened without resistance. Inside the room, it was almost completely dark. The curtains were drawn; the window was closed. After probing the nearest wall with his free hand, he found the light switch. Before hitting it, he gripped the Scorpion tighter and prepared to fire. Then he focused his senses and flipped it upward.

In the weak light, the room appeared to be undisturbed. On the bed, a human form was laying beneath a blanket. Edis pointed his weapon at it. Slowly, he bent over the shaking body and tossed off the cover with authority. Curled below, a young woman was laying face down, trembling with fear. Edis grabbed a shoulder and gently rolled her over. He studied her features. A moment passed before recognition was made. The siblings were mutually surprised. Several months had passed since they had last seen one another. Right away, Edis raised an index finger to his lips, gesturing her to stay quiet. But it was too late. Amra's fragile reflexes overreacted. She released a shrill cry that sounded throughout the house.

XXXI

The guard in the kitchen was chopping vegetables when Amra's cry rang out. Alerted by the shriek, he squeezed his knife tighter and stepped toward his pistol. But before his second foot had touched the floor, he became aware of Lucas's presence and the Berretta pointed at his head. Now standing flat-footed, he was confused about how to react. Lucas spoke bluntly to him in perfect Serbian dialect.

"Don't move, my friend. Just stay still. This will all be over soon. You can walk out of here alive if you do as I say," he said.

Lucas did not know that Saša, the guard on the terrace, had also heard the scream and was moving toward the back door. In a quick, sweeping motion, Saša slipped his solid frame through the entrance and crept up from behind. Step by step, he neared the kitchen with his semi-automatic drawn. Then, in a flash, chaos erupted.

The general's bodyguard was a powerful, broad-shouldered man whose weight shifted unevenly on approach. As he turned the final corner to strike, his secrecy was betrayed by a loose tile that rattled in response to his moving mass. Convinced of his detection, Saša reacted impulsively. Overanxious and undisciplined, he burst toward the kitchen pointing his pistol precariously.

Because his attack began in haste, Saša's sole opportunity to kill the intruder was lost in the time it took for him to adjust. Before his gun could be accurately aimed, Lucas had pivoted, directed his weapon at the guard's head, and squeezed the trigger twice. The Beretta discharged successive rounds that zipped through the air before drilling twin holes through the guard's skull. Instantly, Saša's muscular body fell to the floor with a massive thud. Blood began gushing from his wounds and was soon running across the peach-colored tiles.

The suddenness of the attack caught Lucas by surprise. He stayed locked in a crouched position, struggling to grasp what had happened. Overwhelmed with adrenalin, his concentration was distracted by the event that had just occurred. There wasn't sufficient time for him to react to the next emerging threat. Lucas's senses did not detect the kitchen guard raising his knife, intent on hurling it into his back.

"Lucas!"

Regaining his wits, Lucas's reflexes responded accordingly. His body whirled; the Berretta was set to fire. But his reaction time was too slow. When the second guard was set to heave the blade, another gun blast sounded from behind Lucas's head. As the bullet whizzed past his ear, the gunshot's deafening percussion dropped Lucas to the floor.

Just as the second guard released the knife, the round from Edis's gun crushed his throat and snapped his head backwards. The makeshift dagger, thrown with lethal velocity, was sent flying in a harmless direction. It struck the side of the refrigerator before clattering innocently to the floor.

The guard, now mortally wounded, clutched at his collar and staggered a short distance. Blood squirted from between his fingers – a carotid artery had been shredded. As he gasped for air, a loud gurgle emitted from the gaping hole in his neck. A steady stream of bright, red liquid dripped from the corners of his mouth. Lucas watched the man collapse. There was nothing he could do. Seconds later, he was still.

He should have just stayed put, Lucas thought. *What was he thinking? Was it loyalty? Stupidity? Adrenalin? Bad instincts?* In the end, it didn't matter. The general's bodyguard had performed his duty admirably. Now he was dead.

Lucas turned to Edis, who was still holding the Scorpion as if he expected more danger to crop up. Then he checked the guards' vital signs to confirm they were dead. While he was bending over the bodies, the reason they had returned to the villa popped into his mind.

"Is she here? Is your sister in the house? Is she all right?" Lucas asked.

"She's in the bedroom," Edis answered. "I didn't recognize her at first. She's badly traumatized; probably in shock. I don't think she could handle this scene."

Lucas agreed.

"Go back and take care of her. Get her ready to go. I'll clean up this mess. We're not in the clear just yet, but I think the worst is behind us."

Lucas dragged the corpses into a corner and covered them with a tablecloth he found in the pantry. After collecting their weapons, he unloaded each and stashed them in a cupboard. Next, he walked to the back door and looked outside. The terrace was empty. Memories of his first meeting with the general and his cronies replayed in his mind. *How quickly things had changed*, he thought.

He walked to the terrace railing and looked over the limestone ledge on which the villa was built. The jagged cliff dropped forty meters straight down to the sea. From his elevated position, he searched below for the general.

A steep walk down a twisting concrete staircase was required to reach the beach beneath the villa. Once there, a secluded strip of pebbles eased into the clear blue water. From where Lucas was now standing, not a soul could be seen. The general was not swimming, nor moving about on the rocky shore, so he stepped back from the ledge and walked over to the terrace table. On its top, the deserted cell phone rested next to Saša's cup of coffee. Spotting the briefcase, Lucas lifted its flap. Inside, he immediately saw the general's prized possession. He took the revolver's handle, pulled it out, and then studied its design. While briefly admiring its craftsmanship, he read the dedication etched into the barrel. Transcribed in Cyrillic script, it read:

To General Stevan Parenta; Our Finest Commander
Crvena Zastava Company, Kragujevac, Serbia
March 01, 1992

Lucas set the gun aside and picked through the case. Official papers, documents, and maps were neatly arranged within. After digging a little deeper, he found a large envelope hidden in a zipped pocket on the right. It was addressed to the general. A scribbled, hand-written address identified a village in eastern Bosnia as the packet's point of origin. The Serbian word for 'CONFIDENTIAL' was stamped on both sides. Lucas opened it and removed the documents it contained. He flipped through the pages one by one. Each paper bore the signature of the highest-ranking politician in the Bosnian-Serb government. The dossier included orders to round up male Muslim civilians from various regions in Bosnia and detain them until further instructions were given. Recommended methods of elimination and disposal were requested from General Parenta. Lucas put the papers back into the envelope, folded the file in half, and slid it under his belt inside his shirt. The revolver and the rest of the briefcase contents were put away exactly as he had found them.

Next, Lucas went back into the villa and entered the bedroom slowly. Edis was sitting on the bed helping his sister drink water from a glass. The room appeared exactly as Lucas remembered it, but Edis's sister had changed noticeably. Physically, Amra looked stronger than when he had rescued her from her Sarajevo captors. Her face, now fuller, showed that she had gained weight over the last few months. But little progress had been made in her mental state. The extent of the psychological damage she had suffered could not be determined. Based on her current appearance, Lucas doubted if she would ever fully recover from the emotional trauma she had endured. Putting on an optimistic front, he grabbed Edis by the shoulder.

"That's it...let her drink. She'll be fine in time. Jesus, it's amazing how much stress the body can handle."

Edis wasn't convinced. A subtle rage was growing in his brain. An outward explosion soon followed.

"Those bastards! Look at her, Lucas! Look what those fucking Chetniks did to her!" he howled. "I'll kill every last one of them!"

Lucas knew the situation required immediate defusing. It was the worst moment for such an outburst to occur.

"Edis, calm down!" he said, squeezing the back of his friend's neck. He leaned his head closer. "We've got what we came for. Your sister is going to be fine. This is no time for hysterics. It's time to get your sister, and us, out of here - alive. It will be too difficult carrying her to the Audi. I'll find the keys to the Mercedes parked in front so we can drive her to it. There will be less risk of drawing attention that way. Get your sister dressed. I'll be back in a few minutes to help take her outside."

After a quick scan of the villa's interior, Lucas returned to the kitchen and searched though the cupboards. No car keys were found. After considering all other possibilities, he uncovered the dead bodies and emptied their pockets. The guard from the kitchen had nothing to offer. Saša, the one who had been drinking coffee in the late-morning sun, carried several keys looped to a chain in his front pant pocket. On the main ring, he found one displaying the Mercedes-Benz insignia.

"This should start it," he mumbled.

Relieved by his discovery, Lucas headed out the front door. While walking down the driveway it occurred to him that he should have made a second attempt to locate the general. Lucas's carelessness burdened him deeply. As he neared the parked car, he knew a critical decision had to be made. For a brief moment, he debated whether to return to secure the premises before preparing the car for escape.

This will only take a second, he told himself. *I'll be quick about it.*

Continuing onward, he tried to open the Mercedes, but struggled to get the key to work. After consecutive failed attempts, he adjusted the angle and the alarm beeped three times in a row. He pulled the door handle and it opened smoothly. A broad smile crossed his face. After the engine was started, he left the automobile running and hurried back toward the house.

Only a few more minutes and we'll be long gone, he thought, while retracing his path toward the house.

XXXII

General Parenta was hoping a swim in the sea would calm his nerves, but the water's temperature had become too cold for even the most avid swimmer. Instead, he found a hidden strip of pebbles under the limestone cliff and sat in solitude. After smoking a couple of cigarettes, his temper began to cool. During the break, he reassessed the situation, which until a few hours ago he had thought was under control.

Since Saša had not yet reported, the general presumed Dragoslav Obrenović's status to be worse than expected. After many worrisome minutes had passed, his impatience could no longer be restrained, and he decided to take action. In a huff, he returned to the stairway and stormed the steps upward, swearing fervently as he climbed.

"Where the hell are you, Dragoslav? *Goddamn you! U pičku materinu!*" he barked, alternating curses in English and Serbian. "Must I do everything myself? And where is Saša? He's supposed to be keeping me informed!" he fumed, almost halfway to the top.

General Parenta's robe flailed loosely as he moved. His rubber sandals flopped with each step. At several points along the way, his pace slowed when he felt strong chest pains and had difficulty breathing. Between curses, he promised to cut down on his smoking habit as soon as the money had been deposited into his bank account. It now exceeded three packs per day.

After reaching the top step, General Parenta's eyes beamed at the chair where his bodyguard had been sitting. He was set to fire a flurry of obscenities in that direction, but after noticing the guard's absence, he stood motionless in astonishment.

Saša was not to leave his position except to report to me! roared in his mind. He was certain that his orders had been clear.

With his blood pressure now soaring, the general walked over to the table and looked at the cell phone. No calls had been made, nor received, for quite a while. He studied the scene in greater detail. Everything appeared to be in place. He considered calling out to announce his presence, but decided against it an instant later. His curiosity had trumped his anger long enough to investigate why Saša had disobeyed his orders.

The general stepped vigilantly through the villa's back door. As he walked down the hallway, the smeared blood of the dead guards came into view. His eyes followed the burgundy trail across the kitchen floor until he saw both bodies, piled together under wraps. A distressed fury overcame him. Almost in panic, he kicked off his sandals and hurried back onto the terrace. Once outside, he sprinted to his briefcase and yanked out the revolver that he had admired, but never fired.

Returning to the back door, General Parenta listened for sounds of activity inside. Carefully, he re-entered the villa with his weapon's sight pointed forward. His hands were now shaking worse than ever.

The general's first inclination was to find the girl. He rationalized that his scheme would still be intact so long as she remained under his control. Ever so slowly, he scanned the villa's interior. There was no sign of intrusion except that the front door was slightly ajar. He was about to go inspect it when a female voice coming from the far bedroom snared his attention. Suddenly, it struck him. His hostage was still there.

Without a sound, General Parenta moved down the hallway in his bare feet. When he reached the door, he held the gun in his right hand and pressed his left shoulder against the door's wooden frame. Once properly positioned, he lowered the handle, leaned forward, and thrust the door inward.

At the foot of the bed, Edis was working hard to get his sister ready for escape.

Amra had already been dressed and her belt was about to be fastened when she flinched abruptly. Soon after, she squirmed anxiously and cried out with fear. In a heartbeat, her brother deduced their predicament.

The Serbian general was standing in the doorway, less than two meters away, aiming his revolver at him. Edis considered his options, but there was no way out. The Scorpion, sitting on the nightstand, was too far out of reach. Any sudden movement would surely be his last. There was nothing he could do. General Parenta spoke first.

"I don't know who you are, but you are in a bad way. I saw what you did to my associates. I will never forgive you for that. Nor will I forget. Who are you? I see what you are doing. I want to know why."

Edis thought before answering. His blood was boiling inside.

"This is my sister and we're leaving here together," he answered after several seconds.

"Oh, I see," the general said, sarcastically. "That's quite noble of you, young man. But the girl is worth a lot of money to me. She won't be going anywhere until I've collected what's mine. Now walk your sister out to the kitchen."

From where he was standing, General Parenta spotted the gun that Edis had been carrying. After taking a closer look at it, he recognized the weapon as Dragoslav's.

"Shall I presume that my associate is dead?" the general asked.

Fatigue and disdain made Edis unafraid of the general's deadly intent.

"He's dead. You can also presume that I enjoyed killing the murderous bastard," he responded.

"You've done a lot of damage," said General Parenta. "I'm impressed. You are very resourceful for a *Bosanac*," he added, using the slur intentionally in an attempt to provoke Edis into making a foolish mistake.

The three walked out of the bedroom and down the hallway to where it joined the kitchen. As they moved, General Parenta's revolver stayed fixed on Edis's heart. The general desperately wanted to avenge the death of his men, but first, he needed time to re-evaluate the situation. The circumstances had changed so rapidly. Confusion now clouded everything. After taking a moment to reassess the facts, he continued to believe that as long as he controlled the girl, his plan was intact. Her brother was dangerous; therefore, he was a liability.

●●●●●

After starting the Mercedes, Lucas returned to the house, planning to help Edis evacuate his sister. Before entering, he decided to search the grounds for signs of the general. They would be leaving soon; they could not risk an unexpected surprise.

Lucas walked around the villa's perimeter. When he reached the back terrace, he parted the bushes encircling its foundation and scaled the railing above. On top, he surveyed the site. Everything appeared as he had left it. He quickly moved to the ledge and leaned over the rail, bent forward like a child ready to spit over the side of a bridge. Once again, he saw nothing except an empty beach and undisturbed water. As he examined the picture more carefully, a terse voice from inside the house alerted him of a looming danger. Instinctively, Lucas ducked under the kitchen window. He listened closely, puzzled about the commotion inside. Gradually, he stood erect and pressed his back against the stucco wall. Inch by inch, he moved toward the open back door. Inside the villa, the irate shouting of a disturbed man could be heard.

The moment Lucas recognized General Parenta's voice, dread surged through his brain. His body, however, had been conditioned to avoid panic. Calmly, Lucas removed the Berretta from his waistline while he listened to the tirade from around the corner.

As the general's eruption intensified, Lucas calculated that he was unaware Edis had not come alone; that obvious evidence of an accomplice had been overlooked as a result of the drama's surprise. As the general's rant continued, Lucas heard an evolution take place in the pitch of his voice. The previous tone of self-control was transforming into a volatile emotional state, an almost animal-like rage. Before long, Lucas poked his head through the doorway to evaluate the scenario firsthand. General Parenta's back was turned to him. In his right hand, his decorated revolver wavered erratically as he screamed. His free arm was flailing as he cursed and berated Edis for his actions.

"Did you think you could *destroy* everything I've worked for? You will not ruin it!" he howled. The Serbian officer's face burned an evil red. His mouth foamed in both corners and his speech was slurred. At times, saliva sprayed from his flapping lips.

Edis stood passively, holding his sister, awaiting their fate. Amra cried and clung to her brother. There was little strength left in her withered nerves. Lucas decided to act.

Stepping around the corner, he entered the hallway. As he advanced, a change in lighting cast his shadow, bringing his presence to the general's attention. Lucas purposely held his Beretta at his side, pointed down toward the floor.

"You! I should have known you were involved," the general howled, whirling his weapon toward Lucas's head.

"General, put the gun down. Too many people have died in the past twenty-four hours. It's over now."

"I want my money you son-of-a-bitch. It's mine. I earned it, and I want it!" General Parenta wailed, while cocking back the revolver's hammer.

"General, put your gun down," Lucas repeated. "Your plan is finished."

Diligently, he backpedaled out onto the terrace. The general followed him stride for stride until the terrace railing ended his retreat. Lucas slowly replaced the Berretta under his belt and focused his attention on the revolver pointed at his face.

"This will be over when I say it's over. I should have had you killed in Sarajevo months ago. You could have cost me millions!" the general raged.

Edis watched the drama unfold. Leaving his sister's side, he stepped into the doorway and prepared to pounce on the general from behind. At the last moment, Lucas halted his advance with a wave of his hand.

"Just take care of your sister, Edis. The situation is under control," Lucas said. When the general briefly focused his attention on Edis, Lucas subtly sunk his hand into his front pant pocket.

"No, the situation is not under control, Mr. Martin. Not yet. Not until I have my money!" snarled the general.

General Parenta lowered his weapon's barrel and redirected it toward his nemesis's heart. With his irritation growing, he gripped the gun tighter. The end of his patience was near; his self-control was now overwhelmed by emotion. Lucas swallowed hard. His breathing became faster and his palms began to sweat. The confrontation ended a moment later when the Serbian commander's finger squeezed the trigger.

The revolver's hammer fell forward. The following millisecond seemed to last an eternity. When it ended, General Parenta's gun sounded with a feeble click. The revolver did not fire. The Serbian officer recocked the hammer and pulled the trigger again. Once more, there was no effect. When he tried a third and a fourth time, each subsequent attempt produced the identical, futile result. Almost instantaneously, Lucas's breathing eased.

"You need these, General," he said. Digging deeper into his pocket, Lucas pulled out six .357 magnum rounds and held them in his open palm. Each glistened like a gold nugget in a miner's tin. He took one aside and slipped it into his shirt pocket on the sly. Then in one fluid motion, he tossed the remaining five bullets high into the air. Seconds later, the sea engulfed the deadly chunks of lead.

General Parenta stood at a loss, realizing he had been defeated; that his ambitions were in ruins.

Pulling the Berretta from his waistline, Lucas moved toward the distraught officer and took the revolver from his hand.

"Sit down over there," Lucas commanded. He guided the dazed figure to the same chair where Saša had been sitting less than an hour ago. The dead guard's unfinished cup of coffee was still in place.

General Parenta obeyed the instructions. He could not escape, he had nowhere to go. Lucas left him alone and went into the kitchen to check on the siblings. A relaxed expression had returned to Edis's face, but his pulse continued to race. Lucas spoke first.

"Can you get your sister into the car without me? I have some unfinished business here that I have to take care of. I'll be out in a little while. It will be best if we leave as soon as possible," he added.

"If you need my help, just call," Edis answered, nodding his head toward the general. Then he draped Amra's arm around his neck and coaxed her into shuffling her feet. Together, they walked out the front door.

Lucas wasted no time. Inside, he set the general's revolver on the kitchen counter and moved systematically throughout the villa to remove every trace of their presence. After all their belongings had been collected, he set them near the front door. Before leaving, one final task needed to be performed.

●●●●●

General Parenta sat unmoved, staring out to open sea. His form was shrunken; his hands shook freely. The general's eyes were glazed, almost catatonic. He mumbled incoherently and appeared to be in shock. Lucas pulled up a chair and sat near the stone figure, showing no sympathy.

"General, I have no authority to arrest you, though you definitely deserve to be tried for the crimes that have been committed on your orders. Between you and me, I would prefer to execute you right now. Fortunately for you, I am not a murderer. I am, however, determined to see that you are dealt with by the proper authorities. You will be held accountable for your actions. And whatever grand scheme you had planned can be forgotten about now."

Lucas took out the manila envelope from under his shirt. "I have plenty of incriminating evidence against you to turn over to the impending United Nations war crimes tribunal. Expect an indictment to be forthcoming. Imprisonment as a war criminal is certain to follow. I personally guarantee that you will face the consequences for your actions. And expect to have your foreign bank accounts seized immediately. You can forget about living your life in luxury. Go ahead; breathe in the salt air while you can, General. I want you to remember what freedom smells like," Lucas taunted.

The general did not respond. Little by little, his eyes filled with water as he continued mumbling unintelligibly.

"It appears that all your dreams have *vanished*," Lucas added, placing emphasis on the final word.

Lucas rose from the table, went to the kitchen, and retrieved the revolver. When he returned to the terrace, General Parenta hadn't budged. Lucas placed the decorated weapon in front of his crushed opponent.

"I want you to keep this," he said. Reaching into his shirt pocket, Lucas took out the saved .357 caliber round and placed it on the table's far edge. "You should have this, too."

Turning his back, he hurried out to the Mercedes where Edis and his sister were waiting.

XXXIII

With the use of the general's Mercedes, Lucas, Edis, and Amra reached the Audi in minutes. Once there, Lucas transferred their things while Edis helped his sister climb into the backseat. Before leaving, the men hid the general's car behind some heavy brush. Lucas was certain it wouldn't be found for weeks, maybe months.

Soon the Audi was coasting down the road toward Vela Luka. Inside, the mood was mostly one of exhaustion. Edis drove while Lucas dozed in the passenger seat. As they neared the port village, Edis woke Lucas, who had requested to meet the contact who had helped Edis the month before. After a brief introduction, Lucas thanked the man for his time and effort. The islander, slightly befuddled, asked no questions and expected nothing in return. Just the same, Lucas took his contact information. He would make certain that Morton Riggs rewarded the stranger for his critical support. As the two parted company, Lucas felt certain the man would never understand the true value of his service. Regretfully, the classified nature of his mission prevented Lucas from describing the saga to him in better detail.

The same ferry that delivered them to the island earlier in the day was awaiting their return to Split. After a short stay, Edis drove the Audi aboard and parked in its hull. When the ferry departed, the threesome climbed to the open-air upper deck. The men took turns supporting Amra along the way. On the final flight of steps, a late-season German tourist inquired about the girl's poor physical condition and offered his assistance. Lucas gave a vague response to his question and politely refused his help. The foreigner feigned satisfaction and left them alone.

On the top deck, the temperature was comfortable in the afternoon sun. Amra sat in a plastic chair and sipped a soft drink. With their backs to the sea, the men leaned against the deck rail a few meters away. Edis studied his sister, worried about the state of her well-being. He doubted the psychological damage inflicted upon her would ever be erased. Lucas could offer few words of assurance. Physically, she appeared to be on the mend; mentally, her condition had deteriorated.

"Here's what I can arrange for your sister," Lucas said. "When we reach Split, I'll contact the U.S. State Department. I should be able to get her transferred to a U.S. Army hospital in Germany or admitted onto a navy ship infirmary. She'll get 'top priority' status. When her condition stabilizes, she can be inserted into the refugee program and will probably be relocated somewhere in Europe, or maybe stateside. She'll get the best care available. She's going to need it. As for you... you can go with her. Just tell me where you'd prefer to live."

"Lucas, you know I won't leave. My life is here. I have an obligation to fight. I'll appreciate all you can do for my sister, but I won't leave Bosnia the way it is now. At this point, I have nothing left to lose."

Lucas did not challenge Edis's position on the matter. He knew that his viewpoint was not likely to be swayed by an outsider's logic. From his experience in the Balkans, he had learned that emotional ties and personal bonds often defied Western reasoning in situations like this.

"Okay, if you're sure. I suppose I'll always have powerful connections within the U.S. government. If you change your mind...just let me know," he said.

"What about you, Lucas? What now? Will you return to Sarajevo?" Edis asked.

"I plan to one day, but not until the madness has ended. I still have some unfinished business to take care of - the search for my father and the cause of his disappearance. I don't see any hope of discovering new leads in the current environment, however. So... thanks to you, my assignment is almost complete. I'll likely be debriefed in Split and flown back to Washington, D.C., shortly thereafter. When all is said and done, I intend to resume my life on permanent vacation. Let's arrange to keep in touch. When the fighting finally stops, I'll come visit you and continue my search. Maybe we could go somewhere and eat grilled lamb?" Lucas proposed, with a cheerless smile on his face. Internally, he was deeply concerned for his friend's future. "For the time being, you just worry about staying alive. I'll make sure your sister gets taken care of."

The ferry powered forward. Lucas's short hair blew in the wind. Edis's stringy mane, pulled tightly into a ponytail, flopped occasionally with stronger gusts.

"Lucas, what about General Parenta? He could still arrange to have a private yacht come to pick him up. Does he get to escape? Just return to the war as if nothing happened?"

Lucas pondered Edis's words for a moment. "It's hard to say. He might. If he does, I'll return, hunt him down, and personally deliver him to The Hague. But I don't think he'll go far. All of his glory has been lost, his money will soon be gone, and his dreams have been destroyed."

The warriors turned and gazed out to sea.

●●●●●

General Parenta sat soberly and stared out over the water. He had not moved since the intruders left with the girl several hours ago. He thought about the two dead bodies stacked in the kitchen and contemplated how his could easily have been the third. Simultaneously, he considered his prospects. Only a few realistic options stood out and none of those choices appealed to him.

The general deliberated over lighting a cigarette, but the urge to smoke no longer controlled him. His mind worked feverishly. A constant, annoying buzz sounded in his ears, and it seemed to be growing louder with time. His head felt like it was shrinking from within; as if a minuscule vacuum was sucking at his brain from its core. Below his neckline, his body was useless. His entire spinal cord, from his skull to his tailbone, ached from inflammation. Any attempt to change positions forced him to wince in pain.

Once again, the general's subconscious was refusing to obey the commands his mind had ordered. He wanted to get up and arrange an escape, but all his strength had deserted him. Instead, he sat lethargically and breathed in the salt air. At unpredictable intervals, his eyes filled with water, blurring his vision until multiple teardrops fell onto his shirt. When he tried to speak, only muffled murmurs managed to leave his quivering lips.

Time passed cruelly as he mulled over his past. With every attempt of self-justification for his actions, fewer legitimate explanations now surfaced. With each attempt at self-reprieve, only more self-loathing came to light.

The desire to return to his command was gone. His ambitions were now in tatters. Because his plan had failed, the prestige he held with his superiors had surely been stripped. The general's beloved status of top warrior had been lost along with his respect, reputation, and influence. Exacerbating things, command of the siege of Sarajevo was now far less alluring without Dragoslav Obrenovic's sinister assistance. It was just as well. He had recently become convinced that the city would survive the onslaught and that his superiors' strategy would fail. At this point, the war could not be won, only extended for profit. But the easy money had already been made. It was merely a matter of time before the West intervened and shut the trade routes down forever.

General Parenta was convinced that his offshore assets would soon be frozen, if they had not been seized already. When this happened, his fiscal future would be in shambles and his family's fortune would be a distant memory. In combination with the loss of his command, he would now be financially worse off than the day the war had begun.

Worse yet, he had little doubt that he would be indicted by a U.N. war crimes tribunal for the unlawful acts that had been performed under his authority. Incarceration was a legitimate possibility, despite the protection his political friends had promised. His single hope of lasting freedom depended on the Serbs dominating the region when the fighting ended, and even if that scenario came to pass, the Serbian officials now in place would need to remain in power for many more years to come. At the moment, the chances of that were looking slimmer and slimmer. Despair nearly set in, but before his mind became hysterical, he was temporarily comforted by the thought that the U.N. courts did not execute war criminals. This fact caused a small smile to spread across his face, but the dark humor disappeared as quickly as it came. His head continued to throb from within. He waited, unable to move. More time passed.

By late afternoon, the day's heat had disappeared. The general now sat in the shade, his position unchanged. His body temperature had lowered in concert with the sun's position. He shivered incessantly; his hands shook like those of a retired boxer who had taken too many blows to the head. General Parenta's ego could not survive in such a broken state. A difficult decision now consumed his thoughts and ate at his fragile mind. Before long, a final choice would have to be made.

The JNA general managed the strength to reach for the bullet Lucas had left behind. Grabbing his prized revolver, he inserted the round into the cylinder. The weapon quickly became heavy, so he set it down in front of him. Inhaling deeply, he leaned forward and placed his head in his hands. His buried sense of shame finally dominated his over-inflated sense of pride. With tears streaming down his face, General Parenta made his final decision. He would wait no longer.

In one fluid motion, he lifted the revolver and pressed its barrel under his chin, just above his Adam's apple. As he raised his head skyward, he forced the stainless steel deep into the tissue and angled it upward. After looking out to sea a final time, the general pulled the trigger without hesitating. At last, his tears fell no more.

●●●●●

The war ended early for General Parenta, but it continued on tragically for millions of others. In the following three years, hundreds of thousands of combatants, civilians, journalists, and foreign observers suffered great losses for the gain of a few. In the end, a handful of broken countries with ruined economies and a generation of displaced citizens were all that emerged from the smoke, dust, and destruction.

The survivors often repeat, "It was a lesson that should never be forgotten by the generations to come, not only in the Balkans, but around the world." Time will tell if these hard-learned words will be heeded.

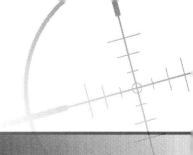

XXXIV

The lone figure was sitting on a balcony chair, puffing on a cigar and sipping red wine. The aged man's eyeglasses were set low across the bridge of his nose. He breathed heavily; a faint whistle sounded from his nostrils with each exhalation of the crisp autumn air. Between puffs, he admired the view in all directions. Presented before him, the Italian Dolomites' cragged peaks jutted upward, and the afternoon sun enticed the forest leaves to flaunt their splendor. He noted how much the scenery had changed since his last visit, only a few months ago. Resting on his lap, an envelope containing classified documents awaited his attention. The U. S. State Department motif was stamped on each page inside.

Within the hour, a black SUV rolled down the private lane in his direction. The vehicle did not have the typical elongated license plates found on most European vehicles. Rather, this one had much smaller tags with black numbers on display over a white backdrop. Above the digits, "U.S. Military" was stamped into the metal. The vehicle's driver wore military attire; its single passenger did not. Minutes later, the SUV stopped in the estate's driveway below.

Lucas got out unaccompanied and closed the door. With his hands on his hips, he looked up at the balcony. Morton Riggs waved down from above.

"Come on up, my old friend. I have a fantastic bottle of Friuli Merlot waiting for you!' the diplomat hollered.

Lucas shook his head in annoyance. He was exhausted. The flight from Split to the Aviano Air Force Base had passed quickly, but the drive from Aviano to Morton Riggs's location had dragged on. Even so, it was the life and death confrontation two days before that had depleted the bulk of his energy reserves. Lucas entered the villa and casually made his way up the stairs.

●●●●●

"Nice view. Nice place. Did you rent it on my behalf?" he asked, after finding the room with the balcony entrance.

The U.S. undersecretary grinned before answering. "No, no...this chateau has been State Department property for quite some time...one of the spoils of the Second World War. It's my understanding that 'Il Duce' himself used to visit here regularly. I doubt many Italians are aware of its existence. Those who do know about it must be clueless to the present ownership. It's a favorite place of mine - I come here as often as my busy schedule allows."

Morton filled two empty wineglasses. "*Salute*! To a job well done."

"*Salute*," Lucas replied.

"Lucas, I read the report of your debriefing...it's right over there," Morton said, pointing at a file next to another bottle of wine. "The Secretary of State will go in front of the United Nations assembly next month. At that time, he'll request the Security Council's permission to allow NATO military intervention in order to stop the fighting in Bosnia. The information you collected should be enough to make the case. In the event that it isn't, the Department of Defense and the NSA have been accumulating additional evidence to support these assertions," Morton said. "I'll be goddamned if I can't count on you when the chips are down, my friend. But then, I always could."

"It wasn't all my doing. I got lucky. I knew some good people at the right time. It was nothing more than that."

"And that's exactly what I'm talking about" Morton added. "One way or another, you always get the job done."

There was a lull in the conversation. Lucas spoke next, "So…are we square?"

"If you're referring to the money that was wired to your Cayman Island account yesterday, the answer is yes," Morton said. "Please double check to make sure the amount is correct. A nice bonus was added by my request. You know, Lucas, I always enjoy doing business with you."

The public servant's flattery was hovering just above Lucas's level of suspicion. He had known the diplomat too long to take the bait. Gulping down his wine, Lucas stood up and prepared to leave. "Then our business is finished," he said. "Thanks for the vino, Morty. I'll show myself out."

"Lucas, wait a moment. Please, sit down. There's something else I would like to discuss with you," said the statesman. When Lucas hesitated, it provided the opening Morton needed. "Come on now, don't always be in such a hurry; sit down over here," he cajoled, pulling an empty chair closer to his. "I have an offer for you. An extremely important project with a very lucrative contract awaits your attention."

"Be very careful what you say next, Morty. You know that I'm easily agitated when I'm tired," Lucas warned. "Well, get on with it. What's on your mind?"

Morton wasted no time. "I've been contacted by some people in our government who are seeking a security specialist for a research installation. This site is already in its developmental stages. This facility will be navigating unexplored scientific territory and using state-of-the-art technology. The entire project is classified and a matter of national security. Knowing that security is your area of expertise, I thought of recommending you for the position right away," Morton said.

The catchphrase "national security" repulsed Lucas. In his experience, it was an overused cliché politicians used to coerce public approval for military funding that would otherwise be rejected. Rarely did anything attached to the term benefit a taxpayer's interest.

"Which people in the government? I want to know with whom I would be dealing - the State Department? The Department of Defense? The NSA?" Lucas asked.

Morton answered, "My friend, please understand that I'm limited to what I can convey because I've been limited by what I've been told. I'm authorized to provide only enough information for you to decide if you are interested in pursuing the matter further. Of course, these prospective employers have requested me to provide them with your credentials, also. They will need to know if you are qualified to perform the job effectively."

"You say this every time, Morty. So, to whom am I being referred?"

"The project is a DOD-private sector, joint operation. The job is located in the remote wilderness of Alaska," Morton started.

Lucas interrupted, "DOD and Alaska? The missile defense initiative? But that's dead in the water."

"In the public eye, it is. But from the DOD's point of view, it's only dead in the newspapers. Once it's in the hands of the private sector, it's still in play."

"So, it *is* missile defense…the 'Star Wars' initiative?"

"Oh…it's much more than that, Lucas. Over the last decade, technology has progressed by leaps and bounds. Warfare, as we know it, is evolving rapidly. It's no longer a primitive missile-to-missile strategy. High power transmissions utilizing particle beams, energy pulses, and high, low, and extremely low-frequency radio waves will soon be able to manipulate the earth's ionosphere. A global weapon system application is being devised as we speak - and once the technology has been perfected, communications anywhere in the world can be intercepted or disrupted with pinpoint accuracy. A climate control theory is in its early stages. From what I understand, this installation will have the capability of changing how Mother Nature works," Morton said, with a coarse cackle.

"Particle beams? Radio waves? Jesus Christ. You're talking about Tesla technology. So, after destroying the man's credibility for decades, the bastards were finally able to harness his concepts?" Lucas uttered.

The corners of Morton's mouth angled downward; his shoulders shot up. "I don't know anything about that. Look, based on what I've been told, nothing yet has been harnessed. The models are still in the experimental stages. That's why security is crucial. Once the environmentalists get wind of the project, God knows the lengths they'll go through to shut the facility down."

"What do you mean 'the experimental stages?' Are you telling me the military intends to tamper with the earth's natural protective shields without knowing the end results in advance? And the public isn't being informed of this? Do these idiots know what consequences could occur if something goes awry?" Lucas asked.

"Lucas, I don't believe you are seeing the broader picture," Morton stated.

"I see plenty, Morton" Lucas snapped.

The diplomat interrupted, "Listen, if what I've learned is true, once this technology has been mastered, the United States will dominate the world...or at least those segments that it doesn't already control."

"So what, Morty? Why is that essential? I want to know who benefits from taking these risks. And at what cost to the public?" Lucas queried.

"Lucas, I am not going to get into a political debate with you on the matter. My career is nearing its end. What happens five, ten, or fifteen years from now is of little concern to me at the moment. You are a security specialist - the best I know. Consider the offer. You would be working for a private corporation with deep pockets. Access to the best resources, equipment, and manpower would be at your disposal. A paycheck beyond any you've ever seen will go to the chosen candidate - and you're at the top of the shortlist. There will be ample excitement in the Alaska wilderness for you to enjoy during your free time - fantastic hunting and some of the best trout and salmon fishing in the world is waiting for you. It will be like a working vacation."

Lucas didn't need time to consider his answer. He stood and shook Morton's hand.

"Thank you for thinking of me, Morton, but no thank you. I have enough money. I think I'd rather go trout fishing in Chile or New Zealand while there's still an ozone layer. Be careful with whom you are dealing, old man," Lucas warned. "Tampering with nature rarely ends with expected results. You should know better at your age."

Spinning quickly, Lucas walked down the stairs and out of the chateau. Then the military chauffeur drove him away.

Acknowledgments

This book could not have been written without the help of several friends, local experts, and other contributors of important information. In particular, Mr. Dimitrij Vasiljev and Mr. Ervin Katalinić generously shared their time, knowledge, and assistance, all of which were invaluable in the writing of this book.

Dimitrij enthusiastically discussed his personal history, knowledge, and background from his years growing up in various parts of the former Yugoslavia. His descriptions of the harrowing experiences he endured during Croatia's Homeland War helped me immensely in developing the book's plot.

I am also indebted to Mr. Ervin Katalinić for his assistance. Ervin kindly devoted much of his limited free time to help this novel become a reality. His suggestions, advice, and in-depth review were greatly appreciated.

I would also like to thank my older brother, Martin Cavanaugh, who offered his time, guidance and encouragement to see this project to completion.

Ognjen Puhovac also volunteered valuable time, suggestions, and encouragement.

This book's front and back cover concepts were created by Mark Broderick and Douglas Cavanaugh, while the brilliant graphics on the book cover were produced solely by Mark Broderick at www.broderickcreative.com. Broderick Creative also designed the maps included in the book.

I would like to thank another local author, Barbara Unković, who offered me plenty of inspiration and insight. A New Zealander-raised Croat, Barbara provided the boost to help me develop the opening scene of chapter one, which masterfully sets the tone for the rest of the book.

This novel's main editor was Andrew Hoogheem of Davenport, Iowa. Additional editing and proofreading were performed by various contributors.

Thank you very much, dear friends. Your efforts have been very much appreciated and without your contributions, this book would have never seen the printing press.

Douglas Cavanaugh
[Rijeka], December 2012

The Author – Douglas Cavanaugh

Douglas Cavanaugh is an American who grew up in the state of Iowa. After several trips abroad in the early 1990s, he arrived in Croatia in 1996, not long after the country's Homeland War had ended, and just after the final shots in the neighboring Bosnia and Herzegovina had been fired.

He has lived in Croatia for seventeen years. Douglas is an outdoor enthusiast whose activities include: fly-fishing, mushroom hunting, hiking, and weekend island getaways.

Printed in Great Britain
by Amazon